THE LEGACY STAND

—•—

THE BARBER BROTHERS' FINAL ADVENTURE

JASON B. BAKER

GREER
BOOKS

THE LEGACY STAND

ALSO BY JASON B. BAKER

—·—

"This writer has a future in the genre."
-RON SCHWAB, Bestselling author of Coldsmith, *Old Dogs*, *The Accidental Sheriff*, and other classic Western novels.

The Barber Brothers' Adventures
The Ace's Bounty
The War Remains
The Legacy Stand

Barber Brothers' Adventures Prequel
The Sheriff's Pursuit

The Vengeance of Reed Caine
Red Canyon Reckoning
River's Fortune
Sins of Santa Fe

Narrative Non-Fiction
Chicago To Appomattox: The 39th Illinois Infantry In The Civil War

Learn more about Jason and his books, and sign up for future updates at JasonBakerAuthor.com

For my boys. Elijah might only have one son in this book, but I hope you both see yourself in him. . .and that I have done as well raising you as Elijah.

-Dad

No legacy is so rich as honesty.

-William Shakespeare

CONTENTS

PROLOGUE

— • —

SUMMER 1869

Bozeman, Montana Territory

D ust from Main Street swirled in the warm, late summer breeze, mixing with the scents of fresh-cut timber, horses, and the faint aroma of evening cooking fires sparking to life. The streets buzzed with activity as miners, ranchers, and merchants went about their business, the town's growth evident in every new building and bustling storefront. Just off the center of Main Street, torches lit the front of the grandest home in town, casting a warm glow over the gathering crowd.

Carriages arrived one after another, depositing well-dressed guests onto the cobblestone driveway. Footmen helped ladies in elegant gowns and gentlemen in fine suits step down, each couple greeted with polite nods and welcomes. The scene was one of refined celebration, a stark contrast to life in Bozeman not long ago—and still much of it now.

Elijah Barber stood outside the mansion, near Jonathan Stratton, helping greet the guests. The collar of his jacket itched against his neck, the starched fabric too stiff for comfort. His boots, though polished, felt out of place on the stone path instead of dirt. It was easier to exchange brief pleasantries and send people inside than to endure the small talk within the crowded rooms, but even standing here left him exposed to praise he didn't feel he deserved.

With his trimmed salt-and-pepper beard, Stratton stood with a commanding presence in a suit any Eastern city would have been challenged to best. He shook hands and welcomed guests with practiced charm, unfazed by the pomp and polish surrounding him.

As Stratton greeted the latest arrivals, Elijah's thoughts drifted. He stared down the street toward the man's office, his mind wandering to the day a year ago when a wagon had pulled up in front. The beautiful woman he now called his wife had jumped down before her father had hardly set the handbrake, running to him with a beaming smile. The memory brought a smile to Elijah's face, something that happened more often these days.

"Elijah," Stratton's voice broke through his reverie, "I'd like you to meet Benjamin Townsend, a member of the territorial legislature from Virginia City."

Elijah snapped back to the present, shaking the important man's hand and offering a polite smile. "Mister Townsend, a pleasure."

"Ben, Elijah Barber manages my ranch for me with his brother, Moses. They've got quite a story and served us proudly in the war." Stratton leaned in and raised his hand as if whispering a secret. "Just don't tell him a bunch of gold-mining rebel sympathizers named Virginia City."

Townsend laughed. "The pleasure is mine, Mister Barber. Congratulations on your position. High praise to be trusted by a man like this." His eyes sparkled with curiosity. "I've heard the stories, you know. Soldiers? Deputy Marshals? Quite impressive."

Elijah shifted his feet, his gaze darting toward the street before he could stop himself. "They were jobs that needed done, sir."

Stratton laughed, clapping him on the back. "Don't let him fool you, Townsend. After all that, I happen upon him on the trail, and he fights off bands of hostile natives, and teaches my men how to fend for themselves. Even learned a great deal about the cattle business in the process."

Townsend leaned in, clearly eager for details. "Very good, Barber, very good. What was it you did in the war?"

Elijah's mouth tightened slightly. He hated these questions. "Cavalry," he said briefly, hoping that would suffice. "I was a captain."

Stratton, ever the entertainer, didn't let it go. "Chased that rapscallion Price all over Missouri, Ben. They were heroes—and that was before the law work."

Townsend nodded approvingly, but Elijah felt the weight of the praise settle heavy on his shoulders. Heroes. The word never sat right. "Like I said," Elijah repeated, "we just did our jobs."

Townsend shook Elijah's hand again. "And we're the better for it." He smiled at Stratton. "If you'll excuse me then."

Stratton introduced a few more guests, each exchange bringing similar accolades and stories. By the time Stratton turned to him with a knowing look, Elijah was already debating slipping away. "You're doing well, Elijah. Keep it up."

Just then, a light touch on his shoulder pulled Elijah from his thoughts, and he turned. She wore her reddish-brown hair pulled back, and her eyes sparkled. Maggie's dress, a deep emerald green with intricate lace detailing along the bodice and sleeves, reflected the evening's elegance. She wore it with the grace of someone who thrived in this environment, even if it was as foreign to her as it was to him.

Elijah's face lit up as he saw her. She was a breath of fresh air, a reminder of everything real amidst the polished veneers of the party. "You look beautiful," he whispered.

"And you look handsome, as always," she replied, smiling. She reached up and touched his beard. "I'm finally getting used to this. How are you holding up?"

"Better now," he admitted, his eyes twinkling with relief. "This place feels like a different world sometimes." He glanced at Stratton, then mouthed, "Save me."

Maggie smiled, slipping her arm inside his. "It does feel different. But it's our world now. And we're making it a good one."

Elijah turned and pointed toward Stratton's office. "You know, I was just standing here thinking about the day you showed up. Such a wonderful day."

She smiled and squeezed his arm. "It was." She rolled her eyes. "Although had I known the law would ultimately realize your outcome far outweighed you going beyond your mandate, I could have just summoned you back to Omaha."

She turned to Stratton. "Jon, I need to borrow Elijah. You can't keep him out here all night, you know."

Stratton chuckled. "Of course, Maggie. Enjoy the party, Elijah."

As they walked inside, Maggie pointed to Moses, who worked the room with his usual charm, laughing and talking to an attractive young woman. "Look at your brother. He's fitting right in. That's Helen Jonesen. Her father and mine have become friends and have plenty of ideas for expanding the livery and freight business."

Elijah grinned. "Well, that's fine for Moses, but I don't need to talk to any women. I have you."

Maggie feigned flattery. "Sweet talker. But this is part of your world now, if only rarely. You need to make acquaintances." She gestured across the room where her father, Patrick, mingled. "If the sixty-five-year-old Irish immigrant can make friends out here, so can you, Elijah."

Elijah smiled and nodded, the knot in his chest loosening as Maggie's presence anchored him. They mingled with the guests, his arm around her, the noise and stares of the party fading into the background.

Later in the evening, Stratton found Elijah with Moses in a corner of the room, a young boy trailing behind him. His face lit up as he saw the Barbers, and he skipped forward, eager to make their acquaintance.

"Elijah, Moses," Stratton said, resting a hand on the boy's shoulder. "I'd like you to meet my son, Edward." He looked down at the young man and smiled, then back at the Barbers. "He has been beside himself that he hasn't met you yet."

Elijah guessed the boy to be about eleven or twelve years old, give or take, though he carried himself with the manner of someone much older. He stood tall for his age, with bright eyes and a wide grin that spoke of admiration.

"It's a pleasure," Edward said, the words tumbling out with excitement. "Father has told me stories about you. About how you— "

Stratton cleared his throat, his smile tight. "Edward, what did I tell you about listening too closely to adult conversations?"

Elijah exchanged a look with Moses, who raised an eyebrow, half amused. "We've had our fair share of work," Elijah said carefully. He looked around, then lowered his voice. "But we're ranchers now, and proud to work for your father."

Edward flushed, realizing his enthusiasm had overstepped. "Sorry, Father. I just think what they've done is. . . impressive."

"One day, you'll have plenty of stories of your own to tell," Stratton replied, recovering quickly. "After all, the sign out front of my land office will someday say 'Stratton and Son.'"

Edward gave a polite smile. "Yes sir."

The elder Stratton looked at the Barbers with admiration. "These men will be a large part of that success, Edward. You'd do well to learn about sacrifice and work ethic from them."

Edward nodded, but his gaze stayed on Elijah, a spark of curiosity still burning. "But also, from books and schooling. That's why I'm going out east, right, Father?"

Jonathan Stratton gave Elijah an apologetic glance. "Yes, that's the plan. There's more to building a future than just hard work. Education will open doors that ranching cannot. But the Barbers though, they— "

Elijah smiled. "It's OK." He looked at Edward. "Your father is just saying that you need the learning just as much as the hard work. We never got that."

Moses chuckled and raised his glass. "I only went to the one-room school 'till I was about fourteen, and even then, only half the time. Imagine if they coulda taught me more."

Stratton laughed, easing the moment. He clapped Moses on the back, his posture relaxing. "Well, we all have our paths, don't we?"

Turning to Edward, Stratton's tone shifted back to its formal cadence. "Edward, why don't you go find your mother? I'm sure she'd like to hear about your impressions of the evening."

"Yes, Father," Edward replied, his enthusiasm dimming as he obediently turned away.

As Edward walked away, Elijah noticed the boy's shoulders slump. He paused a few steps away, glancing back to see his father sharing a hearty laugh with Moses—a side of Jonathan Stratton he knew the boy seldom witnessed. Elijah couldn't tell if Edward's dejection stemmed from being dismissed or yearning for the camaraderie his father shared with him and Moses.

"Eager kid," Moses said after Jonathan excused himself.

"I'd say," Elijah replied quietly, his gaze searching out the boy. "Hope he finds what he's looking for."

As the celebration continued inside, Elijah stepped outside for a moment of respite. The night air was refreshing, a welcome change from the warmth and noise of the party. He took out his pipe, packing it with a practiced hand, and struck a match. The glow of the flame briefly illuminated his face before he took a few puffs, sending wisps of smoke into the starry sky, constantly reminded of his father, Joseph, and mentor, Talbot, when he partook in the ritual.

The view was breathtaking to Elijah, even after a few years in the territory. The moon hung high, casting a silvery light over the landscape. To the east, the rugged silhouette of the mountains framed the valley, their peaks stark against the night sky. The stillness of the night and the knowledge that they'd be back at the ranch in a few days soothed his soul.

As he enjoyed his pipe, he heard the shuffle of small footsteps behind him. He turned and saw Edward Stratton. The boy's face lit up with excitement and curiosity, his cheeks flushed from the party inside.

"You're sneakin' off from the party?" Elijah said, chuckling.

Edward grinned, stepping closer. "Father's inside talking about railroads again. I'd rather be out here, learning something real."

"Well, railroads are plenty real," Elijah said, nodding toward the stars. "But this is about as real as it gets. What's on your mind, son?"

Edward hesitated, his boots scuffing the dirt. Then, as though the floodgates had opened, the questions came all at once. "Is it really true you chased guerrillas in the war? And became deputy marshals who hunted down the notorious Frank Tucker? And chased the Crenshaw gang all the way from Omaha to Julesburg?"

Elijah chuckled, shifting his weight. "That's all in the past, Edward."

"But it's true, right?" Edward pressed, his eyes shining. "You and Moses did all those things? And then you caught on to my father's cattle drive and helped them fight off the Sioux and protect the herd."

Elijah puffed on his pipe, taking a long draw before answering. "We did what we had to do, for ourselves and for others. But it wasn't like the stories you hear." None of the glory and all the horror, Elijah thought. "And we only caught on with your father after he saved us when we were in a bad way."

The boy's eyes glimmered with fascination. "It must've felt good, though. Making a name for yourself. Being someone people respected, maybe even feared."

Elijah's smile faded slightly, and his gaze drifted toward the distant hills. "Respect is earned by the work you do, not the guns you carry. That's what your father's building here—something lasting. My brother and I are proud to help him. That's what we do now."

"But that's how you'll help him, right?" Edward asked eagerly. "Ensure nobody ever takes it from him?"

Elijah exhaled through his nose, growing more uncomfortable. If this young boy, not even his, could put him so ill at ease, how would he do as a father? "We'll ensure your father's ranch is as successful as it can be."

Edward's enthusiasm dimmed, and he kicked at the ground. "He wants me to go East for schooling with my mother's people like you heard. Business, the law, politics, and all of that." He sighed. "Become a gentleman."

Elijah studied the boy for a moment. He recognized the inner struggle, the push and pull of expectations against personal dreams. "Yeah, I gathered that. But it's not a bad path," he said, choosing his words carefully. "It'll prepare you to take over his businesses one day."

"But what if I want to stay here?" Edward asked, his voice dropping. "What if I wanted to do something bigger? Something more adventurous—like you?"

Elijah took the pipe from his mouth. "Adventure isn't always what you think it is, Edward. It's not glory—it's hard choices, risk, and sacrifice. You've got an opportunity to build something that doesn't leave scars." He tapped his chest. "I've got plenty, inside and out, and I wish I'd had the opportunity to be successful without them. Does that make sense?"

Edward lowered his gaze, disappointment flickering across his face. "Maybe." Elijah cocked his head and gave an exaggerated frown, and the boy smiled. "Yes, sir. It does."

Elijah placed a hand on the boy's shoulder, softening his tone. "You've got your own path to carve, Edward. But remember, the best legacies aren't built on how fast you can draw a gun—they're built on what you leave behind for others." He looked the boy in the eyes. "You'll do well to follow your father's plan. Mine wasn't around long enough for me to do so, and he didn't have the resources your father does." He smiled. "But until then, you feel free to ride out anytime your mother lets you and we'll see if Moses and I can't rustle up some adventure for you."

Edward perked up at that, a small chuckle escaping his lips. "That'll have to do for now, then. Thanks for talking to me, Mister Barber."

"Anytime, son," Elijah answered.

The back door creaked, and Harrison Webb, Stratton's butler, stepped out, smoothing his vest as he glanced toward Edward. "Sorry to interrupt, Mister Barber, but Master Edward," he called, "your father's lookin' for you inside."

Edward sighed, his youthful energy dimming at the mention of returning to the affair inside. "Yes, sir," he muttered, brushing past Harrison without another word.

Harrison watched the boy disappear into the house, then turned to Elijah with a nod. "Evenin', Mister Barber. Mighty fine night, ain't it?"

Elijah tipped his hat in greeting. "Evenin', Harrison. And I told you, call me Elijah." He smiled. "Family doin' alright?"

The older man smiled, the moonlight catching the salt and pepper in his hair. "Oh yessir. Wife keeps me in line, and the boys are growin' faster than weeds. Can't complain." He glanced toward the house, where laughter and music spilled through the open windows. "Though I'd take quiet nights over these fancy affairs any day."

Elijah chuckled, puffing on his pipe. "That boy feels the same about these things, don't he? Would rather find some adventure then attend parties and schooling in the east."

"That's a fact," Harrison answered, looking toward the party briefly. "But I believe that's that happiest I seen him, meetin' you and your brother tonight."

Elijah shook his head, unsure what to do with such comments. "Well, I'm glad he enjoyed something about tonight, then."

"Yessir," Harrison answered. He then frowned. "Well, I could speak with you all night long, sir, but I best be gettin' back to work."

Elijah smiled. "I could as well, Harrison. You tell your family I asked after them."

Harrison dipped his head respectfully. "Will do, Mister Barber, and you as well. Y'all have a good evenin'."

Elijah tapped out his pipe a few moments later and returned inside just in time to catch Stratton raising a glass, his voice carrying over the murmur of the guests.

"To new beginnings and the prosperous future of Bozeman. I'm honored to welcome you to my new home after you graciously welcomed me not long ago." He spotted Elijah and waved. "Maybe the next big party will be at the ranch to celebrate the new headquarters buildings."

Elijah smiled and waved, then leaned close to Maggie. "Not if I have anything to say about it," he whispered.

She elbowed him, smiling, and whispered back, "That's your boss, Elijah."

". . . May we continue to grow and thrive together," Stratton concluded.

The room applauded, and Stratton put his arms around his wife and son, soaking it in. All eyes were on the mighty man but Elijah's. He looked at Maggie, a hand on her stomach, thinking of the growing and thriving he sought for his family.

⸻

Scottish Highlands, Moray Firth Region

The wind keened through the glen, whipping through tufts of heather and rattling the wooden fence posts that marked the edge of the Hill family farmstead. The sun was dipping low, casting its golden light over the rolling hills of his surname and the cliffs beyond, where the sea lay just out of view. A lone sheep, its wool caked with mud from the damp earth, wandered near the barn, bleating softly. But to Carson Hill, the once-picturesque view had become a prison.

"Ach, it's a fine night for wonderin' where yer next meal'll come from," Finn MacDonald called out, stepping over the fence with ease and landing beside him. The smell of damp earth and peat smoke clung to him. His grin was lopsided, but not without warmth. "How's the fence, then? Gonna hold, or is this all for naught?"

Hill finished tying off the last rope with a grunt, brushing the sweat from his forehead. His coat flapped in the evening breeze, the fabric fraying at the elbows. "If it holds, it'll be a miracle," he muttered, switching to Gaelic briefly. His words came faster in his native tongue, their rhythm sharper and more biting.

Finn chuckled, leaning against the post. "Ye've a knack fer miracles, ye do. Or ye did, once upon a time. Held out longer than the lot o' them."

Hill sighed, his eyes tracing the outline of the farm, from the sagging roof of the house to the barn where he had spent his youth working beside his da. His ma had kept the place tidy, her laughter filling the kitchen even when the crops failed, or animals didn't sell. But they were both gone now—his da dead from exhaustion after the debts piled too high, his ma not long after, her grief and hunger too much to bear. And his younger brother, Angus. . . Hill swallowed hard, the memory of his brother's lifeless body found in the woods after a "hunting accident" still raw. A hunting accident, no doubt arranged by one of the clearance's most menacing enforcers, Torcall MacLeod—a traitor to the people he came from.

"Aye," Finn said, stepping closer. "If ye cannot save it, no man can. They've already taken so much—and there's only so much a body can stand. Yer family, yer coin, and soon enough, yer home."

Hill exhaled through his nose, his gaze drifting toward the distant hills. "It wasn't meant to be this way," he muttered. "I was supposed to open a proper trade yard by now. Livestock deals, contracts—somethin' bigger than sheep an' a few coos. But the world doesnae give a damn about what was meant to be."

Finn nodded. "Aye, I 'spose not. But ye could leave this place. Ye're too clever a man to waste away here, Carson Hill."

As they stepped inside the stone walls and thatched roof of the small home, the sound of hoofbeats interrupted them, distant but growing louder. Hill's head snapped up, and his breath hitched when he saw three riders approaching from the west road. MacLeod rode at the front, his heavy overcoat flaring behind him, and the two men flanking him carried the cold air of hired muscle.

The fire crackled in the hearth, its warm glow casting flickering shadows that the walls seemed to absorb. Hill paced near it, his hands trembling—not from fear, but from the weight of everything pressing down on him. The deaths of his family. The humiliation of being unable to hold on to what they had built. And the knowledge that MacLeod wouldn't stop until he had wrung out whatever scraps were left.

Finn watched him closely. "What are ye thinkin', then?"

Hill didn't answer immediately. His gaze flicked to the iron poker resting in the hearth, its tip glowing red-hot. The trembling in his hands stopped, replaced by something steadier. He looked at Finn, his voice low but clear. "Are ye with me?"

Finn's brow furrowed. "Aye, always, but— "

Before Finn could finish, the heavy thud of boots sounded on the porch. The door burst open, and MacLeod strode in, his coat damp from the sea mist. His eyes, cold and calculating, swept across the room.

"Carson Hill," MacLeod said, his voice dripping with mock civility. "I thought I might find ye sulkin' by the fire." He gestured to the room. "Awfy quiet in here, eh? Nae ma, nae da, nae brother."

Hill's knuckles whitened. "Ye've taken enough, MacLeod. There's naethin' left I can give ye."

MacLeod clicked his tongue. "Ach, ye say that, but I hear different. There's sheep an' wool in the barn, and a few coos fattenin' on what's left o' yer pasture." He leaned in closer. "And the land an' hoose itself—still worth somethin', aye?" He gave a look of mock disgust and glanced at his associates. "Not that I'd live in it."

Hill felt his face burn. MacLeod's words struck like a hammer, but it was the sneer—the man's satisfaction in his misery—that ignited something in him. All the grief, humiliation, and rage he had buried came roaring to the surface, a tidal wave that wouldn't be held back. His gaze flicked once more to the iron poker.

"I've buried my family here, and can barely make a livin'," Hill said, his voice barely above a whisper. "Isn't it enough?"

"And ye'll join 'em if ye keep refusin' me," MacLeod replied, his tone hardening. I'll be takin' what's owed, one way or 'nother."

The room crackled with tension, the only sound the faint pop of the fire.

Without warning, Hill lunged. His hand closed around the iron poker, and he swung with all his might. The glowing tip connected with MacLeod's jaw, the force of the blow sending him staggering backward. The man cursed, blood pouring from his mouth as the smell of burned flesh filled the small space.

Finn didn't hesitate. He slashed at the nearest thug, his knife biting deep into the man's side. The second thug reached for his gun, but Finn's blade was quicker, slashing across his throat in one swift motion, the gun clattering to the floor.

MacLeod, disoriented and bleeding, fumbled for the pistol in his coat. His fingers closed around it, and he twisted it free. He pointed it at Finn standing nearby, but before he could fire, Hill grabbed the fallen gun, his hands trembling as he raised it. He had never fired a gun, but instinct guided him now.

Hill pointed it at MacLeod's midsection and squeezed the trigger. The shot echoed through the farmhouse, and MacLeod slumped to the floor, his eyes wide and unseeing.

The silence that followed was suffocating. Hill lowered the gun, his breath coming in ragged gasps. The smell of gunpowder and blood filled the room, mingling with the smoke from the fire.

Finn wiped his blade on one of the dead man's coat, the crimson smearing across the fabric. He let out a dark chuckle, the sound low and bitter. "Aye, well," he muttered, glancing at Hill, "that took a wee turn, didn't it?" He stood and eyed Hill. "Didn't know ye had that in ye."

Hill stared at the bodies, his mind struggling to process what had just happened. "Wanted men we'll be," he whispered.

Finn clapped a hand on Hill's shoulder, his breath still ragged from the fight. "Aye, well, it's a good thing we've a ship waitin', then." He crouched down, his fingers digging through MacLeod's coat until they closed around two leather pouches that jingled with the weight of coins. "Ye kept me fed longer than any man wi' sense would've, an' then ye went an' saved my life. Least I can do is cover yer fare to the new world."

Hill stared at him a moment, still regaining his breath, and then a strange calm came over him. "America," he said, his voice firm. "We take what we deserve, and we don't look back."

Finn grinned. "Aye. And this time, we make sure no one ever takes it from ye."

Hill looked at the horses MacLeod and his men rode in on, then at the sparse possessions he would bring with him. He had lost everything here. But in America, he wouldn't lose again.

PART ONE

— • —

FIFTEEN YEARS LATER: SPRING, 1884

RUSTLERS

— • —

T he hay wagon rattled along the rutted trail, its wheels cutting deep into the muddy Montana Territory thaw as melting snow revealed patches of grass beneath the slush, signaling spring was coming. The horses plodded forward, their hooves squelching with each step, while a soft breeze carried the faint smell of damp earth and rebirth.

Clint Thompson guided the team with a loose grip on the reins, his back stiff and shoulders hunched beneath his sheepskin coat. He squinted into the dying light; the horizon glowing orange as the sun dipped behind the distant Absaroka Range. They'd hauled the last load of winter hay to what remained of his herd—scarcely enough to feed them for a week. With the snow melting, he prayed the cattle would find grass in time to spare him from buying more forage on credit he didn't have.

The small line of cows grazing on the freshly tossed hay in the pasture caught his attention, and he pulled the team to a stop, resting the reins against his leg. He counted them, frowning as he realized the number, while low, was higher than expected. He flicked the reins and kept moving, his mind chewing on the thought. A few extra heads of cattle mixed in with his own should've been a good thing, but it left him uneasy instead.

His foreman Ewan rode up alongside him, his mount's breath misting in the cool air. "Oughta' hold them for another week, boss," Ewan said, patting his horse's neck. "Maybe this warm-up will allow 'em to find some cheat grass."

"Maybe." Thompson's voice was distant, his gaze still locked on the grazing herd. His looked past the cows. The Box H ranch wasn't far from here, just beyond the ridge. The spread was still one of the smallest around but was growing fast while other small outfits were struggling. He couldn't help but think of the original Box H spread—a modest operation once owned by a man named Mulligan, who'd sold it for less than it was worth when debt and bad luck squeezed him dry. Now, under Carson Hill's control, it had ballooned into one of the fastest-growing ranches in the region.

Thompson had resisted the new bank's offer to buy him out last summer when First National Bank of Bozeman would no longer extend loans or credit. The growing seasons had been unlike anything anyone had seen, and he'd thought he could get caught up with good grass, mindful spending, and a little luck. He'd taken a loan from newcomer Carson Hill's bank instead, and now that decision felt like trying to bail out a sinking boat with a cracked bucket. The interest had mounted faster than he could keep up with, and instead of bringing relief, spring had only revealed the depth of his problems.

"I should've sold then," he muttered under his breath. But selling back then would've felt like defeat, and pride was hard to let go of.

"You say somethin'?" Ewan asked.

Thompson shook his head and snapped the reins. The wagon creaked forward again, its wheels splashing through shallow puddles. "Where's Clay, Wren, and Jesse? They should've been back by now."

Ewan frowned. "Don't rightly know. Thought they were ridin' in from the western line this morning."

Thompson's unease deepened, gnawing at his insides. He clicked his tongue, urging the horses into a faster pace. As they rounded a bend, the sprawling cottonwood near the property line came into view—and his blood ran cold.

Three men hung from the tree's thick branches; their necks twisted at unnatural angles. One of their horses still lingered nearby, grazing on the sparse grass as if nothing had happened. The other two had likely not stopped after running from underneath the men, leaving only the trampled ground and the creak of the nooses swaying in the breeze. A running iron lay in the mud below them, and someone had tied a crude sign around Clay's neck: *Rustlers*.

"Dear God," Thompson whispered.

Ewan dismounted, his face pale. "What in the. . . Boss. . .What do we do?"

Thompson stared at the bodies, his chest heaving. His hands trembled as he climbed down from the wagon and stumbled toward them. Clay's eyes stared ahead, lifeless and glassy. The rope had bitten so deeply into his neck that it looked like a second mouth.

"Cut 'em down," Thompson said, his voice cracking, his face void of emotion. "For God's sake, cut 'em down."

THE WAGON CREAKED into the yard of the T Bar ranch just as the last light of day faded into twilight. The air was chilly and still, but the tension wrapped around Thompson's chest like a vise. Ewan jumped down first, grabbing a lantern from the porch as he moved toward the back of the wagon, where the bodies lay covered by only their coats.

Thompson climbed the steps to the front door, his boots heavy with mud. He stopped short when he noticed the unfamiliar horses tied to the hitching post—sleek animals with Box H brands on their flanks.

His gut twisted. He pushed the door open, the smell of fresh coffee and warm biscuits hitting him. His wife sat at the kitchen table with their two children, her hands folded in her lap. The fear in her eyes told him everything.

Carson Hill sat at the head of the table, casually sipping from a cup of coffee. "There ye are, Clint. Was beginnin' to think ye'd gotten lost." He gestured toward an empty chair. "Come. Sit. Warm up with some of this fine coffee your wife has so graciously provided me."

Finn MacDonald leaned against the wall near the stove, working a knife under his fingernails. Two other Box H men sat nearby, their holsters adjusted to be on full display.

Thompson didn't move. His eyes darted to his wife, then back to Hill. "What do you want?"

Hill sighed, setting his cup down gently. "Clint, ye've missed yer last three payments. I'm afraid my bank is no longer in a position to extend ye any more credit. Especially not when we bought out First National loans to begin with."

"This is my home," Thompson said through gritted teeth. "Ye can't just—"

"I don't want to take it, Clint. I've been in yer position. I'd much rather ye'd paid what was owed." Hill leaned forward, his eyes softening in a way that felt rehearsed. "But that's not the world we live in, aye? There are other small ranchers reporting losses, cattle gone missing. It's a bad look, especially when their brands turn up mixed in with yer herd." He paused a moment. "No doubt ye seen your herd is bigger than expected in spots. Aye, not big enough to survive, but enough that other spreads feel the struggle too."

Thompson's heart pounded. "You know I despise rustling, that I'm an honest man, and that any beeves without a Bar T brand are in there by mistake."

Hill spread his hands. "Maybe so. But ye'd be surprised what I found—If it were only my own, perhaps we could work something out, but Box H brands weren't the only ones. There's plenty for folks to talk about. Even if ye're a good man, Clint, yer hands might've been desperate enough to help ye out."

Ewan stepped forward. "Lies! Those men we cut down were—"

Finn's knife tapped the butt of his revolver, and the two Box H men shifted in their seats, their eyes hard and unblinking. Ewan stopped, swallowing hard.

Hill didn't even glance at him. "Let's not make this worse. I have the papers here." He gestured to the table. "Sign, and ye can take yer family to Livingston with enough money for train tickets to start fresh somewhere else, out of debt. Somewhere that folks have no reason to associate you with rustling, fair or not. There's a bit of dignity in that." Hill offered his best sympathetic face. "It's more 'n anyone offered me when I lost my farm in the old country, and I came out alright."

Thompson stared at the papers, bile rising in his throat. His gaze flicked to his wife and children, their faces etched with fear. Her eyes dropped, and she nodded.

Thompson's shoulders slumped in defeat, and he picked up the pen.

Hill watched him sign, then slid a small burlap sack across the table. "Not as much as selling last spring might have earned ye, but there's enough in there for yer journey."

Thompson didn't respond. His hands trembled as he stood, his mind numb.

Hill stood as well, adjusting his gloves as he prepared to leave, his voice turning colder. "Good luck, Clint. I doubt we'll cross paths again."

Finn opened the door, and the frosty night air rushed in as the Box H hands exited. As Hill stepped outside, he paused on the porch, his gaze lingering on the bodies in the wagon. "It's a shame some folks feel justice need be taken care of in such a cruel way. Ye've got my sympathies."

He mounted his horse, settling into the saddle with practiced ease. Finn followed, glancing at the doorway, where Ewan stood stiff as a fence post. "Don't make me regret forgivin' yer outburst," Finn said, his tone low but deadly. His eyes shifted to Thompson's wife and children, then back to the rancher. "We move in day after tomorrow."

Summit Valley

— ❖ —

E lijah Barber's eyes narrowed, his hand hovering near the grip of
his Colt Peacemaker. A bead of sweat trickled down his temple,
but he didn't dare move. This wasn't a moment for blinking, not now.
He stared down his opponent, his posture tense, every muscle coiled
like a spring ready to snap.

From the corner of his eye, he saw Moses approaching, his brother's
long shadow stretching across the ground. Moses halted, recognizing
the intensity of the standoff. Elijah waved him off with a slight motion
of his free hand, signaling he had it under control.

"Back off, Mo," Elijah hissed, never taking his eyes off his adversary.

Moses hesitated, but then stepped back, a knowing grin tugging at
the corners of his mouth. "You got it, brother," he said, his voice laced
with amusement. Over forty now, his thick red beard had a bit of silver,
but his jovial demeanor was the same as ever.

Elijah's focus sharpened, his eyes locking onto the figure before
him. The sun's glare was blinding, but he could still see the determination etched into the youthful face across from him. His opponent's
hand twitched near the holster, and Elijah braced himself for the
inevitable.

"Ready, boy?" Elijah asked, his voice calm.

His opponent swallowed hard, eyes wide with anticipation. "Ready, Pa," came the steady reply.

A heartbeat later, the boy's hand flew to his gun. But Elijah was faster, his Colt out and aimed before the boy could get the barrel up.

"Bang," Elijah said, lowering his weapon with a satisfied smile.

Moses whistled, shaking his head in admiration. "You're gettin' closer, JT," he called out. He stepped forward and clapped his nephew on the shoulder.

Joseph Talbot Barber, named for Elijah's father and his mentor Talbot Jones, dropped his hand to the side. "Thought I had you that time, Pa."

Margaret Hennessey Barber appeared from the direction of the horse corral, wiping her hands on a cloth and shaking her head as she walked toward the house. She wore sturdy work clothes: a faded chambray shirt tucked into well-worn trousers, sturdy boots, and a bandana tied around her neck. Her reddish-brown hair was pulled back into a loose braid, seeming to glow in the sunlight, Elijah thought. He couldn't help but admire her; she looked as beautiful in her work attire as she did in a dress.

A dog bounded behind her, barking happily. The dog had a striking brindle and black coat, much like his sire, Brutus. Also like his sire, he was a mix of breeds, but with the strong characteristics of mastiff and herding breeds. The dog circled JT before sitting at Elijah's feet.

"Easy there, Scout," Elijah said, giving the dog a pat. Scout was a regular reminder of the loyal companion who had saved them more than once, both in Nebraska and then in Montana Territory.

"Just what I love to see, husband and son dueling instead of getting washed up for noon dinner, and their dog to protect them from me."

Elijah touched the brim of his hat to his wife and motioned his son over. JT handed the revolver and belt to him, and Elijah checked it.

JT rolled his eyes. "It ain't loaded, Pa. I always check."

"Isn't," Elijah corrected. He holstered the weapon and held both belts at his side. "Beginning to think we spent too much time and money building a school and hiring a teacher."

Moses looked at JT. "You're gettin' there, kid. Won't be long before your Pa has to let you start carryin' for real." The deal had long been that Elijah would not let his son carry a weapon on his belt when working outside the headquarters until he could outdraw his father.

JT brightened at the encouragement, heading off to wash up as instructed. Elijah and Moses watched him go, both taking in the sight of the boy who looked so much like a younger version of Elijah. At six feet tall already, with thick brown hair and a broad frame that favored his uncle Moses, the fourteen-year-old JT was growing into a man faster than Elijah was ready for.

"He's gonna get there," Moses said. "And you're gonna have to honor your word." He pointed at the gun belts his brother held. He stops flarin' it as he clears leather, and he'll have you.

Elijah scratched his beard, now with plenty of white mixing with the brown. "I'm getting awful close to having to go as fast as I can to prevent that. Not sure I want him to know how fast either of us really is."

"Or was," Moses replied with a grin. "I think Billy McCray would have us both licked these days. I'm gonna stay on his good side."

Billy McCray, a stout, barrel-chested red head with a fiery temper, had come on at Summit Valley as an orphan—when not much older than JT was now—doing odd jobs for the Barbers a few years back. Elijah and Moses took a shine to him and gave him more responsibilities as the years passed. Everything Billy knew about cattle he'd learned from Travis Carrington, but everything he knew about being handy with a gun had come from the Barbers.

Elijah gave a disapproving frown and shook his head.

Moses chuckled. "JT will figure everything out soon enough," he said. "It ain't the best kept secret in Bozeman or the valley, even all these years later. He'd be proud. Maybe even understand why you are the way you are with him. 'Course, he won't understand why you taught Billy but not him."

Elijah shook his head. "It's been pleasant not having to think about such things for my son. Let's not spoil it just yet."

"Who walked away from the duel?" called a voice in a Texas drawl that had mellowed some since the brothers first heard it nearly eighteen years ago.

Travis Carrington, one of Stratton's cattle drive hands who first encountered the Barbers as they wandered for help after killing the notorious Crenshaw brothers in Julesburg, Colorado, approached. Moses had been close to death, but the encounter had led to a lifelong friendship. Hank Stephens, the other hand who had helped them, had returned to Texas in the spring of 1867, but not before imparting all his ranching wisdom to the Barbers.

Travis, a decade younger than Elijah at thirty-eight years of age, had stayed on, wanting no part of management and just happy to be a foreman and spend a lot of time in the saddle around cattle and the mountains. He was tall and lean, with sun-weathered skin, a thick mustache, and piercing blue eyes that always seemed to squint against the Texas sun he once knew so well.

Moses pointed to Elijah. "Still the king for now."

Travis shook his head as he joined them. "Oughta just put him in his place and show him who the fastest 'round here is," Travis said.

"Don't know that I still am," Elijah responded.

Travis appraised Elijah's statement and nodded. "You're right, boss. I reckon it's Billy."

Elijah scoffed as they heard the chow bell being rung from the headquarters house and walked that way.

As they walked, Scout trotted alongside Elijah, his ears perked up and tail wagging. They passed various buildings essential to the ranch's operations. There was a bunkhouse for the single ranch hands, a simple yet sturdy wooden structure. Cabins for those with families dotted the landscape, each with a small garden and a sense of home that spoke of permanence. Maggie's horse breeding barn and corral were a flurry of activity, with mares and foals moving about, overseen by attentive ranch hands.

Beyond the living quarters, the blacksmith's shop rang with the clang of metal on metal as he crafted and repaired tools and horseshoes. The large barn held supplies and equipment essential for the ranch's daily operations. Above it was the hayloft, stacked high with bales of hay and a granary for storing the feed.

A carpenter's workshop was busy with men crafting everything from furniture to wagon wheels. The laundry building was alive with the activity of women washing clothes and linens, the scent of lye soap wafting through the air. A smokehouse cured game meat to add to the copious amount of beef, ensuring a steady food supply for the long Montana winters.

The central building, a hub of activity, housed offices, a kitchen, and a dining hall. The dining hall was used for guests and weekly communal meals. Today, Saturday, was noon dinner with the foreman and top hands. Elijah usually demanded they finish any chores and spend time with their families the rest of the day, which he ensured to do himself. Sunday dinner, after services in the church they had built on the ranch, was always the family of a hand or two, or perhaps visiting guests, and Sunday supper was a Barber family affair.

Summit Valley was a small town, a self-sufficient community nestled in the Paradise Valley. Every structure and every person played a vital role in maintaining the sprawling operation, ensuring that the ranch not only survived but thrived in the rugged Montana Territory.

Elijah took it all in, as he always did. This was their world, built from the ground up, and it was a world worth protecting. On paper, this was Jonathan Stratton's world. In practice, it was run by the Barber Brothers, with their cattle foreman, Travis Carrington. Elijah, everyone including Moses knew, however, was the boss.

As they neared the dining hall, the pleasant aroma of home-cooked food wafted through the air. The door swung open, and Moses's wife, Helen, stepped out, her three young daughters, Ruth, Hannah, and Abigail, trailing behind her. Helen had a warm smile and a sturdy build, her brown hair tied back. Helen, along with a few wives of hands, did all the house cooking, a job she took on seriously and with love.

She greeted her husband and brother-in-law with a nod. "Cleaned up, are we?" she asked.

"Oh, yes, ma'am, or soon will be, rather," Elijah answered. He smiled as his brother greeted his wife, forever happy to see him settled down. "Are the girls helping you today?"

Helen laughed. "Always. And keeping them out of trouble is a full-time job beyond the cooking."

The three girls, ranging in age from young Abigail at six to Ruth at ten, giggled and waved at their father and uncle. Moses stooped to give each of them a quick hug before they scurried off to join the other children playing nearby.

Elijah's two younger daughters, Molly and Bridget, ran up to him, their skirts swishing around their legs. "Papa!"

Molly, the older of the two at twelve, had her mother's reddish-brown hair, while eight-year-old Bridget sported a shade closer to Elijah's own brown. They hugged their father tightly.

"Wash up, now," Elijah said, nudging them toward the washbasin.

As the families gathered for the meal, Elijah looked around at the assembled ranch hands. There was Horse Goes Ahead, who was called Henry most of the time, a member of the Crow tribe who had found a place among them as a skilled horseman. He helped Maggie with breeding and breaking horses, and was called upon to scout or break a trail whenever required.

Jackson "Jax" Turner was a Black former Buffalo Soldier who had joined the ranch after leaving the army. He saw that Travis's orders were carried out by the hands when it came to cattle and oversaw just about any other work happening on a daily basis. Jax, with his easy smile and quick wit, greeted Elijah with a firm handshake.

"Good to see ya, Boss." Heard about the duel. JT gettin' faster?"

Elijah smiled. "Too fast for my liking."

Long wooden tables were set with hearty fare: roast beef, potatoes, beans, fresh-baked bread, and pies cooling on a sideboard.

"Smells wonderful, Helen," Elijah said.

The other men all echoed their agreement and thanks.

Billy McCray, one of today's invited young hands, appeared in the doorway, wiping his boots and removing his hat. The redhead grinned as he caught sight of everyone.

"Well it smells mighty fine in here. I reckon my turn at Saturday dinner is one of my favorite days of the month."

"Billy," Travis said with a shake of his head as he eyed two low-slung pistols, "how many times do I have to tell you—take those things off before comin' inside here. You tryin' to make me look bad in front of the boss?"

Billy's eyes lowered for a moment, but then his easy smile came. He removed the belts and hung them on a high peg, then stepped inside as he smoothed his hair. "My apologies Ms. Maggie, Ms. Helen."

Both women smiled and waved him off, and Elijah gave Travis a look of approval for taking care of his man.

As was the custom, the youngest hand grabbed a plate first and moved down the line, everyone else following. As was also custom, the men could not avoid talking about work.

"Another week of solid weather, it might be time for spring round-up like we been sayin', boss," Travis said. "Seen some cows gettin' after cheat grass in one of the wind break pastures."

Elijah nodded. "May will be here the end of next week. Reckon that's as good a time as any if the weather continues."

"'Till we get snowed on again," Moses added. "I tell you one thing, this place has it on Illinois for scenery, but 'least we always knew when winter was over."

Travis turned to Billy. "Well, Billy, you'll make sure the hands know to start getting' prepared. Won't you, son?"

Billy grinned as he found a seat, admiring his full plate. "Yes, sir."

JT, sitting nearby, looked up eagerly. "Pa, can I take part in the round-up this year?"

Elijah contemplated the question, his eyes meeting Maggie's. She seemed to wonder herself what he would say. Elijah decided not to have the discussion in front of everyone during the meal, however.

"We'll talk about it, son."

JT's face showed a mix of anticipation and slight disappointment, but he nodded.

Elijah smiled and patted his son's shoulder. "Now, son, how about you say the prayer for us?"

"Yessir," JT said, bowing his head.

As JT prayed, Elijah said a silent prayer of his own for a peaceful and successful season ahead for the Summit Valley Ranch and this blessed life he had.

News from the Circle C

— ✦ —

E lijah sat on his front porch, the rhythmic creak of the rocking chair providing a soothing counterpoint to the sounds of the morning. He puffed on his pipe, the fragrant smoke curling upwards and disappearing into the clear blue sky. The morning sun was shining on the peaks of the Absaroka Range, their snow-capped tops gleaming in the light.

While Sundays were normally quiet days, there was always some work to be done, and he had already been out to say good morning to some of the younger hands feeding horses or chickens, and tending to chores. Now, however, it was time for his Sunday morning ritual, a ritual Scout always laid at his feet for.

The view from the porch was breathtaking, with the Yellowstone River winding its way through the valley, water sparkling in the early morning sun. The pastures of the Summit Valley Ranch spread out before him were greening up, and soon they'd move the cattle out of the sheltered areas, no longer needing to perform the arduous winter chore of hauling out hay.

Elijah sipped his coffee, savoring the warmth that spread through him. The spring air was still crisp in late April, but the cup of coffee and his Sunday suit kept him comfortable. The suit alone reminded him of how far he had come. Twenty years ago, he and Moses would have considered a Sunday suit to be the cleanest one with the fewest holes. Now, it was a fine, tailored garment from the haberdashery in Bozeman.

The sound of the door opening interrupted his thoughts. Scout briefly looked up as JT stepped out, dressed in his Sunday best as well. Elijah couldn't help but smile at the sight of his son and the young man he was becoming.

"You clean up nice, son," Elijah remarked, a twinkle in his eye. "Hoping the Collins family will be at church today? Emily is the daughter, right?"

JT's face reddened, and he dropped on the porch steps, scowling. "I don't wanna talk about that, Pa."

Elijah chuckled, taking another puff of his pipe. "Alright, then. What do you want to talk about?"

JT looked out at the ranch, his expression serious. "I want to talk about the spring round-up like you said we would. I want to be a part of it this year, Pa."

Elijah's smile faded as he studied his son's earnest face. He took a moment to choose his words carefully. "There's still school left, son."

JT frowned. "You didn't go to school past fourteen. To get my high school certificate, I'd have to go all the way into Bozeman. Thirty-odd miles to Livingston then the train to Bozeman. You wanna be the one to tell Ma she won't hardly see me on account of goin' to school?"

Elijah felt a pang of impatience but tried to keep his voice steady. "Your mother would love for you to get more education. There's more to life than learning how to ride, shoot, and herd cattle." He stuck the pipe back in his mouth and then spoke around it. "And watch how you speak to me." He had long wanted to start better introducing JT to ranch operations, but he and Maggie's desire for the boy to get more schooling than Elijah did, and Elijah's own stubbornness toward the boy's demands, had prevented him thus far.

JT shot back, his eyes flashing. "You stopped goin' to school and went from a poor farmer to the head of the biggest ranch in the territory. Plus, we got a livery, and a freight business and. . . Well, you let Billy go on round-ups when he was— "

"*We* ain't got nothin', boy," Elijah cut him off sharply. "Your uncle and me run this ranch. Travis Carrington runs those cattle. Your ma runs that horse business, and your granddad, God rest his soul, is the one that started that freight outfit. It's what pays to feed you, clothe you, and keep you safe and warm. And not an ounce of it woulda been possible if not for Mister Stratton saving your uncle's life and giving us a fresh start." He pointed at JT with his pipe. "*You* don't have anything but a smart mouth. As for Billy, that boy needed work. He didn't have a ma or pa—or anyone—taking care of and providing for him."

JT stood his ground, but Elijah could see the hurt in his eyes. He softened his tone, only a bit. "You're right, though. I stopped going after grade eight, but that was because my family would have starved if I didn't. . . And we almost did anyway. Your uncle Mo and I. . . we learned things in other ways."

"You always talk about how you learned other things, or these experiences you had, but I don't know anything about it. All these men on the ranch, folks in town, even Mister Stratton—-they all seem to have this respect for you. . . somethin' they all know, and I don't."

Elijah stared at his son a moment, then looked toward the trail leading onto the ranch where the wagons of neighbors coming to church were rumbling in. Finally, he removed his pipe and rubbed his forehead.

"JT, I have made myself clear time and again that it is a wonder your uncle and I still walk God's green Earth after the struggles our family faced, then the war. . ." He trailed off. He didn't want to talk about the war, and he most certainly didn't want to talk about what came after. "I work hard, your mother works hard, so that you won't face that. But I also regret that it seems I've allowed you to take some things for granted."

JT began to speak again, but Elijah held up his hand. "We can talk about it more later."

JT bounded off the steps toward the church as Moses and his family exited their house and walked toward Elijah. Maggie soon stepped out of the house with the girls and a worried look.

They greeted each other warmly, with Moses's booming laugh and the girls' giggles filling the air as Scout ran around their feet. Elijah complimented the girls, and his wife, on their beautiful dresses and picked up Bridget, his smile returning.

Maggie's eyes followed her son's sulking form, however. "What's the matter with JT?" she asked.

Elijah shook his head, then set his daughter down, and offered Maggie his arm for the walk. "He's too much like me."

THE SUMMIT VALLEY RANCH'S CHURCH sat on a gentle rise overlooking the expansive valley pastures, framed by the majestic Absaroka Range in the distance. It was a modest, white-painted building, built with care and dedication. The morning sun cast a long shadow of the steeple and illuminated the well-tended flower beds that bordered the path leading to the entrance.

Elijah could see the buckboards and carriages of neighboring ranch and farm families arriving, the largest crowd since before the first snow last fall. The church was a symbol of the community they had built, a place where they gathered to give thanks and seek guidance, and the ranch made it clear their neighbors were always welcome. As Moses always told folks: 'Maggie is Catholic, Elijah is Methodist, and I hardly ever paid attention growing up. There's a seat for everyone.'

As they approached, Elijah noticed Reverend Jacob Harris standing by the entrance, greeting the arriving families with a warm smile. Elijah always marveled at the man's social stamina. Most preachers greeted their congregation on the way out, but Reverend Harris loved to interact with people both coming and going.

He was a middle-aged man with a kind face, his graying hair and spectacles giving him a scholarly appearance. He had arrived at the ranch several years ago with his wife when their daughter had become the one-room school teacher. The addition of the church and the school had made the ranch feel even more like a small town, a testament to Elijah and Moses's commitment to their community.

Reverend Harris waved as the Barbers approached. "Good morning, Elijah, Maggie, Moses, Helen. It's a fine day the Lord has given us."

"Morning, Reverend," Elijah replied. He removed his Sunday bowler hat. "It sure is. Looks like we have a full house today."

The Reverend nodded, his eyes twinkling. "Indeed. Folks are eager to be out and about after the long winter. It's good to see everyone coming together again."

Elijah watched as more families arrived, the buzz of conversation and laughter filling the air. He felt a deep sense of satisfaction seeing the fruits of their labor and the strength of their community.

Inside the church, the simple wooden pews filled with families. The interior was plain but welcoming, with sunlight streaming through the large windows providing light. The modesty of the building reflected the values of the people who had built it—a focus on faith and fellowship rather than grandeur.

Elijah and his family found their usual seats near the front. JT sat beside his father, still looking sullen from their earlier conversation. Elijah placed a reassuring hand on his shoulder, hoping to ease their tension.

Reverend Harris began the service with a hymn, his voice strong and clear. The congregation joined in, their voices rising in harmony. As the service progressed, Elijah glanced around the room, taking in the faces of his friends and neighbors. Each one had a story, a connection to the ranch and the community they had built together.

Reverend Harris stepped forward to read a lesson and deliver his sermon. He spoke of gratitude, of the blessings they had received, and of the challenges they had overcome. His words spoke of renewal, invoking the spring and the new ranch season.

As the sermon came to a close, the congregation bowed their heads in prayer. Elijah felt a profound sense of peace wash over him, a reminder of the strength and resilience of the community they had created. He prayed silently for guidance, for the wisdom to lead his family and bring prosperity to the ranch.

The service ended with another hymn, and as the congregation filed out of the church, Elijah exchanged warm greetings with his neighbors. He noticed James Collins, the bordering rancher, approaching him. Collins was a stout man with a weathered face, a testament to the hard work he put into his land. His hat was in his hands, and the somber look on his face told Elijah that this would not be a friendly conversation about spring grazing.

"Elijah," Collins said, shaking his hand firmly. "Good to see you. Beautiful service today. How's life at the Slash V?" The Summit Valley brand was a broken slash attached to an upside V, representing a trail to the summit. To avoid a mouthful, it had become Slash V over the years.

"Good to see you too, James," Elijah replied. "We're doing just fine. How about the Circle C?"

Collins hesitated for a moment, glancing around before lowering his voice. "I got some news. Carson Hill bought out Thompson and the T Bar spread."

Elijah's eyebrows rose. "I didn't even know Clint was selling."

"Didn't seem like he planned to," Collins said grimly. "But word is, Hill came callin' with the bank papers, and Thompson didn't have much choice. Then the family packed up and left fast—too fast." Collins looked around, then stepped closer and lowered his voice further. "I hear tell that three of Thompson's men were strung up before he signed over the deed."

Elijah's expression hardened. "Hanged?"

Collins nodded. "They'd been rustling. . . supposedly. But anyone who knew Clint or his hands would find that mighty suspicious, no matter how bad a fix they were in." Collins shifted, glancing at the ground. "We've had a lot or riders we don't recognize, on Box H mounts, workin' awful close to where our range butts up to yours."

Carson Hill had come to America fifteen years ago, making his start in the East as a livestock broker before working his way west. His early investments in cattle for the Army had turned enough profit to buy a stake in a bank, which allowed him to finance other ventures—mercantiles, mining claims, and further cattle operations. The expansion of the railroads had been his golden opportunity, and he had seized it with ruthless efficiency. While he'd always operated within the bounds of the law, Hill often found ways to "encourage" struggling folks to part with their land or businesses when debt overwhelmed them.

Elijah and Moses had first heard of him when Stratton mentioned the man's presence in Virginia City. Hill's smaller outfits served mining camps, towns like Butte, and other developing areas, but Stratton had thought his presence in Bozeman and the Valley would keep Hill out of both—an assessment that had proven false.

Elijah's gaze settled on Collins. "Thanks for tellin' me, James. You reckon Hill'll keep pressin' you on that shared range?"

Collins exhaled through his nose, his lips thinning into a hard line. "He already is. I don't want trouble, but I also can't afford to give up that grazing land."

Elijah nodded. "We'll keep an eye on things. Round-up's as good an excuse as any to take a look. When are you planning to start?"

"End of next week, weather willing." Collins hesitated again before adding, "Elijah, if Hill's men push further, we might need more than just a friendly word between neighbors to settle this."

Elijah placed a reassuring hand on Collins's shoulder. "Let's hope it doesn't come to that, but if it does, you won't be standing alone."

"Much obliged, Elijah."

Elijah nodded. "We're looking to start later this week. I'll send a man over to chat with your foreman in a day or two." He smiled. "Why don't you and the family stay for dinner. Been too long since we socialized other than talking ranch work."

"Well, now I'm doubly obliged," Collins said. "I've never had a poor meal at the Summit Valley House."

Elijah shook his hand and smiled. "Head on up, we'll be there directly."

Elijah found Maggie and the girls, and let her know who this week's Sunday dinner guests would be, and she let him know she had invited Reverend Harris as well.

"I'll be right up, dear. Need to talk to Mo and Travis."

"No work on this fine Lord's day, Elijah Barber."

He held a hand up. "Just talkin' some real quick." She raised an eyebrow, then gathered up the girls and headed for the house.

Elijah caught Moses and Travis's attention, motioning them over.

"We need to start the roundup sooner," Elijah said, relaying his conversation with Collins. "Carson Hill is making moves. I don't want to be left wondering about this."

Travis nodded. "Jax says we're down a hand, though. The Shafer kid up and quit."

Elijah's eyes shot open. "Quit? We've never had a problem with that."

"Wouldn't take it personal, boss. He wasn't cut out for it," Travis said. "Reckon he skedaddled before more hard work came."

"Lot of work to be down a man," Moses said. "I know they pull their weight, but we usually provide the bulk of the punchers when we work with Circle C, and Jax has already been sayin' we've probably needed one or two more for a while."

Elijah thought for a moment. Running 7,000 head of cattle and growing, Summit Valley had five times as many cattle as Circle C. They always cooperated during round-ups, however, as it was good to ensure you had helpful neighbors, and the cattle tended to ignore imaginary lines on the ground and rock piles that denoted ranging boundaries.

Elijah's gaze shifted to JT, who was nearby helping a departing neighbor with a heavy load on their wagon. He watched as JT effortlessly lifted a crate into place, his strength evident.

Elijah turned back to Moses and Travis, biting his lip as he glimpsed Maggie walking to the house. "One man ain't much, but every pair of hands helps. I think I know where we can get an eager substitute if I swallow a bit of my pride."

A NEW HAND

— ◆ —

E lijah welcomed James Collins and his family, including his daughter Emily, who JT fancied, along with Reverend Harris's family, to a hearty Sunday dinner. The meal overflowed with laughter, stories of spring calving, friendly teasing about JT and Emily, and the comfort of neighbors who had shared both hardship and prosperity for years.

While it was a regular Sunday custom, Elijah also hoped to get more information from James Collins about the recent developments with Carson Hill, although he learned little more than he already had between Collins's limited knowledge, and the glares of their wives for talking business at the table.

After the meal and socializing, Elijah and Moses sent word to Travis, Henry, and Jax to come to the office in the headquarters building. The office was a modest room with wooden shelves lined with ledgers and books. A large, sturdy desk dominated the space, with a few smaller ones nearby. A few mounted hunting trophies, a framed map of the ranch, family photographs, and a calendar marking the days adorned the walls.

A careful eye would also observe the army trunks of Elijah and Moses, unopened for quite some time.

Elijah leaned back in his chair and spoke around his pipe. "Thank you for taking the time on a Sunday. I know it's a day for family and rest and that I'm breaking my own rule."

Henry nodded solemnly while Jax leaned against the wall, and Travis crossed his arms, listening intently. Scout laid in the sun near a window, never far from the action when these men were together. The central headquarters portion of the house was the one place he had the run of going wherever he pleased. Maggie loved the dog, but she only allowed him in the entry portion of the living area when too cold outside, or to collect his scraps after mealtime.

Elijah continued, "I filled Travis in already, but I want Henry and Jax to hear this. James Collins came to me after church. He told me Carson Hill bought out the Thompson spread and his men are already claiming range that hasn't been theirs. They've been surveying and marking territory."

Moses added, "Elijah and I, along with Travis, think it's best to start the roundup early. The weather's holding up, and the grass is getting green. No reason to delay."

"Mo is right," Elijah said. "It's time for a roundup anyway, and Circle C is ready to move, so we can help each other. On top of scouting what it is they're up to, I like the thought of them seeing the way we do things out here. Different brands on the beeves, but we're all in this together in a lot of ways." He puffed on his pipe. "Mo and I will take the train into Bozeman after and give Stratton the lay of things."

Travis's expression hardened. "Never good when your first intro-duction to a new neighbor is them snatching up a struggling man's spread then tryin' to claim land that ain't theirs."

Elijah agreed but didn't want to stoke any aggression. "As for doin' the work, we'll send out the hands to track the usual suspects to hire on, but every new body helps, so I'm going to bring JT along."

Jax rubbed his chin. "Cookie just got back with supplies for the chuck wagon last week, so he'll be ready to go." Jax played with his hat for a moment. "The boy ready for it? I know you'll treat him like any other until he proves himself."

Henry spoke up. "The boy is ready. I sense it in his spirit. But is Fierce Heart?" Fierce Heart was what Henry often called Maggie as a sign of respect for how she protected the family.

Travis grinned. "That's the real question."

"That'll be my battle to fight, but we'll plan on having him," Elijah said. "He's a strong boy and eager to prove himself." He looked at his foremen. "Travis, Jax, treat him like any of the hands, though. Like you said, no special treatment."

They discussed the logistics, going over what needed to be done in the next couple of days. Elijah proposed, "How about we move out on Wednesday?"

"Can we have everything ready by then, fellas?" Moses asked.

"Henry, make sure any horses that need shod have that done, and let's figure out what mounts we want for a remuda," Travis said.

"I'll have Maggie help you with that," Elijah added.

Travis continued. "Jax, make sure the hands have their gear together and in good order, and I'll get a list of chores ready. We'll let Cookie know to get the wagon stocked and send someone over to let Circle C know."

"Read my mind," Elijah said. "Thank you all. Go be with your families and carry my apologies for pulling you away."

Boots shuffled and knocked on the wood floor as the men departed, pulling their hats back on their heads. Elijah and Moses followed them, stopping in the doorway.

Elijah sighed, glancing at Moses. "I hope this thing with Hill is an overreaction."

Moses clapped him on the back, looking toward their families enjoying the sun in the yard. "Reckon that ain't your worst unknown right now," he said. He tipped his chin toward Maggie.

Elijah and Moses stepped outside and played with the girls for a while. Elijah then joined Maggie, who was sitting on a blanket in the grass, watching the children.

She looked up at him, her expression knowing. "I already know what you're going to say."

Elijah sat down beside her. "I wanted to talk to you first."

Maggie sighed. "I love and support you, but you've already told your men what the plan is." She smiled in a way that always flustered him, where she knew she was right and that he could never be mad at her. "I wasn't the first to be told, but I knew first."

Elijah began to apologize, but Maggie cut him off. "It might have been eighteen years ago, but you forget I've seen you operate and lead. I always know what's coming." She pointed to the stable, where JT was mending some of his gear. "He's already caught wind of it, so if you don't want things to be even more contentious between you two, you best stick to that plan."

Elijah looked and saw JT at work and nodded. "I'll let him know tonight."

She looked at him for a moment, studying him. "Why now when you've so recently lectured him about school and such? Do you really need one more?"

Elijah picked at some grass and tossed it. "With everything we've been working toward to fully take this over from Stratton. . ." He paused, surveying the ranch. "The thought of someone coming in here and leaning on us made me want the boy involved if it's gonna be his someday. Hopefully it's just a misunderstanding, though." He shook his head. "And I just plum need the help."

She gave him a warm smile. "Perhaps you should talk with him about all of that, too. He looks up to you." Elijah shook his head. "No, listen to me. He looks up to the version of you that he knows. He knows there is more to your past, and he'll learn it all soon enough. But right now, he looks up to a man who works hard for a good thing, and loves his family, and enjoys life."

Elijah stood, dusting himself off. "You're right."

"I usually am. You might also talk to him about other things, too." Elijah cocked his head. "I'm sure I wasn't the only one seeing how much the Collins girl has taken to him. He might think the same, but Lord knows he isn't sure how to go about that."

Elijah grimaced and rubbed his neck. "Maggie, I don't know that—"

"Can't just teach him riding, roping and shooting, Elijah." She batted her eyes and smiled. "I believe I heard you telling him there was more than that to life only this morning."

Elijah bent and kissed her forehead, then walked back to join the playing children. As he did, Maggie called after him, "Just remember, when men upset me on that adventure through Nebraska, I dealt with them."

Elijah shook his head and waved as he walked away. "Prayin' I don't put you in that fix again, dear."

SUNDAY SUPPER was always a lively affair for the two Barber families. This week, it took place at Elijah and Maggie's home. The five girls, Ruth, Hannah, Abigail, Molly, and Bridget, all loved to play with each other, filling the house with their laughter and the occasional squeal. JT, who used to take the opportunity as the only boy to torment them, had lately preferred sitting with his father and uncle, seeking the company of the men.

If the boy wanted to sit and talk with the men and act like one, Elijah took the opportunity for it to be a learning affair. Though he might not have trusted himself or Moses fifteen years ago to do such a thing, especially Moses, he now tried to ensure the boy saw there was more to a man than wearing a hat and gun and riding a horse.

Elijah and Moses settled into Elijah's study just off the front parlor, awaiting the call for supper. The small room was comfortably furnished, with high-back leather chairs, a settee, and a small desk. A well-worn rug lay on the wooden floor in front of a fireplace, and shelves lined the walls, filled with books, maps, and a few photos and mementos. Elijah and Moses regularly remarked that they now each had personal space used only for a desk that was nearly as big as the cabin they grew up in.

Elijah called for JT to join them, and the boy eagerly entered and took a seat. He surveyed the room, sensing a weighty discussion.

"JT," Elijah began, relaxing in his chair, "you know we've got a big week ahead with the roundup."

JT's eyes lit up. "Yes, sir. I've been hearing you talk about it."

Moses chuckled, leaning forward. JT leaned forward as well, looking at his uncle, then back at Elijah.

"We've decided you're going to come with us," Elijah said.

JT's face broke into a wide grin. "Really? You mean it?"

Elijah nodded. "But let's ensure we understand each other, son. You're going to work hard, just like any other hand. No special treatment. Travis, Jax, and Henry will be your bosses out there, and you'll follow their orders." Elijah rubbed his beard, then added, "And this isn't me saying the ranch work is more important than your schooling either."

JT straightened up, his expression serious. "I understand, Pa. I'll do my best."

Elijah exchanged a glance with Moses before continuing. "There's more to it than just the work. You've got to understand the responsibility that comes with this job. The safety of the herd, the men, and yourself. It's not just about being strong or quick; it's about making smart decisions and working as a team for the good of the outfit. Every man rides for the brand, not himself."

Moses nodded in agreement. "And listen, JT. There's a reason we're letting you come along. We trust you're ready, but this ain't for fun. We need the help."

Elijah's tone grew serious again. "You remember the Shafer kid, right?"

JT nodded. "Yeah, Tim. He was working with us during the winter."

Moses sat back with a grin. "Well, I dunno how much work he was doin'."

Elijah shook his head. "Well, he up and quit a few days ago," Elijah said, sighing. "He struggled through calving season and hauling hay to the herd during the winter. Seemed like he missed town life, and wasn't cut out for this. When he sensed spring round-up was coming, he decided it was time to leave."

Moses added, "It's a hard life, JT. Not everyone can handle it. The work can be grueling, and it takes a special kind of person to stick it out."

JT's expression grew more serious. "I understand. I won't let you or the Slash V name down Pa, Uncle Mo."

Elijah nodded. "Good. Now, go wash up for supper. Your aunt will be calling us in any minute. Try not to let your mother see how excited you are to run off and do grown man's work."

JT stood and shook each of their hands, surprising Elijah. He thought the boy looked older and taller than when he'd come into the study a few minutes earlier, and remembered what Maggie had said to him.

"JT, hold up a minute." He looked at Moses. "Mo, you mind givin' JT and I a minute?"

Moses raised an eyebrow, but then stood. "Sure thing. I need to wash up anyhow." He slapped JT on the back as he exited the study, his boots echoing down the hall toward the kitchen.

"Sit back down for a second, son." JT chose the seat Moses had just vacated, and Elijah smiled. "This doesn't change anything about our discussion this morning about school, understand? You'll still earn your way in the world and respect me when I talk to you about such things."

"Yessir."

Elijah studied JT's earnest expression. "There's something else you need to know, something only your mother, aunt, and uncle know."

JT raised an eyebrow, his curiosity piqued. "What is it, Pa?"

Elijah took a deep breath. "We're in the process of buying the ranch out from Mister Stratton."

JT's eyes widened. "Really? I thought we just ran it for him."

"We do, for now. But Mister Stratton has his reasons for eventually wanting to turn it over to us. His son, Edward, doesn't seem inclined to leave the East Coast even with his schooling done. He had always dreamed of passing the ranch onto his son, but since that's unlikely, he views it going to us as the next best thing, and a reward for all we've helped him build. Don't get me wrong, son, he has and will continue to make great profit from this ranch, sell the businesses he's built for a fortune, and enjoy his retirement with a legacy well earned. He's a good man, and with his wife gone, no other family, and an estranged son, he wants to know that legacy lives on in some way. Folks will know who built this ranch, and his name will be on buildings in Bozeman and in history books. . . but all that's also about money."

JT chuckled.

"So, your uncle Mo and I proposed we agree over a period of years to work toward acquiring it from him."

"Like actually own it all and not just run it?" JT asked.

Elijah nodded. "Yes, actually own it. It's still a bit off, but the thought of someone encroaching on this land. . ." He hesitated, choosing his words carefully. "I've been cross with you about things this past year because I wanted you to have opportunities I didn't have. I envisioned you being some businessman or lawyer who helped me run that end of things. . . and I'd like that still. But I guess I just want you to understand it better than I've let you. Plus, I'm your pa and I always have the right to change what I've said in a day's time as required." He scratched his chin. "So don't go smart mouthing me like you did this morning and make me regret it." He grinned.

JT nodded, absorbing the information. "I understand, Pa. I won't let you down."

"Now, one more thing, Elijah said. The Collins girl."

"Oh, Pa." JT's face turned bright red.

Elijah held a hand up. "Your mother has pointed out. . ." JT rolled his eyes. "And I agree," Elijah continued, "that Emily has set her cap for you."

JT shifted in the chair. "I 'spose that's so. But we're too young for all that."

Elijah nodded. At least he understood that much. "Son, I did not have the luxury of spending time thinking about such things when I was your age, as we were just trying to survive. Even as a grown man, I was quite the fool when it came to such affairs. If your mother were not so confident and forward, you might not be here."

JT laughed, and Elijah decided not to add that he and his mother's bond had also grown out of their shared experience of danger.

"I'll tell you two things, son. If you like the girl, try to respectfully let her know. Or rather, just be respectful. As you said, you're too young, but you don't treat her properly right now. . ." He tapped his fingers on the leather chair, deciding if he needed to say more. "In fact, respect her, Mister and Missus Collins, and your mother, and you'll be all set."

Elijah stood; thankful he had navigated the discussion without causing either of them much embarrassment. He clapped JT on the shoulder, and they headed for the kitchen.

"What about you, Pa, how do I respect you?"

Elijah stopped and put his arm around JT. "Do all those things I just asked and help me build a Barber legacy. There's never been such a thing, and you, me, and your Uncle Mo are the last men our family has."

As they joined everyone at the table, Elijah made eye contact with Maggie, a silent understanding passing between them that JT was coming on the roundup and that Elijah had spoken to him about his young love.

Elijah and Moses each took a seat at either end of the table, their wives beside them. Elijah and Maggie's oldest daughter, Molly, smirked at JT.

"What has you smiling so much?"

Moses and Helen's oldest, Ruth, chimed in. "I bet he's thinking about Miss Emily!" The girls erupted into giggles, making exaggerated kissing noises.

JT handled it well, his cheeks reddening, but his smile unwavering.

"What, you girls don't like kissin' and such?" Moses leaned toward Helen and gave her a peck on the cheek.

The girls squealed, their shouts growing when Elijah did the same to Maggie.

"Alright, that's enough," Elijah said. "I suppose we all forgot our table manners for a moment." He cleared his throat. "JT is stepping in to help with the spring roundup. You should be proud of him for helping the ranch."

Elijah and Maggie's youngest, Bridget, huffed, "I don't care about roundups."

Maggie jumped in, "You better care, young lady. It's our livelihood. And besides, when these men are all gone, who do you think takes care of the headquarters? Those cows don't milk themselves, and I've yet to see the chickens or horses put out their own feed."

Elijah smiled and reached under the table and squeezed his wife's hand. As they bowed their heads to pray over the meal, his mind wandered, and he peeked at his wife. He hoped his words to JT helped the boy understand the weight of his responsibilities and guided him to one day choose and respect as wonderful a partner in life as he had found in Maggie.

DEPARTURE

— · —

E lijah awoke with a start, his heart pounding from a vague, shadowy dream of violence that lingered just out of reach. Shouts, gunshots, people calling out for him. He marveled at his ability to always wake up when required, even if it too often was at the end of a nightmare.

Laying still for a moment, he performed a mental check of all the preparations they had completed over the past two days. Hands ensured they had the supplies to repair or replace their catch pens and temporary corrals. They had shod the horses, and the remuda was ready, each mount selected for its endurance and reliability. The chuck wagon was stocked with provisions, thanks to Cookie's diligent work. Each cowboy checked and packed his gear and equipment. Jax had overseen the hands, making sure they were ready and understood their roles.

Turning his head, he saw Maggie still sleeping beside him, her bare torso peeking out from under the blanket. The preparations had exhausted him, but he would never leave on a roundup without their intimate ritual. Elijah marveled at his wife's beauty, the way she looked so peaceful in her sleep. He noticed she was curled up and looked cold on the cool spring morning. Gently, he covered her with the blanket.

He had already packed his bedroll and saddlebags. Anticipating the early start, he had set his clothes on a chair near their bed. As he quietly got out of bed to grab them, Maggie stirred and woke up.

"Sorry to wake you," Elijah whispered.

Maggie smiled sleepily. "I'm getting up with you."

She lit a lamp for him, and he got dressed. The round-up weather called for layers: denim jeans, a thick wool shirt, and his worn canvas vest. His saddlebag included an extra pair of jeans, some undergarments, and a lighter-weight shirt.

He pulled on his boots as he ensured he had packed or laid out everything he needed. Sheepskin jacket, rain slicker, chaps, bed roll, neckerchief, and gloves. When you added in some food and water, a gun belt, and pistol, and the rifle for his saddle scabbard, it was a wonder they didn't need an army quartermaster to ensure everyone left fully outfitted.

Catching him staring at her as he buttoned his shirt, Maggie threw the blanket aside. "Get a good look before you go," she teased.

Elijah flushed. "That's one way to get me to hurry back."

Maggie laughed, then put on her nightgown, robe, and moccasins. They walked downstairs together, only to find JT already dressed and preparing coffee on the cookstove.

"You're up early," Elijah remarked.

JT grinned. "Wanted to be ready."

Elijah looked him over. Their attire was almost exactly the same, although JT already had his neckerchief tied around his neck and was wearing Elijah's old Stetson Boss of the Plains hat, handed down a few years back when Elijah gained a new one. The boy was eager. There was no doubt.

Maggie glanced at her son and then at her husband. "I know Cookie will have a quick bite for you before you get moving, but I want to sit and talk a spell with my two men before you depart." She smiled. "JT, have a seat next to your father."

JT obeyed, sitting down at the kitchen table. Maggie finished preparing the coffee and got out three mugs and served them, pausing in front of JT and laughing. "My goodness, here I am making you a grown man already."

Elijah chuckled. "You better get used to it, son."

JT sipped, grimacing at the strong taste. Maggie and Elijah laughed, the sound filling the room with warmth. They enjoyed the moment, the three of them sipping their coffee in companionable silence. Elijah noticed that in just a few brief minutes, Maggie's expression shifted from worry for the both of them, to pride in her husband and son, and back to worry again.

The first light of dawn crept through the windows, accompanied by the distant sounds of men, horses, and wagons moving outside. Elijah stood up, stretched, and peeked out the kitchen window.

"It's about that time," he said, strapping on his gun belt. JT looked at him expectantly, but Elijah shook his head. "Nope. But take my old Spencer and put it in your scabbard."

"Yessir," JT said.

He walked off, but Elijah called after him. "Son, you're so eager about a rifle that you aren't even gonna hug your Ma and kiss and tell her goodbye before you head out for three or four weeks?"

JT rushed back to his mother, embracing her tightly. Her head fell in underneath his as she whispered, "My boy is all grown up. You listen to your father, uncle, and all those men, but I don't want to hear about you losing money playing cards at night."

Elijah stood by the door, pulling on his coat. "What a man does with the money I pay him is his own business, dear." He smiled briefly, then looked at JT with a serious face. "Unless he's my son."

JT smiled, a bit embarrassed, but nodded. "I'll listen, Ma. I promise."

"Go find Jax and get your assignments," Elijah instructed. As JT departed, Elijah walked over to Maggie, putting his arms around her waist and pulling her close. "Should I wake the girls?" he asked.

"No, you said your goodbyes last night." She laid her head on his chest. "They already think cows are smelly and take too much of your time, anyway."

"They are, and they do," Elijah said with a chuckle. "But soon enough, it'll be wholly ours."

She pushed his hat up, and they shared a kiss. Then she looked at him for a moment before pulling the brim back down. "Thank you for what you do for this family, those men out there, and everyone that counts on you. But now I need you to add minding that boy to the list of things I'll thank you for."

He touched the brim of his hat. "Yes, ma'am." His boots knocked on the floor as he slung his saddlebags over his shoulder and headed out the back door. "I love you."

"I love you, too," she replied.

Elijah caught her gazing out the window toward the distant stone in the ranch's cemetery and thought about the date. "Five years?" he asked. She nodded and wiped a tear away. "Your father was, and is, very proud of you," Elijah added.

She smiled. "I know. And you too, for helping it all come to be, and allowing him to see me happy." She laughed. "And that he lived long enough to meet his grandbabies."

He smiled, blew her a kiss, and stepped outside. The faintest bit of morning light showed him the way, and the cool air carried the scents of fresh earth and horses. The sounds of the ranch waking up surrounded them: the neighing of horses, the clatter of hooves, and the murmurs of men readying for the roundup.

From the open door, Maggie called out as Elijah joined Moses, the brothers walking toward where their mounts were stabled. "You two see that my boy retains at least some of his innocence on this trip."

Elijah waved, and Moses hollered back, "Ain't no women comin' with, Miss Maggie, just us and some cowboys."

"It's you and the cowboys I'm worried about," she said, laughing before closing the door.

The brothers walked briskly toward the stable, their boots crunching on the path. The building was a large, well-kept structure with wide doors and sturdy wooden walls. Inside, the comforting scent of hay and the soft sounds of horses filled the air. Moses grabbed a lamp from a shelf, lit it, and hung it from a hook.

They moved about, saddling their horses, attaching their saddlebags, and placing their rifles in the scabbards.

"She worried about JT?" Moses asked as they worked.

Elijah tightened the cinch of his saddle. "Sure is."

"To be expected," Moses said. He hung a canteen on his saddle, tossing another to Elijah. They'd fill them with cool, clean Yellowstone water on the way out.

"Told JT about the long-term agreement with Stratton to acquire the ranch," Elijah said.

Moses paused; his hands thrown across his saddle. "Good that he knows. He's got to understand what we're working toward."

Elijah nodded as he patted his horse's neck. Duke, a strong bay gelding, nickered.

Moses's horse, a spirited chestnut mare named Ruby, tossed her head, eager to get going. He looked across at Elijah. "I recall nineteen years ago, we stood just like this, talking to each other over our horses, preparing to leave home forever. We had nothing behind us, no money or anything to our name. Now we're talking about your son helping us create a legacy for future Barbers."

Elijah shook his head, a smile coming to his face. "I do recall that. Didn't know you were capable of such deep thought."

Moses chuckled. "Surprise myself sometimes. Why if I was the crying type, I reckon that woulda done it."

They led their horses to the exit, looking across the yard to see JT loading the last bits of equipment onto a wagon.

"Lot of pressure to put on him with talks of legacy and such," Elijah mused.

Moses nodded, then turned to Elijah with a mischievous grin. "You're right. Maybe I oughta talk Helen into trying for a boy yet again."

Elijah laughed and shook his head. "You're too old for that."

"*She* ain't." Moses winked at Elijah. "And I may be too old for a lot of things, but not for that, brother."

As Cookie's chuck wagon rumbled out of the yard, its wooden wheels creaking under the weight, they led their horses toward Travis, Jax, and Henry.

Travis tipped the brim of his cattleman hat. "We're all set, boss. Circle C fellas should be nearby when we get there."

Jax nodded in agreement. "Everything's in order, boss."

Henry looked up at the sky, his eyes scanning the horizon as he secured a feather in the band of his open crown hat. "We are blessed with good weather."

Elijah turned and looked at the various ranch hands and cowboys, both permanent and hired on, giving a slight nod when he saw JT mounted among them.

"Let's head for the south winter pasture first. Tell the men I'll be moving among them throughout the morning to say hello and introduce myself to the new ones."

Travis tapped the brim of his hat and wheeled toward the group, shouting orders as Jax and Henry followed. Elijah and Moses turned back toward the valley before them, the first light of day casting a glow over the landscape. The rolling hills, dotted with pines and firs, led to the distant mountains standing tall against the pale morning sky. Elijah took a deep breath. There was the old familiar scent of horse and man, now joined by the smell of pine and evergreen and the emerging green grass that was his herd's lifeblood.

Moses smiled. "Off we go yet again, brother."

Elijah nodded, feeling the familiar mix of excitement and responsibility that always came with the start of the roundup. "Off we go." The brothers spurred their horses forward, leading the way into the dawn.

ROUNDUP

———— ◆ ————

A s the Slash V spread out across the south winter pasture, the rhythmic pounding of hooves, lowing cattle, and whoops and shouts of cowboys filled the air. The morning sun appeared over the peaks, casting a glow over the rolling hills and distant mountains. The fresh scent of pine mingled with the earthy aroma of the grasslands, creating a sense of serenity despite the bustling activity.

The team spent the first day setting up temporary corrals and catch pens, observing the herd, and moving stray and injured cattle back to the main group. Now, with the initial preparations complete, the men focused on herding the Slash V cattle from the south winter pasture toward their staging area. They had linked up with James Collins and his Circle C outfit, the combined forces working together.

Paradise Valley was alive with activity. The summer pastures stretched out before them, greening up, and dotted with cattle already happy to use it for grazing. In the distance, the Absaroka Range stood tall, its snow-capped peaks glistening in the early morning light. The Yellowstone River meandered through the valley, its waters sparkling in the sunlight.

Elijah rode alongside Moses, scanning the horizon. The men had been working tirelessly, driving the cattle toward the roundup pens. Elijah spotted JT riding ahead of him, his posture tense and his focus locked on a small pocket of cattle straying toward the hills. He could see the boy working hard to keep up—but working hard didn't always mean working smart.

"JT, on your left—left!" Elijah called out, urgency creeping into his tone. JT's horse hesitated as he over-corrected before spurring forward to guide the wayward calf back toward the herd. The calf darted the wrong way before JT finally brought it back in line. Elijah exhaled, watching one of the older cowboys tip his hat in mild frustration before riding over to help.

Moses leaned closer. "He's got heart, but he's still learnin' how to read the animals. That'll take time."

Elijah nodded but couldn't shake the thought gnawing at him: Had he brought the boy out here too soon? Were the hands being patient because they respected JT, or because he was the boss's son?

The day wore on, with the sun climbing high overhead. The cowboys took brief breaks to water their horses and grab quick bites from the chuck wagon before returning to round up stragglers or push the main herd. JT sat with a few of the men during one break, trying to absorb their advice, even as a few cowboys exchanged knowing glances when the boy wasn't looking.

"You're doin' good, kid," one puncher said, clapping JT on the back. "But remember, it ain't just about pushin' hard. You gotta learn to read the animals, know what they're gonna do before they do it. You keep watchin' the older fellas, and you'll learn."

JT nodded eagerly, but another hand chuckled, scraping the last of some beans off his tin plate. "And when readin' them don't work, sometimes you just gotta muscle through it. Wait till we start branding calves and you see Billy manhandle those critters." He winked. "Then you'll see the fun."

Elijah sat nearby with Moses and James Collins, sipping water and watching JT. He wanted to feel proud—and part of him did—but seeing the boy struggle weighed on him. He didn't want JT thinking this was just about impressing his pa or the men. He knew firsthand that ranch work could chew up a man's pride as quickly as any gunfight. Was it fair to throw his son into it all at once?

Moses seemed to read his mind. "Don't go second-guessin' it," he said. "Every man here was green once, just like him. Ain't one of 'em that won't let him stumble a little if it means learnin' somethin'." He nodded toward a group of hands. "It's a good outfit we got."

Elijah nodded, grateful for his brother's words, but he still watched JT as the boy mounted up again, his posture a little too stiff, his determination written all over his face.

The sound of approaching hooves pulled Elijah's attention.

"Bossmen," a cowboy named Red called down from his horse. "We found somethin' you might wanna take a look at. You too, Mister Collins."

Moses raised an eyebrow, pulling his hat down against the glare of the sun. "Right now?"

"Yessir."

The three men exchanged glances and then headed for their day's mounts, which were staked nearby. They followed Red for a bit, and when he stopped at the peak of a small rise, they saw a group of cattle milling around, a mix of Slash V and Circle C brands.

Elijah scanned the area, recognizing it as part of Summit Valley's grazing land. "Looks like some of your cattle got mixed in with ours, James," he said.

Collins nodded, then looked at Red. "It's not unusual for beeves to wander though."

Red shook his head. "No sir, but that ain't what I mean to show you. It's why they've wandered. Or more likely, got pushed."

They rode further until they came upon fresh survey markers and a rock pile seeming to act as a boundary. Elijah turned to Collins. "This should be yours, right?"

Collins confirmed it with a grim nod. "Sure is."

"And you haven't been doing any surveying? I reckon you haven't been trying to close off the water to the rest of us."

"Sure haven't, Elijah."

"Looks like Hill's men have been busy," Moses muttered, his brow furrowing.

"They're pushing their luck," Elijah added. He dismounted and inspected the markers and rocks more closely. "What would they need to be surveying for?"

As they looked, another cowboy everyone called Slim approached. He reined up just short of the men. "Bosses, Mister Collins. We found some fencing supply just on the other side of that rise." He pointed in the direction he'd come from.

Elijah squinted toward what used to be the Thompson Bar T ranch.

"We're gonna need to address this."

———— ⚙ ————

NIGHT SETTLED over the roundup camp, a canopy of stars blanketing the sky. Small cook fires dotted the immediate area, their flickering flames casting a warm glow on the faces of the men gathered around them. The sounds of the nearby cattle, lowing in the cool night air, mingled with the distant singing of the circling outriders attempting to keep them calm.

Elijah, Moses, Travis, Jax, and Henry sat around their fire, relaxing a bit after eating. The scent of cooked bacon, beans, and coffee lingered, adding to the familiar aroma of horse and man.

Travis took a sip from his tin cup and looked at Elijah and Moses. "You wanna talk about the cattle work first, or the business with Hill?"

Elijah leaned back against his saddle, stretching his legs. "Reckon we ought to discuss the cattle first. I suspect the business with Hill will take longer."

Travis nodded and updated them on their progress. "We're makin' good headway. We've gathered the main herd and most of the smaller pockets. I'll send a few men out in the morning to make a last sweep for any loners. Not many sick or injured, which is good, but we'll make another check to see if more need to be cut out."

"Any issues?" Moses asked, stirring the embers with a stick.

"Just the usual," Travis replied. "A few groups that don't seem to want to stick with the herd. We'll start cutting out the calves tomorrow and maybe do some branding if we can get to it by nightfall. It's gonna be a long day."

"We got a good group, boss," Jax added. "No issues with the men yet. I know we pay well, but even so, we ain't had to get after any to earn their keep."

"Even the newest one?" Moses asked, as he smirked at Elijah.

Jax smiled. "Even the newest one."

Elijah nodded. "Sounds like we're on track. Keep pushing to get the work done, and make sure the men stay sharp."

They shifted the conversation to Hill's encroachment. Elijah told the men what they'd found earlier in the day, and he could see Travis seething in the firelight.

"I'm tellin' ya it's trouble when someone buys up an outfit and don't even bother to introduce hisself before he goes about doin' somethin' like that."

Moses finally asked, "What's the plan then?"

Elijah took a deep breath. "I talked it over with James. Mo, you, me and him are riding out in the morning to try and track down Hill's men working their supposed new boundaries. Henry, I'd like you to come with us for help tracking."

Henry nodded. "I will be ready."

"Travis, you're in charge tomorrow, Jax, be sure to back him up. Let the fellas know we're headed to the boundary to talk with the new neighbors so they don't think we are out gallivanting. Let's keep the details out of it for now, though."

The fire crackled as they sat in contemplative silence for a moment. Elijah looked around at his men with a bit of apprehension. He sensed they all wanted to hear more, Travis especially.

"Let's address this head on but try not to stir up any trouble. We'll see what they're up to and take it from there. We've had no trouble in the valley the entire time we been here that talking things out hasn't solved. I know Mister Stratton wouldn't want to see a misunderstanding lead to some kind of range war." He rubbed his beard. "We all have cattle wander or make use of access to water but patrolling it like it's their own isn't something we can ignore."

"A range war?" a voice asked from the dark.

The men turned to see JT approaching the edge of the firelight. Elijah felt a surge of agitation at seeing his son there, knowing he had been listening in on the conversation and interrupting the bosses, something most brand-new cowboys wouldn't dream of doing. He then noticed Moses and Travis's hands had gone toward their guns.

"You need somethin', son?" Elijah asked, his voice steady but firm. "Good way to get some lead thrown at you, sneakin' up on fellas in the dark."

JT hesitated, glancing at the other men before answering. "Sorry. Just wanted to say hello and goodnight before I head out for my turn circling the herd."

Moses seemed to sense Elijah's agitation. "Everything alright, JT?"

"Yessir, Uncle Mo. Just thought I'd check in."

Elijah nodded. "Hello and goodnight, then."

Jax, sensing the awkwardness, added, "You're doin good, JT. Keep it up."

"Yessir, I will." JT lingered for a moment, then headed toward the remuda to collect a horse for his shift.

Jax rubbed his forehead. "Boss, I ain't the one in charge, and I ain't got any youngins' myself, but the boy just wants to make sure he's doing his pop proud, you know?"

Elijah packed his pipe, struck a match, and nodded as he puffed to get it going. "I know it," he said. "But I also don't aim to show him any favor over the rest—not yet at least."

"But one day?" Travis laughed.

Moses chuckled. "That's right, but we'll make sure he keeps you on as foreman, Travis."

The men all laughed at this, but Hank turned and watched JT walking away and stood with his plate and mess kit as the men continued chatting.

As JT reached the remuda, he selected a bay gelding named Storm. The name reflected not a stormy disposition, but a mild one that could weather any storm—a good choice for the night watch. JT led Storm away from the rest of the horses, preparing to saddle him for his shift.

Henry approached quietly, his presence unobtrusive. He watched JT for a moment before speaking. "Storm is a good choice for tonight," he said. "Strong heart and steady spirit. He will guide you well in the dark."

Henry's presence startled JT, who looked up. "Oh, thank you, Henry. I've always liked him."

Henry nodded, his features barely discernible in the moonlight. "In my tribe, we say that a horse like Storm is not just an animal but a partner. He sees what you do not, hears what you cannot, and feels the world in ways you do not understand."

JT paused, considering Henry's words. "I guess I've never thought of it that way."

Henry smiled. "Most do not. But those who understand find their way easier."

JT's nod showed gratitude, but also some confusion. He continued to prepare Storm, adjusting the saddle and checking the straps.

Henry stood quietly for a moment longer, watching JT's careful movements. "Your father is the same way, JT."

JT looked up with a raised eyebrow. "Whaddya mean, Henry?"

"You are disappointed your father did not have more to say to you just now, or when he speaks of you earning your way, or things you are not ready for." He raised an eyebrow. "And are unsure of how you have been performing in his eyes."

JT paused. "Is it that obvious?"

Henry smiled. "Do not play poker with the cowboys, my friend." JT laughed, and Henry continued. "Do you know how I came to work at Summit Valley?"

"You left the Crow reservation to find work, right?"

"Yes, that is part of it. But there is more to the story." Henry took a deep breath, his gaze distant. "The Treaty of Fort Laramie established the Crow Indian Reservation, reducing the traditional lands of my people. My family tried to maintain our lifestyle, but it became difficult as the buffalo dwindled. We worked together with the government, but it did not mean life was easy."

JT listened intently.

"When I was little older than you, it became clear our way of life was unsustainable. The Battle of Little Bighorn further impacted us. My older brother was one of Custer's Crow scouts and died in the battle. His loss scarred me."

"I'm sorry to hear that," JT said.

Henry nodded. "My father died in battle with the Sioux as well, and my mother died of sickness while forced to move so many times. Seeking stability and new opportunities, I approached the Summit Valley ranch for work the next year. Your mother taught me more of your language. But that is not the main story I want to tell you."

JT looked at Henry with curiosity.

"Your father and uncle brought a delivery of cattle to the reservation for a contract Mister Stratton made with the Indian Agent. The amount of cattle paid for was not the amount of cattle brought, but your father did not know this. When he said he would make it right, he was also told that this had happened with other deliveries from other sellers. While they trusted your father did not do it on purpose, they knew others had. When he returned a week later, he had fulfilled the Summit Valley contract as promised and extra, to make up for those who had shorted us."

JT's eyes widened. "I never knew that."

Henry continued, "I have never heard from your father, nor has anyone else, how he accounted for this with Mister Stratton, but it has never been spoken of since. I rode after your father and told him I wanted to work for a man like him. Since coming to Summit Valley,

I took the name Horse Goes Ahead from my brother, named for his skills in scouting the enemy. My original name was *Ahote*, meaning 'Restless One.' Now, I am no longer restless."

JT took this in. "Wow. I never knew any of that."

Henry placed a hand on JT's shoulder. "I tell you all this for two reasons. Your father is an honest and respected man. He is training you not just to replace him but to do it in the same way—to be a leader with integrity and honor. You want to move fast and become a man. You will. But it is okay to be restless and wander first, *Ahote*, so long as you pay attention to the lessons of life."

JT nodded, the weight of Henry's words settling in. "I always thought he was so overly-strict, and maybe even selfish." JT frowned, as if he questioned the word choice. "It's just that he is always talking about success and securing the family's future."

"Both important to your father," Henry replied, "But he wishes this for others as well."

JT nodded, then suddenly looked Henry in the eyes as if a thought struck him. "Do you know more about my father's past? I know there is something beyond all of this. Why does it seem men either respect or fear him? Why do even strangers seem to listen to him without question?"

Henry patted JT on the shoulder, then turned to walk away. "That is not for me to tell you. He will impart that to you in his own time."

RANGE MEETING

— · —

E lijah woke in his bedroll, the chill of the early morning air making him pull his blanket tighter around him. Above him, the starry sky still stretched vast and dark, a canopy of twinkling lights that never ceased to amaze him. He stared into the heavens for a moment, reflecting on the countless nights he had spent under the stars, surrounded by men and animals. It was a way of life that had become second nature to him, a peaceful routine that contrasted with the tumult of his past.

Elijah sat up and stretched, shaking off the last remnants of sleep as he pulled on his boots. He glanced around at the other bedrolls scattered about, the shapes of his men beginning to move in the pre-dawn stillness. He moved to wake Moses, giving his brother a nudge with his foot.

Moses grumbled but roused himself, sitting up and rubbing his eyes. "Mornin' already?" he muttered.

"Yep," Elijah replied. He marveled that in the over forty years he had been on Earth with Moses through farm work, war, duty as lawmen, and their ranching life, his brother had never once woken before him. "Let's get some coffee going."

Moses nodded and set to work, stoking the coals from their previous night's fire. Elijah gathered their coffeepot and filled it with water, setting it near the fire to heat. They moved with the practiced efficiency of men who had done this countless times before.

As the coffee percolated, they dressed for the cool morning ahead. Elijah added a wool shirt over the thin cotton one he'd slept in. He then pulled on his vest and a jacket, knowing he'd want it until the sun was warming the day in earnest. He secured his gun belt around his waist and checked his rifle before sliding it into the scabbard on his saddle.

The brothers took their saddles and saddlebags to the remuda, selecting Duke and Ruby, their faithful mounts, for the day's ride. The horses, having gotten a day's rest, were eager to get moving. They saddled them with care, making sure everything was secure before leading them over to the chuck wagon where Cookie was at work.

The scent of sizzling bacon and fresh coffee filled the air as they approached the chuck wagon. Cookie, an eccentric old man with a long white beard and a penchant for colorful language, was bustling around as if he ran the entire camp. The brothers let him, knowing full well that a happy cook made for happy cowboys.

"Tie 'em off over there," Cookie barked, pointing to a nearby post. "I know you two always eat after the night's riders, but that red-headed ox McCray ain't been through yet, and you're lucky I don't toss what I saved for all three of ya."

Moses chuckled as he took a plate and began eating in earnest. "I always enjoy your pleasant nature in the morning, Cookie." He then saw the concerned look on Elijah's face. "I'm sure he's fine, Eli. Somebody woulda woke us if there was trouble."

Elijah frowned. Billy wasn't just one of the most reliable hands, but a reliable eater as well. If he was missing breakfast, it meant something had happened during the night shift.

"Ain't seen your boy yet, either," bossman," Cookie added.

Now even Moses had a look of concern on his face, and Elijah sent him in one direction while Elijah headed in the other. Eating a piece of ham and a biscuit as he walked, irritated his breakfast was being rushed, he encountered Slim. "Seen Billy or JT?"

Slim rubbed the back of his neck and gestured toward the remuda. Just saw Billy rubbin' his horse down and puttin' him up with the others, boss."

Elijah raised an eyebrow, then thanked Slim and headed toward the remuda, finding the sturdy hand as he carried away his saddle and tack. He had just set his things down and was wiping sweat and dirt from his face with a bandana. His shirt clung to him, and the weariness in his posture spoke of a long night. Billy straightened when he saw Elijah approach, offering a tired but respectful nod.

"Mornin', boss," Billy said, though his tone was cautious. He could already sense Elijah's mood.

"Didn't expect to see you already looking like you put a day's work in, Billy," Elijah said, crossing his arms. "Cookie's about ready to toss your breakfast, and you look like you've been working harder than you should've had to."

Billy rubbed the back of his neck, choosing his words carefully. "Had to spend a little time roundin' up a few cows." He looked around, then lowered his voice. "JT dozed off in the saddle. I found him a bit off our loop, and by then, a few had strayed."

Elijah sighed. "How long?"

"Not too long," Billy said quickly. "I caught it before any real damage was done. We didn't lose any cattle, just had to spend some extra time pulling the strays back in and the dark didn't help."

Elijah exhaled sharply, frustration bubbling beneath his calm exterior. "Billy, I appreciate you covering for him, but the boy's gotta learn. If you always fix things for him, he won't."

Billy nodded, but his gaze didn't waver. "I get that, sir, I do. But I figured stoppin' the cattle from wanderin' was more important in the moment than lettin' it go further to teach a lesson. I've been the low man all too recently, and I know what it's like to feel as if you're climbin' uphill every day, wonderin' if you'll ever measure up." He bit his lip. "And I know what it's like when you're the one the bossman is carin' for."

Elijah's shoulders eased somewhat, but the tension didn't leave him. "I know you were trying to help, Billy. I do. But I can't let him think someone will always be there to clean up after him."

Billy smiled. "He knows. I could see it in his face when I found him. You don't have to drive the point too hard. He beat himself up proper the whole time we were workin' to fix it."

Elijah ran a hand over his beard and nodded. "Go get your breakfast, Billy. I'll talk to him."

"Yessir," Billy said, tipping his hat before heading toward the chuck wagon. Stopping, he turned. "He asked me again about helpin' him get faster with his shooting iron." He smirked when he saw Elijah's reaction, turning back to the chuck wagon as he called out, "But I didn't."

Elijah walked toward a creek, where JT sat on a rock, splashing water onto his face and staring at the rippling surface as if it held answers he couldn't find. His shoulders were hunched, his hat resting beside him on the ground. Elijah's boots crunched on the ground as he approached, and JT stiffened but didn't turn around.

"Billy told me what happened," Elijah said, stopping a few feet away.

JT lowered his hands, letting the water drip from his fingers. "I'm sorry, Pa."

Elijah crouched next to him, resting his arms on his knees. "I know. But sorry doesn't keep cattle from wandering. Plus that's askin' to get yourself hurt, or have somethin' even worse happen to us when outriders aren't alert."

JT nodded, but his gaze stayed fixed on the water. "Billy covered for me."

"I know," Elijah said. "But that's not the point. You can't rely on that."

"I wasn't tryin' to," JT said quickly, his voice cracking slightly. "But that's the point. I just—Billy always seems to know what to do. He's strong, and even the older hands listen to him. . . You listen to him."

Elijah frowned, sensing where this was going. "You think I treat Billy different than you."

JT hesitated, then nodded. "He's not your son, but you trust him like one. You let him do things I'm not ready for. He succeeds, and I always mess up."

Elijah sat back on his heels, the boy's words hitting harder than he expected. "Billy's had years to earn that trust, JT. He made plenty of mistakes when he was your age, but he learned from them." He looked toward the water. "If you're thinkin' you'd rather be him, the Billy McCray that came to us at your age would have loved to make that trade."

JT swallowed hard, still staring at the water. "Henry told me last night that it's okay to stumble as long as you pay attention to the lessons. I know I'm supposed to learn from this, but it's hard when it feels like I'll never catch up and earn your trust."

Elijah felt the weight of those words settle in his chest. He wanted to say the right thing to make JT understand he was proud of him, but the words didn't come easily. Instead, he placed a hand on his son's shoulder, squeezing gently.

"You don't have to catch up to Billy," Elijah said finally. "You just have to be the man you're meant to be. And that's not something that happens overnight."

JT nodded, though the doubt still lingered in his eyes. "I just want to make you proud."

Elijah's grip tightened slightly. "I know. You're out here working hard, and that's what matters. Just don't forget that part of earning respect is knowing when to ask for help—and when to admit you've reached your limit."

JT took a deep breath, as if trying to let those words sink in. "I'll do better, Pa. I promise."

"I know." He helped the boy up and pointed toward the chuck wagon. "Go on and get your vittles then check in with Travis. Your uncle and I will be away for the day."

***

THE MORNING SUN was just beginning to rise over the Absaroka range as Elijah and Moses gave Travis and Jax a few last instructions, leaving most decisions to them. Along with Henry, they then mounted their horses and rode the short distance to where Collins and his men camped. The plan was to return to the area where they had seen the survey markers and fencing equipment, hoping to cut sign that lead them to the men doing the work. Their intent was to stay on Collins's range, avoiding baiting arguments about who was on whose spread.

As they rode, Elijah marveled at the beauty of the surrounding valley. The landscape was a breathtaking mix of rolling hills and pastures that were greening up, with the two mountain ranges framing things on either side. The early morning light shimmered on the Yellowstone River, winding through it all.

Elijah broke the silence. "This valley is so different from where we grew up in Illinois, but the first time I saw it, I knew we'd never leave."

Moses nodded, his gaze sweeping across the landscape. "Ain't that the truth. Close enough to civilization when we need it, but not so close we need to contend with city life. And now with a railroad down valley in Livingston, getting cattle to market don't involve a drive all the way to Miles City or further."

As they continued to ride, the morning sun cleared the Absaroka range, shining in their faces as they traversed the valley floor. Paradise Valley's beauty was undeniable. It was a tranquil haven that belied any tension brewing beneath its serene surface.

Henry, riding ahead, dismounted and kneeled on the ground, examining faint tracks in the dirt. "Looks like they moved on recently. Tracks heading west."

Elijah and Moses dismounted, joining Henry to inspect the tracks. "We'll follow them," Elijah said, mounting back up. "Let's stay on James's range as best we can. I'd like to start our chat from the high ground." He hoped his statement only required being figurative.

They followed the tracks west as they wound through a series of gently sloping hills and dense clusters of pine trees, their shadows riding ahead of them through the grassy land. The trail led them closer to a stand of trees, the peacefulness of the valley only disrupted by the occasional chirping of birds and rustling of leaves in the breeze.

Henry pointed to a set of tracks leading into the trees. "They camp in there."

"Well, now that's old Bar T range. Box H now, I guess," Collins said.

Elijah took a deep breath. "You or me, James?"

Collins adjusted his hat. "I reckon I'll let you."

Elijah shifted in his saddle. "Hello the camp. Good morning. We're from Summit Valley and the Circle C and would like to talk."

Elijah's voice carried through the trees, his tone firm but calm. For a moment, there was silence, broken only by the rustling of leaves and the distant call of a bird. Then, the sound of movement echoed through the stand of trees, followed by the appearance of four men on horseback, their figures emerging from the shadows. They trotted toward Elijah, Moses, Henry, and Collins, reigning up a few yards in front of them.

The apparent leader of the group, a stocky man with a broad chest and a face weathered by years in the sun, guided his horse forward. His hair had a red tint, and his accent, when he spoke, was unmistakably Scottish. He tipped his bowler, or as he likely called it, a derby hat.

"Mornin', gents," he greeted them, a smile on his face. "What brings ye to this part of the valley?"

Elijah noted the man's casual demeanor, but there was an undercurrent of tension in his voice. "Morning. We were following some tracks on James Collins's Circle C spread," Elijah replied evenly. "Seems there's been some surveying and fencing going on. Thought it best we have a chat about it. We all keep to our own spreads but have never closed any land off or saw the need to do any surveying."

The Scottish man's smile widened slightly, but his eyes remained cold. "Aye, well, that would be Mister Hill's doing. We've been tasked with makin' sure his range is properly marked. Can't have folks and cattle wandering where they don't belong, now can we?"

Moses, sensing the tension, spoke up. "This here's James Collins," he said. "And this land we're on is range his cattle have been on, same with the area where your boys were placing rock piles and putting up fencing."

The leader turned his gaze to Collins, nodding. "Mister Collins," he acknowledged. "Name's Finn MacDonald. Pleasure to meet ye', but I'm afraid there's been a wee bit of misunderstanding. This land here, accordin' to long ago arrangements the Bar T made when they first come to the Valley, was theirs—and now that of Mister Hill and the Box H."

Elijah began to introduce himself, but before he could finish, Finn cut him off.

"Aye, we know who ye are and who ye work for," he said. The way he spoke made it clear they knew the Barbers for more than just running Jonathan Stratton's ranch.

Elijah fought to keep his composure. "Then you know we've always kept peace in this valley. If there's a misunderstanding, we're here to clear it up. No need to go doing such work without conferring with neighbors."

Finn leaned forward in his saddle, the leather creaking as his expression turned serious. "Misunderstanding or not, Mister Thompson and the Bar T might've been fine to let things be as they always were, but this is historic Bar T range, and we aim to restore it as such for the Box H. There's land and water access that should've always been his."

Collins narrowed his eyes. "That may be true, and I'm not saying it ain't, but 'round here, we don't go about things like this. You could've come and talked to us."

The Scottish man's smirk returned, colder this time. "So ye do speak for yerself sometimes, then. Mister Hill is nae lookin' to do things the way they've always been done around here. Seems that has only benefited the business of Jon Stratton and Summit Valley." Finn looked at Elijah. "So it's the largest outfit that can share range with others, but the small need to keep to themselves. Is that how it is then?"

Elijah noticed the other men hadn't spoken a word. They sat silently, their hands folded on their saddle horns, eyes locked on him and Moses. Their rough appearances, the way they carried themselves, and the way they wore their guns told Elijah everything he needed to know—they weren't businessmen or ranch workers. They were gunmen, there for a very specific purpose.

Elijah kept his voice steady. "We're not lookin' for trouble. We'll take this up with Mister Stratton and Mister Hill directly if need be." Elijah eyed them for any kind of reaction.

Finn MacDonald glanced back at his men before turning his attention to Elijah. "You do that, Mister Barber. But in the meantime, we've work to do. I suggest you and your men keep clear of our business, as we, of course, will of yours."

His tone was laced with sarcasm, the challenge clear. Finn touched the brim of his hat, then turned his horse, signaling for his men to follow. The silent gunmen cast one last lingering look at Elijah and Moses before turning their mounts.

As they rode off, Finn called back over his shoulder, "Good luck with yer roundup. We'll be seein' ye around."

Elijah watched them go, the tension in his chest refusing to ease. He exchanged a glance with Moses, Hank, and Collins, all understanding that this was far from over. The beauty of Paradise Valley surrounded them, but for the first time, Elijah felt the weight of something dark looming on the horizon.

Moses broke the silence, his voice low. "They're pushin', Eli. And they know exactly what they're doing." He watched the men ride for a moment. "He was prepared for that talk. Knew exactly what he was gonna say."

Collins shook his head. "And I came off like a fool that can't speak for himself." He removed his hat and ran a hand through his hair.

"You know, when I first come out here, Thompson ran a small part of his herd on this range, but mine needed the water and so he let me on. That was all there was to it." He looked after the retreating riders. "Guess that's not how we're doing it anymore."

"Don't worry about that, James," Elijah said. Elijah did worry about what Hill's men were capable of, though, if they sensed Collins wasn't ready to stand up for himself. "We've always got your back."

"Alright then," Moses said as he turned Ruby around. "Gotta finish this roundup regardless of that. I'm sure we'll find a way forward."

"Thanks fellas," Collins said.

Elijah turned, casting one last look at the retreating figures of Hill's men before adjusting his hat and spurring Duke back toward the roundup. The ever more crowded valley had never felt so quiet.

LIVINGSTON

— · —

H igh in the clear blue sky, the sun cast a warm glow over Paradise Valley. Across the open land echoed the sound of cattle lowing and the occasional shout of a cowboy. The summer pasture stretched out before them, a wide expanse of grass bordered by the towering Absaroka Range to the east and the Gallatin Range to the west. The Yellowstone River meandered through the valley, its waters glistening in the sunlight, providing a natural boundary and a much-needed source of water for the herd.

Elijah sat atop Duke, looking out over the expanse of land. It was an ideal spot for summer pasture, with plenty of fresh grass to keep the cattle fat and healthy until the fall. The valley was more than just land to him—it was a place of peace and prosperity, something he had worked hard to maintain for the past eighteen years.

As he surveyed the scene, Elijah couldn't help but feel a twinge of regret. He had driven the outfit hard since their encounter with Hill's men two weeks ago. He knew he had pushed them, but he was determined to get the work done quickly so that he and Moses could head to Bozeman and, more importantly, return home. The tension from that encounter had been gnawing at him ever since, and he was eager to set things right, clear up any misunderstandings—or, if required—figure out what they would do about it.

He rode over to where Travis, Jax, and Henry gathered, giving them their final instructions. "You three did good work getting the herd here," Elijah said. "We've got the cattle settled, but you know as well as I do that's only half the job. Get the outfit back to Summit Valley and pay the hands. You've got my approval for the extra pay we talked about."

Travis nodded, tipping his hat. "We'll handle it, Boss."

Jax chimed in, "We'll make sure everything gets back in order."

Henry, who had quietly listened, added, "You want line riders left with the herd?"

Travis and Jax looked at him expectantly, as if they'd been afraid to ask the question. Summit Valley had never felt the need to keep men with the herd at all times, looking out for rustlers, predators, sick or injured cattle, and the like. Sure, there were regular line-riding rotations, but immediately following a roundup had never been considered.

Elijah removed his hat and ran a hand through his hair before pulling it back on. "Why don't we get three or four volunteers, offer them some extra pay, and have them stick with the herd until they are settled in?" He stared past the cattle into the distance. "And maybe don't tell them about the business with Hill."

"You think they'd try somethin'?" Travis asked.

"Don't think so," Moses said. He looked at Elijah, then back at the men. "But things feel different. . ."

"Mo's right," Elijah said. "I wouldn't mind having a presence out here until we get this all cleared up."

As the men prepared to break camp, Elijah spotted JT off to the side, busy preparing his horse. He dismounted and walked over to his son, who looked up at him with a look Elijah realized was pride in his work.

Elijah studied JT for a moment, noticing how much the young man had changed. He seemed leaner and stronger from the work, his tanned face somehow older and wiser. A sly smile came to his face as he feigned close inspection. "Might need to start shaving soon, son."

JT grinned. "Maybe. Been working hard, Pa."

Elijah nodded. "Glad you stuck with it, JT. All the fellas have declared you earned your keep."

JT gave a small smile, then hesitated, as if perhaps waiting to hear what his father's own assessment was. "You and Uncle Mo headin' to Bozeman to see Mister Stratton?"

"Yes, we are. It's important we check in after a roundup, make sure everything's squared away and keep him informed."

JT hesitated, then asked, "Can I come with you? I'd like to see Bozeman again, and I've never ridden on a train."

Elijah shook his head. "I need you back at headquarters, son. You've got responsibilities there, and I need you to be the man of our house until I get back."

JT looked like he wanted to protest but stopped. "Yessir. I'll head back, then."

Elijah placed a hand on JT's shoulder, giving it a reassuring squeeze. "You're doing good, JT. Keep it up." He watched as JT mounted up, then reached over and shook his hand. "Tell your ma and aunt Helen we'll be back as soon as we can. A few more days."

With that, Elijah found Moses and rode over to James Collins, who was preparing to depart with his own men. Elijah tipped his hat. "James, we're headed to Bozeman now. We'll get word to you after we've spoken with Stratton."

Collins nodded, his expression serious. "Appreciate that, Elijah. We'll be headin' back ourselves. Thanks for the help. All things considered, I reckon we did well."

Elijah gave a slight smile. "We did. Give my best to Martha and the family."

Collins smiled at the mention of his wife's name. "I will. You tell Maggie and the girls I said hello."

Just as Collins was about to ride off, JT, who had been lingering near the men as they spoke, suddenly called out, "Mister Collins. . ."

Collins turned in the saddle, his eyebrows raised in curiosity. JT hesitated. Then, gaining confidence, said, "And could you also give your family my best, and tell Miss Emily especially that I send my greetings?"

Elijah and Moses exchanged amused glances, stifling their laughter as they watched Collins's reaction. Collins looked at JT, a mixture of surprise and amusement on his face, but also a protective glint in his eye. He nodded. "Alright then, JT. I'll do that."

Collins tipped his hat to the brothers again, this time with a hint of a smile, and rode off, leaving Elijah to marvel at how much JT had grown up in such a short time.

⚜

ELIJAH AND MOSES spent the rest of the afternoon following the Yellowstone River as it wound its way north through the valley. Frequent use by cowboys, travelers, trappers, and traders over the years had worn the trail they rode. The sun dipped lower in the sky, throwing shadows that matched the various mountain peaks across the landscape. As they rode, the brothers spoke little, each lost in his own thoughts about the task ahead in Bozeman.

By the time they reached Livingston, the sun was setting behind the mountains, painting the sky in shades of orange and pink. The town was bustling with activity, a stark contrast to the peaceful valley they had left behind. Livingston was a growing town, spurred by the arrival of the Northern Pacific Railroad. Cowboys, miners, merchants, and travelers filled the streets, each pursuing their business. The clatter of wagon wheels, the braying of mules, and the shouts of townsfolk created a lively atmosphere that was both invigorating and exhausting after their long day's ride.

The brothers guided their horses toward the Albemarle Hotel, a grand three-story building on the corner across the street from the railroad station. The hotel was one of the finest in the region, a sign of the town's growing prosperity. Its brick façade and large, inviting windows made it a beacon for weary travelers.

They dismounted, handing the reins to a groom who approached them, and walked into the hotel lobby, their boots echoing on the polished wooden floors. The lobby was bustling with guests, and the rich scent of tobacco smoke and leather mingled with the smell of fresh coffee being served in the corner.

Elijah approached the front desk, where a young man in a neat suit and bow tie stood behind the counter. The clerk eyed their dusty attire with a raised eyebrow. "Good evening, gentlemen. How can I assist you?"

Elijah removed his hat and placed it on the counter. "We'd like a room for the night. How much?"

The clerk, still scrutinizing them, replied, "One dollar and fifty cents per night, gentlemen. An additional fifty cents for hot water if you wish to bathe."

Moses grinned. "Reckon we'll need that hot water, seein' as we've been out in the dust and dirt for a while."

The clerk cleared his throat. "Very well, sir. We also offer supper in the dining room for fifty cents and breakfast in the morning for the same price."

Elijah nodded, reaching into his coat and pulling out a worn leather wallet. He counted out the money and handed it to the clerk, who seemed slightly surprised at how easily Elijah paid. "We'll take it all," Elijah said.

The clerk nodded and handed over a brass key attached to a small wooden block. "Your room is on the second floor. The bathhouse is at the end of the hall. I'll have someone bring up hot water shortly."

"Much obliged," Elijah said as he took the key.

They made their way upstairs, the wooden steps creaking under their weight. The hallway was quiet, a stark contrast to the lively lobby below. They found their room and pushed open the door, revealing a modest but clean space with two beds, a washstand, and a small table with a basin and pitcher. A large window looked out over the railroad station, where the faint sound of a train whistle could be heard in the distance.

After dropping off their things, the brothers washed up as best they could before heading back downstairs to the dining room for supper. The meal was simple but satisfying—roast beef, potatoes, and freshly baked bread, washed down with coffee. They ate in companionable silence, the weariness of the day beginning to catch up with them.

Once they finished supper, they crossed the street to the railroad station to inquire about the next day's train to Bozeman. The station was a busy place, with travelers coming and going, and the scent of coal smoke lingering in the air.

They approached the ticket window, where a middle-aged man with a bushy mustache and wire-rimmed glasses greeted them. "What can I do for you, gentlemen?"

Elijah placed his hands on the counter. "We'd like two tickets for the morning train to Bozeman. What time does it leave?"

The ticket agent consulted a schedule pinned to the wall behind him. "Train departs at eight o'clock sharp. Should get you to Bozeman by half past nine."

Elijah nodded. "We'll take the tickets, and while we're at it, we'd like to send a wire to Bozeman."

After accepting their payment, the agent slid two tickets across the counter. "You can send your wire at the telegraph office just down the platform."

They thanked the man and made their way to the telegraph office, a small room filled with the steady tapping of telegraph keys. The operator, a thin man with sharp features, looked up as they entered. "Evening, gents. Need to send a message?"

Elijah nodded, taking the small notebook and pencil the man handed him. He wrote out a brief message to John Stratton, letting him know the roundup was complete and they would arrive the following morning and were looking forward to a meeting. He returned the notebook to the operator, who began transcribing the message.

As the operator tapped out the message, he paused, his eyes narrowing as he looked down at the name. "You're Elijah Barber?"

Elijah exchanged a glance with Moses, then nodded. "I am."

The operator's face lit up. "Well, I'll be. There's already a message here for you, Mister Barber. Came in 'round a week ago or so. Said to make sure you saw it as soon as you came through." The man reached into a drawer and pulled out a folded piece of paper, handing it to Elijah. Elijah unfolded it and read the message, his brow furrowing as he did so.

The message was from Stratton, asking them to come to Bozeman as soon as possible and to wire back their arrival time. The urgency in the wording was apparent, and Elijah's concern deepened.

"Looks like he's expectin' us," Moses said, reading over Elijah's shoulder.

Elijah nodded, handing the message back to the operator. "Scrap my message. Send word we'll be on the eight o'clock train."

The operator nodded, quickly tapping the reply as the brothers exchanged a glance. The tension they had felt since their encounter with Hill's men was back and as they left the station and returned to the hotel, Elijah couldn't shake the feeling that whatever awaited them in Bozeman wouldn't be good.

BOZEMAN

— ◦ —

The low rumble of the train carried Elijah and Moses west from Livingston, toward Bozeman. The rhythmic clatter of wheels on steel tracks sped them along the journey in just over ninety minutes—a far cry from the day's travel it had required before the railroad arrived. From their seats, the brothers watched the familiar landscape shift and evolve, the miles between past and present blurring like the scenery outside the window.

The late spring sun bathed the rolling terrain in golden light, coaxing life back into the high plains and valleys after a long winter. New grass stretched across the open land in waves of vibrant green, and wildflowers dotted the hills like splashes of paint on a canvas. The nearby mountains, still clinging to patches of snow, stood like silent sentinels over the valley, casting cool shadows over ranches, settlements, and fields bustling with fresh activity.

But it wasn't just the land that had changed.

Bozeman was coming into view; more alive and more complex than the quiet town they had first known almost twenty years ago. Now, it sprawled, expanding outward like a living thing, hungry for more space. Every passing moment sharpened the town's outline, its buildings standing taller, its streets busier, its air tinged with the scent of sawdust and progress.

Elijah leaned toward the window, narrowing his eyes as he spotted a newly built wooden structure near the train station. "That wasn't there last fall."

Moses followed his brother's gaze and grunted. "Hill's new mercantile." He pointed further down the street, where a small building with a prominent sign reading Mining Supplies & Assayer stood out among the newer constructions. "And there's something else he's added—a mining supply shop. Guess the man's branching out."

Elijah frowned. "Not sure there are enough prospectors with claims to keep a place that size open."

"I bet there will be as soon as Carson Hill figured out how to make it worth his while," Moses replied, his voice carrying a mix of skepticism and unease. "Bozeman's always been about cattle and ranches, but Hill seems dead set on adding more to that picture."

Elijah stood, adjusting his coat as he prepared to disembark. "A picture I'm not sure I'll like given how fast it's changing."

The train slowed as it pulled into the station, the hiss of steam and the squeal of brakes cutting through the early morning air. When they stepped off the platform, the rush of warm spring air hit them, carrying with it a mix of familiar and new scents. The smell of freshly sawn lumber mingled with the earthy undertone of nearby livestock pens, but there was something sharper in the air now—a sense of motion, of purpose, like the town itself had picked up speed and wasn't planning to slow down.

They walked down Main Street, boots clacking against the wooden boardwalks as they passed by bustling shops and construction crews raising wooden frames for new buildings. Laborers hauled beams, and the steady thunk-thunk of hammers rang out, punctuated by shouts from foremen. A new bank was going up across from the train station, its brick exterior half-finished but already promising permanence. The faint strains of piano music floated from a nearby saloon, one of several new ones that had opened their doors since last fall.

Elijah scanned the surroundings, noting the contrast. The Bozeman they'd first arrived in had been simpler, humbler—a town of dirt roads, small-time merchants, and ranchers gathering supplies or sharing news over a drink. The faces back then had been familiar, whether friendly or wary, but always grounded. Now, there were more unfamiliar faces in the crowd, and many of them were men in suits or workers moving too fast to tip their hats or offer a nod. Business had overtaken familiarity.

"There's a harder edge to this place now," Elijah said, his tone measured. "Fifteen years ago, we could walk Main Street and know just about everyone we passed. Now, I can barely tell who's a rancher and who's here to make a quick dollar."

Elijah wasn't a man who feared progress. He'd fought for it during the war, sought to protect it during his days as a lawman, and ensured the ranch community had a school and the latest equipment to make work easier. But progress, unchecked and driven by men who saw it as nothing more than a means to fill their pockets, was a different matter altogether. His concern wasn't what was being built—it was who would benefit and whether Bozeman would thrive or simply be carved up by those hungry for profit.

As they neared the end of Main Street, their destination came into view: Stratton Land Management. Unlike the buildings springing up around it, Stratton's headquarters was well-established, a monument to his years of success. The whitewashed trim gleamed in the morning sun, and tall windows reflected the bustling street below. Stratton had built this office years ago when Bozeman was still finding its footing, and for years it had stood as a symbol of stability and growth.

But as Elijah stood before it now, something about that vision felt different—less certain. Stratton was still the most powerful man in town, but the town wasn't the same place he had built. There was a name other than Stratton on many people's lips now, a name that seemed to come up every time progress was mentioned: Carson Hill.

Inside, the air was cooler, contrasting with the growing warmth outside. Stratton's assistant greeted them with a nod and a hurried expression, leading them into the large, elegantly furnished office where Jonathan Stratton waited. The man stood by the window, looking out over the bustling street, his arms crossed over his chest.

When he turned to greet them, Elijah noted a strain in his face, a weariness that hadn't been there the last time they'd met. Stratton's once-vibrant complexion was now a bit pale, and his sharp blue eyes held a trace of fatigue, though he masked it with a welcoming smile.

"Gentlemen," he said, stepping forward and extending a hand. "So good to see you both. I believe not seeing you during the winter kills me a bit every year."

"Good to see you, too, Jon," Elijah replied, gripping his hand firmly.

"How's the Barber clan?" Stratton asked. "JT still growing?"

Elijah smiled. "Yes, sir, he is. Even helped with the round-up."

"My goodness," Stratton said with a chuckle. "And the girls? You two ensuring they grow up tough behind those pretty dresses?"

Moses laughed and extended his hand to Stratton. "I reckon their mothers handle that just fine." They all laughed. "Bozeman's grown since we last set foot here," Moses added.

Stratton gave a slight nod as he shook Moses's hand, though his smile didn't quite reach his eyes now. "Yes, it has. And faster than I'd anticipated. Carson Hill has brought in quite a crew—more men than I'd have thought possible, given the weather we had this past winter. He's been raising funds, buying up buildings and land, and getting to work with little regard for the town's natural pace." He gestured toward the window, where the new bank was being erected across the street. "The man's wasting no time." While many in Bozeman might have marveled at the process, Elijah sensed Jonathan Stratton did not join them in such feelings.

Moses exchanged a glance with Elijah as Stratton gestured for them to sit, both aware that Hill's rapid expansion could bring trouble. Elijah finally spoke. "We saw the signs of it ourselves. Ran into one of Hill's men during the round-up. Looked like they were pressing some of the range lines of the Circle C. . . and ours."

Stratton's face darkened as he fell into his oversized chair, and his head fell back. "I was afraid of that, and that's why I set the wire. The man's a force, no question. Where he's getting the funds for all this, I can't say, but he's had no shortage of folks eager to follow and do business with him."

Elijah finished packing his pipe and spoke around it as he lit it, studying the lines of worry in Stratton's face. "What do you make of him? This Hill fella?" He shook out the match. "Troublemaker?"

Stratton hesitated, then looked at each brother. "Hill's the type who sees an opportunity and seizes it, no matter who stands in his way. He's ambitious, with a drive that's unsettling, even to a man like me." He paused, and his tone became almost reflective. "Bozeman has always needed men with vision, but I'm not sure his aligns with ours."

"Reckon I know a man who might have been just the same fifteen years ago," Moses said with a grin. Stratton gave him a look of disapproval before smiling. "Not that we and the town ain't the benefactor of that," Moses added.

"Fair enough," Stratton said. "But I didn't have to move in on anyone to accomplish what I did," he said. Stratton gestured out the window. "I built all this from nothing."

The brothers nodded, each mulling over Stratton's words. Elijah cleared his throat. "Aside from Hill's ventures, the round-up went well, mostly as expected. Our herd's in good shape, and we're looking strong as ever heading into the growing season."

"Things have been good, and the weather's cooperating, but we're thinking we should put extra time and effort into getting hay put up," Moses added. "Don't want to be caught flat-footed when this string of fortune ends."

Elijah looked at Moses and nodded. "He's right. When times are good, you can't forget they might get hard. Our mother thumped that into our brains."

Stratton managed a faint smile. "Good to hear, and yes, I agree. It's always a comfort knowing you two are watching over things. You and Travis have my blessing, as always, to do what's best for the ranch."

Moses added, "That said, we did run into Hill's men where they shouldn't have been. Looks like they've even been putting up some fencing and doing some surveying. For what, we have no idea. They ain't got the word, though, that cattle don't always know where men draw their lines. Said Bar T had been ceding ground to Collins they shouldn't have been."

Elijah pulled his pipe from his mouth. "If they aren't willing to talk friendly with us, it's only a matter of time before that causes trouble."

Stratton sighed, rubbing a hand across his forehead. "I expected this. I knew he'd push his luck but hoped it'd take longer." He paused for a moment, then added, "It's times like this I wish Edward were out here."

Both brothers stilled, the mention of Edward catching them off guard. They hadn't heard Stratton mention his son in some time. "Edward?" Elijah asked.

Stratton nodded, exhaling through his nose as if the thought weighed on him. "He wrote me recently. It surprised me, to be honest. It's been a long while since he showed any interest in coming back west, but now. . . well, I confided that I'd lost a step, and he's concerned my health is failing. The boy seems worried."

Moses raised an eyebrow. "Did you tell him he's worryin' over nothin'?" Elijah could see his brother having a hard time grasping the force of a man speaking freely about slowing down.

"I did," Stratton said with a small chuckle. "But maybe it's time he came. I could use his legal mind and it seems he's developed a knack for business deals and he could put that legal training to work as well."

Elijah and Moses shared a brief look of curiosity. Edward Stratton had once been a boy who admired them, asking endless questions about ranching and cowboy life. But over the years, their perception of him had shifted as he seemed only to want to use Stratton family money to better himself in New York, and stay away from his father and their holdings in the Montana Territory.

"Do you think he's really coming out of concern?" Elijah asked.

Stratton leaned back, tapping his fingers on the armrest. "He says he wants to reconnect with me—but yes, he mentioned Hill. Seems he's been keeping an ear to the ground about what's happening out here. He's curious about how Hill's investments could affect things." Stratton chuckled softly, though there was something faintly introspective in the sound. "Maybe that's the business instinct in him." He eyed the brothers and seemed to sense something in their silent reactions. "This did used to be all he ever wanted a part of, if you remember."

Elijah puffed on his pipe as he thought, but his expression was neutral. Stratton's last comment had seemed defensive, and he tried to put his boss at ease. "If Edward's taking an interest, I suppose it's better late than never."

Stratton leaned forward. "If he comes, I'd appreciate you two keeping an eye on him—helping him adjust, showing him what we've built here." He smiled. "I know he's lost some favor with folks, being gone so long, but maybe you can show him a little adventure like old times?"

Moses smiled faintly. "Wouldn't mind seein' the kid grown up. Let's hope he's ready to get some dust on his boots."

Stratton seemed to reflect for a moment, then smiled. "I hope so too." He rose with a grunt and great effort. "I'm sure you need to check on things at the livery, but I hope you'll join me at the house for supper tonight before you leave town in the morning?"

They each shook his hand. "Wouldn't miss it, sir," Elijah answered.

As they stepped outside into the dust of Bozeman's bustling Main Street, Elijah adjusted his hat and lit another match for his pipe. He stole a glance at Moses, who was watching him with a knowing look.

Elijah spoke around the pipe as he re-lit it. "What?"

"What do you make of it?" Moses asked.

"Not much to make anything of just yet," Elijah replied as he shook out the match. "If Edward's comin' west, we'll see soon enough whether he's here to help—or whether he's lookin' to make his own mark."

Moses nodded as they began to walk. "And you're not worried the young man's decided he wants a piece of the ranch after all?"

Elijah shrugged. "Can't say for sure, but I like to think that given how much he respected us and the kind of man his father is, we'll be secure."

Moses let that settle a moment before he said anything. "Yeah. . . I reckon you're right."

Elijah clapped his brother on the back. "I usually am."

But as he exhaled a slow puff of smoke into the warm spring air, Elijah's gaze lingered on the growing number of buildings bearing

Carson Hill's name. Whatever was coming next, they'd face it—just like they always had.

But this time, the ground beneath them didn't feel as steady as it once had.

PART TWO

—◦—

Summer

CHESS

— • —

The sun hung low over Bozeman, its last light fading as lanterns flickered to life along Main Street's arcade. The settlement, still finding its footing between frontier rawness and the structure of a growing hub, was a curious mix of refinement and grit. Wooden boardwalks bustled with ranchers, cowboys, merchants, and drifters, their voices mingling with the clatter of wagon wheels and the distant strains of a saloon piano.

At the far end of the thoroughfare, the Stratton Land Office stood like a sentinel, its polished windows reflecting the fading light. Across from it, Carson Hill's Bozeman Trust and Banking loomed in muted defiance. Its freshly painted facade gleamed, a deliberate display of Hill's rapid rise—his foothold in a town that, until recently, had been another man's domain.

Most folks didn't see it yet, but Bozeman was shifting. The old hands who'd built the town still held their grip, but Hill was tightening his own—one quiet deal, one strategic purchase at a time. His bank, his land office, the expanding Box H ranch, the land in the valley—these weren't just business ventures. They were the foundation of something bigger. This time, Hill wasn't just passing through. He was here to stay.

Carson Hill and Finn MacDonald had spent fifteen years on the move, climbing westward like the tide, sweeping into one town after another—always making their mark before moving on, before questions grew too sharp and opposition too determined. Hill had played every role a man might use to get ahead: financier, speculator, rancher, politician when it suited him, and, if need be, the man who had no problem removing an obstacle by any means necessary.

From St. Louis to Denver, they'd carved their way through boomtowns and failing settlements alike, taking fortunes others hadn't realized were there for the taking. Cattle outfit here, a business there, stakes in railroads, freight lines, and land speculation—always a step ahead, always gone before things soured.

But now, Hill wanted more than money. He wanted permanence. Influence. He was no longer just another man chasing wealth—he intended to become a pillar of it. The valley held more than cattle and homesteads; it held resources that could build an empire. And an empire needed a sound foundation.

Inside The Grand North, the town's finest hotel, Hill stood at the window of his private suite, surveying the town below. The entire top floor belonged to him, a reflection of the wealth and power he intended to cement here. His office, a study in refinement, bore no trace of frontier ruggedness—rich leather armchairs, a polished oak desk, and heavy drapes that muffled the street noise below.

Hill himself was as meticulously arranged as the room—waistcoat fitted perfectly over his broad chest, his finely manicured mustache adding to his air of measured control. His pale eyes scanned the town like a general surveying a battlefield.

Movement caught his attention. Down on the street, Finn Mac-Donald rode into town, the dust of weeks of travel clinging to his coat and derby. He dismounted with his usual ease, hitching his horse outside the hotel before taking the broad steps two at a time. A moment later, the heavy oak doors swung open, swallowing him into the opulent lobby.

Hill turned from the window just as Finn's boots sounded heavy on the stairs.

"Ye been gone longer than I expected," Hill remarked as Finn entered.

Finn tossed his hat onto a side table, sending up a small cloud of dust, then poured himself a glass of Scotch from the decanter on the desk. "Aye, the valley's a big place, and I'm just one man," he said. "Had to take my time, get the lay of things proper."

Hill motioned to a chair, his pale eyes narrowing slightly.

Finn sat opposite him, one boot resting on his knee as he swirled the glass of Scotch. While he wore clothing a cut above most in the area, his dusty coat and worn boots were at odds with the surrounding luxury—though his sharp eyes made him seem perfectly at home. A fresh stack of papers sat between them—maps, deeds, and ledgers detailing the valley's layout.

"Good whisky," Finn said, breaking the silence after he drank. "Almost makes a man forget about ridin' back and forth across that bloody valley."

Hill turned from the window, his lips curling faintly. "I take it yer travels yielded something useful. I sincerely hope ye've visited for more than a drink."

Finn chuckled, leaning forward to refill his glass. "Useful enough. Collins is diggin' his heels in, stubborn old goat that he is. Keeps Summit Valley's Barbers close whenever talk of land comes up, like they're his damn bodyguards. Makes a man wonder who's really runnin' that ranch."

Hill raised an eyebrow of curiosity and smoothed his mustache. "You met them?"

Finn's grin widened, more teeth than humor. "Aye. Elijah and Moses Barber. Older now than in the stories we read. Quieter. The kind that want peace but have the look of men who remember how to fight. But Collins? He's nervous as a hen in a fox's den. Let's them do all the talkin'. I'd wager he knows his days are numbered if he don't go all in with them." Finn scratched his beard. "Felt like he knew that Bar T spread rightfully included some of what had been passin' as his."

Hill's fingers tapped against the desk. "Which we've confirmed?"

Finn nodded. "That lawyer of yours, Greaves, got together some signed affidavits from folks. . . motivated. . . to recall that it was historic Bar T range." He gestured out the window toward the bank. "Collins keeps up on his payments, but his spread ain't big enough to keep from gettin' squeezed."

Hill nodded approvingly, then spread a map across the desk. His fingers traced the ranges of the valley's major ranches—the Bar T, now part of the Box H, the Circle C, Summit Valley. His pale eyes flicked to Finn as he spread a hand across the Slash V holdings.

"Go on... I pay ye for more than what ye've told me so far."

Finn swirled his glass, his grin fading into something more serious. "The Barbers are loyal to Stratton, that much is clear. They respect him, and the valley respects them." He chuckled. "Maybe more than they respect Stratton. That makes them tricky. As for Collins, he's soft, and soft men are easy to break. He knows he's surrounded."

Hill studied Finn for a moment, his gaze sharp. "Can they be swayed?"

Finn leaned back, his grin returning. "Everyone's got a weak point, Carson. Collins wants out, even if he don't know it yet. The Barbers?" He tapped his temple. "They're not eager to return to their past. Protecting their family is most important to them. They've got history, and history's heavy. Play it right, and you can use it to bring them down."

Hill set the map down, his fingers resting on Summit Valley. "Their past is their weakness," he hissed. "Men like that don't forget. And the people who look up to them don't either. When the time comes, we'll remind this valley who they were before they became respectable ranchers." He dropped into his chair and sat back. "No, you don't go directly after men like that, Finn. You let them see what's in their best interest."

Finn raised his glass in a mock toast. "Aye, and the cracks'll show soon enough."

Hill didn't return the gesture. Instead, he glanced back at the papers on the desk. "Collins will follow in time. But Summit Valley. . ." He trailed off, his expression hardening. "They're the key to the whole thing. Without them, the rest is meaningless." He glanced across the street at the new mining office.

Finn set his glass down with a clink. "Yer still buildin' somethin', though. Stratton or the Barbers might not care much for your kind of progress, but I see plenty in town who do. That bank of yours—plenty folks're already usin' it over Stratton's. And those miners who came from elsewhere in the territory that you're putting to work? They'll remember who gave 'em their coin when the time comes."

Hill's lips curved into a faint, calculating smile. "Loyalty forged by necessity," he said. "It's the only kind that endures. And those miners. . . When the time comes, they'll be more useful than just diggin' color out of the ground."

Finn chuckled. "Aye. Useful for diggin' graves, if need be. And puttin' folks in 'em."

Hill didn't laugh. Instead, he returned to the window, watching the lanterns flicker along Main Street. "The Barbers are hosting a gathering soon. Inviting all their neighbors, I'm told."

"A party?" Finn raised an eyebrow. "Didn't take 'em for the festive type."

Hill's smile turned cold. "A show of strength, no doubt, cloaked in the banner of celebrating this young experiment of a country they fought for—an attempt to remind the valley who holds its trust. Neighbors can build you up—or bring you down. Let's see which they choose."

Finn stood, adjusting his hat as he moved toward the door. "Shall I start makin' moves?"

Hill shook his head. "Not yet. This isn't the time for boldness. Let them have their party." He gestured to the papers on the desk. "We continue as planned. Plus, am I not a neighbor now, and do you not enjoy a good party, Finn?" He gazed east toward the valley. "I believe I'd like to see what it is I am acquiring."

Finn paused, tipping his hat with a smirk. "Aye. You'll have your empire yet, Carson. Never a doubt."

Hill didn't reply, his gaze still fixed on the town below. The valley was a chessboard, and the pieces were moving into place. Carson Hill always played to win.

IN IT TOGETHER

— • —

High above Paradise Valley, the summer sun cast its golden glow across the rolling pastures of Summit Valley Ranch. The grass had come up thick and tall, swaying gently in the warm July breeze. The scent of fresh-cut hay mixed with dust kicked up by animals and workers moving through the day's chores. A chorus of cicadas droned, their hum stretching across the valley, broken only by the distant call of a meadowlark.

The cattle had settled into the summer pastures, spreading across the vast stretches of land beneath the shadow of the Absaroka Range. This was normally a season of steadiness, a time when the ranch could breathe after the intensity of spring and before the fall roundup and drive.

But this summer felt different. An unseen tension hung in the air like the rumble of distant thunder, leaving one to wonder if, or when, a storm would arrive.

Elijah leaned against a fence post as he puffed on his pipe, his gaze sweeping over the valley, then back to the ranch yard. He saw animals grazing by a creek that branched off the Yellowstone. Moses and JT were inspecting some recently broken horses with Maggie, and men scattered across the ranch going about their work.

It was a scene he'd grown to cherish, a world he'd built with his brother and their families. But something gnawed at him. It was like looking at a well-built fence and noticing, for the first time, that the wood had splintered, or a few posts were leaning—not enough to collapse, not yet, but enough to see where the damage might spread.

Moses approached, wiping the sweat from his brow with a worn bandana. "Collins was here earlier," he said, his tone grave. "Showed me some papers from a lawyer in town. Handful of old-timers signed their name to affidavits saying that's historic Bar T range."

Elijah nodded, processing the news. "Figured that was going to be the outcome. What good is there to come when fancy lawyers get involved in where cattle graze?" He held the pipe away from his mouth as if he might say more, then replaced it and puffed again. He knew there wasn't anything of value to add.

"Collins is fit to be tied," Moses said. He leaned over the wooden fence alongside his brother. "He always thought a spot like that, overlapping so many spreads, could be shared peaceably."

"Him and me both," Elijah said.

They stared up the valley silently for a few minutes, almost not needing words to communicate at this point in their lives. Eventually, they made their way toward the main barn. Elijah noticed the way the ranch hands stole glances at them as they passed—respectful, but uneasy. It wasn't just the rumors of Hill's encroachment anymore. The Slash V riders had encountered Hill's men more and more often on the range, and every one of them had been carrying iron. That wasn't unheard of, but even the few Slash V riders who never carried a sidearm had started wearing one on their hip. That fact alone was enough to trouble Elijah.

Jax had mentioned a scuffle at a saloon in Livingston—two Box H riders had squared off against some Circle C boys over a dispute that started over a hand of cards and ended with talk of fences and cattle grazing on the wrong side of declared boundaries. No actual damage had been done, and defending the brand was always to be expected, but the encounters were becoming more frequent.

And then there was Billy.

The sharpest eye on cattle of any man in the valley, Billy McCray had returned from a few days riding the line swearing up and down that they were missing cows. Not many. Few enough that most men wouldn't have noticed. But Billy did.

And Billy was angry.

Jax and Travis had brought the matter to Elijah and Moses, and Elijah had told them to have Billy monitor it—but keep his wits.

Elijah's gut told him Billy was right, though. A few steers missing wasn't uncommon, but given everything else, it didn't sit right with him.

As they reached the barn, Henry nodded in greeting, his calm demeanor assessing them. "Bosses," he said. "Heard about Hill's expansion. Not much good will come of it, I fear."

"No, I don't reckon it will," Elijah replied. "But I don't have to tell you about losing land that's yours because of what some paper might say. Collins is feeling the pressure though, and with the Independence Day barn dance coming up, I have half a mind to worry about trouble with so many neighbors—old and new—coming around."

Henry gave a nod, his face unreadable. "People like Hill do not settle for what is fair and will only use decency, the law, and its paper when it serves them."

"We still talkin' 'bout Hill and the Circle C, Henry?" Moses looked at him, squinting into the sun with a grin.

The three of them talked about the topic of what had happened to Henry's people and other tribes often. "They will take and take until someone makes them stop. . . and yes, I am talking about Carson Hill." He grinned. "This time."

Elijah shared a look with Moses before he spoke. "I ain't looking to be the one to make them stop. I don't want to do anything without the law behind it, Henry."

"I know, boss."

Jax joined them near the barn door, his broad frame covered in dust from the day's work. "Bosses," he said, adjusting his hat. "Travis and I were goin' over the plans for the soiree, making sure we're set up for the crowd, but. . ." He hesitated, then gave a low chuckle. "I'd be lying if I said I didn't half-expect some folks to show up to see how they were received. With Hill's men working right up to the edge of our spread, a lot of the boys are talkin'."

Elijah looked past Jax, his eyes settling on the open expanse of pasture that stretched toward the low ridge marking their boundary with Hill's claimed range. "We're set on having the dance," he said firmly. "It's a tradition here, as is the knowledge that any neighbor that knows we're here is invited. If we let the likes of Hill chase us off our own land, or change the way we do things, what does that say about us or to our neighbors? No, we'll have it as we always do."

Moses clapped Jax on the shoulder. "You and Travis make sure things are in order. If Hill's men show up looking for trouble, we'll handle it then. But until then, its business as usual."

Henry and Jax departed, and Moses turned to Elijah. "Usually, no guns at this thing. You talked to Maggie about that?"

Elijah scoffed. "Did *you* talk to Helen?" he asked sarcastically.

JT interrupted, wiping his hands on his pants as he approached. The boy had grown taller over the summer, and Elijah noted the way he carried himself—a little more sure-footed, a little more like a man.

"Need any help setting up?" he asked, a glimmer of excitement in his eyes.

Elijah forced a smile and gave him a nod. "It's set. Pending whatever other chores your foreman gives you. Ready to help see it through?"

JT's face brightened. "Yes, sir. Looking forward to seeing all our neighbors like the Collins," he added, trying to hide the smile that tugged at the corner of his mouth.

Moses caught Elijah's eye and grinned. "Oh, I see now. He's more eager for this dance than he lets on."

JT flushed, but didn't deny it. "Pa, could I maybe wear one of your suits? I think they might come close to fitting, and ma said she could do some altering."

Moses whistled. "Heaven's sake, boy. You want for us to get the preacher over here too?"

Elijah saw a flash of embarrassed anger in JT's eyes and shook his head at Moses before putting a hand on JT's shoulder. "Well, you just remember there's work to be done, too. You can think about Emily after the chores are finished." He puffed on his pipe. "But tell your mother that whatever she thinks will look good on you is yours."

JT nodded, sheepishly, but Elijah could see the determination in his eyes as he ruffled the boy's hair and then watched him depart with Moses. JT was eager to prove himself as a man, and with the situation at hand, Elijah knew that the world he was raising his son into was fraught with risk.

ELIJAH WAS ABOUT to head for his office when the sound of a closing gate caught his attention, and he turned just in time to see Maggie stepping out of the barn. Sweat and dust from working with the horses stained her hands, yet she moved with a grace that seemed to make the earth pause beneath her feet. The setting sun caught in her auburn hair, making it glow like fire as she closed the distance between them, and Elijah felt that familiar warmth spread through his chest.

She smiled as she approached, and Elijah couldn't help but return it, even as he fought to maintain his composure. "Everything alright?" she asked, her eyes assessing him with that sharp, knowing gaze. She could read him better than anyone, and though he tried to hide it, he knew she could see the tension that had coiled inside him.

He exhaled slowly, pretending to take a last puff from his pipe, then let it fall from his mouth as he tapped it out on the edge of a post. "Yeah. You were right about JT and the Collins girl."

"I know." Her smile softened into something more knowing, though her expression did not express judgment, but understanding.

Elijah chuckled and shook his head, leaning back against the post. "He asked about wearing one of my suits." He paused, watching Maggie as she stepped closer. Her steps were light and assured, always the same, no matter the weight of the day.

She met his gaze, tilting her head with a slight smile that stirred his heart. "And what did you say?"

He grinned, the corners of his mouth tugging upwards despite the shadows of concern lingering in his chest. "Told him to ask you for help."

Her lips quirked. "Well, I do hope you're not planning on letting him wear any ratty old thing of yours." She reached out and adjusted the collar of his shirt, her fingers lingering for a moment before dropping back to her side. "Of which there are still plenty in your wardrobe, might I add."

Elijah stood there momentarily, watching her, taking in the way the light danced off her features, the beauty of the woman he'd married despite the odds stacked against them. His life, their life, hadn't been easy, but they had made it work. And yet, as always, his heart tightened with the knowledge of the struggles ahead, and he knew Maggie sensed it.

"But what is it that's really on your mind?"

He cleared his throat, tapping out the remnants of his pipe with a snap of his fingers, then looked at her again, more seriously this time. "Mo and I were talking about the dance."

Maggie raised an eyebrow. "What about it?"

Elijah's gaze hardened just a touch, a flicker of the old fire still burning beneath his steady surface. "We were thinking maybe a few of us should wear guns. Not everyone might be coming to catch up with neighbors."

Maggie crossed her arms over her chest, eyes narrowing slightly. "Elijah, you said yourself that we weren't going to let Carson Hill change the way we do things. We've always had these dances—no guns, no fighting. It's the way it's always been."

Elijah let out a breath, his shoulders sinking momentarily as if the weight of his decision hung heavy on him. "I don't disagree with you, Maggie. I don't want that life anymore, 'specially not at my home. Not at a party, not when our friends and neighbors are here." He paused, meeting her eyes. "But we can't ignore what's happening out there. Hill's men have been pushing their way through Bozeman and this valley. Collins feels it. Hell, we all feel it."

Maggie's gaze softened for a moment as she stepped closer, her hand brushing against his arm. "I know, Elijah. I know what it's like to carry the weight of this land, this family, all on your shoulders." Her voice dropped a bit, a hint of tenderness breaking through the firmness in her tone. "But you said we wouldn't change who we are, no matter how much things shift around us. You promised me that."

He stared at her, his heart swelling with admiration. "And I haven't gone back on that promise. I don't want to carry a gun around at our own party. But I can't ignore what's happening, either."

She stepped back, looking him over with that same thoughtful, unyielding gaze. "Then show them, Elijah. Show them who you are. Show them that you're not afraid to stand your ground with no need to hold a gun. Without scaring them into being good neighbors. That's the man I married."

Elijah felt the heat of her words settle deep in his chest. She was right, of course—she usually was. He didn't want to be the man who resorted to violence when he didn't need to. But the world had changed, and things were coming to a head.

He gave a slight, resolute nod, lifting his chin. "I'll show them."

Maggie reached up, cupping his face in her hands and planting a soft kiss on his lips. "I know you will," she murmured, pulling away just as quickly as she had come. "And Elijah... don't carry that weight alone. You've got me, you've got your family, you've got your brother, and all these workers who love you both."

As she turned to walk back toward the barn, Elijah stood there for a moment, watching her. He knew she was right, and he was hopefully making something out of nothing. She was everything he needed. Strong, fierce, and unshakable. His better half that had seen him at his worst and brought him through to the other side.

<hr />

THE DAY PRESSED ON with preparations for the dance. The men worked to string up lanterns around the barn and nearby buildings, clear open space for the musicians, and set up long tables for the food.

A current of anticipation ran through the ranch, the excitement of the event mingling with the unspoken tension of Hill's encroachment.

Near sunset, as they loaded barrels of cider and crates of supplies onto wagons, James Collins rode up, his face drawn and eyes steely. He dismounted and walked over to Elijah and Moses, nodding a greeting but getting straight to the point.

"Everything looks in order for tomorrow," he said, his voice tight. "Mighty good of you to carry on with it, but Hill's men. . . I just come from talking to two of my steady hands who had words with them while they worked awful close to our cattle. He took off his hat, grimaced, and beat it against his leg, dust flying off. "Well, dammit, Elijah, they're puttin' up fencing, cutting me off from direct access to the water." He shook his head. I don't like the way they're looking at things. They're talking as if they own the valley."

Elijah's gaze fixed on the horizon. "None of us have ever thought a man could own water, or the access to it, and prevent a neighbor from caring for man or beast."

Collins gave a grim nod. "I agree. But the truth of it is, Hill's got men and money on his side, and the law's favoring him lately. Folks are saying he's already bought his way into Bozeman's council."

Moses scoffed, glancing back at the ranch workers moving about, too busy to hear their conversation. "So he's bought himself a few allies. We'll deal with him like we would any man who thinks he can come in and take what he pleases."

Elijah held up a hand. "I don't disagree with either of you, but I have to believe what's right will win out if we hold our ground, and that starts with us having this party, and being good neighbors." He could see both men wanted to respect him but had their doubts. "I'm confident in that," Elijah added with a resolute nod.

But the confidence was tinged with unease. Hill's influence was spreading, and the man himself was becoming more than just a neighbor—they knew he was a threat. They could see it in the way the ranch hands exchanged wary glances, in the way James Collins spoke, his tone tense and clipped.

Elijah put a hand on each man's shoulder. "Whatever comes, we'll face it together. And we'll stand up for ourselves and way of life."

BARN DANCE

— ◦ —

The summer evening settled over Summit Valley Ranch, casting a warm, golden light across the rolling landscape as neighbors, ranch hands, and families arrived from all over the valley and beyond. Wagons lined the edges of the yard, horses grazed from staked out positions, and families greeted each other with laughter and warm handshakes. For many, the yearly Independence Day barn dance at Summit Valley was the highlight of the season, a time for food, music, and a rare chance to forget the daily hardships of ranch life.

The Barbers had gone all out, as they did every year, to make the occasion special. Long tables were set up outside the barn, laden with fresh pies, roast beef, baked beans, corn on the cob, and pitchers of lemonade. Children ran around in their Sunday best, playing games and darting between the adults. Lanterns strung from the barn beams cast a soft glow on the red, white, and blue bunting, mingling with the fading sunlight, as a group of fiddle players tuned up near the open doors.

Elijah and Moses, dressed in their finest three-piece suits and immaculate Stetson hats, moved among the guests, greeting friends and neighbors, and helping the hands settle horses and wagons. For the Barbers, this event was more than just a celebration; it was a way to remind their neighbors of the unity and community that had grown up around the ranch—and of their various sacrifices for a young country still recovering from the awful war.

Scout padded alongside Elijah, sniffing around the children, who squealed in delight at the sight of the big brindle dog. Maggie walked over, her hair pinned up with care and her dress simple for the ranch but elegant enough for the occasion as host, catching Elijah's eye.

"I'm a lucky man," he said, admiring her beauty. She was a modest woman, but when she wanted to, could turn heads as she was this evening. "And you look beautiful."

She clutched his arm. "You are, and I am," she smiled. She reached up and adjusted his tie. "But I'm a lucky woman, and you look very handsome."

"Elijah!" The voice was deep and familiar. Turning, Elijah spotted Jonathan Stratton approaching, his frame slightly frailer but still exuding that unmistakable Stratton strength. His suit, though a more rugged one fit for the ranch, was crisply tailored, and he moved with the deliberate steps of a man used to commanding attention.

Elijah extended a hand, genuinely pleased. "Jonathan, good to see you here. Wasn't expecting you to make the trip out."

Stratton shook his hand firmly, a slight smile crinkling his eyes. "Couldn't miss your famous Independence Day gathering, could I?" He looked to Maggie and removed his hat, bowing slightly and reaching out his hand. "Or seeing your beautiful wife."

She took his hand. "You are too kind, and we are so grateful you're here. It's been too long, but your guest room is available as usual."

"Excellent," he said, before glancing around, his gaze settling on the barn and the distant ridgeline. "There are few places I feel more at home than here." Then, with a slight shift in his tone, he turned back to them, adding, "I brought my son with me."

Elijah's brow furrowed. "Edward?"

"I was as surprised to see him as you are now," Stratton replied. He gestured to a tall figure making his way through the crowd.

Elijah followed his gaze, taking in the man approaching. Edward Stratton cut an imposing figure, the years of university and law school in the East having refined him into something distant, more polished than the boy who once idolized the Barbers. His suit was finely tailored, his hair neatly parted, his bearing just a shade too stiff for ranch country. He carried himself with confidence—perhaps too much of it—and though his smile was polite; it didn't carry the same warmth it once had.

"Edward, it's good to see you again," Elijah said, extending his hand. "It's been a while since you were last out here." Elijah took his hand, noting the firm grip and the way Edward's gaze flicked over him—not as a young man greeting an old mentor but as an equal taking stock.

"Thank you, Mister Barber. I've heard a lot about Summit Valley over the years. Glad to finally see it again."

Elijah's head shot back at the formality, and he sensed something guarded in Edward's words. "Please, call me Elijah."

For a split second, hesitation flickered in Edward's eyes, as if the offer of familiarity unsettled him. Then he merely nodded.

Elijah introduced Maggie before turning back to Edward. "The ranch has held up well, thanks to your father's support and trust in us."

He glanced at the elder Stratton, noting the pride in the old man's eyes as he looked at his son. But there was something else there too—something harder to place.

The three exchanged a few pleasantries before Jonathan cleared his throat. "Elijah, could we have a word in private? There's something I'd like to discuss." His eyes darted to Maggie, and he did his best to show contrition. "If you'll grant us leave to do so, Maggie, with my deepest apologies."

Maggie rolled her eyes and patted Elijah on the arm. "Make it quick, gentlemen." She then smiled. "It is very good to see you, Jon."

Elijah motioned for them to follow, leading them toward his office in the main headquarters building. As they walked, Elijah glanced over the crowd, spotting Moses in conversation with some of the ranch hands near the cider barrels. He caught his brother's eye and gave a subtle nod, gesturing toward the headquarters building.

Moses raised an eyebrow, then excused himself and made his way over, his curiosity evident as he approached.

"You know the way, Jon," Elijah said, watching the elder Stratton point out various points of the surrounding landscape to his son. "I'll gather Moses, and we'll catch up."

Stratton touched a finger to his hat and continued toward the main building. As he walked, Edward remained quiet, his eyes scanning the ranch with an expression Elijah couldn't quite read.

Moses tipped up his hat and watched the two men walking ahead of them. "That Stratton's boy with him?"

"Not a boy anymore, Mo." Elijah said, now watching the pair walk as well.

Moses gave a low whistle. "Surprised to see Jon come all the way out here for this. He seem like he's lost the spring in his step to you?"

Elijah exhaled slowly. "Not as surprised as I am to see that Edward came after all," he answered. Then, quieter, as if admitting something he didn't want to say aloud—"And yes, he has lost a step."

They caught up to the Strattons just outside the office, and Moses stuck out his hand. "Good to see you, Jonathan."

Stratton returned the handshake with a smile to match Moses's. "Likewise, Moses. And you remember my son, Edward?"

"How do you do?" Edward said as he offered his hand."

Moses waved dismissively before offering his hand. "Goodness, Edward, drop all that formality business, but I do well. Good to see you after all these years." Moses clapped him on the back, causing Edward to jolt forward. "Maybe we saddle up a few of Maggie's wilder mounts and try to break 'em for old times' sake? See if we can't find some mischief?"

Edward straightened his jacket and gave a forced smile. "I should think not, I'm not a boy anymore."

The smile fell from Moses's face. "No, I reckon not, then." Elijah couldn't help but sense a bit of disdain in Moses's voice and could see Edward noticed as well.

As they entered the office, the hum of the dance and the laughter of the crowd faded, replaced by the intimacy of the wood-paneled room. Scout sneaked in behind them all, and Elijah left the door ajar to bring in the cool evening air.

Elijah gestured for the elder Stratton to take the oversized chair behind his desk, then offered a chair in front of the desk to Edward. He and Moses then settled into chairs along the wall, facing the Strattons. Elijah's gaze moved between Jonathan and Edward with mild suspicion, seeming to sense a heavy conversation was coming.

Jonathan Stratton adjusted himself in his chair, glancing at his son before addressing the Barbers. "I won't beat around the bush, Elijah, Moses. My health. . . it's not what it used to be." His voice betrayed a vulnerability that neither Barber had seen in the older man before. "I wrote to my son about my health and, truth be told, wasn't sure what to expect. I know I told you he wrote me back, but he still surprised me with a telegram shortly before his arrival. He says he has taken an interest in the ranch and the Stratton name in Bozeman and wants to ensure I can secure it. We've come to an understanding about the future."

Elijah kept his expression neutral but exchanged a brief look with Moses, both of them sensing the gravity of Jonathan's words.

Edward leaned forward, his posture assertive as he folded his arms. "Father's been running this place single-handedly for years. It's time I stepped in to secure our legacy."

Elijah held Edward's gaze, keeping his own steady. "The ranch has done well under your father's care. But I might add that it's been an honor to help build it into what it is today by performing the day-to-day management for the last eighteen years."

Moses took a less tactful approach. "All due respect, Edward, and especially to your pa—seeing as how I'm alive and still have this arm 'cause of him—he ain't done it by himself."

Elijah scratched his beard, then pulled out his pipe and packed it. There was a time not long ago where he would have jumped in to chastise his brother for his reaction, but he didn't disagree with Moses, nor did he find him out of line.

Jonathan held up a hand to stop his son from responding. "I'll be forever grateful to you both. But Edward's future will be using his experience from out East to forge alliances that will benefit Summit Valley, and my business in Bozeman. When he says I've done it alone, he means only the purely business side. Much of it concerns things in town or separate from the ranch."

Elijah and Moses exchanged another glance, and Elijah chose his words carefully. "Your father's legacy means a lot to us, Edward. We've invested our lives here, and we'd hoped to continue building it the way we've always known. Beyond the ranch itself, that's our own doing putting up that school and church you saw." He puffed on his pipe. "And I assume he's made you aware that we were arranging to—"

"Indeed," Edward interrupted, causing Elijah to bite down on his pipe. "That's precisely why I'm here as well—to ensure that this place thrives in the years to come." His gaze drifted to Elijah's desk, eyeing the paperwork there as though sizing up the business side of the ranch. "The country is changing rapidly, even Bozeman and the valley. With the right structure, we can turn this land into something that not only sustains itself but also drives prosperity across the region." He paused and took a breath, as if the next part of his speech took great effort. "Now being that you have already invested money into an ownership stake," he turned to his father with a look of what Elijah assessed as disapproval, "I'm sure we can come up with an effective cost and profit-sharing plan that is fair."

Moses, sensing the tension in Edward's words, crossed his arms and leaned back. "We're gettin' awful close to a lot of lawyer speak here, Edward. More than I like to think people with as much history and trust as your pa and us have should need."

"Mo. . ." Elijah interjected, speaking around his pipe.

"We've worked a long time to build up this place, Edward," Moses continued. "It's been more than just a business to us. We want to see it thrive, sure, but truth be told, we've sank a lot more blood, sweat, tears, and now money into this place than you have." He looked at Elijah as if expecting to be stopped, but Elijah only puffed on his pipe. "Now we lost our pa young, but got kids of our own now and understand the notion of legacy and leavin' something behind. We ride for the Stratton family and the Slash V, but we won't be pushed aside as if we're just the help."

Elijah admired his brother for a moment, wondering how it came to be that the smart-mouthed younger brother who had caused so much mischief in the past had grown into the man now sitting beside him.

Elijah turned to the Strattons. "All my brother is saying, is that we believe we've earned being equal partners, but we understand family as well as anyone. I'm sure we can make this work." He didn't altogether believe what he was saying, but respected Jon Stratton too much to argue further, and also wasn't sure how much he believed Edward Stratton could stick with this life anyway. "I am sure your father appreciates your help in town and will be better for it."

Jonathan looked between the brothers and his son, a flicker of fatigue crossing his face. Then he smiled at the Barbers while casting a look of admonishment toward Edward that would have left an onlooker wondering if Elijah and Moses weren't the ones that were his blood. "We've been through a lot together, you two. I trust you'll support whatever needs to be done." His tone came across as if he were pleading as much as instructing.

Before Elijah could respond, Scout, who'd been lying near the door, suddenly sprang up, his ears perked as a low growl rumbled in his throat. He let out a sharp bark, his body tense and alert. The dog turned to Elijah and Moses momentarily, then shot out the open door. The men fell silent, and a beat later, the faint strains of fiddle music outside stopped abruptly.

The three men exchanged wary glances, and Elijah moved to the door, his hand instinctively brushing his belt before realizing there was no weapon there. He stepped outside with Moses and the Strattons close behind, searching the yard for the source of the disturbance.

A crowd had gathered, murmurs rippling through as heads turned toward a group of men standing near the edge of the barn. At the center was Carson Hill, looking dapper in a dark suit and wide-brimmed hat, his expression one of twisted amusement. Around him stood several of his men, each one exuding a rough, menacing air that contrasted sharply with the jovial atmosphere of the gathering.

"Evenin', folks!" Hill called out, his voice carrying the lilting Scottish accent that seemed to emphasize his foreignness to the valley in the quiet Montana evening. He tipped his hat with a mockingly cordial air. "Heard there was a gatherin' fer all the neighbors, and well, I can't deny we're your closest ones now. How happy we are to celebrate the founding of this wonderful land of opportunity."

Elijah felt a flash of anger surge through him, but he kept his face neutral, concealing the hostility simmering beneath the surface. He was not opposed to the man's presence all together, only to his desire to interrupt the evening. He strode forward, keeping his tone even. "Mister Hill. Didn't expect to see you out here tonight." Elijah looked around at the crowd, however, and chose the high road. "Not that you are not welcome."

Hill's grin widened, his eyes remaining cold, like sharp cut glass. "Well, what better way to formally meet and celebrate bein' new neighbors, aye? And call me Carson." He cast his gaze around, eyes flicking over the crowd as if sizing them up. "Besides," he added, glancing back at Elijah with feigned admiration, "it's always wise to keep things friendly 'tween folks who range alongside each other." He reached his hand out. "A pleasure to meet the men who have run this valley for so long."

"Elijah," he said as he shook Hill's hand and then stepped back. "We don't claim to run it, only share it with others." He knew Hill's words were a challenge to their perceived future ownership of Paradise Valley. Elijah turned and gestured to the Strattons, noticing a worried look on Jonathan's face, but a bemused one on Edward's. "You know Jonathan I gather, but this is his son, Edward. That there is my brother, Moses."

Hill's smirk never faltered. "A real family affair out here, aye?" He turned slightly and gestured behind him. "This is my associate, Finn MacDonald."

Finn didn't move right away. He stood a half-step behind Hill, hands resting easily at his sides, his expression unreadable. When he finally inclined his head, it was slow, deliberate.

Elijah let his gaze settle on Finn, allowing a small, humorless smile to flicker across his lips. "Oh, we've met."

Finn's only response was a slow, knowing nod.

"A talker this one." Hill chuckled, clapping Finn on the shoulder before turning back to Elijah. "And nonsense," he continued, with mocking ease. "Run it you do—just like Bozeman—and done well, might I add. But always room for more, eh?"

The crowd shifted uneasily, murmurs rippling through the gathering as the tension bled into the warm evening air. Elijah's sharp eye caught the telltale bulges beneath jackets and waistbands of Hill's men, then spotted Travis, Jax, and Henry moving along the barn walls, their postures growing taut as they positioned themselves within reach of weapons should things turn ugly.

Across the yard, his eyes found Maggie, standing next to JT, his daughters, and the Collins family on the other side of the crowd. They all had nervous looks on their face, save for JT, who appeared excited, and Maggie, who stared at Elijah with a look he knew served as a reminder to keep his cool.

Forcing a cordial smile, Elijah maintained a practiced friendliness. "You're right, Carson. Neighbors ought to get to know each other better." He tilted his head, allowing a small, cold smile to cross his lips. "Though I'll admit, we're usually a bit friendlier than bringing armed men along to a dance. . . especially after stretching onto new land."

Elijah regretted the last part as soon as he said it and saw Maggie lower her eyes and shake her head slightly.

Hill let out a low chuckle, his gaze hardening with a dangerous glint. "Ah, ye misunderstand, Elijah," he replied, his accent sharpening. "It's just for show, ye ken? Wouldn't dream of ruinin' your fine event." His eyes flicked to Edward Stratton, landing on him briefly with a look that was calculating. "As for the range, well, that's just business."

Moses stepped forward; his face set in a grim line. "We don't need any 'shows' here tonight. We got musicians for that. This is a family celebration, not a saloon."

"Aye, you're right, Moses," Hill said. "And I know ye know much about shootin' up saloons now, you and your brother do."

There it was again, Elijah thought. References by Hill and his men to his and Moses's past.

Hill gave a slight, mocking nod toward the American flag bunting draped along the barn, his tone almost sneering. "But I'd hate for anyone to feel I wasn't showin' the proper respect for your fine customs."

Elijah felt his patience thinning, his voice taking on an edge as he replied, "Respect or not, I won't have my family or my neighbors feeling threatened. So, if you and your men are here to enjoy the evening, then by all means, make yourselves at home—guns off. But if you're here to start trouble. . ."

His gaze flicked to Maggie again—her silent plea stopping him from saying more.

He exhaled sharply. ". . . Well, there's no need of it."

For a moment, Hill's smile wavered, his eyes flashing with something unreadable—irritation? Contempt? But then, just as quickly, he masked it beneath that same empty grin.

"Understood, Barber," he said, his accent thick and deliberate now, as if settling into something more natural. "Just here to enjoy the evenin', naethin' more."

Elijah didn't reply. Instead, he gave a brief, curt nod and turned away, moving back toward his family and neighbors. He didn't have to look to know Hill and his men weren't leaving.

Across the yard, he met Moses's gaze—his brother's expression reflecting the same unease.

The fiddle players hesitated, then cautiously resumed their tune. But the music had lost something—some of its life, some of its energy. The lively cadence from earlier had dulled, replaced by a more cautious rhythm.

Elijah took a slow, deep breath, feeling the weight of the night settle on his shoulders.

Hill's arrival hadn't been a friendly gesture.

And they both knew it.

Rumors and Worries

— ◦ —

The late August sun hung heavy over Summit Valley, casting long golden beams across the vast stretches of land that made up the Slash V. The gentle rustle of wind carried the faint scent of warm earth, pine, and the distant lowing of cattle dotting the land. Yet, for all the beauty and familiarity of the scene, a current of unease ran through the ranch. Something about the air felt different—heavier, unsettled.

Elijah Barber stood near the barn, wiping his hands with a faded rag after fastening a stubborn hinge. He stepped back, his eyes drifting to the distant ridge that marked the farthest boundary of the ranch. Beyond that ridge lay Carson Hill's Box H. Even without seeing it, he could feel the tension it brought. The man's name was a thorn, and rumors of rustling had begun to carry more weight than idle talk.

"Pa!" JT's voice cut through his thoughts. Elijah turned to see his son trotting toward him, the boy's stride confident, even if his shoulders still bore the uncertainty of youth.

"Son," Elijah said, tucking the rag into his back pocket. "What is it?"

"Uncle Mo said there's a meeting in the office," JT replied, his face serious. "Travis is there. Says Collins came by."

Elijah sighed, brushing the dust off his hat as he set it back on his head. "Alright, let's go see what's stirring."

JT fell in step beside him as they made their way toward the office, the boy glancing up at his father occasionally. Elijah noticed, but he said nothing. He had learned that the right question would surface if you let a boy sit with his thoughts long enough.

"Pa," JT finally said, "do you think Hill's men are really rustling cattle?"

Elijah's lips pressed into a thin line, his gaze fixed on the path ahead. "I think Hill didn't buy up the Thompson place just to sit on it. Men like him don't spend money unless they plan to make it back twice over, and some say that's how he built and grew his herd. Men like him, they don't care who they trample along the way." He gathered his thoughts as they walked before continuing. "That being said, I'm not sure why he or his men would be so bold now that they are well known. Could be someone else altogether."

JT frowned. "So, what do we do about it?"

"We'll figure that out," Elijah said. "But for now, you better finish any chores and get up to the house."

JT's face fell. "But Pa, I want to be part of the meeting. I can help."

Elijah stopped and placed a firm hand on his son's shoulder. "The hands don't sit in on meetings of the bosses, JT. You'll have your time, but it's not today."

The boy's shoulders sagged, and he looked down, scuffing his boot against the dirt. "Yes, sir," he muttered, turning to walk away.

Elijah watched him go, a pang of guilt tightening in his chest. He questioned if he should bring the boy more into the family business, allowing him to learn the ropes firsthand. This uncertainty weighed on him as he approached the office door.

The room was already crowded when Elijah stepped inside. Travis stood near the desk, his wide-brimmed hat in his hands, his face set with the hard lines of a man who had seen more than his share of trouble. Moses leaned against the far wall, his arms crossed, his expression unreadable but tense. Jax and Henry sat on a bench near the window, their boots dusty from a morning ride.

"Boss," Travis said, nodding as he stepped forward. "We got a problem."

Elijah closed the door behind him, the weight of his exchange with JT still lingering in his mind. He glanced around the room, noting the serious expressions on the men's faces. "Let me guess," he said, trying to focus on the matter at hand. "Hill's men."

Travis nodded. "Collins rode over this morning and said they spotted some Box H riders on their spread, then found some tracks the next day. Said some of his herd's gone missing. Not a lot—just enough to make him take notice."

"That's not all, boss," Jax said, his voice low but steady. "Henry and I rode the east line this morning. Found fresh tracks—too many to be strays. Whoever it was, they were moving fast."

Moses's eyebrows shot up. "We got beeves missing too?"

Henry nodded. "We did not count, and it is hard to tell. But they crossed back over into Hill's land, and did not bother covering their tracks. It is like they wanted us to see them."

Elijah frowned, his mind working through the implications. "Hill's poking at us," he said finally. "Seeing how far he can push before we push back."

Moses looked at Elijah. "Wants to see how far our good neighbor patience will go," he said. "What do you reckon we do?"

"We don't do anything rash," Elijah replied. "Last thing this valley needs is us chasing our cattle to turn into open conflict. We'll keep an eye on our herd and tighten up the watches." He scratched his beard and thought for a moment. "We'll start the fall roundup early. Prices are good, they're fat on the grass we've had, and they can eat it all the way to Livingston. The railhead being just down valley makes it a far easier task than it used to be."

Travis exchanged a glance with Moses. "Roundup and drive is still a big job," he said. "Even if we don't gotta ride to Miles City no more."

Before anyone could say more, the sound of hoofbeats echoed outside. All heads turned toward the window as a figure rode into the yard—sharp, polished, and out of place. Edward Stratton.

"What in the hell is he doing here?" Moses muttered, pushing off the wall.

Edward dismounted with the practiced ease of a man who was learning how to play the part of a cowboy. His tailored coat and polished boots, however, stood in stark contrast to the dust-streaked workwear of the men watching him.

"Elijah?" Edward called out as he knocked, then stepped inside without waiting for a response. His voice was smooth and unhurried. "Oh. Gentlemen."

"Edward," Elijah replied, his tone neutral. "Didn't expect to see you out this way. It's not exactly a casual trip from Bozeman."

Edward smiled faintly, as if amused by the observation. "Family business brought me to Livingston. Thought I'd take the opportunity to check in on the ranch."

"Still funny how you're suddenly interested in that after all these years," Moses said, his voice sharp.

Edward ignored him, turning his attention to the room at large. "I hear there's been trouble with Hill's men and perhaps some rustling as well?"

"That's one way to put it," Elijah said. "And we aren't ruling out that it's one in the same." Elijah cocked his head. "What do you know about it?"

Edward's smile didn't falter, but his eyes narrowed a touch. "I know Hill's been making moves to solidify his holdings. It's nothing unusual in a growing economy." He looked around the room.

"Rustling isn't 'usual,'" Elijah said evenly.

Edward shrugged. "Sometimes cattle wander. It happens." He glanced around the room. "Do you all truly believe he would rise to that level of provocation? A rancher and expanding businessman stealing cattle from his neighbors?"

The tension in the room thickened as the men all shifted their weight uneasily. Elijah studied Edward for a long moment, weighing his words carefully. "Hill's not just moving cattle. He's testing the boundaries. And I don't take kindly to anyone testing mine."

"*Our* boundaries." Edward's smile faded, replaced by a calculating expression. "Then perhaps it's time to take a more proactive approach. Organize a watch, set up patrols. The formation of a livestock growers association is taking too long in the territory, and law enforcement seems not to care about what happens in the valley. We need to be our own advocates. I am not inclined to think it is Hill doing the rustling, but regardless, perhaps Hill and his men might be more willing to negotiate if they see we're serious."

"And by 'negotiate,' you mean what exactly?" Moses asked, his tone biting.

"Whatever keeps the peace," Edward replied smoothly. "The last thing this valley needs is a feud or range war. A show of strength might dissuade such a thing."

Elijah held Edward's gaze, his jaw tightening. "Or encourage it, and nobody here is advocating for a war, Edward. I've seen enough war and fighting to know if you threaten folks with armed men, they tend to strike first."

Edward smiled faintly, tipping his hat as he turned toward the door. "Suit yourself. But don't say I didn't warn you." He glanced around the room. "You were all soldiers once. . . on one side or another." His gaze fell on Travis as he spoke, no doubt acknowledging the Texan's experience on the Confederate side. "No matter what anyone on either side wants, conflict usually prevails if anyone at all wishes to see it." He turned to Elijah. "And I am sure you want to prevail and see that my father's ranch and legacy are not lost to rustlers and an intruding immigrant."

"I'll take it under advisement," Elijah managed. "Need a room in the house for the night?"

Edward made a face that betrayed he thought very little of staying on the ranch overnight, then sought to mask it. "Thank you, but no. I can make Livingston by evening."

The office was quiet after Edward's departure; the tension lingering like smoke after a fire.

"Long way to come for a ten-minute meeting," Elijah muttered.

"Don't seem like he was thrilled to see more than just Elijah and Moses in here," Jax said.

Moses looked at Travis and winked. "Guess he don't like you, Johnny Reb."

Travis rolled his eyes and whistled a few notes of Dixie.

Elijah grinned and shook his head, then turned to the others, his expression now stern. "We keep a close watch on the herd. Start getting the full-time hands ready for a round-up, and hire on the usual help. And we don't give Hill or his men any reason to think we're backing down."

Travis walked to a window, watching Edward ride away. "Hate to say that daddy's city boy has a point, but," he turned away from the window, "you reckon we need to look into the rustling?"

Elijah sighed and rubbed his beard. He looked at Moses, who nodded, his eyes closed. "Get up a few more pairs of line riders. We need counts before the round-up anyway." He felt like he was giving orders in the war again, but the familiar feeling was not a desired one. "Nobody does anything without talking to us, though." Travis nodded.

"And if they push harder?" Moses asked in a low voice.

"Then we push back," Elijah said. He saw Moses raise an eyebrow. "Smartly," he added.

THAT EVENING, Elijah found Maggie in the kitchen, her hands busily kneading dough while the younger children played in the parlor. He leaned against the doorframe, watching her for a moment before speaking.

"You look beautiful," he said. "Even when do something like rolling out dough."

"Thank you dear," she said as she continued to work. "So, what is it you need to tell me then."

Elijah bit his lip. "We might be starting the round-up and drive earlier than usual this fall," he said finally. "Need to send some hands out to ride the herd as well."

Maggie glanced up, her hands never stopping. "Because of Hill and the rustling?"

"Because of Hill and the rustling," Elijah confirmed.

She nodded, her back still turned to him as she worked the dough. "And our son?"

Elijah was quiet for a moment, watching her beautiful form. She knew the answer, yet he was compelled to respond. "Coming with."

When she didn't respond, he added, "And he'll need to take his turn on the line. I need all the hands I have, and then some."

She dropped the dough and turned, brushing her red hair away from her face with the back of her hand. "So this is what he does, now?"

Elijah hung his head briefly, then looked her in the eye, sighing. "Maggie, I wanted him to do more schooling as much as you, but—"

She held a hand in the air. "We are not quite so privileged that our son doesn't have to pull his weight to ensure our future." She bit her lip. "But you are the one that has so recently sought to keep him from it. And has he earned your blessing to carry a weapon to defend himself, or do you still seek to protect him from what you fear is some terrible version of yourself?"

Elijah's head shot back. "I thought you didn't want him carrying a weapon as much as I didn't, dear."

She found a towel, wiped her hands, then stepped forward and put her hands on his shoulders, looking up. "You are a good man for trying to make me think this will not come to violence soon, but a foolish one to think I'll believe it." She forced a smile. "You can't keep asking him to be like you without being like you."

Elijah's eyes welled up and his voice cracked as he spoke. "I wanted to be done with this, Maggie. Mo and I. . . we had finally left it all behind. Everything was set. Now Hill, the rustling. . . and Stratton's son butting in." He looked at the floor. "I thought I was all done worrying about money or seeing men wind up in pine boxes."

"I know." She gave him a knowing look of understanding. "Any progress on a new agreement with Jon?"

Elijah sighed. "Turns out we'd made payment on almost half of what was originally agreed to. He convinced Edward to call it such." He rubbed the back of his neck. "A quarter each for Moses and I, and the rest remaining with Jon and passed on to Edward." He shook his head. "A quarter each to do all the work. Mo says we oughta turn them down and take ourselves and any man that would come with over to join in with James Collins."

"Before it was nothing owned and all the work," Maggie said softly. "And that sounds like Moses, but you know this is still the better situation."

Elijah bit his lip. "You aren't wrong, dear. But it was supposed to be full ownership, full acknowledgment of everything we've done." He hesitated, then raised his voice slightly. "A future for our family, and everyone who works for us. A life I could have never dreamed of not just for myself, and my family, but for others."

She pulled him close. "I know." They hugged tightly and she rubbed his back. "You're a good man, Elijah Barber. Edward wants this now only for greed, and you want it so you can provide for others."

They held their embrace for a moment until young Bridget interrupted. "What's wrong, mama?"

They stepped away from each other, and smiled at their youngest daughter, Maggie wiping a tear from her eyes. "Oh I was just telling your papa how much I love him, and want he and your brother to be careful working with those critters out there."

"You have to leave again, papa?" the young girl asked.

Elijah bent and scooped her up, holding her face to face. "Yes ma'am, soon enough, but then it will be done for the year and we'll be home. . . and not smelling like stinky cows."

She laughed and held her nose, then her look became more serious. "But you'll be careful, papa?" Maggie stuck out her lower lip and held a hand over her chest.

"Always," Elijah said, setting her down and stroking her hair. "And I'll keep an extra eye on your brother."

The girl smiled and ran off, and Maggie looked at Elijah, her eyes searching his. "I trust you, Elijah. Just make sure you both come back to me. You're more important to me than any ranch or legacy could be."

"We will," Elijah promised.

As the sun dipped below the horizon, casting the valley in hues of red and gold, Elijah stepped out onto the porch, puffing on his pipe, his gaze fixed on the distant ridge.

The sound of distant thunder pulled his attention, and he looked across the yard at Moses's porch and saw his brother leaning against a railing. Moses looked back at him with a look Elijah had seen too many times before—but not for a long time. The storm was building, and he knew the coming days would test them all in ways they couldn't yet see.

THE BIG MONTANA

— · —

T he lamplight from the Stratton Land Office spilled onto the
street later than usual, their flames dancing in the window as
a cool wind swept through Bozeman, promising that fall would soon
arrive. Inside, Jonathan Stratton leaned back in his chair, staring at
the papers on his desk without truly seeing them. The room smelled
of tobacco, leather, and ink, the trappings of a man whose legacy was
etched into ledgers and deeds stacked in neat piles. But tonight, there
was no comfort in the routine.

Edward stood by the window, his silhouette framed against the
bustling activity outside. The saloon across the street was alive with
laughter, boots scuffing against wooden floors, and the occasional
burst of raised voices. Edward watched it all, his expression distant, as
though calculating something only he could see.

"You should rest," Edward said without turning. His voice was
calm, almost indifferent.

Jonathan sighed, running a hand through his gray hair. "Rest is for
men without responsibilities. Things don't run themselves, Edward.
And lately, I've been feeling like it's slipping through my fingers."

Edward finally turned, leaning against the windowsill. "Slipping
through your fingers? Sounds like dramatics to me. The valley's

changing, yes. But change is opportunity. An opportunity to let things run themselves and allow you to retire."

Jonathan sighed as he set down his pen and looked at his son. "Carson Hill is not opportunity, Edward. He's a predator. A man like that doesn't build, he takes. And I won't see him take from this town and that valley."

Edward crossed his arms, his casual stance a stark contrast to the tension in his father's voice. "What if he's not taking, but reshaping? You talk about Hill as if he's some villain. But maybe he's just... ahead of his time."

Jonathan's eyes narrowed, suspicion creeping into his gaze. "What exactly are you saying, Edward?"

Edward's face remained unreadable, though a flicker of something—defiance, perhaps—passed behind his eyes. "Nothing, Father. I'm only saying that the Barbers aren't as untouchable as you think. They've built their reputation on being larger than life, but reputations can be a burden as much as a shield. Carson Hill sees that there are more ways to do things than how you or the Barbers see it."

Jonathan leaned forward, pointing a finger at his son. "The Barbers have been loyal to this family for years. I won't have their names dragged through the mud. Do you understand me?" He stacked some papers. "Why, I'd be dead somewhere in the Dakotas, full of arrows with no cattle around me, if it weren't for Elijah Barber."

Edward straightened his jacket, offering a tight smile that didn't reach his eyes. "Of course, Father. And you know I'd never do anything to jeopardize our legacy."

Jonathan watched him leave, unease settling in his chest like a stone. Edward's boots on the stairs faded into the night, leaving the room silent but for the distant hum of Bozeman's nightlife.

THE BIG MONTANA Saloon held a packed crowd, its polished oak bar lined with ranch hands eager to spend their summer wages on a few days in town before the busy ranch work of fall. A cacophony filled the room: clattering billiard balls, raucous cowboy laughter, and a tinny piano melody underscored the scene. The air was thick with the scent of sweat, tobacco, and spilled whiskey.

Finn MacDonald stood near the bar, leaning against the counter with a glass in hand. The low light softened his sharp features, but his eyes glinted with mischief as he surveyed the room. A group of ranch hands—Summit Valley, Circle C, the Box H, and others from smaller spreads—gathered nearby, their laughter carrying over the din.

Finn raised his glass, his Scottish lilt cutting through the noise. "Funny thing about the west and this valley" he said, his voice loud enough to draw attention. "Men here have a knack for big talk. Always goin' on about their ranches, their cattle, their loyalty."

One hand, a wiry man with a cocky grin, chuckled. "What's wrong with loyalty, mister?"

"Not a thing," Finn replied, his grin widening. "Unless o' course, it's loyalty to a name that nae deserve it. Take the Barbers, for instance. Aye, fine ranchers, sure. But did ye ever wonder how they got that spread in the first place? It's Jon Stratton's, no? Lawmen back east, weren't they? And not the kind who always stuck to the rules I hear. Why'd a man like Jon Stratton give such men such power?"

The room quieted a bit, and the piano music slowed as the player watched the scene in the mirror above him. A Circle C hand leaned forward, narrowing his eyes. "Whaddya tryin' to say, fella? You take umbrage with the Barbers or Mister Stratton? They're fine neighbors."

Finn chuckled, shaking his head. "Not at all. Just sayin' men like that—men with a past—they don't always leave it behind."

Near the back of the saloon, Jax Turner nursed a beer, his hat pulled low over his brow. He'd been watching Finn from the moment he walked in, sensing the man's intent. But it was Billy McCray, the broad-shouldered, red-headed Summit Valley cowpuncher with a fiery temper, who spoke up.

Billy straightened to his full height—well over six feet—his voice cutting through the indistinct murmur of the crowd. "No, what is it exactly you're tryin' to say about the Slash V, Mister MacDonald? Maybe I ain't takin' your meaning right, what with that funny voice and you bein' a newcomer and all."

A ripple of laughter moved through the room, but Finn's grin didn't falter. "Just makin' conversation, friend. No need to get riled."

Billy pushed his hat up a bit and stepped closer, his hand resting on his belt. "Riled? I ain't riled. Just don't take kindly to outsiders talkin' big about things they don't understand."

The tension in the room thickened as a few Box H men stood from a table, their movements slow and deliberate. One of them, a burly man with a scar across his cheek, rested his hand on the butt of his revolver.

Billy narrowed his eyes, stepping forward. "Easy there. I thought we was just talkin'. Unless you fellas want me to shut up so bad you're gonna pull those irons."

"Yeah. Maybe we ought to shut your mouth," one of Finn's men said.

The piano stopped, replaced only by the sound of rubbing chair and table legs as men moved away, then silence. Jax stood and moved off to the side, where he had a clear view of Finn and the Box H men.

"Alright, Billy. No need to be callin' 'em out."

"I ain't, Jax." Billy looked at Finn a moment, then back to his toughs. "But, I don't doubt my words have made 'em sore, what with their foreman who don't know spit about this business runnin' his mouth." He looked back to Finn. "Speakin' of business, have y'all been havin' trouble with rustlers this summer too, or that just us and the Circle C?"

There were gasps through the saloon as everyone took Billy's meaning for the thinly veiled accusation that it was.

Finn took a drink. "That's a loaded question, lad."

Billy stared at Finn for a moment and nodded slightly. "I 'spose it is." He then turned to the hands. "He didn't answer me, though. You three are the muscle. . . what do you know about it?"

The scarred man scowled, his fingers twitching. In a flash, he moved to draw, but Billy was faster. His Colt barked once as the scarred man cleared leather, the shot echoing through the saloon as the man grabbed his mid-section and staggered back, then buckled forward.

The room froze.

The other two toughs shot hands toward their guns, but Jax had drawn and covered both while Billy's gun remained raised.

"In or out?" Jax asked in a low voice.

Both men looked at Finn, who shook his head slightly, then spread their fingers and moved their hands away.

"Guess I'm out," one said.

"I ain't in it," the other added.

Jax scanned the room, motioning for Billy to holster. "That's enough, then. Anyone see anything about that they didn't like?"

The tension broke as men muttered.

"Fair fight."

"Box H feller drew first," another added, nodding at Finn's dead man on the floor.

"Tough words, but McCray was defendin' himself."

Jax holstered his pistol and straightened his coat. "I expect that'll be what anyone tells the marshal when he comes askin', then."

Even Finn raised his hands, his grin returning. "Fair's fair," he said. He looked at his dead man and shook his head. "Seems the Box H needs to learn how things work 'round here." He motioned to the remaining two toughs. "Get him out of here, fellas."

But as the men set about their grim task, and the room relaxed, Finn added, his tone just loud enough to carry, "Shoulda known when you ride for the Slash V, you're bound to be a gunslinger. Makes a man wonder if the Barbers keep what's theirs by force."

Billy stiffened, but Jax placed a firm hand on his shoulder. "Let's go," Jax said, his voice brooking no argument.

The two men pushed through the batwing doors, leaving Finn and his crew behind. As they stepped into the cool night air under the arcade, Billy muttered, "That son of a gun acted like he wanted that to happen."

Jax nodded, scanning the street. "Yeah. Exactly. And you ain't heard a word the boss has been sayin' about not giving into that."

Billy bit his lip and beat his hat against his leg. "Dammit Jax, I couldn't just get myself shot, though."

Jax sighed. "Don't I know it? I'll make sure they know the whole story." He pointed toward the city marshal's office, where a deputy had just stepped outside. "C'mon, we best go tell him ourselves."

From across the street, Edward Stratton stepped out of the shadows, his gaze following Jax and Billy as they headed toward the marshal, then shifting to meet Finn's as the man exited the saloon. For a moment, neither moved. Then, Finn tipped his hat, his grin as sharp and crooked as a knife's edge, before disappearing into the night.

Edward lingered, his expression unreadable, before turning toward the Stratton home, his boots crunching against the quieted street.

The shooting at the Big Montana would echo far beyond the saloon walls, carried on whispers through Bozeman's streets and out into the valley. No one knew it yet, but the first shot in the Gallatin County Range War had been fired, and the echoes of violence would soon find their way to every ranch, every corner of the valley, and every man or woman who dared to stand in the way.

PART THREE

— · —

Fall

It's Business

— • —

T he suite at the Grand North Hotel was quiet, save for the faint crackle of a dying fire in the hearth. Carson Hill stood by the window, his hands clasped behind his back as he surveyed the town below. The streets of Bozeman flickered with life—a mix of warmth spilling from lantern-lit windows and the occasional shadow passing under the arcade.

The season's shift was unmistakable: the air carried the crisp bite of fall, and the departure of ranch hands and farmers for their busy season left the town feeling industrious but also exposed. A community in transition, Bozeman wore its growing pains uneasily, the tension between its traditional frontier roots and its emerging ambitions visible in every corner. To most, the town was a vision of prosperity, but Hill saw it for what it was: a fractured battleground.

Behind him, Finn MacDonald lounged in a chair by the fire, his whiskey glass dangling from his fingers. The sheen of polished boots and a fresh shave had replaced weeks of trail dust, but his sharp eyes still held the rough edge of a man lately more at home in the saddle. He watched Hill. "You're brooding again, Carson."

Hill turned, his expression sharp but calm. "The shooting at the Big Montana," he said finally, his voice clipped. "It should have been enough. Is this country not past saloon shootouts?"

Finn raised an eyebrow, sitting up. "Oh, but it got people talkin'. Plenty in town starting to see the Slash V for what we want 'em to see."

"But not everyone, and not folks in the Valley," Hill answered. His gaze drifted back to the window. "McCray. What's this I hear about a nickname already?"

Finn chuckled, clearly amused. "Billy Irons."

Hill rolled his eyes.

"Because he's a cowboy who uses branding irons, but also shooting irons. . ." Finn stopped, realizing his boss understood.

Hill continued to look out the window as he spoke. "I prefer not to dignify theatrics like that. This isn't some dime novel, Finn. It's business."

"Business, aye," Finn replied. "But nicknames have a way of stickin'. Like it or not, it gives a man a reputation. And 'Irons'—well, that sounds like someone folks either respect or fear, and we can work with the fear part."

Hill turned and studied Finn for a long moment before striding to the table at the room's center, brushing aside correspondence to reveal a map of Gallatin County. "I hope you're holding back better guns than the one McCray put in the ground."

Finn tipped his glass back, savoring the whiskey. "Poor lad wasn't my best, no sir, but he served a purpose. Besides, McCray's reputation doesn't make him bulletproof. You needn't worry of that."

Hill's tone grew colder. "I worry when I see opportunities wasted. The Barbers have rallied the valley. They've made the ranchers feel emboldened—too emboldened." His eyes snapped to the window toward the valley. "Like they've brought along a new generation of heroes to protect them."

Finn leaned forward, swirling his glass. "The valley's old blood, Carson. Set in their ways, the lot of 'em. You're too much change too fast. They see you as a threat to their way of life."

Hill scoffed. "And yet they'll use my bank, drink my liquor, and buy my goods. Hypocrites, all of them." He tapped a spot on the map, his tone darkening. "The Slash V and Circle C have held their ground." He trailed off, exhaling sharply. "And now they fancy themselves protectors of the old ways. Guns on their hips, thinking that makes them right."

Finn smirked. "Well, it ain't just them. Town's full 'a men who still believe in settling things the old way." He took another sip.

"The town council already bends to me. The mayor? He likes my money, and he likes not having trouble," Hill said. "If Bozeman aspires to be a civilized place, then let's make it one. It's time we propose a ban on carrying firearms within town limits."

Finn let out a quiet laugh. "You think folks will turn in their pistols when they come in? You think they'll go for that?"

Hill sat, tapping a cigar against the edge of his desk before striking a match. "Not at first," he admitted, the flame flickering as he lit the cigar. "But this is about control, not compliance. The Earps did it in Tombstone."

Finn scoffed. "Aye, and it didn't exactly go smooth for 'em."

Hill exhaled a slow ribbon of smoke, his gaze dark "No. But it forced the fight. The Cowboys had to test the law, and when they did, they were buried." He glanced at Finn. "Ye understand me?"

Finn grinned, the firelight catching the sharp edge of his teeth. "Oh, aye."

Hill nodded, satisfied, then stood and paced as he puffed on his cigar. His steps were deliberate, as if each was a process in developing his thoughts. "The sheriff rode out to the valley. What did he achieve?"

Finn shrugged. "Grant poked around, made enough noise to look busy, then rode back to town proud as a rooster. Told the Barbers to keep McCray on a leash, though. Told others to mind their manners."

"Including you?" Hill asked.

"Aye, including me."

Hill paused his pacing. "And you believe Grant will stay neutral?"

Finn tilted his head, considering. "For now, and that's a good thing for you. Especially when the Barbers had him figured for being on their side. Neutrality is fragile, though, like ye said. Push him right, and he'll lean where it's safe."

Hill walked to a large map on the wall, and his gaze fell on it. "The valley respects tradition. That's their weakness. It blinds them to change. We need them to act out—bigger, publicly."

Finn chuckled. "More rustling it is, then. Not just whispers or small handfuls this time—a proper bit of chaos."

Hill nodded, his voice cold. "Their fall drives are a perfect opportunity. The small-scale cattle theft has agitated them, but we'll have to escalate. Be more direct. They'll either seek the help of the law, and the town—having to mind their manners as you said, or they'll act out, and expose themselves."

Finn stood, his grin wolfish. "And when they do, Sheriff Grant won't have a choice. He'll take the side of law and order—our side."

Hill's expression hardened. "Make it clean. No ties to us. Nobody from the ranch. Use outsiders, drifters. The miners. Let them take whatever cattle they please for themselves. If they're caught, though, I don't know them."

"I've got just the men," Finn said.

Hill returned to the window once more and was about to dismiss the man when he looked down the street toward the Stratton Land Office. "What of your new friend? Learning anything more?"

"Just that Jon Stratton is not a healthy man, but not yet on his deathbed either. He continues to want no part in using ranch land for mining and is set on building and maintaining a legacy here. He's got no interest in sharing to keep the peace."

Hill exhaled smoke from his cigar. "Keep after it."

Finn stood and adjusted his coat, tipping his hat. "Aye, sir, back to the Valley I go."

Hill watched him leave, the room falling silent once more. Turning back to the window, his gaze drifted beyond the town to the dark expanse of the valley. The cigar smoke curled around him like a storm cloud.

"The valley will bend," he murmured. "And if it doesn't, it will break."

UNWELCOME COMPANY

—— ● ——

P aradise Valley spread out like a painting, its grasses rippling in
the crisp breeze of early fall. Trees along the ridges had begun
their slow turn to fiery oranges and reds, standing in stark contrast
to the pines that clung to their green. The air carried a sharpness, a
reminder that colder days were on the horizon. Summit Valley ranch
hands worked steadily; the usual rhythm of preparation punctuated
by bursts of anxious chatter as the fall cattle drive loomed.

Elijah Barber stood near the barn, his gaze sweeping the valley with
a practiced eye. To an outsider, he might have looked like any rancher
on the cusp of a season's work. But his shoulders carried the weight of
something more. He had spent the past weeks moving between worry
and resolve.

The shootout at the Big Montana still lingered in the minds of the
ranch hands. Billy McCray had kept to his duties, but the incident had
changed him. He was quieter, his usual humor dulled by the weight of
what had happened. They'd all seen Billy wield quick pistols to shoot
an object off a fence post for sport or use a rifle to drop a wolf or coyote
chasing a cow, but never a man. Elijah had seen it before—men who
had taken a life, even in self-defense, carried it in different ways. Some
buried it deep. Others let it change them. He wasn't yet sure which
way Billy would go.

Maggie had been the one to voice what Elijah and Moses wouldn't. One Sunday after a Barber family supper, her sharp eyes fixed on Elijah, she had said, "You know they're setting you up, don't you?"

Elijah had looked at her, surprised by the bluntness of her words. "What do you mean?"

"They want you to act out," Maggie said. "That Finn and the rest of Hill's men. They're pushing you, trying to make you look like the aggressors." She looked to the parlor where the children played and lowered her voice. "Remind folks of your past. And with Billy, they're halfway there."

Maggie was rarely wrong when it came to reading people, and he knew better than to dismiss her concerns.

Elijah sighed and shifted his weight, turning his gaze toward the lane leading to the headquarters building. The Gallatin County sheriff had ridden out not long after, the shooting flanked by a pair of deputies. Sheriff Grant rarely left Bozeman, preferring the convenience of law from his desk, so his arrival in the valley had been noteworthy.

The visit had been a show of law and order, he'd said, but Elijah couldn't ignore the sheriff's careful neutrality. Grant had spoken to each rancher with equal care, his tone heavy with warnings about further violence. Clearly, he intended to keep the peace at all costs—or at least give the appearance of doing so.

Elijah turned at the sound of approaching hoofbeats. Edward Stratton rode into the yard with a flourish, his polished boots, and immaculate coat a striking contrast to the dust-streaked hands around him. His arrival snapped Elijah from his thoughts and drew a muttered curse from Moses, who stood nearby saddling Duke.

"Great," Moses said under his breath. "Just what we need."

Edward dismounted, his sharp gaze taking in the yard. "Well," he said, striding toward Elijah and Moses, "I see you're finally ready to move. About time, I'd say."

Moses glanced at Elijah but said nothing. Elijah forced a polite smile, stepping forward. "We always leave in the afternoon and make the first night's camp near a portion of the herd. Sort of a tradition." Elijah grinned. "Start first light tomorrow morning."

"Didn't expect you to ride out with us, Edward," Moses said condescendingly.

Edward waved a hand. "If I'm going to understand this business, I need to see it firsthand."

Elijah's patience strained, but he managed a calm tone. "We run a tight operation. Hard work isn't something you can pick up by watching."

"Which is why I'll be learning by doing," Edward countered sharply. "Surely there's room for one more."

Elijah hesitated, glancing at Moses, who was studying Edward with an expression of barely concealed disdain. Finally, Elijah gave a curt nod. "Fine. But you ride with us, you work with us. No exceptions."

Edward smirked. "Excellent. I knew you'd see reason."

JT approached from the bunkhouse, Scout trotting obediently at his side. He stopped a few paces from Edward, his expression wary. "Why's he here?"

Elijah frowned. "JT, this isn't your concern."

JT's gaze didn't waver. "I just don't see how he's gonna help—"

Edward turned, his face tightening. "I beg your pardon?"

JT stood his ground, his voice steady. "Respectfully, Mister Stratton, you're not a hand. You're not a foreman. You're not here to work." He glanced at Elijah. "What good's he gonna do, Pa?"

Elijah flushed, both from his son's boldness and the truth of his words. "That's enough, JT," he said, his tone firm. "Go check on your mount."

JT hesitated but finally turned toward the stables. Edward watched him go, his expression a mixture of annoyance and amusement.

"Well," Edward said, adjusting his coat. "Fine manners."

Elijah's eyes darkened, but Moses stepped in, his tone light but pointed. "You'll have to forgive the kid, Edward. He's just got his pa's knack for cutting through nonsense." He turned and watched JT helping a hand with his horse. "Plus, he's already done quite a bit of work for this ranch."

Edward shot Moses a glare, ignoring the implication over his own contributions. "Yes, well, I suppose he's better behaved than some other hands," Edward said. "At least he didn't shoot me over it."

Elijah's eyes narrowed, and his nostrils flared, but he held his tongue and allowed Edward Stratton to have his verbal victory as the man turned back to his horse.

LATER, as the yard bustled with final preparations, Elijah spotted Billy and JT leaning against the corral fence after saddling their horses and attaching their bags. He saw them speaking in hushed tones, JT's hands curled into fists, and he knew what the conversation was about before he even got close.

"I ain't sayin' he's right, JT," Billy said, his voice calm but firm. "Just sayin' there ain't sense in lettin' him get to you. Words don't hurt you, just actions. Your pa taught me that."

JT scowled. "He insulted you. He insulted all of us."

Billy shook his head. "What you want me to do? Punch him? *Shoot* him? What would that do?"

JT opened his mouth, but Elijah's voice cut in first. "Nothing but make us look bad."

Both young men turned, surprised by his approach. Elijah leaned over the fence, his arms dangling as he watched the crew assemble in the yard.

"You let men like Edward Stratton get under your skin, and you'll spend your whole life fightin' battles that ain't worth fightin'." His gaze settled on JT. "Boy, you think words from a man like that are worth this much of your time? He ain't the first boss, or fella higher up on the ladder, that doesn't treat the working man right, and he damn sure won't be the last." He straightened and crossed his arms. "And where do you get off talking like that to an adult anyhow?"

JT didn't answer, still simmering.

Billy exhaled and spoke first. "I was just tellin' him all that, sir."

Elijah studied Billy for a moment, seeing something different in him. He had feared the young man would turn reckless after the shooting, but instead, Billy was the one talking sense into JT. It surprised him. It also gave him hope.

"Good," Elijah finally said. "Because I can't have men who act first and think later. That goes for both of you. I need good hands, not troublemakers right now, especially out of my youngest hands. He looked at Billy. "The one that got in a saloon shootout, and," he stared at JT, "the one who's the boss' son."

Billy nodded. "Understood, sir."

JT hesitated, then gave a grudging nod.

Elijah turned his ear toward his son. "Couldn't hear you."

JT looked him in the eyes. "Understood, sir."

Elijah jerked his thumb toward their horses, dismissing them, then turned to see Maggie standing near the house, holding up her hand against the sun as she watched the scene unfold.

Elijah adjusted his hat and walked to the porch, his boots knocking up the steps to stand beside his wife.

"He's a lot like you," she said softly.

Elijah raised an eyebrow. "How so?"

"I saw him talking to Edward in front of you. He's got your values. Your sense of what's right and wrong. But he hasn't learned how to temper it yet." She smiled faintly. "Don't be too hard on him. He's watching you more than you think. Both of them are."

Elijah kicked a porch step, knocking dirt off his boot as he watched Billy and JT mount up. "Lot of good it has done me. I don't feel like a good father sometimes. I don't always temper myself or take time to understand."

Maggie laughed, reaching up to adjust his collar. "You didn't use to, but age has done wonders for you, husband. Maybe you and JT can work on it together."

Elijah smiled, but his expression grew serious as he glanced toward the bunkhouse. "I'm leaving a few more men behind than usual," he said. "Just to make sure everything is all right."

Maggie placed her hands on his shoulders, both of them ignoring that his decision was more about safety than chores. "Fine idea, dear."

"We make do every time you're gone, and this will be the shortest drive yet," Elijhah said. He kissed her forehead, then took his usual long look to ensure he never forgot her face.

As Elijah stepped down from the porch, Travis Carrington's sharp Texas cry brought the yard to life. Elijah and Moses mounted their horses, their figures silhouetted against the shadow of the mid-day sun, and led their outfit into the valley.

THE DRIVE

— · —

The drive began smoothly, with the herds moving steadily under the watchful eyes of riders, while others worked to cut out the cattle bound for the railhead. The lowing of the cattle mixed with the rhythmic clop of hooves, a cadence that seemed to echo off the distant ridges. Dust rose in soft clouds, hanging in the crisp fall air as the trail wound its way through the valley. Overhead, the sky stretched endlessly, its pale blue scattered with a few drifting clouds, while the golden light of early fall illuminated the expansive landscape.

Moses rode alongside Elijah, his gaze sweeping the horizon. The sun cast long shadows across the grasses, highlighting the slight movements of the herd. The brothers had done this so many times before, but today, there was an unease neither could shake.

"Numbers feel low," Moses said, his voice carrying just enough to reach Elijah over the noise of the drive.

Elijah nodded, his eyes scanning the herd as if willing the missing cattle to appear. Reports from outriders earlier in the day had confirmed their suspicions—cows were missing. Tracks suggested rustling, and one cow in particular told a story.

Travis rode up and gestured toward a young steer trotting along the outskirts of the herd, its hide marred by something unnatural. "Somebody tried to alter its brand." His voice was laden with frustration. "Didn't finish the job, though."

Elijah narrowed his eyes, spotting the deep slashes in the hide, the telltale signs of a running iron. A crude attempt to twist a Slash V into something else, but the work had been abandoned, likely when the animal broke free.

"Gettin' bolder," Moses muttered.

Before Elijah could respond, the sound of hoofbeats interrupted them. Edward Stratton rode up, his polished boots now dulled by dust and his immaculate coat showing the faintest trace of trail grime. Despite the rugged setting, he carried himself like a man inspecting rather than contributing to the work.

"Something wrong?" Edward asked, his tone casual, though his sharp eyes betrayed a deeper curiosity.

"Nothing we can't handle," Moses replied curtly, barely glancing in Edward's direction.

Edward's lips twitched, his expression tightening for an instant before smoothing into practiced indifference. "I did want to ask," he said, turning to Elijah, "why you insist on practically giving away cattle to the Crow. Surely, they can pay full price with their government contracts."

The statement hung in the air like a challenge. Henry Horse Goes Ahead, riding a few lengths behind, straightened in his saddle. The reins in his hands didn't falter, but his posture shifted, his calm demeanor now edged with a quiet tension. Elijah caught the movement and shot him a warning glance.

"Because it's the right thing to do," Elijah replied firmly, his voice even but carrying an unmistakable authority. "We've got a history with the Crow—one I don't intend to tarnish over a few dollars." He turned in the saddle, nodding to Henry. "Neighbors help neighbors, Edward. Always have."

Edward's scoff was soft but audible. "Charity's a fine sentiment, but it won't keep this ranch running. Surely you see that."

Moses's hand tightened on the reins, his knuckles whitening as he held back a retort. His eyes darted to Elijah, silently asking how much longer they'd humor Edward's condescension.

Henry didn't wait for Elijah's reply. With an unhurried motion, he nudged his horse forward until he was riding level with Edward. Though his expression remained calm, there was no mistaking the steel in his gaze. "We respect the Barbers because they understand what it means to be neighbors. Not because they ask for a tally sheet whenever they lend a hand. He once righted a wrong that allowed my people to survive a harsh winter. He has never asked us to return the favor, but we do not forget such kindness."

Edward's face flushed, the veneer of civility cracking briefly before he recovered. "A noble sentiment," he said with a tight smile, "but nobility doesn't pay the bills."

Elijah, sensing the tension rising further, spoke with the measured tone of a man used to calming disputes. "The cattle sent to the Crow come from the cut to Moses and me. It doesn't touch what's owed to your father or take a cent from any hand's pay or supply needs."

He shifted his gaze to Henry and then to JT, who had ridden up alongside them. JT sat straight-backed, his growing attachment to Henry clear. "The Crow wranglers meet us partway," Elijah continued. "Henry represents us in the dealings, and this year, JT's learning alongside him."

Edward's eyes darted to JT, and a flicker of something darker crossed his face—annoyance, perhaps even suspicion. "Ah yes," Edward said, his tone sharp. "The future of the ranch secured by charity, an Indian, and a boy."

The words hit like a slap. Henry's shoulders stiffened, but he kept his head high. Moses's eyes flashed with barely contained anger, and his mouth opened, but Elijah raised a hand to stop him. The elder Barber fixed Edward with a look that was cold but controlled.

"Secured by family, neighbors, and hard—honest—work," Elijah said. His voice carried over the drive, silencing even the distant murmurs of the hands. "That's what keeps this place running."

As if on cue, James Collins rode closer, his presence a reminder of the ranch's long-standing alliances. He tipped his hat slightly, his expression grim as he surveyed the exchange.

Edward seemed to falter under the combined weight of their stares. He tugged on his reins, his horse sidestepping in agitation. "So be it," he muttered, his voice quieter now. With a forced air of nonchalance, he spurred his horse ahead, putting distance between himself and the others.

As Edward disappeared into the dust, Elijah exhaled slowly, his hand brushing over his beard. Moses broke the silence, his voice low and cutting. "A man like that don't run a ranch—he runs his mouth."

Elijah didn't respond. His gaze followed Edward's retreating figure, fighting to hold back the storm of thoughts swirling in his mind.

THE DRIVE SETTLED into its rhythm, days blending together under the expansive Montana sky. Dust hung in the air as the herd pushed north through the Valley, the golden grasses stretching out in all directions. Crisp mornings gave way to warm afternoons, and the sound of lowing cattle was constant, punctuated by the sharp calls of riders keeping the cattle in line.

Henry Horse Goes Ahead had parted ways with the drive two days earlier, leading a smaller herd toward the Crow reservation. The Crow wranglers had met them as planned, a stoic group riding in with the precision of seasoned horsemen. JT, bursting with excitement, rode tall in his saddle, ensuring his father he took the opportunity seriously. Though reluctant, Elijah had sent his son off with a firm warning to listen to Henry and learn the relationship the Slash V had with the Crow.

"Boy was grinning like a catfish hooked in the lip," Moses had remarked as they watched JT disappear over a ridge with Henry. "Segundo on his own little drive."

Elijah had chuckled but said nothing, his thoughts divided between pride and worry. With JT and Henry gone, the drive continued, but the weight of their absence lingered at the back of his mind.

Edward Stratton, meanwhile, had grown increasingly irritable. The polished veneer he'd maintained upon arriving was long gone, replaced by the demeanor of a man out of his depth. He struggled with even the simplest tasks—saddling his horse, keeping his position in the line—and when he wasn't offering unsolicited advice, he was complaining about the conditions.

By the third day, Edward's grumbling had reached a fever pitch. "I still don't see why we bother with this," he muttered during a midday break, wiping his brow with a handkerchief. "Surely there's a more efficient way to do this than driving cattle through miles of dust."

"Efficient don't always mean better," Moses shot back, not bothering to hide his irritation. "This is how it's done."

Elijah fought back a grin at his brother's disdain for Edward. "Unless they branch that railroad off down the valley," he said, Moses is right." Elijah pointed east. "We used to trail them for nearly a month to find markets and railheads and had to cut some out to Bozeman and the west as well." He was silent momentarily, then joined all the others who had made veiled slights toward the younger Stratton. "Used to be much harder than this."

Edward huffed, unimpressed, and wandered back toward his horse, where he lingered, fiddling with his reins.

Later that afternoon, as the sun began its descent and the golden hues of the Valley deepened, Edward's dissatisfaction reached its peak. While the bosses gathered to regroup and discuss the next leg of the drive, Edward approached Elijah and Moses, his expression grim.

"I've decided to leave," he announced abruptly, his voice clipped. "I have pressing matters in Bozeman that require my attention. I trust you can manage without me."

Elijah straightened. "You're leaving? Just like that?" he asked, his voice carefully neutral.

Edward's irritation was evident. "I've seen enough for now," he replied, glancing dismissively at the assembled riders. "It's clear this operation will carry on fine without me."

Moses let out a short, dry laugh, shaking his head. "Yeah. We'll try our best to manage without you."

Edward's eyes flickered with something unreadable before settling into a practiced calm. "I wish you all the best."

"You think that's a blessing or a curse?" Travis muttered under his breath, earning a snort of laughter from James Collins.

Elijah, however, remained serious. "Want us to check in with you and your father after we sell?" he asked, his gaze steady on Edward. "That's what we usually do." He didn't care for Edward being along but knew he had to do business with the man. "I know you were awful eager to have a say in the sale."

Edward bristled, his tone growing colder. "I don't see why you're questioning me. I've already told you—I have responsibilities that extend beyond this little adventure." He sighed. "If you are able, then yes, feel free to bring a report."

"Adventure," Moses repeated with a low chuckle, shaking his head. "Go on, then. Ain't no one holding you back." He nodded toward a trail. "You stick to the wagon road and keep a good pace, and you can sleep in a bed in Livingston tonight."

Edward mounted his horse with a stiffness that betrayed his annoyance. "Good day," he said curtly before turning his horse and riding off, his figure growing smaller as the dust swallowed him.

As silence settled over the group, Moses broke it with a sardonic drawl. "Lasted longer than I thought, I 'spose. He sure has changed since before he went East. Was a good show to see him try and hide how miserable he was."

Travis leaned on his saddle horn, watching Edward's retreating figure. "Good riddance," he said. "Man's been nothing but a thorn in everyone's side since he got here."

James Collins nodded but added, "Still, feels wrong somehow. A little too sudden, even for a man like him."

Elijah remained quiet, his gaze lingering on the horizon long after Edward disappeared from view. Finally, he shook his head and turned back to the group. "Let's not waste time worrying about what we can't fix. We've got a herd to move."

Moses glanced at his brother, no doubt noting the tightness in his jaw. "You don't think he's just running from hard work, do you?" Moses asked as they rode side by side.

Elijah sighed, his voice low. "I don't know. But something about the way he left—it don't sit right."

Moses gave a small nod, his expression darkening. "Then I reckon we keep an eye on the road ahead. Trouble's got a way of finding us, whether we're lookin' for it or not."

The brothers fell into silence, the rhythmic clop of hooves filling the space as the drive pressed on. Though no one said it aloud, the absence of Edward's grating presence relieved the group. Yet Elijah's unease lingered, a faint shadow against the fading light of the day.

THAT EVENING, the drive camped near a shallow creek; the cattle spread out under the watchful eyes of the outriders. The chuck wagon's fire crackled, and Cookie ladled out stew as the hands settled in for the night. Laughter and low conversation filled the air, but beneath it all was an undercurrent of tension.

Elijah and Moses sat near the fire with James Collins, discussing the state of things in Bozeman. Collins's face was drawn, his usual good nature replaced by a look of concern.

"Things ain't right in town," he said. "Hill's got his fingers in every pocket he can reach, and folks are too afeared to push back. I've heard talk—things are escalating." He shook his head. "He's got my men all stirred up, searching out rustlers and trespassers."

Collins looked down at his bowl of stew and stirred it before continuing. "They're gettin' strong words when they're in town, then worried anytime they ride about an additional threat to their livelihood." He took a bite, as if thinking about what he would say next. "And what's with all these miners suddenly in town? I know things have calmed down in Virginia City and the like, but ain't anybody doing anything but some small-time claim digging and panning around here."

The trio was quiet for a moment, taking in Collins's words.

Collins sighed, then looked at the Barbers as if he'd been contemplating something for a long time. "Well, shoot, fellas, I'll just say it. A good deal of my hands and those from other outfits know your past, and while they don't care much for Stratton's son, they do wonder if he's right we should be tryin' to put a stop to all this trouble."

Moses raised an eyebrow. "The implication being *we* should be the ones to lead that effort?" Collins rubbed the back of his neck, then nodded as if reluctant to admit the point he was trying to make.

Elijah sat back and puffed on his pipe, then brushed his beard on the spot where his scar was covered. Somehow, people wanting him to lead efforts to stop violence was the story of his adult life, even after so many years of relative peace.

"The rustling is concerning," Elijah said finally. "There's no doubt of that."

"Rustling's just the start," Moses muttered. He stood and walked toward the chuck wagon. "We're all being pushed, little by little, but if we're gonna do anything about it, I'll be needing more of this stew in my belly." He held his bowl out to Cookie, patting his stomach.

Cookie cocked his head and stared past Moses, straining to hear something.

"I said the stew is good—"

"Quiet, dammit. You hear that?" Cookie said in a sharp whisper.

The group went silent, ears straining. Faint hoofbeats echoed in the distance, growing louder. Elijah and Collins stood, now straining their ears as well.

Elijah joined Moses at the back of the chuck wagon and was about to speak when he felt the familiar snap of a bullet near his head, then a loud metallic clank as the round impacted one of Cookie's hanging skillets.

"Cattle might be runnin', but I'm doubtin' they're the ones shootin', Cookie yelled, stooping to retrieve a rifle.

Then, a sharp cry cut through the night: "Stampede!"

STAMPEDE

— · —

The stampede roared to life, a rolling thunder that enveloped the valley. Cattle surged forward in a frenzied tide, their hooves striking the earth like hammers on a drum, each beat rattling the ground beneath them. Shouts from the camp tangled with the bawling of terrified cattle, while gunfire cracked through the night like snapping branches. Dust billowed into the air, thick and choking, turning the moonlight into a pale, flickering haze that barely outlined the chaos unfolding below.

"Rustlers!" came a shout.

Elijah ducked low, adrenaline surging as he got his wits about him. His mind was back to the war, now almost twenty years behind him. The muscle memory was there, but the sharpness had dulled. He levered a round into his Winchester, saw a masked figure riding hard toward the chuck wagon, and fired. The shot kicked up dirt in front of the horse, sending him scrambling away.

Elijah cursed under his breath. "Dang it—I wish I had my old Spencer," he muttered. He then remembered JT had it and pictured his son riding alongside Henry. *Was he safe?*

The thought gnawed at him, but another silhouette flitted between the cattle, and Elijah snapped back to the present. He steadied his breath, lined up the sights, and fired again. This time, the figure crumpled and fell out of the saddle, tumbling across the ground as the riderless horse continued apace.

"Hold the line!" Elijah bellowed, his voice straining to cut through the din.

Moses scrambled for his horse, narrowly dodging a stray shot that sparked off the iron rim of a wagon wheel. "Eli, they're pushing hard from the east!" he shouted.

Shadowy figures darted among the herd, their features obscured by the dark and swirling dust. They fired indiscriminately, their bullets kicking up dirt and ricocheting off rocks. Elijah glimpsed one—a bandana covering his face—before the man disappeared into the sea of cattle.

Cookie, rifle in hand, fired off a shot from behind the chuck wagon. "Lousy rustlers picked the wrong damn herd!" he yelled with sharp fury.

Elijah dove toward Duke, pulling himself into the saddle as another bullet zipped past, tearing through the canvas of the chuck wagon. He urged the gelding forward, weaving between panicked cattle and scattering ranch hands. "Moses, ride with me! We've got to get ahead of this mess!"

Moses swung up onto Ruby and followed. Their voices carried as they barked orders to the men. "Get to the edges! Turn 'em!" Moses hollered, his voice raw.

Amid the dust and confusion, Elijah spotted Billy riding hard toward them, his hat gone, hair plastered to his forehead with sweat. Dirt streaked his face, but his eyes were sharp and clear. "Seen two men down already! They're pushing the herd toward the gulch!" Billy shouted, pulling his horse alongside Elijah's.

Elijah didn't answer right away, his mind working furiously. It was harder now, harder to slow down, to think tactically instead of just reacting as he used to. He blinked away sweat and dust, forcing himself to focus. *Slow down enough to think straight, Elijah.*

"They're trying to bottleneck us," Elijah finally gritted out. "Moses, circle wide to the east! Billy, grab two men and flank them on the west!"

Billy gave a sharp nod and wheeled his horse around, disappearing into the fray with a shout. Moses spurred Ruby eastward, rifle in hand, while Elijah kept Duke moving, eyes sweeping the shifting shadows for signs of the attackers. A familiar silhouette caught his attention—James Collins, rifle raised, braced behind his horse and firing over the saddle, covering the hands struggling to turn the herd.

"James!" Elijah shouted, pulling Duke up short next to the rancher. "Where's Travis?"

Collins fired off a shot before turning to Elijah, his face grim. "Up there with Jax and some men in front, trying to cut 'em off and get 'em turning before they reach the gulch!"

Elijah shouted his response. "Ain't gonna be any of us to drive those cows if we don't stop these shooters. Come on!"

Collins hesitated, his gaze flicking toward the men struggling to gain control of the stampede. Elijah saw the conflict in his eyes, but the rancher didn't argue. Together, they rode into the fray.

The herd splintered as the men worked furiously to turn it. A group of ranch hands, led by Travis, rode hard along the edges, trying to redirect the cattle toward open ground. Even in the fading light, Elijah could see the determination etched on Travis's face.

Another shot cracked through the night, and one hand fell from his saddle with a cry, disappearing beneath the surging herd. "Damn it!" Elijah growled, gripping his reins tighter.

"Keep moving, boys!" Travis shouted, spurring his horse forward. His voice rang out like a beacon amidst the chaos. "Turn 'em like you know how and let others do the shootin'."

Elijah scanned an opening in a stand of trees, catching movement in the moonlight. Another shot rang out, throwing up dirt in front of Duke, and rearing the animal onto his hind legs. "There!" Elijah shouted, pointing as he regained control of his mount.

Moses appeared, rifle raised, his expression fierce. "I see 'em!" he yelled. With a sharp crack, his shot echoed, and one figure on the ridge toppled from his horse.

All four feet back on the ground, Elijah wrapped the reins around his hand, levered in a round and fired a shot at a rider streaking away from the one Moses dropped, sending the horse tumbling forward as the rider flew over its head.

Billy reappeared, flanked by two other hands, their horses lathered with sweat. "They're pulling back, but some of the herd's already in the gulch, and I saw cattle moving east. Six riders heading off hard toward the ridge!" he shouted.

Elijah's head snapped toward the east, his mind racing. "They're splitting us up."

"Reckon we stick with the riders," Moses said, his voice steady despite the surrounding shouts, hoofbeats, and scattered gunfire. "Travis, Jax, and the Circle C foremen will handle the cattle."

James Collins was struggling to catch his breath but spoke up. "Sounds right to me."

Elijah rubbed his beard, mentally tracing the lay of the land. "They'll go for the wash by Wolf Ridge."

"Sure as shootin'," Billy said. His grin was sharp despite the tension. "You all circle behind—I'll head them off."

Elijah considered briefly, then nodded. "Go. Don't let them out of your sight. Don't take any risks." He looked at the two hands with Billy. "You two find Travis and help him round things back up." Billy spurred his horse forward, disappearing into the night, and the hands headed off toward the cattle.

Elijah, Moses, and Collins galloped toward Wolf Ridge. The rhythmic pounding of hooves and the rush of wind against their faces filled the air as the terrain shifted beneath them—from the open grasslands of the valley to the rocky outcroppings and twisting paths leading toward the ridge. Moonlight bathed the landscape, turning it into a patchwork of shadow and silver.

As they crested a rise, they saw the group of bandits moving below. Their laughter and shouts carried on the wind. Elijah raised a hand, signaling the others to hold back.

"We can't leave the herd too long," Moses said grimly. "Let's make sure they don't double back, then head back ourselves."

Elijah nodded. "Come daylight, we'll— "

One of the riders below pitched violently from his saddle, the sharp crack of a rifle following a heartbeat later from somewhere ahead. The remaining bandits jerked their mounts to a halt, confusion rippling through their ranks.

Moses leaned forward in the saddle, squinting into the moonlit shadows. "I'll be dammed," he muttered. "Billy must've gotten ahead of them and found a perch."

Two more shots split the night, spaced just enough apart to show patience, not panic. Another rider tumbled from his horse, while the third spurred his horse and wheeled around, charging away from the shots.

"Damn," Elijah breathed, watching the improbable scene unfold. "That boy moves like a snake in tall grass."

The third rider didn't make it far. From a dark clump of pines ahead, Billy exploded into view, reins loose, rifle balanced across the saddle. He didn't shout or hesitate—just leaned forward, drew his revolver, and fired. The last bandit slumped sideways, the horse galloping off without its rider.

Moses shook his head. "We used to move like that," he breathed. "I thought you said no risks."

"I know I never moved like that," James Collins said, exasperated relief in his voice.

"I'm not sure anyone moves with a weapon like him," Elijah replied. "And I don't reckon he considered it a risk."

The momentary stillness was shattered when movement flickered to their left. The click of a hammer cocking was all the warning Elijah had.

"On our right," Elijah roared, reaching for his revolver.

Two bandits had doubled back, using the terrain to flank them while their retreating counterparts served as a distraction. Blasts erupted in the dark as shots rang out. Elijah wheeled Duke hard, firing a quick shot toward a muzzle flash that dropped one bandit from his horse. Moses fired in tandem, his shot sending the second rider sprawling to the ground.

The echoes of gunfire faded, leaving an uneasy silence in their wake. Elijah gritted his teeth, his heart pounding. "Damn it," he muttered under his breath. "Should've known better than to follow them in the dark."

Moses exhaled sharply, lowering his gun. "Ain't your fault, brother. They knew this land just enough to try something slick."

Elijah didn't answer, his eyes scanning the horizon for any sign of further danger. "Let's get back to the herd," he said finally. "If they've scattered— "

"Eli. . ."

Elijah turned to see James Collins swaying in the saddle, his head bowed.

"James!" Elijah dismounted swiftly as Collins slid from his horse. Together, he and Moses eased the rancher to the ground.

Elijah saw the dark stain spreading across Collins's chest in the moonlight. Blood soaked his shirt, and he gasped for breath.

"James," Elijah said, his voice cracking. "Hold on. We'll get you back to the— "

Collins coughed, and his eyes fluttered. "No. . . won't make it," he rasped.

Billy rode in hard, cursing as he jumped down from his horse. He unwrapped his bedroll and laid it out underneath Collins's head.

"Damn them all!" Billy yelled as he paced. He stopped and looked at Elijah. "I can ride for a doc. "Cookie did a bit of medical help in the war and might be able. . ." He trailed off as James Collins shook his head.

"I'm so sorry James," Elijah said. It had been eighteen years since he held his friend Matt Hobbs as the man lay dying after a gun battle Elijah had gotten him into. The feeling of every decision he'd ever made that led to men dying rushed to the front of his mind. "I'm sorry," he managed again

Collins lifted his head slightly, weakly grabbing Elijah's coat and pulling him close. "Sorry for nothin'," he said. He fell back and caught his breath. "I woulda been finished years ago without you two." He swallowed hard, then coughed, and Elijah saw blood. "Take care of my family, Elijah. The men, my wife. . . they'll listen to you. Make sure they do right by me."

Elijah kneeled beside him, his hands trembling as he gripped Collins's shoulder. "We'll do right by all of them," he said, the words barely escaping his lips.

Collins coughed, then groaned, and he shook his head. "Listen to me babble. I bet all those fellers in the war. . . I bet they died braver 'n this."

Moses dropped his head and cleared his throat. "No, James. This is as brave as it gets, and about like any man I ever known who found himself shot in the dark."

Collins's breath became staggered and shallow, and his eyes opened and closed a few times, looking from man to man. He groaned, then was suddenly, if not momentarily, alert as he looked at Elijah and clutched his friend's hand.

"And tell your boy—tell JT—he's got my blessing with Emily when the time comes."

Elijah had been holding it together until then, but now he bit his lip and cleared his throat. "I'll tell him, James."

Collins nodded as if he'd said all he needed to, then closed his eyes, and his breathing slowed until it stopped entirely. Moses and Billy removed their hats, and Elijah followed suit as he offered a brief, quiet prayer.

Elijah sat back on his heels, his jaw tight, as he stared at his old friend's still figure. The weight of the moment pressed down on him like a physical force. He stood slowly, his gaze hardening as he stared across the valley. The thundering sound of cattle, horses, cowboys, and gunfire had faded.

But the weight of what had occurred roared in Elijah's ears.

THE CROW

—·—

T he sun dipped low in the sky, casting the mountainous Montana landscape in a rich amber glow. JT rode alongside Henry Horse Goes Ahead, his youthful eagerness tempered by the seriousness of his task. A small herd of cattle plodded ahead, their bellows mixing with the soft sounds of the horses and the occasional murmur of Crow phrases. Scout trotted at JT's side, his tongue lolling as he matched the horse's pace.

The Crow wranglers worked with quiet efficiency, their commands to the cattle fluid and rhythmic. JT tried mimicking their words, earning a soft chuckle from Henry.

"You are getting there," Henry said, his weathered face breaking into a rare smile. "But if you are going to say 'héhe'—slow—don't yell it like you are trying to scare the poor cows."

JT grinned, his cheeks reddening. "Just trying to sound like I know what I'm doing."

Henry nodded. "Listen first—learn—then speak. That's the Crow way." He was quiet a moment before adding. "The way of your father as well."

JT laughed. "That much is true."

The group moved through a narrowing trail flanked by steep ridges. As the shadows stretched long across the land, Henry's keen eyes scanned the horizon, where the golden hues of late afternoon painted the rocky outcrops and scattered pines. The other wranglers rode ahead, speaking to one another in Crow. Their casual demeanor belied the sharpness in their gazes, always alert.

One of the men spoke to Henry in Crow, and Henry called to JT. "They would like to make camp soon. We will find a spot and you will learn our ways for the evening."

JT smiled and was about to speak but noticed a shift in Henry's watchful eyes. Henry muttered something in Crow to the men riding ahead, who nodded and quickened their pace.

JT noticed the shift in the group's demeanor. "Something wrong?" he asked, keeping his voice low.

Henry shook his head, his expression unreadable. "Could be nothing. Could be something. Keep your eyes sharp."

Henry reined in his horse when they crested a hill, his hand raised. Below, six riders appeared, silhouetted against the fading sunlight. They moved at an easy canter, their posture relaxed but deliberate. JT felt his stomach tighten as the riders he hadn't even noticed until now fanned out as they pulled neckerchiefs over their mouths, slowing to block the trail.

Henry's jaw tightened. "Stay close," he said quietly to JT, his voice heavy with warning.

The group's leader, a tall man with a scraggly beard and a worn hat pulled low, tipped his head as he approached. His eyes lingered on the cattle, then on the wranglers. "Evenin'," he drawled, his voice casual. "Mighty fine-looking group of beeves you got there. Small herd, but they look strong."

Henry nodded, his face impassive. "They've been sold. Driving them to the Crow."

The man chuckled, his gaze drifting to the brands on the cattle. "That so? Slash V beeves, eh?" He leaned forward slightly in his saddle, his grin widening. "Well, that makes sense. You must be Henry Horse Goes Ahead, then. Unless this valley has more Indians speakin' good English than we thought." He turned and chuckled to his companions.

Henry straightened. "Speaking English well," he enunciated. "And yes, I am Horse Goes Ahead."

The man's grin faltered, and he pointed toward JT. "And that must make him the Barber boy."

JT tensed, his hands tightening on the reins, attempting to control his nervous horse as Scout growled at his side. He noticed the Crow wranglers were still as stone, staring at the group blocking their path.

"Name does not matter," Henry said evenly, his voice carrying a warning edge. "We have work to do, and he is helping us, so if you will let us pass— "

The man held up a hand. "Hold on now. No need to get prickly." He looked at his companions, who chuckled darkly, then back at Henry. "We don't want trouble. Maybe we can parlay a bit. Ain't that how we've all made friendly out here? Makin' trades?"

"Is that what you think has happened?" one of the Crow thundered, surprising everyone.

Henry's gaze hardened. "We are not interested."

The man leaned forward in his saddle, his grin returning, now cold. "Hear me out, now. You hand over the boy, and we'll let you and your cattle go. No harm done to you. No reason to get mixed up in this feud brewing in the valley. You stay safe and sound, and your tribe gets some fresh beef on the rez."

JT's breath hitched, but Henry's voice remained calm. "And what happens if we do not comply?"

The man's grin disappeared. His hand drifted toward the butt of his revolver. "Then I guess we see if you fare any better 'n when your kind helped Custer down the road."

Henry's eyes flicked to the other riders, spreading out subtly, their hands resting on their weapons. He turned to the Crow wranglers, speaking quickly in their language. JT caught only a few words: "*Awakkáawasa. Akbáak*"— "protect" and "run."

One of the Crow wranglers muttered something under his breath, kneeing his horse forward a step, and JT saw the leader across from them stiffen, his hand closing on his pistol. Another rider lifted a rifle across his saddle, angling it toward JT and the Crow men. Henry caught it all—the shift in posture, the glance between men, the silent signal of an ambush about to spring.

He turned back to JT, his voice low and urgent. "Ride. Now. Back to the drive. Tell your father. I fear there is even more danger." He looked at the Crow wranglers, then back at JT. "Your father has given me too much not to protect you. Now go."

JT hesitated, his heart pounding. "I can't just leave— "

One of the riders walked his horse forward, cutting the distance between them. The man's lips twisted in a sneer. "That boy ain't goin' nowhere."

Henry didn't flinch. He raised his rifle, eyes never leaving the man. "He will if you want to walk away from this alive." His tone, cold and certain, seemed to freeze the man momentarily. The brief hesitation was all Henry needed. He snapped his head toward JT, voice sharp and commanding.

"Go!" Henry barked, his tone brooking no argument.

JT turned his horse and spurred it into a gallop, Scout leaping to follow. The sound of hoofbeats and labored breaths filled his ears as he streaked away. Behind him, voices rose sharply and then came the crack of a gunshot.

JT glanced back just in time to see Henry fire his rifle, the shot dropping one bandit from his saddle. The other Crow wranglers charged forward, their war cries piercing the air as they engaged the riders. Scout barked, snapping JT's attention back to the trail. He leaned low over his horse's neck, urging the animal faster.

Gunfire erupted behind him, the sharp reports echoing off the rocks. JT's mind raced, torn between the instinct to turn back and the desperate need to reach safety. The clash of shouts and shots grew fainter as he pressed on, the pounding of his horse's hooves drowning out everything else.

Ahead, the trail twisted, disappearing into the shadowed hills and bringing JT to a trot. Scout yipped, keeping close, but JT's grip faltered as doubt flooded his mind. Everything his father had ever told him, Henry's urgency, and the bloodshed behind him churned together in a rising storm.

He slowed his horse to a walk, glancing over his shoulder at the distant chaos. His breath caught. What if they needed him? Could turning back make a difference? What if alerting his father and uncle was the right choice? As the thoughts flickered, the cries of the Crow and the bandits' shouted curses seemed impossibly far away now, muffled by the growing distance.

Scout barked again, almost as if in protest of his hesitation. JT straightened, his resolve shifting. He gripped the reins tightly, the growing darkness a veil over his decision to all but himself.

HEADQUARTERS

— ◆ —

The kitchen was warm and filled with the scent of apple pie and coffee. Maggie smiled as she gathered the last of the plates, watching the girls play in the parlor while Helen wiped down the table. The sound of boots on the porch caused them to pause, and a knock followed.

"Evenin', Missus Barber," Teddy Jones, one of the more experienced hands that Elijah left in charge, said as Maggie opened the door. He tipped his hat, his expression easygoing. "Just wanted to thank you both for dinner. The fellas are all much obliged. That pie was a fine way to end the day."

"You're welcome, Teddy," Maggie said with a smile. "I'll be sure to save you another slice next time."

Jones nodded with a grin. "We're all finished up for the night and headed to the bunkhouse. You need anything, ma'am, you holler. Somebody'll always be ridin' the property through the night like always."

"We'll be fine," Maggie replied. "But we appreciate it dearly. Good night."

Jones tipped his hat again and disappeared into the darkness. Maggie shut the door and turned back to Helen, who was smiling faintly.

"Nice to know there's someone keeping watch," Helen said, though her hands still fidgeted with the edge of her apron.

"They've been doing this for years," Maggie said gently. "We'll be just fine."

The two women worked quietly, tidying up, while the girls giggled and played with their dolls in the parlor. Ruth and Abigail argued over which doll was prettiest while Molly practiced her reading. The moment's warmth pushed away the weight of the empty ranch house, if only for a little while.

But then, a sound broke the peace—a sharp crack from the yard.

"What was that?" Helen froze, her eyes wide.

Maggie straightened, her heart quickening. "Stay here," she said firmly, moving toward the window. She peeked through the curtains, but the yard was dark, the lantern by the barn swaying in the breeze.

"Maggie?" Helen whispered.

"I don't see anything," Maggie began. Maybe one of the hands shooting a critter by the—"

Another crack split the night, followed by the sound of a man shouting.

"Comin' up toward the corrals!"

The shouting outside grew louder, punctuated by gunfire. Maggie heard a man bellow, "Bring 'em out, boys! They ain't got but a few left here!"

Maggie turned. "Get the girls away from the windows and doors." She threw the bar on the door near her, then rushed to the front of the house and did the same.

The women scrambled as Helen gathered the children, while Maggie retrieved a rifle from the closet. The sharp report of gunfire erupted again, followed by the flash of lantern light as shadows darted in the yard.

"Maggie!" Helen called, panic rising in her voice. "What's happening?" Her eyes shot open. "Do you know how to use that?"

Maggie levered a round into the rifle and crouched low by the window. She spotted movement—a group of riders circling the yard, firing and shouting at one another.

"They're trying to draw out the hands," Maggie said, her voice steady despite the pounding in her chest. "I think our men are trying to seem as if they have more numbers than they really do."

A man yelled from the bunkhouse. "Get outta here, you bastards!" Shots rang out, and the flash of rifles from the yard revealed a handful of ranch hands firing from cover.

Maggie ducked low as a stray shot shattered the front window. The girls screamed, and Helen pulled them closer.

A second flurry of shots erupted and Maggie buried her head in her chest, looking across the room toward the girls, attempting to convey a look of confidence.

"Stay down, girls," Maggie ordered, her tone firm. She crawled toward the broken window, peering out just as Jones sprinted toward the house.

"Maggie! Missus Barber!" he shouted. "They're—"

Another shot cut Teddy Jones's words short. He stumbled, clutching his side as he dropped to the ground. Helen gasped, clutching the girls tighter. Maggie's stomach twisted, but her grip on the rifle remained steady.

She crawled toward the back door, her breath catching as heavy boots thudded across the porch. A husky voice called out. "Come on now, ladies. We don't wanna hurt ya—just open the door, nice and easy."

Maggie positioned herself near the door, her rifle leveled. "Stay back. There are no more men in here for you to worry about, but you come through this door, I swear I'll shoot."

Laughter answered her. "She's got spunk. I like that."

"I ain't sure which part I like to get paid for more," came another voice. "The killin' or the spoils."

Maggie glanced toward the parlor, where Helen held the girls behind an overturned table in the corner. Their wide, tear-filled eyes met Maggie's.

The faint creak of boots on wooden steps sent her heart pounding anew. Shadows passed across the windows, and Maggie steadied her breathing. The door shuddered under the weight of a heavy blow. Another came, and then another.

The bar holding the door splintered.

"Maggie!" Helen cried.

"Quiet," Maggie whispered harshly, keeping her focus on the door.

A final crash sent the door swinging open. Maggie fired, the recoil slamming into her shoulder. A man fell, clutching his chest, but another figure lunged forward. Maggie worked the lever, but the man reached forward, clamping down on her wrist with one hand and pushing away the barrel with the other. He was wide-eyed, with a sickening smile on his face, his hot breath repulsing her as she struggled in vain to get away from him.

A deafening shot rang out from behind her, and the man stumbled, blood blooming across his chest. As the man fell, Maggie looked past him to see Teddy Jones, pale, and swaying, his revolver still raised.

"You. . . keep 'em safe, Missus Barber," he gasped. His knees buckled, and he dropped to the ground.

Maggie scrambled toward him as the sound of boots echoed closer. "Teddy!" she cried, reaching for him.

He looked up at her, his eyes glassy. "Tell. . . your husband. . . I tried."

The front door now shuddered, and voices shouted from outside. Maggie's head snapped toward the sound, her heart racing.

Maggie stood and positioned herself halfway between each door, the rifle gripped tightly in her hands. She levered a round, and her breath came in quick gasps, her eyes fixed on the broken door as the sounds of the night closed in around her.

HOMECOMING

— • —

E lijah hadn't slept for more than an hour since the attack. His body ached, yet his mind refused to relent. After leaving Travis to oversee the remaining drive to Livingston, he and Moses set out for the ranch with the bodies of James Collins and two other hands who had died in the rustler ambush. They commandeered a small buckboard normally used to carry supplies, loading up the men for the somber ride home.

The two brothers rode silently, Moses handling the wagon's reins while Ruby traveled free rein behind Duke as Elijah's gaze lingered on the horizon. Despite the crispness of the morning air, the weight of his thoughts burned hot. The image of James, his friend and neighbor, falling from his horse haunted him. And then there was JT. He had sent his son off with Henry and the Crow, and the decision gnawed at him. *Was he safe? Would he rejoin the drive with Henry?*

After an hour of quiet, Moses spoke, his voice breaking the tension like a hammer on an anvil. "So, we ain't gonna talk about how Edward left just before all that happened?"

Elijah's jaw tightened. "You think I didn't notice? He rode out like a man on fire, only a few hours before the shooting started."

"And that don't sit wrong with you?" Moses pressed, his tone edged with disbelief.

"'Course it sits wrong," Elijah retorted. He tugged at the brim of his hat. He looked at his brother, only able to see his form in the early morning darkness. "That's a heavy thing for us to say out loud, though."

Moses gave him a sidelong glance. "I know you don't wanna think it, Eli, but Edward's been trouble since he came back here. He ain't the kid we remember." He paused for a moment. "A man changes, Lord knows we have. . . but it's his character that don't sit with me. You saw it just as plain as I did. You really think he's got no hand in all this?" He stared straight ahead, holding the reins loosely. "He wants this land for himself."

"I don't want to think it," Elijah replied. "But wanting and knowing are two different things."

Moses shook his head. "Well, you best figure it out quick, brother. 'Cause Hill and Finn are already bold enough. We don't need to add Edward causin' trouble to our list."

"You think I don't know that Mo?" Elijah snapped. "And why's it always gotta be me doing the figuring?" He regretted the sharpness in his tone, but his frustration boiled over. He had spent every day over a decade and a half ensuring their old life was over, their new life prosperous, and their future life secure. Now, it felt as though not a day had passed since the last time violence forced its way into their lives.

They fell silent again, the sound of the wagon wheels and the steady clop of the horses filling the air. They'd had so many spats like this over the years, and Moses always came to realize where his brother was coming from. Silence, without provoking each other further, was their way of apologizing and letting it go.

As they crested the last rise before the ranch, the first light of day crept over the mountains, the long shadows stretching across the yard.

Elijah froze at the sight below. The house and barn stood intact, but the yard bore the signs of a battle. A broken window glinted in the morning sun. A rifle lay discarded near the porch. And worse yet—bodies sprawled across the yard like discarded dolls.

"Hellfire," Moses muttered. He threw the hand brake on the wagon, jumped down, and ran to Ruby. "They wouldn't."

Elijah's breath came fast and sharp as he scanned the property. "Maggie. . ." he whispered, the name almost a prayer.

They spurred their horses forward, leaving the wagon and bodies behind. Moses peeled off toward his house, his hollered call of "Helen! Girls!" carrying across the yard. Elijah galloped toward the headquarters house, slowing only as he reached the porch. He dismounted in one fluid motion, his boots crunching on broken glass.

The sight of Teddy Jones's body lying in the doorway, and another pair of boots alongside him, stopped him cold. He edged toward the back door, revolver raised. Peering inside, he caught the glint of a rifle barrel pointed straight at him. Elijah ducked back instinctively, his heart hammering in his chest. Then he processed what he had seen.

"Maggie!" he called out, his voice tight with fear. "It's me!"

The sound of the rifle clattering to the wooden floor made him move again. He stepped into the house cautiously, the only sound his boots knocking as he approached the door. Maggie's voice came soft and trembling from the shadows, disassociated from reality. "We're in here."

Elijah holstered his gun and called for Moses. Stepping over the bodies of two men just inside the doorway, he found Maggie in the parlor, the overturned furniture, spent shells, and blanket-covered body of one more man telling the story of the night's horror. She looked up at him, her face pale, with dark circles under her eyes.

Without a word, she rose on unsteady feet and walked into his arms. Her body trembled against his, and Elijah gripped her.

"I didn't have a choice," she whispered, her voice cracking. "I— "

"You did what you had to," Elijah murmured, stroking her hair. "You kept them safe. That's all that matters."

Moses appeared in the doorway, his face grim. He then saw Helen and the girls and hopped over the bodies and clutter and rushed to them, taking them all into his arms and kissing the tops of their heads. He paused and looked around the house. "Lord almighty."

Maggie explained what happened with a clinical detachment, and as Elijah began explaining the ambush, Maggie suddenly gasped. "Where's JT?" she demanded, her voice rising in panic. Her hands clutched Elijah's coat as she stared at him, waiting for an answer.

Elijah did his best to hide his own apprehension. "He's with Henry and the Crow wranglers; they left before it happened, taking cows to the reservation. He's safe with them."

"How do you know?" Maggie shouted. "We were supposed to be safe here, too!"

The words cut Elijah to his core, and all he could do was reassure her that Henry would protect him. They moved the girls upstairs, shielding them from the sight of the bodies in the doorway, and Elijah and Moses began the grim task of moving the dead men outside and straightening up the mess.

When the girls settled upstairs, Maggie and Helen prepared some coffee and warmed some food. They were all eating in silence when a dog's bark, distinctively Scout's, brought them all to their feet.

They rushed to the porch, and Scout's figure appeared on the ridge, followed by two horses. Maggie's hand flew to her mouth as the horses came closer.

One was a pony with a tired but stoic Crow rider in the saddle. The other, they could all now see, was JT's horse, tethered alongside the pony, a body slumped over its saddle.

Maggie let out a strangled cry and rushed forward, dropping to her knees and bawling. Elijah hurried to catch up, a feeling of guilt overwhelming him. He stopped at Maggie's side, put a hand on her shoulder, and buried his face in his other hand, unable to look.

When Maggie let out a loud wail, a figure poked its head from behind the Crow rider. Maggie stood and shielded her eyes from the early morning sun. The figure behind the Crow jumped down from the horse, stumbling, then rose and ran toward Maggie. JT fell into her arms, trembling. "He saved me," he said, his voice breaking. He pointed at the body laying across the horse. "Henry saved me."

Elijah removed his hat and looked to the sky, then approached the Crow warrior, his face hard. "What happened?"

The Crow rider dismounted slowly, his voice calm but heavy with sorrow. "Found by wicked men. Horse Goes Ahead fought to give us time. He died with honor."

"Followed?" Moses asked.

The Crow man shook his head, then used a mixture of hand signals and speech to make his point. "Not followed or found. Knew where we would be. Waiting for us."

Moses beat his hat against his leg and walked away, cursing, before turning back suddenly and pointing toward the valley. "Three attacks in one night, Eli. That ain't coincidence. I don't need another ounce 'a proof that Edward is workin' with Hill." Helen motioned for the girls to head toward her home, and put a hand on her husband's shoulder, attempting to calm him. Moses bit his lip and forced a smile for the girls as they departed.

The Crow man looked around the yard as if suddenly realizing the carnage. "More fighting here?"

Elijah grimaced. "Hit us on the drive last night and came here before we got back." He looked at JT, who had stood and moved toward the men. Elijah could see Maggie's pain. He looked back at the Crow wrangler. "What'd they say they wanted?"

The man looked at Maggie, hesitating, then answered. "The boy."

Maggie's head dropped, and she sobbed.

The Crow man looked at JT a moment, then spoke in a lower voice. "Horse Goes Ahead told your boy to leave, but he came back. Horse Goes Ahead saved your boy, but your boy saved me."

Maggie's eyes fell to the blood smeared on her son's shirt, then the gun at his hip. Her boy—who had always carried his father's fire but her gentle heart—had crossed a line they'd worked so hard to keep him from.

Elijah looked at his son, his face drawn in a way that made him look far older than his years. He had seen that same look on young men during the war. Their expressions revealed a first brush with death; unharmed in body yet deeply marked.

"You alright?" Elijah said, his voice catching.

"Yessir," JT answered.

Elijah nodded. The words 'good job' were almost out of his lips, but he held them back for Maggie's sake. There was nothing good about this. He turned to the Crow wrangler. "Thank you."

"He should be buried with honor," the man said. "This place was his home, but I would be grateful if you help me do it in our way."

"Of course," Elijah said.

Maggie looked at JT, seeming to want to change the subject. "Go clean yourself up," she said firmly, her voice shaking but resolute. "I'll check you over and get some food in you."

"Then you can ride with us to the Circle C to return James's body," Elijah said. "Emily will be glad for your comfort."

"Yessir."

The boy turned and trudged toward the house, Scout trotting loyally at his side. Maggie watched him go, her hands trembling as she turned back to Elijah. "I told myself this day wouldn't come," she whispered, her voice cracking.

"I know," Elijah said. He pulled her close. She sobbed, and he held her tighter. "I don't. . ." He cleared his throat and regained his composure, then looked toward the bodies in the wagon and those lying in the yard. "I don't like it any more than you."

Later in the day, after the grim task of burying the killed Summit Valley hands and their attackers, Elijah, Moses, and JT saddled up for the somber procession to the Circle C with James Collins.

Maggie stood at the edge of the yard, her hands clenched around a shawl. The wind tugged at her hair, carrying with it the faint smell of dust and horses. She watched them disappear over the ridge, her heart heavy knowing the valley's peace was shattered and her son was no longer the boy she raised, but a man forged by violence and loss.

TROUBLING NEWS

— • —

The days following the attack were a blur of repairs and whispered fears. Though the ranch's physical scars—splintered doors, shattered windows, and trampled fences—were mended, its emotional wounds ran deeper. The girls refused to stray far from their mothers or the house, clinging to Moses or Elijah when they ventured outside. Scout paced the yard with a nervous energy, his sharp barks at any movement snapping through the air, setting nerves further on edge.

Elijah worked beside Moses that morning, his hands busy while his mind churned. Together, they refitted a barn door, their conversation sparse, the silence between them laden with unspoken thoughts. Every so often, Elijah's gaze wandered to the Summit Valley cemetery, now dotted with new graves. Until recently, it had held only Maggie's father, and a young ranch hand lost in a horse accident. Now it stood as a grim reminder of what had happened.

What had happened? Elijah thought over and over.

Moses, hammer in hand, followed Elijah's gaze. "This place don't feel like home no more," he muttered, his voice low but weighted.

Elijah didn't reply immediately. He drove a nail into the doorframe. "It's still ours," he said finally. He gazed around the yard and saw the wives of the few married hands—some awaiting their husband's return, and some now widows. The blacksmith was at work, and a few other workers who came to the ranch during the day were there as well. But Moses was right. It was different.

Elijah looked toward the church and saw Reverend Harris inspecting a bullet hole in the church exterior. He'd spoken to the pastor after the funeral services, and told him he would be right to consider leaving for the time being. The man had only smiled, and told Elijah this was exactly where he needed to be right now.

Moses spat to the side, his cursing breaking Elijah's train of thought as he gestured toward the cemetery, then north. "We oughta be ridin', Eli. To Livingston, or even Bozeman for that matter. Sittin' here patchin' boards ain't gonna fix what's broke."

Elijah stood still for a moment, the hammer heavy in his hand. "We don't know enough yet," he mumbled. "What happened. Why they hit us. Until we do, we can't ride pell-mell into the wrong battle. Or maybe you don't remember how that's gone for us in the past?"

Moses' frustration boiled to the surface. "What more do you need to know? They came at us, guns blazin'. Killed James. Killed young men in the dark who were just tryin' to do their jobs. Came after your boy and our family!" Moses scoffed and shook his head. "You know who done it, right?"

Elijah turned to face his brother, his eyes shadowed with anger and something deeper—uncertainty. "Sure I know who probably done it, but why? Why would he go that far? We're missing something, Mo." He sighed. "We ride off half-cocked, we lose more than we already have." He turned and pointed at the house. "Plus you want to be the one to tell those women, those girls, we are headed out again already? Maybe I'll give the preacher, the blacksmith, and my boy a rifle—wish 'em luck." He returned to his hammer and nails.

"Eli, I'm just sayin' that—"

"We'll head to Livingston in two or three days to meet the drive, then on to Bozeman. Just let me get my wits about me, Mo." He shook his head and drove a nail home. "Of course we can't just sit here and pretend nothin' happened, but if Travis don't get those cattle sold first, then what's any of this matter?"

Before Moses could reply, the sharp sound of galloping hooves interrupted the tension. Both men turned to see a rider barreling into the yard, his horse lathered and blowing hard. Tommy Morris, one of their seasonal hands, swung down from the saddle with a hurried, clumsy motion, his face flushed and streaked with dust.

Elijah stepped forward, handing his hammer to Moses. "Tommy, I hope to God you're not bringing more trouble." He cast a glance at the heaving horse. "But if you ran that critter that hard, it'd better be something worth the risk."

Tommy pulled his hat off, wiping sweat from his brow. "Mister Barber," he began, breathless. "There's trouble in Livingston. Billy McCray's been arrested."

Elijah stiffened. "Arrested? For what?"

"Fightin'," Tommy replied. "Him and Jax rode ahead with Travis to arrange the sale and file a report on the ambush. But when they got there, Billy and Jax spotted some fellers they swear were part of the rustler group that hit us. Things got heated."

Moses's jaw tightened. "He shoot one of 'em?"

"No, sir," Tommy said quickly. "But he beat one damn near half to death and pulled his gun on another who tried to step in. Other feller never drew, though."

Moses looked at Elijah, his voice low. "Fella goes after rustlers that kilt his friend, and he's the one who gets locked up?"

Tommy nodded, his gaze darting between the brothers. "Marshal's got him in the jail, but there's more. Sheriff's deputy is involved now, and they've locked up three of the men Billy and Jax called out, but he said Billy had to stay locked up, too."

Elijah lit his pipe, his movements deliberate, though his knuckles were white. "Alright then. So seems like they cool Billy off, and this all comes out the right way."

Tommy's face betrayed he hadn't got to the catch in the story. "They let Jax go free on account he was just tryin' to stop the melee, but the marshal and deputy told Travis and Jax they don't want any Slash V or Circle C riders leavin' town after they bring the cattle in. Not 'fore they get some more information, leastways." He looked at each brother. "I reckon they wanna speak with you."

Elijah's jaw clenched around his pipe. "Alright. What about the drive then?"

"Still on its way," Tommy said. "Jax stayed with Billy and Travis rode back to the herd after it all went down. They coulda made Livingston by tomorrow, but he sent me to ask what you want done while he holds 'em outside town. Told me to ride hard and get word to you." He pointed to the horse. "Third one I swapped with neighbors to get here in a hurry."

Elijah took a long draw on the pipe, the smoke curling around his head. His gaze drifted toward the house, where Maggie stood on the porch, her hands twisting in her apron. He looked at Moses and shook his head, neither speaking. He knew Moses was thinking like him. *Why was the law wanting to detain the cattle outfit in town?* The law had always sided with ranchers when it came to dealing with rustlers.

"Alright," Elijah finally said to Tommy. "My thanks for bringing the word. See to your horse, and we'll get you a meal and a place to rest. We'll head out in the morning."

Tommy grabbed his horse's bridle and walked him to the barn as Elijah turned on his heel for the headquarters building, Moses following.

Tommy looked as if he was talking to himself, shaking his head, then halted. "Bosses?"

Elijah and Moses stopped and turned, and Elijah removed his pipe from his mouth. "Yeah, Tommy?"

The young man rubbed the stubble on his face. "Them Circle C boys is fit to hang anyone they get their hands on and name responsible for their boss bein' kilt. Reckon plenty of our own, too." He licked his lips. "They get into town, I ain't sure how well they're gonna behave."

Elijah glanced at a stone-faced Moses, then nodded subtly. He stuck his pipe back in his mouth and spoke around it as he turned. "Get that horse taken care of."

THAT EVENING, the family gathered around the dinner table, the glows of a warm fire and oil lamps dancing on the walls. The meal was subdued, the scrape of forks on plates and the clink of cups the only sounds for long stretches. The girls sat quietly, their usual chatter absent, as if even their young minds sensed the weight pressing on the household.

Maggie tried to maintain a sense of normalcy, urging Bridget to finish her vegetables and helping Molly steady her hand as she poured milk into her cup, but her smile was thin, her movements brisk and strained. Helen glanced between Maggie and Elijah, her face pale, her fingers twisting her napkin until it was a crumpled mess.

When everyone finished, Elijah set his cup down and cleared his throat. All eyes turned to him.

"Moses, Tommy, and I have to go to Livingston tomorrow," he began, his voice steady.

Helen stiffened, her breath catching as she gripped the edge of the table. The girls looked up, their wide eyes darting between Elijah and Moses. Maggie's lips tightened, but she said nothing, her hands folded and still.

"And you," Elijah said, turning to JT, "will stay here."

JT froze. "Why can't I come?" His tone carried a note of defiance, his young pride bristling.

Elijah leaned forward, his voice calm but firm. "Because I need someone here I can trust. You're the only one left to keep things running, and to protect the ranch if there's more trouble."

JT's eyes flicked to Moses, then back to his father. "You don't think I'm ready," he said, the hurt plain in his voice. "Or is it you still don't trust me, even now?"

Elijah pounded the table, startling everyone and causing plates and utensils to jump. He then closed his eyes and took a breath before speaking quietly. "That ain't it, boy. It is about trust—me trustin' you to follow orders and do what needs to be done here."

JT's frustration didn't ebb entirely, but he nodded stiffly. "Yes, sir."

The weight of the moment settled heavily over the room. Helen reached for Moses's hand.

Moses gave her a soft look, squeezing her hand. "We'll be alright."

Helen pressed her lips together, her gaze dropping to the table. Ruth climbed into her lap, her little hands clutching Helen's arm as she stared at Moses. "Don't go, papa," she whispered. "What if the bad men come back?"

Maggie's hand moved instinctively to Bridget's hair, smoothing it down as the girl leaned against her side. "They'll be safe," Maggie said, her voice steady even as her eyes shone with unshed tears. "The bad men are gone. We'll all keep each other safe."

Elijah glanced at Maggie, seeing the determination in her face despite the fear she was holding back for the sake of the others. He nodded, silently acknowledging her strength.

When the others began drifting from the table, Maggie lingered, her hands resting on its worn surface. "Will they come back?" she asked, her eyes fixed on the oil lamp's flickering flame.

"I don't believe so," Elijah replied, stepping closer and resting a hand over hers. He had tried to talk to her about what had happened during her defense of the house, not wanting to act like everything was fine and normal, but she had avoided it. "We'll handle this," he added. "I'll send word if it looks like it'll take more than a few days. "We'll send hands back as soon as we can. JT, the preacher, and some of the others will do what they can here."

Maggie nodded, but didn't meet his eyes. "We can fend for ourselves once more. Just come back."

"We always do," Elijah said, his voice firm but gentle. He stooped, kissed her forehead, and lingered for a moment before stepping away.

***

LATER THAT EVENING, Elijah sat in his study, the low fire in the hearth warming the chilly fall evening. The day's events weighed on him as he packed his pipe, his hands moving slowly. He looked up to see JT hesitating in the doorway.

"You wanted to see me?" JT asked, his voice cautious.

"Come in, son," Elijah said, gesturing to the chair opposite him. JT obeyed, sitting stiffly, his eyes fixed on the floor.

Elijah studied his son for a long moment, noting the tension in his shoulders. He'd seen it for days now, ever since JT had returned with Henry's body and the lone Crow rider. It wasn't the first time Elijah had seen that weight on someone's back. It was the look of a man who'd done what was necessary, then had to live with it.

"You think I don't trust you," Elijah said finally. "Or that I somehow blame you for what happened to Henry?"

JT glanced up, startled, but didn't speak.

Elijah leaned forward, resting his elbows on his knees. "You're wrong. I trust you more than you know. That's why I need you to stay."

JT frowned. "I don't understand."

"You're growing into a fine man, JT," Elijah said, his voice steady. "Capable, strong. You've proven you can handle yourself." He paused. "But right now, I need you to do somethin' harder than ridin' off into trouble. I need you to stay. Keep this ranch runnin'. Keep your mama, your aunt, and your sisters and cousins safe."

JT's frown deepened, but there was no mistaking the flicker of pride in his eyes. "You really think I can do all that?"

Elijah nodded. You are capable. I'm not just askin' you as your father—I'm askin' you as a hand of the Slash V. This place needs you, son. I need you."

JT sat back as he absorbed the weight of his father's words. Slowly, he nodded. "I'll do it."

Elijah's lips quirked in a faint smile, but it faded as he noticed JT's expression shift, as if he were wrestling with something unsaid.

"What is it?" Elijah asked.

"What do I do if. . ." JT wrung his hands and gazed around the office before looking back at his father.

Elijah gave him a knowing look. He didn't want to think about it either. "You know more than you think about running a ranch. And if there's anyone you need to talk to about anything at all, your ma knows the answer, or knows who does."

The young man nodded, but Elijah could see there was more on his mind. He cleared his throat, working to find the right words. Not as the boss. As a father. "How you holdin' up?" He rubbed his beard. "What happened when you went back?"

JT blinked, the question seeming to catch him off guard. "I decided I couldn't just leave them. It was like you said—a man rides for the brand, and I couldn't leave Henry behind, even if I was the one they wanted. I circled around, and saw all the Crow but Henry and the one I came back with were dead, and all but two of the attackers the same. Henry and the other Crow were pinned down, and I could see the attackers from their cover. Scout and I charged them, forcing them out, and Henry rose up and shot one, just before he shot at me."

He paused to gather himself, and Elijah could see he was putting all his effort into keeping his composure. "Then the other one turned and took a shot at Henry. Just before he fired at the other Crow, I. . ."

Elijah sat quietly, the silence stretching between them. His chest tightened—not just with sorrow for Henry, but for the boy sitting across from him, who now sounded like one of the hardened young soldiers Elijah had once commanded. He wanted to say something fatherly, comforting. But all that came out was a boss's response.

"I see," Elijah said quietly. He removed his pipe and looked at it as he spoke. "Sounds like you done right as you could in a dangerous situation. That's all any man can do."

JT lowered his head and nodded.

Elijah looked up and tilted his head. "What else, son?"

JT hesitated, then took a deep breath and looked up. "What is it you haven't told me? About. . . your past?"

Elijah's brow furrowed. "What makes you ask that?"

"Tommy said some things today," JT admitted, his voice quiet. "About the attack. About you and Uncle Mo. And it's not just that. It's the way people look at you—like they're scared of you almost. I just. . . I want to know what you're capable of, what you've done. Why this is so easy for you?"

Elijah's gaze drifted to the fire. For a long moment, he said nothing. Then he leaned back, exhaling slowly. "Son," he said, his voice low, "you'd be surprised what you're capable of when it comes to justice and protectin' your own." He puffed on his pipe, then spoke around it. "And I assure you, it's the farthest thing from easy. The moments are few in my life where these things don't occupy my mind."

JT stared at his father, questions lingering in his eyes, but he didn't press further. Elijah stood, clapping a hand on JT's shoulder. "Get some rest. Tomorrow, you take charge around here."

JT nodded, rising to his feet. "Goodnight, Pa."

"Goodnight, son."

As JT left the study, Elijah sank back into his chair, staring into the dying embers of the fire. The past he'd sought to keep from his son was colliding with his present.

REVELATIONS

— • —

E lijah and Moses left with Tommy before dawn, their horses' breath visible as their hooves crunched the frost-kissed ground. The land around them lay quiet, the predawn light bathing the hills in a soft pink glow. The only sounds were the rhythmic clop of hooves and the occasional rustle of wind through the dry grass.

Moses broke the silence. "You think Billy's done somethin' real bad this time?"

Elijah glanced over, his brow furrowed. "Maybe. But what I can't figure is Hill's men being locked up with him, but saying they don't want any of *our* men leaving town once they come in. It's like the law believes one thing but also like we're to blame as well."

Moses grunted. "If this was cut and dry, they'd've let Billy cool off some, pardon him for beatin' on a nare-do-well, then taken those lousy rustlers to the county."

Elijah sighed, gripping the reins tighter. "That's what worries me. This ain't ever been a place that did much law work at all, very well pretending to see it from both sides when they do."

They rode all day, each man lost in thought. They were pushing their horses to the limit of a day's travel in this country, but the cool weather and plentiful water and grass during the breaks eased Elijah's concerns.

In the last bit of light, the trail curved to follow a bend in the Yellowstone, just south of Livingston, where the Slash V herd was bedded down. Cattle milled about, their lowing breaking the stillness. They had called from a distance, easing the nerves of the men riding the edge of the herd. Travis eventually spotted them, raising a hand in greeting as he rode out to meet them.

Travis glanced at Tommy. "Figured you'd get here tonight," he said, his tone brisk but tinged with relief. "Jax is still in town, keepin' close to Billy. But I'll tell ya, things ain't lookin' great, boss."

Elijah climbed down and adjusted his hat, his expression hard. "Tell me everything."

Travis tipped his chin toward Tommy. "Why don't you ride in and have Cookie get the three of you a plate." The young man headed for camp, and Travis continued as they led their horses toward the remuda.

Travis took out the makings, then rolled and lit a cigarette before he began. "I rode in with Billy and Jax ahead of the herd to arrange the sale and report the ambush. We'd no sooner got off our horses at the rail yard's cattle office when they spotted some fellas they said they recognized from the raid. Tempers flared—which seemed to confirm it a bit—and Billy went after one of 'em. Didn't shoot, but mighta been cleaner if he had—beat the man half to death, and then drew his gun."

Elijah's lips thinned. "The law stepped in?"

Travis blew out smoke and then scoffed. "Eventually." Jax was the one who kept there from bein' another body. The marshal and a Gallatin County deputy locked Billy up after one man he was agitating hollered about him being the killer, Billy Irons. Jax talked 'em outta lockin' him up too, claimin' he brought things to a stop, but barely.

Now, word's goin' around that there's men of Hills who weren't involved that are sniffin' for blood."

Moses scowled. "And what about our outfit and James's guys?"

"Oh, them too," Travis answered. He sighed deeply. "I warned em, though. 'Specially after the lawmen said they didn't want us leavin' after we come in." He took a long drag on his cigarette. "They know it's a powder keg."

Elijah scratched his beard. "So, what of the rustlers who got into it with Billy?"

"The one is still breathin', locked up with Billy and two others. The rest skedaddled."

Elijah exchanged a glance with Moses. "Alright, thanks for handling it the best you could." He scanned the camp as they reached where the horses were staked out. "Unfortunately, we don't have any better news."

Elijah and Moses recounted what they discovered upon their return to the ranch and broke the news of Henry's death."

"Henry. . . dammit," Travis said. "How's JT?"

Elijah was quiet for a moment. "He'll be alright."

Travis nodded. "Three attacks in one night, that ain't no coincidence, boss."

Elijah shared a glance with Moses. "Don't we know it?" He looked toward the horizon and the dots of cattle. "Ready to bring 'em in come morning?"

"Yessir," Travis confirmed.

Elijah nodded. "Good. Once we've dealt with this mess, we'll meet you at the pens."

The three of them unsaddled their horses and handed them off to a hand, then the brothers watched Travis head off to prepare his crew for the morning. The foreman stopped suddenly, then turned, walking back toward them.

"Listen, I ain't doin' my job if I'm not honest with you about what the men are saying." He hesitated, as if unsure if it was his place. "But Stratton's son. . ."

"We know," Elijah said.

Travis bit his lip, seeming to wait for more, but when Elijah said nothing, he turned and departed.

Elijah gestured toward the chuck wagon, and he and Moses walked.

Moses raised an eyebrow. "You didn't exactly shut down what he was gettin' at. You alright with everyone accepting that Edward was involved?"

Elijah's silence was answer enough.

———— ⚜ ————

LIVINGSTON GREETED THEM with its usual bustling energy, but something felt off. The town, always lively with ranchers, merchants, and passersby—especially now with the railroad during cattle drive season—seemed on edge. Conversations hushed as Elijah and Moses passed, wary eyes tracking their movements.

They stabled their horses and approached the marshal's office, their boots loud on the wooden walkway. Jax was leaning against a post outside, his face grim as he tipped his hat in greeting.

"Bosses," Jax said.

"Billy?" Elijah asked.

"He's in there," Jax replied as he jerked his head toward the door. "Marshal's keepin' him in the back, but the Gallatin deputy's runnin' the show. And them fellas Billy went after? They're singin' many different tunes, but all claimin' they was nowhere near the Slash V herd."

Moses snorted. "Liars, the lot of 'em."

"But we're sure about who they are?" Elijah asked. He peered through the marshal's window.

Jax nodded. "We told 'em we know it was dark, but a man's prone to remember details about fellas who aimed to steal their cattle and kill you to boot." Jax spit tobacco off the boardwalk. "The fellas look and act the part, and Billy is a lot of things, but he ain't a liar, and he don't forget a man who wrongs him."

Moses chuckled. "'Spose that's true."

Jax turned his back to the office and lowered his voice. "Word around here is Hill and that Finn character been curryin' influence with the law. Folks are scared to cross 'em, and the deputy's leanin' hard on the marshal to make sure that nothin' escalates, and there's no favoritism shown."

"Bribes?"

Jax bit his lip and squinted. "Nah, it seems more careful than that. Just a lot of makin' sure they know where their bread is buttered, Hill's growing influence. . ."

"Quid pro quos," Moses said.

Elijah and Jax both looked at him.

"Well, that's what our old pal Matt Hobbs used to call it."

Elijah sighed.

"Well, whatever it's called," Jax said, "seems like they are also gettin' folks to see a downfall of Jon Stratton with his health and the new competition. They also are workin' hard to remind folks about the two 'a you's past."

Elijah grimaced, then nodded toward the marshal's office. "So, what's the lay of things in there?"

"Trial for 'em all in Bozeman, I reckon. Billy included. Pretty tight-lipped otherwise."

Elijah squared his shoulders. "Alright. Let's get inside."

The marshal's office was small but tidy, the air thick with the smell of tobacco and sweat. Marshal Phil Harlan sat behind his desk, his lined face set in a grimace as he looked up from a stack of papers. The Gallatin County deputy, a younger man with sharp features and a hard expression, stood near the window, arms crossed.

"Mister Barber," Harlan greeted, his tone guarded.

"Marshal," Elijah replied, tipping his hat. "We're here for Billy McCray."

Harlan sighed, gesturing for them to sit. "It ain't that simple. Your man made a mess of things."

Elijah didn't sit, standing and packing his pipe as he spoke instead. "My man went after rustlers who killed our friend. Seems clear to me who oughta be locked up." He looked at the deputy and back at Marshal Harlan. "I ain't the first rancher to come in and get a man who acted in the right—even if overboard—released into his custody with a promise to keep a lid on him."

The deputy stepped forward, his voice cold. "Your man assaulted an unarmed man then threw down on him unprovoked. That's a crime, Mister Barber, no matter what he thinks those fellas did. We can't play sides here."

"Since when?" Moses asked. "Now there ain't been much trouble in this Valley, but when there has been, it seems like the law has been on the side of lettin' folks who've been wronged take care of things."

"Didn't catch your name yet," Elijah said to the deputy.

"Sam Whitaker," the man answered.

Elijah met the deputy's gaze, his voice steady but edged with steel. "Deputy Whitaker, those men locked up with our guy are taking orders from Finn McGovern, and you know it."

The deputy smirked. "No, I don't rightly know that yet. Even if they are, there's no proof they were involved in the raid on your outfit. Now he, or your man here, or any of the rest of you can testify they were, but come on, Mister Barber, it was a firefight in the near dark." He eyed Elijah a moment. "And you aren't doing yourself any favors insinuating anyone working with your competition is, by default, a bad guy."

"Those men fit the descriptions of rustlers we fought off during the raid. My men remember their figures, their voices. That's more than enough to hold 'em accountable coming from reputable men," Elijah said.

Moses leaned forward, his voice low and dangerous. "And you don't think folks are going to take the word of Jon Stratton's men who are fixtures in the county?"

The deputy chuckled. "Well, that's the thing then, isn't it? Folks have set to wonderin' on how it is you've all been so successful for so long, with hardly a bother. Then you get Billy McCray shoot a man in town, and you fellas. . ." He trailed off, and Elijah saw him look at the guns on their hips. "Well, clearly you've still got it."

Elijah removed his pipe and pointed it at the deputy. "What are you tryin' to say?"

"I'm sayin' that you just have to see it from the law's perspective—that these men only allegedly did what you say—"

Elijah cut him off. "How about the fact that near the same time that night, Henry Horse Goes Ahead and my son were also attacked delivering cattle to the Crow? Henry killed. Our headquarters also hit with six hands dead, and a house full of women and girls having to defend themselves. That not enough evidence for you?"

The room fell into a tense silence. Jax's eyes widened slightly, the news hitting him like a blow. "Henry's dead?" he asked quietly.

Elijah took off his hat and ran a hand through his hair, sighing. "Jesus, Jax, I'm sorry. That's not how I intended to tell you about that." Jax pursed his lips and closed his eyes, and Elijah thought it looked like he was praying.

The deputy's face betrayed a flicker of unease before he caught himself. "We didn't know all that, Mister Barber. And I'm awful sorry to hear about your man. We'll surely look into it, but I just need you to—"

"Don't need me for nothin'," Elijah shouted. He slammed a fist on the marshal's desk. "This ain't just a bar brawl or some random cattle theft. This is a coordinated attack—on my family, my ranch, and my men. And if you think it stops here, you're blind. You got some of their comrades locked up, and likely able to tell us where the rest are."

"Don't lecture us, Barber," Whitaker interrupted, his voice sharp. "We can't afford to take sides in this. The law don't play favorites, no matter how tragic your story is—and it truly is."

Elijah stepped forward, his voice dangerously calm. "You think I want your damn pity? I want justice. And if you won't give it to me. . . Then don't stand in my way when I take it for myself."

Whitaker grinned and shook his head. "Just like I was sayin'."

Harlan raised a hand. "Enough. McCray stays here until we get more word from Bozeman. The other man's still recovering, and when he's fit, we'll get his side of the story same as we done with his friends." He rubbed the back of his neck. "We can lean on them with this information as well."

"And if Hill's men come callin'?" Elijah asked, his voice sharp. "You're tellin' my outfit to stay in town while we are catching word they may yet be targets."

Harlan hesitated, then glanced at Deputy Whitaker. "Allegedly Hill's men." He sighed. "Your outfit's free to go now that we talked with you. As for if anybody comes for you again. . . We'll cross that bridge if we come to it."

Elijah's eyes darkened. "You'd better hope we don't get to that bridge, because this is all rotten, and we won't sit around and take any more violence directed against us."

"No, I expect you won't," the deputy said.

"What's that?" Elijah said, speaking around his pipe. Deputy Whitaker eyed him for a moment, and Elijah could sense that the man realized he might be getting too big for his britches, but didn't want to back down.

"I know you fellas have gone off ridin' for justice before, but I want to make sure I remind you that you don't have badges now. . . Much as that didn't always stop you in the past."

Elijah's nostrils flared, and he cocked his head and stared at the deputy, but Moses and Jax guided him out of the office, the door slamming shut behind them.

As they stepped onto the street, the weight of the situation settled over them like a storm cloud. Jax fell into step beside them.

"Jax, I shoulda told you before we went in, I got caught up with—"

"I understand, boss. You got a lot on your mind and ain't none of it good. What now?"

Elijah's gaze swept the town, taking in the uneasy glances of passersby and the subtle movements of men loitering near the saloon. "Well, we don't leave Billy to rot alone," he said, but I ain't gonna hold all our men here to waste away and cause trouble."

Moses grunted. "Fellas will be awful upset to not get their night in town to spend their money and blow off some steam."

Elijah nodded. "They'll be even more upset if they wind up in jail or dead."

"I can stay and keep a few cooler-headed hands with me. That way Billy ain't left alone and we can keep you updated," Jax offered.

Elijah nodded. "We'll go over to the pens and confer with Travis and get the sale taken care of. Get the men paid out and let them get a drink and a meal but break the news they'll camp outside town and ride back tomorrow. If they want to do any shopping, tell them to make it quick, and not make me regret anything."

Jax frowned. "I'll pass the word. How about you two?"

"We always send word to Stratton after a sale anyway, so this won't be any different. Although I might wait for a wire back on whether he wants us to come in, and what he thinks about what's going on."

Elijah glanced at Moses and then at Jax. "Jax, you mind goin' on ahead and giving Moses and I a minute?"

"Sure thing, boss."

The brothers watched the man walk away, then Elijah turned to Moses. "That was the worst, dropping it on him like that about the ranch being hit and Henry being killed. And then I went and made that lousy comment about getting justice on my own." He beat his hat against his leg.

"You mean it, though?" Moses asked, glancing around casually as if to mask the magnitude of the conversation they were having.

Elijah fixed a stare on his brother. "Well, I reckon I sure don't want it to come to that."

Moses shook his head. "No. We don't." He looked around once more. "What ya gonna say to Stratton about his son?"

Elijah rubbed his beard. "That we need to know what's going on."

As they walked down the dusty street, the weight of what lay ahead pressed on Elijah. His senses told him that there would be no shared victories or solutions that came out well for everyone. And Elijah feared being the winner would come at a cost.

He thought about JT's question before he'd left. Wondering about his past. He knew what he had done, but he wondered about the boy's other question, and whether he knew the answer. What *was* he capable of?

⚓

BACK AT THE RANCH, JT leaned on a corral gate, staring at the valley, the weight of responsibility pressing heavy on his shoulders. His father's parting words echoed in his mind: *I'm counting on you*.

He turned back toward the house. The yard was quieter than usual, the few remaining workers going about their day with a subdued efficiency. Even the sounds of the animals seemed subdued, as though they too felt the absence of the ranch's two guiding forces. JT inhaled deeply and walked inside.

The house was warm, the air heavy with the smell of baking bread. Helen and the girls were gathered around Maggie in the kitchen, their quiet chatter an effort to mask their unease. JT walked past them, then paused at the door to Elijah's study, hesitating before pushing it open. He told himself he was just checking to ensure there was no business left unattended to during the recent events. Still, it felt strange entering his father's private domain alone.

The study smelled of pipe smoke and leather. JT stepped toward the desk, running his fingers over the worn surface. A ledger sat open next to a leather bound sheaf of paper. Columns of figures were in the former, various notes in the other, all in his father's neat handwriting.

JT scanned the numbers and notes, but found nothing that appeared to require immediate attention.

Emboldened by his current station on the ranch and sitting in his father's sanctuary, he opened drawers, his recent questions about his father's past in the back of his mind. Most opened easily, revealing papers and supplies—but one drawer near the bottom was locked.

JT frowned. His father rarely locked anything in the house. Glancing toward the door to ensure he was alone, JT crouched down, testing the drawer again. The lock held firm. His heart pounded as he searched the desk and shelves for a key. It took him several minutes to find it, tucked inside an old tobacco box on the bookshelf.

With trembling hands, JT unlocked the drawer and slid it open. Inside were items that immediately caught his eye: a tarnished badge, folded and yellowed newspapers, and a handful of letters tied with twine. JT picked up the badge first, holding it to the light. Its edges were worn, the engraving faint, but there was no mistaking its purpose. It had once belonged to a lawman—a deputy U.S. Marshal.

His breath caught as he opened the newspapers. The headlines told stories of gunfights, arrests, and bloody vengeance. One article mentioned the name Elijah Barber, though the details were vague. JT set the papers aside and reached for the letters. The handwriting was unfamiliar, the tone terse and formal. They referenced bounties and justice but hinted at something darker—decisions made in the heat of anger, actions taken without the law's blessing.

JT's mind reeled. He had always known his father had a past, but this evidence painted a picture far more violent than he had imagined. His fingers brushed the badge again, and he wondered what kind of man Elijah Barber had once been—and what kind of man he still was.

"What are you doing in here?"

JT flinched, turning to see Maggie standing in the doorway. Her arms were crossed, her expression stern.

"Find what you were looking for?"

"I—I was just looking for something about the ranch," JT stammered, hastily closing the drawer. "I didn't mean to. . ."

"No. You weren't. Maggie stepped into the room. "I am amazed it took this long." She reached out, taking the badge from his hand.

JT hesitated. "Is it true? All of it? Was he a war hero?"

"He would tell you it was just the opposite." Maggie sighed, sitting on the edge of the desk. "Your father hasn't told you much about those years, has he?"

JT shook his head. "Not a thing. But I've heard things—what Tommy said after the attack, what the men on the ranch and people in town sometimes hint at. I just don't understand... why would he keep all this from me?"

"Your father has always tried to leave the past behind. He wanted to build something better for all of us—for you and your sisters. He and your uncle barely survived as kids after their father, your granddad, died young." She held up the badge, turning it over in her hands. "The things they did to survive, and the war and time as lawmen? It made him and your uncle who they are."

JT looked down at his hands. "Is that why people act the way they do around him and Uncle Moses? Why they're so. . . afraid?"

"Fear and respect can look similar." Maggie nodded. "But yes, your father and Moses have done things—hard things, necessary things—but they carry that weight with them every day. They've tried to shield you from it, JT. Not because they don't trust you, but because they hoped you'd never have to know what that kind of life feels like."

JT frowned. "But I already do, don't I? After everything that's happened. . . after Henry. . ."

Maggie placed a hand on his shoulder. "You're stronger than you realize, JT. And your father knows that. He's proud of the man you're becoming, but he dreaded the day it ever affected you. To his credit, he's not showing it right now, but he's in agony."

JT swallowed hard, his mind a tangle of emotions. "How do I live up to all that?"

Maggie smiled faintly. "You don't have to, and to be honest, he doesn't want you to. But you can learn from him. And one day, when the time is right, he'll tell you everything, and you can apply his lessons to whatever you set your mind to. And one of those lessons should be not going through your father's desk." She frowned. "We won't tell him but do it again and I can't protect you."

JT chuckled, then looked up at her. "Was he the one who taught you how to shoot? How you were able to defend the house?"

She might have smiled had the thought of that night not haunted her. "Believe it or not, that was my brothers and your grandpa Hennessey who taught me." She motioned to an Omaha newspaper clipping on the desk. "Maybe read that one."

JT didn't reply, his gaze lingering on the faded newspaper. His eyes went wide when he read the portion detailing a posse from Omaha, including the daughter of a local livery owner.

Maggie winked and squeezed his shoulder before standing. "Come on," she said. "The girls are waiting for supper."

FATHER AND SON

— • —

T he crisp crackle of the fire was the only reprieve from the steady drum of rain against the windows in Jonathan Stratton's wood-paneled parlor. The cold fall storm clawed at the house with gusts of wind, rattling the shutters and making the room feel smaller, more confined, as Jonathan reviewed the telegram for the fifth time. Its contents were brief, almost dismissive in tone, but the weight of it had rooted him to the chair.

> TROUBLE IN VALLEY. IN LIVINGSTON
> DEALING WITH IT AND CATTLE. MULT.
> FATALITIES. HENRY AND CROW BUYERS
> KILLED. HQ ATTACKED. ASK EDWARD
> SHARE WHAT HE KNOWS OF RECENT
> EVENTS. CAN TRAVEL 1-2 DAYS. BARBER.

Jonathan folded the telegram carefully, setting it on the mahogany desk alongside his spectacles. His hand lingered on it for a moment, the faint tremor in his fingers betraying the steady facade he struggled to maintain. He reached for his cane, rising with deliberate slowness, his knees protesting with every inch. The fire's warmth did little to ease the chill that had settled into his bones. Jonathan had already sent a summons to Edward, though he hadn't yet decided how he would confront his son—or if he even wanted to know the truth.

The door creaked open moments later, and Edward entered with the confidence of a man who had long since mastered appearing in control. He shrugged off his rain-slicked coat and hung it by the door. His polished boots made no sound on the thick rug as he crossed to the armchair opposite his father, his expression betraying only faint curiosity.

"You called for me, Father?" Edward's tone was devoid of the deference he once showed, his voice tinged with impatience as if he were indulging an old man's whims.

Jonathan gestured to the chair with a weary nod. "Sit."

Edward obliged, lowering himself into the chair with deliberate nonchalance. His eyes flicked to the telegram on the desk. "I assume this is about the trouble in the Valley?"

Jonathan nodded. "Elijah Barber seems to think you may have insight into whatever is going on."

Edward's brow furrowed. "I've been here managing our affairs in Bozeman for days. What would I know of what's happening out there?"

Jonathan studied his son carefully, searching for something familiar about the man he barely recognized anymore. "That's precisely what I'd like to understand, Edward. They've suffered multiple attacks—organized, violent. These are not the actions of mere rustlers. And yet, when I ask for your perspective, you feign ignorance and indifference." The elder Stratton pounded the desk with his free hand, the sharp sound cutting through the rain's relentless rhythm. "Is that not why you claim to be here? To spend time in the Valley? To learn about this business? You either approve that it has happened, or do not grasp the seriousness of the matter!" He paused for a breath. "Your mother would be appalled at what you've become."

Edward stood abruptly, anger flaring in his eyes. "Please, don't evoke Mother to cover for your own failings. You did not object when she sent me away to school, and you chose not to bring me back even for her funeral, saying the journey was too harsh for a boy."

Jonathan recoiled, the mention of his late wife striking a deep nerve. "I did what I thought was best for you. It was a hard decision, made of love, not abandonment. But clearly, you've grown to resent what I provided you."

"Resent? No, Father. I've simply outgrown the quaint notions of family and loyalty you cling to. You're the one living in the past, romanticizing the rugged life of Elijah and Moses Barber—men you wish were your sons because they don't challenge your outdated ways." He straightened his jacket. "I'm sure they provided you comfort in your time of need."

The words struck Jonathan like a slap, their callousness leaving him staring at his son in silence.

Edward shifted, his polished demeanor slipping for a moment. "Now as for those Barbers, if they have enemies, perhaps it's a consequence of how they conduct themselves. They've grown complacent, too comfortable in their supposed invulnerability."

"You speak as though their losses are a matter only of business, not blood," he said, his voice low but sharp. "And forgetting that, it is *our* business! Men dead, including Henry Horse Goes Ahead. Have you no sense of what this means? Is that what you've become? A man who values profit over humanity?"

Edward moved to the window, his hands grasped behind his back. The storm outside rattled the glass panes, and lightning cast fractured light across his face. "What it means, Father, is that the Barbers have always acted as though this valley belongs solely to them. As though the Strattons should be content to linger in their shadow as they take credit for what should have been *our* legacy." He turned, his eyes blazing with ambition. "They've become an obstacle. Hill and MacDonald see it. I see it. And if you were honest, you'd admit it too."

He turned and locked eyes with his father. "The valley has changed, Father. It demands a firmer hand, which you're too frail to provide. If that means making hard choices, then yes, I am the man to make them."

Jonathan straightened best as he could, his hand trembling as he gripped the cane. "You talk of hard choices, but I see only hard consequences. You're gambling with our legacy, Edward, turning it into something unrecognizable."

Edward's expression hardened, his patience exhausted. "Maybe it's time for you to step aside and let me save that legacy from your sentimentality. I am not your obedient son anymore; I am the man who will ensure our survival."

"What are you saying?" Jonathan managed.

Edward met his father's gaze without flinching. "I'm saying that this valley doesn't run on sentimentality, Father. Carson Hill understands what it takes to secure a future for this—"

"A future built on blood and betrayal?" Jonathan interrupted, his voice trembling with a mix of anger and disbelief. "Do you think they care about the Stratton name, about preserving what we have built? They'll bleed this valley dry, Edward, and when they're done, they'll discard you like chaff. Do you honestly think you'll be the exception?"

Edward's lips curled into a faint, bitter smile. "Perhaps. But better to be the one holding the reins while it lasts than to be trampled underfoot like the Barbers. Is it only you, Father, who's allowed to see opportunity in hardship?" He brushed some lint from his jacket. "I've seen the world, and I know how it works."

The words hit Jonathan like a blow, forcing him back into his chair. For a moment, he saw not the man before him but the boy he'd once sent away, his eager eyes now replaced by a cold, calculating gleam. His grip tightened on his cane, his knuckles white as he slammed the bottom into the ground. "You were raised to protect this family, not destroy it."

Edward turned back to the window, studying the rain streaming down the glass. "You raised me to survive, Father. That's all I'm doing. Then you sent me away and replaced me with men more in your own image."

Jonathan's hands trembled, not from age but from fury. "How dare you?" he rasped, his voice hoarse with betrayal. "I gave you everything. Every chance to succeed. You think you built a name yourself?" He shook his head. "I didn't replace you with men in my image, they became such men. You. . . you have become something else."

Edward said nothing. He didn't turn from the window. His silence, colder than the storm outside, spoke more plainly than any denial could.

"You've nothing to say to me? No retort? Can't even face me?"

Still, Edward didn't turn. He simply adjusted his cuffs, his posture ramrod straight.

The old man's temper broke. With surprising force, Jonathan snatched the silver ashtray from his desk and hurled it across the room. It struck the wall beside Edward's head, sending shards of porcelain from a nearby vase skittering across the floor.

Edward flinched, more from surprise than fear, and finally faced his father. For the first time in the conversation, he looked uncertain.

Jonathan's breath came ragged. His anger ebbed as quickly as it had flared, replaced by something far worse—despair. He sank back into his chair, shoulders sagging under the weight of years and regret. His next words were scarcely above a whisper.

"Edward, those men have set events into motion that no one will be able to stop. And when the reckoning comes—if you've done more than just sought business with these men—God help us," Jonathan murmured, shaking his head. "I condemn myself in choosing our family and our name. I damn myself for my weakness in doing so. It will not be Carson Hill or Finn MacDonald that ends us, Edward. It will be Elijah or Moses Barber." He signed and lowered his head. "Damn you, Edward. Damn you for doing this to me."

Edward's face hardened again, his momentary uncertainty vanishing like smoke. Understanding that his father would not stand in his way, he said nothing more, smoothing his jacket and walking out without another word.

Jonathan listened to the measured footfalls fading down the hall, each step echoing like the ticking of a clock running out. The fire crackled weakly in the hearth, its warmth failing to touch the icy knot in his chest.

THE SECOND DAY OF RAIN against the windows had lessened to a soft patter by the time Jonathan Stratton stepped out of his parlor as Harrison walked to the front. The Barber brothers stood in the entryway, hats in hand, their faces lined with exhaustion. Stratton took in the sight of them—alive, whole—and his tired face showed relief.

"Elijah. Moses." Stratton stepped forward, clasping Elijah's hand firmly. "It's good to see you both. When I heard of the attack—" His voice faltered, and he cleared his throat.

Elijah nodded solemnly. "We've had a rough few days, but we're standing."

Stratton's grip lingered for a moment before he turned to Moses. "I'm sorry, truly. About Henry. And the others. I know what they meant to you and your family." He shook his head. "Oh, and your wives and daughters. My heart goes out to them."

Moses inclined his head slightly, his expression unreadable. "Thank you."

"Come," Stratton said, stepping aside to let them in. "Let's sit." He motioned to Harrison, the long-time butler, to take and hang up their rain slickers and hats. "Some coffee too, please."

Elijah smiled at the kindly butler they'd come to know over the years, then saw the man glance at their hips as he took their coats.

"Yeah, about that," Elijah said. "Didn't realize we were no longer allowed to wear guns in town."

Moses snorted. "Guess we missed somethin'. Can't say I enjoyed the attention from the deputy when we came in."

Stratton exhaled sharply, rubbing his forehead as he turned toward the parlor. "Oh, that. . . another fine idea of Carson Hill," he said, his voice thick with sarcasm. "A show of 'progress' and 'safety,' as he put it. Passed the proposal in the wake of the saloon shooting—no firearms carried inside the town limits unless you're law."

"Or Finn MacDonald, I assume," Elijah said under his breath.

Moses folded his arms as he stepped into the parlor. "And here I thought it was a man's own business whether he carried or not."

Stratton sighed as he settled into his chair by the hearth, a cane leaning against it. "That was the argument, but Hill convinced enough folks otherwise." He gestured toward the chairs opposite him. "Please. Sit."

Elijah studied Stratton's frailty as he entered the parlor, the warmth of the fire seeming to offer little relief from the chill in his aching bones. Elijah settled in across from him and pulled his pipe from his coat.

Stratton looked at the brothers with a weary sadness. "Tell me everything. How bad is it?"

Elijah leaned forward, resting his elbows on his knees as he packed his pipe. He recounted the events of the attack in stark detail—Henry's death, the ambush at the ranch, and the near-decimation of their workforce not out on the drive. He spoke steadily, his voice calm but weighted, while Moses remained silent, his eyes fixed on the flickering flames.

Stratton listened intently. He nodded occasionally, his fingers tightening on the armrest of his chair as Elijah spoke. When the recounting was done, Stratton let out a long breath, his shoulders sagging.

"I can't imagine the toll this has taken," he said. "And the Crow buyers? They were killed as well?"

Moses swallowed some coffee he had had just sipped. "Cut down just as Henry was. A message, plain as day. Real personal it seemed."

Elijah shook out the match from lighting his pipe and spoke around it. "They were targeting JT. Said it straight out, according to JT and the only other survivor."

"Oh my," Stratton mentioned. His gaze dropped to the fire, the shadows playing across his face. "It's a tragedy," he murmured. "I've known Henry since he first came to us." He looked up, and Elijah studied him. "Since he came to *you*," Stratton clarified. "Awful. Senseless."

The room fell into a heavy silence, the drizzle on the windows filling the void. For a moment, it seemed neither side was willing to speak what was truly on their minds, each waiting for the other to broach the subject. Finally, Stratton straightened, his hand resting on the telegram still folded on the table beside him.

"Edward. . ." Stratton began, his voice hesitant. "You mentioned him specifically in an otherwise brief message considering the situation."

Elijah's eyes flicked to Moses, then back to Stratton as he puffed on his pipe. "I did."

Stratton frowned, his fingers drumming against the chair's arm. "I've asked him. Pointedly. He denies knowing anything. Says he's been here in Bozeman for days. Surely you don't think he had a hand in orchestrating something like this?"

Elijah sat back, his expression unreadable. "We don't have proof, if that's what you're asking. But we've seen signs—Hill's men emboldened, movements in the valley that don't add up. And Edward. . . Edward has shown himself to be more than friendly with them, or at the least, seeming to know an awful lot about them."

Stratton winced, his free hand brushing over the top of his cane. "Friendly or not. . . I mean, yes, he has admitted to seeking business with them." He cleared his throat. "But accusations without evidence—"

"Evidence will come if it's there," Moses cut in, his voice sharp. "It always does. What matters is what you'll do if it points back to him." Moses glanced at Elijah, who gave no reaction and continued to study Stratton. "He lit out real sudden like only hours before it all happened. More than just a fella not cut out for a drive deciding to quit."

Stratton flinched at the bluntness, his hand tightening on the arm of his chair. "I don't need you to tell me how to manage my son," he said, his voice low. "Or make such vile implications about—"

"Don't you?" Moses shot back, leaning forward. "Because it seems like Edward's managed to put this entire valley at risk, one way or 'nother, while you've sat here, hoping he'd straighten out on his own."

"Moses." Elijah snapped. He removed his pipe. "It gives us no pleasure to come to you with this, Jon."

Stratton's gaze hardened. "You think I don't know my son's faults? Do you think I don't see what he's capable of? But he is still my son."

"And how many more sons will die because of him?" Elijah asked quietly. The question hung in the air like smoke, suffocating and impossible to ignore.

Stratton closed his eyes, his hand trembling as he gripped the cane. "You're asking me to betray him. To betray my legacy and the only one left to carry our name."

"No," Elijah said. "There's still time to do the right thing. We're asking you to see him for what he is." He stuck his pipe in his mouth. "And if it's what we fear, we ask that you stand with us as you always have."

Stratton's eyes opened, filled with despair. He gestured toward the desk, where a leather-bound ledger rested alongside a pouch of coins. "Take it. Money. Take it and go. Leave this valley behind before it takes more from you. Regardless of who is responsible, it seems the die has been cast against you and your future here." His eyes dropped. "Name your price so that I may know you are safe and cared for."

Elijah's expression darkened. He rose slowly, his presence towering over the seated man. "We earn our money, and we don't run. Not from Edward, not from Hill, and not from anyone else who threatens what's ours." He took a step toward the door, then paused. "The Jon

Stratton we came to this territory with would never pay a man off to protect his name from his sins."

Moses followed Elijah to the door, pausing just long enough to cast a glance back at Stratton. "Trials coming up here in town, and I fear our man and some rustlers won't be the only thing getting judged. You'll have to live with your choices, Jonathan. Don't make the wrong ones."

Stratton looked up at them, his face lined with the weight of years and choices he could no longer avoid. "God help us all," he whispered.

Elijah retrieved his rain slicker from the hook and donned his hat, his voice cold. "Mister Stratton, you'll need more than God if Edward is behind this."

ULTIMATUM

— ◆ —

E lijah leaned back in the rickety chair, the scent of damp wood and hay filling the small quarters above Hennessey Livery and Freight. The rain had softened to a faint drizzle; the droplets tapping lightly against the single window that overlooked the muddy Bozeman streets. Maggie's father had built this livery that she bred horses for, and the modest living quarters above it now served as a makeshift home for the brothers—just as similar quarters had in Omaha, and countless other places before.

Moses sat across from Elijah, his boots propped on the edge of the low table between them, his hat pushed back. The lamp hanging from the ceiling cast a warm, uneven light, illuminating the rough-hewn walls and the simple furniture of the room. The smell of coffee brewing on a small cookstove in the corner mingled with the faint tang of leather and horse sweat rising from the stable below.

"You were sharp back there," Moses said, breaking the silence. "Didn't have much to go on, but you made him show his hand."

"Jonathan Stratton's a proud man," Elijah said finally. "Pride's a weakness when you know how to use it. Couldn't help himself—had to defend Edward, and the Stratton name, without realizing we didn't have much but suspicion to go on."

Moses chuckled, shaking his head. "You knew he'd do it too. The way you leaned on him, asked about Edward straight out—like you already had proof."

"Didn't need proof," Elijah replied, his voice calm. "Just needed him to believe I had it." Elijah shook his head. "A real shame, though. Seen the actions of a lot of important men when it came to self-preservation, but I thought Jon was different. Didn't think he had it in him to try and buy us off like that."

Moses leaned forward, the humor fading from his face. "So, what's next? We ride back or stick it out here?"

Elijah packed fresh tobacco into his pipe, his hands steady. "We stay. Too many pieces moving—Hill, MacDonald, the Strattons. Don't like the idea of riding back and forth while they're scheming under our noses. And I don't trust the trial to go straight, not with Hill's influence growing."

Moses nodded, his face settling into a grim expression. "Sent that wire to Travis earlier. Response said they were all settled up in Livingston, and just waiting to her from us before returning to the ranch. Jax is gonna come in on the train with the lawmen and their prisoners."

Elijah struck a match and lit his pipe, the soft glow reflecting in his eyes. "That's the only thing keeping me settled right now—knowing we'll have men back at the ranch soon. JT'll feel better too. Maybe it'll keep his mind off all the rest."

The brothers sat in silence, the sounds of horses shifting in the stalls below mingling with the distant murmurs of the Bozeman streets. Moses stood and checked on a pot of beans, then poured coffee for them and sat back down. Finally, he broke the silence.

"Funny how it always comes back to this. You and I holed up somewhere, trying to outlast whoever's got it in their head to cause us trouble."

Elijah allowed himself the faintest smile, the corners of his mouth twitching as he held the pipe in place. "Seems to be what we're best at."

Moses laughed, shaking his head. "Maybe one day we'll get to live like normal folk."

"Maybe," Elijah replied. Even he wasn't sure whether it was hope or doubt in his voice. He puffed on the pipe again, the smoke curling upward. "I know one thing though. I'm gettin' too old for this."

※

THE RAIN HAD THICKENED again by nightfall, a cold, steady drizzle that seeped through every crack and crevice of frontier Bozeman. The Stratton home stood cloaked in shadow, its grand facade lit by the flicker of the only gas lamps in town.

Jonathan Stratton sat alone near the fire, his cane resting against the arm of his chair, his gaze lost in the flames. A freshly poured drink sat on the table, and he took a long sip. The remnants of the day weighed heavily on him—the piercing accusations from Elijah, the damning silence of Edward, and the inescapable truth that the valley he'd spent a lifetime building was slipping from his grasp.

A sharp knock at the front door pulled Stratton from his reverie. He glanced toward the clock on the mantle—it was late for visitors. His butler, moving with the weariness of the hour, appeared at the doorway.

"Mister Hill and his associate are here to see you, sir," came the announcement. He paused, as if sensing the gravity of the visit. "Shall I send them away, sir?"

Stratton hesitated, his hand brushing against the cane. "No, Harrison. Show them in."

"Very well, sir."

Moments later, Carson Hill strode into the room with an air of practiced refinement, his tailored coat shedding droplets onto the polished floor. Behind him, Finn MacDonald loomed, his rough edges a stark contrast to Hill's polished demeanor. Finn's coat hung heavy with rain, and his boots left damp prints on the rug as he followed Hill toward the fire.

"Mister Stratton," Hill began smoothly, removing his hat and offering a faint smile. "I trust the evening finds you well."

Stratton gestured roughly to the chairs opposite him, though his face betrayed no warmth. "It's late for social calls."

Hill chuckled, settling into a chair as Finn remained standing, his broad frame casting a shadow in the firelight. "Well, I would normally be inclined to send an invite, but I know you're not one to get out much these days." His eyes glanced at the bottles on a nearby table. "But this is not a social call, I'm afraid. More of a business matter."

Stratton's hand gripped the armrest, and he scoffed. "If it's business you're after, you'd best come to the point." He stared at Hill. "Although isn't my son the Stratton you've schemed to do business with?"

Hill leaned forward, ignoring the remark, his expression calm but deliberate. "You've had quite the day, I imagine. Conversations with Barber men have a way of doing that." He steepled his fingers, his tone as smooth as the rain tapping against the windows. "We understand you've been handed a. . . difficult situation."

Stratton's gaze darkened. "If you've come to gloat, you can turn around and leave. I've no patience for it."

Hill smiled faintly, ignoring the jab. "No gloating, Mister Stratton. Just a proposal. One that might ensure your legacy remains intact."

Finn snorted, stepping closer. "More like one that keeps ye outta the dirt wi' the rest o' the Barbers' men."

Stratton's head snapped toward Finn, his voice sharp. "Watch your tongue. You may have sway with the weak-minded ranchers and drifters, but don't think you can speak to me that way."

Hill turned and glared at Finn.

"Why would I give you so much as the time of day after what you just did in the Valley?" Stratton added.

"Enough, the both of you," Hill said with a clipped voice. "We're here to make a deal, not to play at threats." Finn grunted but stepped back, his broad shoulders radiating menace.

Hill turned his attention back to Stratton. "You're a smart man, Jonathan. Surely ye see how things are shifting. The Barbers are a storm waiting to break, but storms like that can be weathered—with the right allies. That's what we're offering ye. An alliance. Between us, Edward, and you."

Stratton straightened in his chair, his cane digging into the rug as he leaned forward. "Why on Earth would I align myself with you?" He sighed. "And my son. . ."

Hill's smile faltered for a fraction of a second, but he recovered. "We both know Edward's ambitions have. . . accelerated things. But that's not a bad thing. The Barbers have held this valley in a stranglehold for too long—held you and any newcomers from growth. This is an opportunity to carve out a future where the Stratton name thrives."

Stratton's eyes narrowed, suspicion and anger flickering behind them. "You think I'd align myself with the men who've brought bloodshed to this valley? To my doorstep?"

Finn's voice cut in, low and cold. "Aye, and bloodshed ye'd best not have the law sniffin' too close to. We know who gave the order to target the Crow, the boy, and the ranch. Would nae look too kindly on you or Edward if that came to light, now, would it?"

The weight of the words landed heavily in the room, the fire crackling in the silence that followed. Stratton's grip on his cane tightened as his chest heaved with restrained fury. "You'd blackmail me? You come into my home— "

Hill's voice interrupted, firm but polished. "No blackmail, Jonathan. Just reality. The truth doesn't need leverage when it's already there, waiting to ruin everything you've built. I am an ambitious man and want what I want, but I'm no monster. Targeting a boy? A man's family?"

Stratton's eyes went wide. "What are you saying to me?" His eyes shifted between the two men. "No. No, I can believe his ambition led him to seek business with you, but. . . I don't believe it."

Stratton gave a look that carried the faintest trace of sympathy, though the smirk tugging at the corner of his mouth belied his true sentiments. He spoke with calculated care, his voice low and smooth. "Let's just say, Jonathan, that while I may know something about the rustling, the deeper cuts—the ones that truly bleed—are purely the work of your progeny. I deal in land and cattle, not cruelties."

Hill paused for a moment, watching the hollow note of regret seep into the dying man as he grappled with the abyss his son had dug.

"But we're offering a way forward," Hill continued. "Edward's actions. . . rash as they may have been. . . can be managed. We can ensure this trial goes smoothly, that the Barbers' influence is contained, and that you and your family remain untouched."

Stratton leaned back, his face pale, his breathing uneven, as he came to grips with what his son had orchestrated. Far worse than anything he'd imagined. He felt as though the room had shrunk. His mind flitted back to Edward as a boy, chasing fireflies in the yard, his laughter untainted by ambition. Now, that boy was gone, replaced by a man capable of this.

"And what happens when Elijah Barber decides he's had enough?" Stratton asked. "That man's no stranger to retribution. You think your 'influence' will stop him?"

Hill spread his hands, his voice calm. "The trial will set the tone. Barber may bluster, but the law will temper him. And should he prove less inclined to heed it. . . well, Finn and I have ways of handling men like him."

Stratton shook his head, his voice trembling with anger and despair. "You don't understand what you're dealing with. Elijah Barber isn't just any man. When I came upon him on my cattle drive from Texas, the world had thrown every last thing it could at that man, and everyone around him. And here he still is. No matter the cost, he'll see this through to the bitter end. If it's to be his end, he'll take everyone responsible with him."

Finn sneered. "Then let him try. The end is what we seek, aye? He's no' the first gunslinger to think he's untouchable."

Hill rose, adjusting his coat as he looked down at Stratton. "You have a choice, Mister Stratton. Ensure your legacy and Edward's safety. Let the Barbers take the fall. We'll make it look like you were part of a noble effort to save the valley from them, preserving your name and keeping your son unharmed. Keep your cattle and your ranch—I care very little where grazing is done, my interests lie below the ground. Stand with us and ensure your family's legacy."

Stratton sighed. "Or?"

"Or the fallout from this will reach far beyond your ranch," Hill warned. "This isn't just about land or cattle anymore. It's about survival. Your legacy and your son's future are at stake. I fear if you can't cooperate, that the Stratton name will join the Barbers in being to blame for all the recent troubles in this county. We'll give you time to think it over, but not too much. The trial will be the turning point, one way or another."

Stratton didn't respond, his gaze fixed on the fire as Hill and Finn made their way to the door. The rain had picked up again, drumming against the windows as the sound of their boots faded.

When the door clicked shut, Stratton sank back into his chair, his hand covering his face. The fire crackled, casting dancing shadows that seemed to mock him. The walls of his world were closing in, and for the first time, he wasn't sure he had the strength to stop them.

TRIALS AND TRIBULATIONS

—·—

T he slow footsteps came up the narrow back staircase late in the evening. Then a knock, sharp but hesitant, cutting through the muted hum of Bozeman's streets below. Elijah glanced at Moses, who gave a slight nod and drew his pistol—allowed due to the livery being a private place of business—before Elijah opened the door. Standing in the doorway was Harrison Webb, Jonathan Stratton's butler. His posture was slightly stooped, his weathered hands clinging to his straw hat like a lifeline as he removed it to reveal tightly coiled salt and pepper hair. His face, though lined with years of toil, showed resolve.

"Harrison," Elijah greeted with curiosity but warm recognition. "Come in."

The man stepped into the cramped quarters, his boots scuffing on the wooden floor. His eyes flitted over the modest furnishings—the sturdy table, mismatched chairs, and the small stove where coffee simmered. Moses leaned back in his chair, setting down his revolver, his gaze wary but not unkind.

Harrison offered a faint, nervous smile. "Evenin', Mister Elijah. Mister Moses. I reckon it's a surprise I'm here. I'm afraid I'm riskin' my loyalty to Mister Stratton by doin' so."

Elijah gestured to the chair opposite Moses, offering a cup of coffee to Harrison, who waved it off politely. "Take a seat, Harrison. You've been with the Strattons for nearly twenty years. That's a lot of loyalty to step away from, if that's the case."

Harrison sat, resting his hat on his knees. "I known you both almost as long, though. First time I met you boys, you'd come in off the trail with a busted wagon wheel. Mister Stratton had you over for supper while I fixed it up." He smiled faintly, the memory warming his tone. "Treated me with respect, and even helped me. First folks Jon Stratton ever had over for a meal that worked alongside me."

Moses nodded. "We aim to treat folks the way we'd want 'em to in return."

Harrison hesitated, his hands trembling as he looked at the brothers. "That's why I'm here tonight. You always asked after my family when you came by the house. Never looked down on me like some do 'round here. I owe it to you to tell you what I've heard."

Elijah leaned forward, his expression steady but encouraging. "Go on, Harrison. Whatever it is, we'll hear it."

The older man exhaled slowly, as if gathering the courage to continue. "I've worked for Mister Stratton a long time. He's not a bad man—always treated me fair enough—but lately, things ain't been right. Hill's been visitin'. Him and that brute, MacDonald. Edward, too."

Elijah straightened at the mention of Edward, but he said nothing. "Yes, we've become concerned about business Edward might be doing with Mister Hill."

Harrison wrung his hands. "It ain't just business they're talkin'. I overheard them. Hill and his man MacDonald were talkin' about what happened in the Valley—the Crow buyers, your boy, your ranch. They had their men escalate the trouble you had with your herd, but it wasn't Hill who gave the orders to make it personal. It was Edward.

He was the one who had men target the Crow, hit the ranch, and try 'n take your boy."

Moses stiffened, his knuckles whitening as he gripped the table. "You're sure?" His voice was sharp.

Harrison nodded solemnly. "I'd stake my life on it, Mister Moses. And mebbe I done so by comin' here. Edward wanted to break you."

"And Jonathan?" Elijah asked, his voice low and hard. "He knows?"

Harrison nodded again, his gaze dropping. "He does now. Hill's got his hooks in deep, and Stratton's desperate to keep Edward, and their name, safe. He mighta thought he could outmaneuver them, but I reckon he's only sinking deeper."

The room fell into a heavy silence, broken only by the faint creak of the floorboards and the muffled sound of horses shifting in the livery below. Elijah's face darkened, his hands tightening into fists. Moses stood, pacing to the window, his back rigid with fury.

"Thought you should know the truth. I'm not sure what you'll plan to do with this, but Hill and that MacDonald feller. . . well, they don't leave loose ends. I'd prefer not to lose my life as well if I don't soon have a job, if you catch my meaning."

Elijah nodded, his eyes narrowing as he processed the revelation. "You've done the right thing, Harrison. We won't bring this to light—not yet. That won't be what the trial is about. But when the time comes, we won't reveal our source."

Harrison stood. "Thank you, Mister Barber. For what it's worth, I believe you'll see justice done. I just hope it don't cost more than it already has."

Elijah stepped forward, clasping the man's shoulder briefly. "We'll see it done, Harrison. One way or another."

As Harrison left, the door clicking softly behind him; the room fell silent again. Moses waited for the steps to fade away, then turned from the window, his expression grim. "Hill was just playing cattle games. Tryin' to run us off. But bad as that was, it don't hold a candle to Edward."

"But Hill will gladly exploit it, and Jon will let it happen," Elijah growled. "He's thrown everything decent about himself into the fire for that son of his."

Moses nodded. "It wasn't just the ranch and gun carrying hands, Elijah. It was family. He went after your son. Our wives and kids put in the crosshairs."

Elijah's fists unclenched, then clenched again. His voice was a low rumble, cold, and resolute. "You asked me if I was going to take justice into my own hands."

Moses stared at him.

"Regardless of what comes from this trial. I fear we'll have to."

⚎

THE DAYS LEADING UP to the trial saw a cold front come to Bozeman, that brought not only a chill, but a layer of heavy tension to the air.

The Barbers' decision to secure a lawyer for Billy through a recommendation from the circuit court prosecutor, Franklin Dale, sent ripples through the town. Though Edward Stratton was a known legal mind and seemingly well-positioned to defend Billy, the brothers did not even send a response when Jonathan Stratton sent a messenger to offer his son's services.

Bozeman's legal circle was small, and Elijah and Moses, wary of Hill's far-reaching influence, approached Dale directly. The prosecutor, a modest, middle-aged man they had dealt with in the past and trusted for his honesty, was hesitant to involve himself in what was becoming a volatile situation—one that forced him to recuse himself from prosecuting Billy's case because of his acquaintance with the Barbers. Still, he believed every man deserved competent representation and suggested Samuel Trask, a defense lawyer from Helena.

The Barbers' decision was seen as deliberate, and the townsfolk took notice. Whispers spread through saloons and general stores, speculating on the reasons behind the rejection of Edward Stratton. For some, it was a sign of the Barbers' unwavering integrity. For others, it confirmed suspicions of a deepening rift between the Barbers and the Strattons, one that seemed to grow more irreparable with every passing day. Further yet, for some, it signaled the waning power of the men so long connected to Jon Stratton.

Trask arrived from Helena two days before the trial. Known for his meticulous attention to detail and biting cross-examinations, Trask exuded a quiet confidence that reassured Elijah. As they reviewed the case, Trask raised an eyebrow. "I'll be honest. I was surprised when I heard you didn't go to Edward Stratton for this. Surprised, but not disappointed." He glanced at Elijah, waiting for an explanation. Elijah offered none, merely nodding as Trask continued. "Your man Billy's got good character witnesses, but we're up against more than just evidence here. Hill's got long arms, and they reach deep into this town." He twisted at a wiry mustache. "The saloon shooting, while. . . justified by custom, perhaps, does not help his cause."

JT, meanwhile, worked tirelessly to rally Billy and the Barbers' supporters, riding to the smaller farms and outfits in the Valley. Ranch hands trickled into Bozeman over several days, their presence subtle but unmistakable. Kept in line by Jax upon his arrival, they didn't loiter in the saloons or boast in the streets; instead, they moved deliberately, their focus on supporting the Slash V. When Billy got word of their arrival, and saw the familiar faces of some ranch hands who gained entry to visit him, he gave a faint smile, the first in days. Maggie, arriving with Helen and the girls by train, always had a hand or two by her side. Not because she asked, but of our respect for her husband and her actions in defense of the ranch.

In stark contrast, Hill's influence seeped into the town like a slow poison. Men who weren't openly associated with the Bar T ranch appeared on street corners and in the back rows of saloons. They lingered near the courthouse, their rough exteriors and sharp eyes leaving little doubt about their purpose. Though no one could definitively tie them to Hill or Finn, their silent intimidation was not subtle—even without guns on their hips. Every glance, every muttered word, added to the growing sense of dread.

Jonathan Stratton, meanwhile, grew more haggard by the day. He rarely left his home, the strain of Hill and Finn's pressure and his own failing health carving deep lines into his face. Edward's smug indifference grated on him, but Jonathan was too weakened and detached to confront his son. Hill's visits became more frequent, each one leaving Jonathan further ensnared in their scheme, with less capability or desire to escape.

Elijah received a wire from Travis at the ranch late one evening. The message was brief but troubling:

> Mining eqpmt into valley. Camps building on old Bar
> T land abutting Circle C. Racing winter to be ready
> spring. Armed outriders.

The words hung heavy in Elijah's mind. The Bar T land bordered the Circle C, and it took little imagination to see where this was heading. Hill wasn't just content with intimidation and manipulation; he was laying the groundwork for something more permanent. Elijah knew Hill's ambitions likely extended beyond cattle—he was looking to solidify a foothold in the valley's untapped resources, no doubt planning to use the coming months to quietly build his operation while everyone else was preoccupied.

Elijah shared the wire with Moses over a late-night drink. Moses scowled as he read it, his hand tightening around the glass. "Hill's scheming for more than just pushing us out," he said, his voice low but sharp. "Mining equipment ain't cheap, and camps mean he's planning for a long haul. He's planting roots."

Elijah nodded, the weight of the message adding to the burden already on his shoulders. "And if it's mining he aims to do, those roots will spread and destroy everything in their path." He took a drink. "It's more than just a move against us. He's trying to box us in. The Circle C is the next target."

Moses leaned forward, his eyes narrowing.

"This trial's just a skirmish, Mo. The real fight's still to come. I wired back to Travis to begin the preparations."

Moses exhaled slowly, his fury tempered by Elijah's calm resolve. "Guess we'll need to be ready, then," he said, tipping his glass.

THE COURTHOUSE WAS PACKED to its limits the day the circuit judge arrived. A sea of hats and anxious faces spilled onto the muddy street, voices hushed in anticipation. Ranchers, townsfolk, and drifters gathered to watch the trials, their expressions a blend of curiosity, judgment, and trepidation. Inside, the gallery reflected the simmering divide within the town.

On one side sat the Barbers, flanked by JT, Maggie, and a contingent of loyal ranch hands. Their presence was deliberate and unified. Maggie's steady gaze anchored JT, her occasional touch on his shoulder the only thing keeping his frustration in check.

Opposite them, the back rows were filled with rough-edged men. Though unaffiliated by name with Hill or Finn, their sharp eyes and looming silence sent an unmistakable message. They were enforcers, a shadowy reminder of the unseen influence that held the town in its grip.

Amos Greaves, the rustlers' lawyer, wasted no time commanding the room. A polished outsider with a tailored suit and a voice as smooth as silk, Greaves wielded charm and venom with equal precision.

Sheriff Rob Grant was the prosecution's key witness, with Greaves relishing the opportunity to cross-examine him. He described the attacks on the Summit Valley ranch, the Crow buyers, and the cattle drive in methodical detail. Though his professionalism was evident, tension lined his face, and more than once, his gaze flicked toward Elijah, a silent acknowledgment of the injustice unfolding.

"We questioned every survivin' witness," Grant said, his tone measured. "Spoke to the Barbers, their hands, and their families. The Barber boy gave us useful information on the Crow ambush." He hesitated, the weight of his words sinking into the room. "The testimony and evidence clearly show these were targeted attacks. But with the attackers masked, and none of the bodies identified as someone known. . ." He trailed off, his frustration palpable. "It's hard to say who they were."

Greaves pounced on the hesitation. "So, Sheriff, to confirm: no one could positively identify these men as locals, or anyone with ties to the community or any business?"

Grant bit his lip, then shook his head. "A few thought they recognized one or two—out-of-work miners, maybe drifters seen around town. Desperate men."

Greaves turned to the jury, his tone thick with feigned empathy. "Desperate men. Victims of circumstance, drawn to trouble by hunger and hardship. Perhaps, in their desperation, they made poor choices—but that doesn't mean these men," he gestured to his clients, "were the culprits."

He swept the room with a practiced glance, pausing momentarily on Maggie and Helen in the gallery. His voice dripped with false sincerity. "Men moved their cattle as they've done before, making their living. And they were violently attacked. And everyone here feels for the horrors Summit Valley and the Circle C endured. No one deserves such terror. Least of which, helpless women."

Maggie stiffened, her expression hardening as her hands gripped her skirt. Helen shifted, her composure faltering briefly.

Greaves continued. "But we must ask: might the aggression of the Summit Valley ranch—men like Billy McCray, known for his temper—have invited such tragedy? The Barbers are known gunfighters are they not? Former vigilante lawmen?"

"Objection!" Dale shouted. "The Barbers are long time members of this community, running the Summit Valley Ranch, and operating a livery here in town. They have built a school and church for valley residents. And if you must mention their past, you might add that they are responsible for bringing two notorious criminals to justice, with President Grant himself declaring their actions just."

"The judge, an aging man whose tired eyes reflected the weight of the day's events, sighed heavily. "Sustained." Mister Graves, please ensure we are characterizing things accurately."

"Of course," Graves said. "My apologies to the Barbers and the fine General and President's moral judgment. However, ladies and gentlemen, it is not difficult to accept what kind of men the Barbers draw in. Not long ago, Billy McCray murdered a man in one of Bozeman's saloons. Perhaps their actions provoked unrest? Drew the ire of men in the valley?"

Franklin Dale stood. "Objection. Again! Inflammatory. A man drew on Mister McCray, he defended himself, and no charges were filed. Numerous witnesses agreed it was a fair fight."

"Sustained. Mister Greaves, please make your argument with the proper facts," the judge said lazily.

Greaves raised his hands in mock surrender, a knowing smirk playing on his lips. "Of course, Your Honor."

By this point, the trial had dragged into the late afternoon, the air in the courthouse as thick with tension as with the smell of the frontier crowd growing more fatigued by the minute. The prosecution called Elijah Barber to the stand, followed by Moses, Jax, JT, and other hands from the Summit Valley ranch. Each offered their account of the attacks—the masked men, the precision of the strikes, the brutality inflicted on their people and property. Their testimony painted a vivid picture of the chaos, but as witness after witness admitted they hadn't seen a single face clearly, the defense seized every opportunity to twist their words.

Elijah's frustration was palpable as he explained how his men knew who the attackers were despite the masks. "These weren't strangers to the area," he said firmly, his eyes locking on the jury. "They knew the valley, the ranch, our movements. Drifters don't pull off something like that. And if they do. . . it's because they had local help."

Greaves pounced. "So, Mister Barber, let me understand. You're asking this jury to convict these men based not on facts or evidence, but on your feelings? Your assumptions?"

Elijah leaned forward and glared at Greaves, then looked past him to the toughs sitting in the back. "I suppose it's hard for those who aren't experiencing it to understand the truth."

Greaves smirked, his eyes sweeping the room as if sharing a private joke with the jury. "The truth," he echoed mockingly. "And yet, for all your testimony, not one witness could identify the accused. Not one."

The jury shifted uneasily, and the judge, who had been growing more impatient with the rising tension, interrupted. "Let's move this along, gentlemen."

Moses' testimony fared no better under cross-examination, his direct and unyielding demeanor clashing with Greaves' slick veneer. Even JT, whose account of the attack on the Crow buyers was passionate and detailed, struggled to make an impact. His youth and anger were used against him, with Greaves painting him as a shaken young man—impulsive and unreliable.

The steady parade of witnesses, meant to bolster the prosecution's case, seemed only to play into Greaves' hands. Each man's inability to definitively identify the accused attackers reinforced the defense's narrative. Elijah shook his head as he realized the effort to tell their story—the truth—was unraveling under the weight of doubt and calculated manipulation.

The gallery stirred uneasily as the judge called for closing statements. The room was charged with the unspoken fear that the verdict had already been decided.

Greaves delivered his final remarks with polished ease, his voice dripping with false compassion. "We all feel deeply for the losses suffered by the Summit Valley ranch. No one here denies the horror of those attacks. But you have heard the words of the prosecution's witnesses, unable to hold up under scrutiny, and the alibis of the defendants—unchallenged by Mister Dale. This court is not here to punish nameless ghosts or to soothe the wounds of vengeance. It is here to uphold justice, and justice demands evidence. Without it, these men must walk free."

A swift verdict came: not guilty. The lack of evidence and the masked identities of the attackers sealed the rustlers' acquittal. Addressing the room, the judge first glanced at the prosecutor, then at Greaves. "The burden of proof lies with the prosecution. And while the attacks on the Summit Valley ranch and its people are undeniable, this jury found insufficient evidence to convict the accused."

The three men walked free, their smug grins taunting the Barbers. JT muttered a curse, his fists tightening at his sides. Maggie placed a calming hand on his arm, her presence keeping him from rising.

As the rustlers exited the courtroom, the judge remained seated. Clearing his throat, he signaled for order, his gavel striking once against the wood. The room fell into a tense silence as the judge turned his attention to Billy McCray.

"Now, regarding the matter of Mister Billy McCray," the judge began, adjusting his spectacles. "Ordinarily, a charge of public affray and assault would be handled by a bench hearing, with no need for a jury, and that would be the next case on my docket. I was not slated to hold court here this month, but given the passions this case has ignited, a request from influential members of this community fetched me from my usual circuit. For the good of the town and county, of course."

Elijah exchanged a sharp glance with Moses.

A murmur ran through the gallery, and the judge cleared his throat loudly. "Order," he said sharply. "Mister McCray, you stand before this court for your conduct in this matter—conduct that has now been tied to a trial in which the principal defendants were exonerated. The jury found them not guilty, and thus, we must consider your actions in that light."

Billy stood tall, jaw set, though Elijah could see the tension in his shoulders. Beside him, Samuel Trask, his lawyer, stepped forward.

"Your Honor," Trask began, his voice calm but firm, "I must object. While a ruling from the bench may be warranted in a case such as this, it is highly irregular to sentence a man based on the outcome of an separate trial. Mister McCray was acting under the belief that he was aiding law enforcement and protecting property. The fact that the rustlers were found not guilty doesn't—"

The judge held up a hand, cutting him off. "I'm well aware of how the law works, Mister Trask, but in this court, I don't see fit to rehash every scrap of testimony already laid out during the trial of the now-exonerated rustlers. The facts, as presented there, spoke plainly enough."

Trask opened his mouth to argue further, but the judge leaned forward, his gavel tapping once against the bench.

"Unless," the judge continued, "the state wishes to present additional evidence? Or perhaps you, Mister Trask, can provide compelling testimony regarding Mister McCray's character, that wasn't already discussed at length? Anything beyond the objections I already sustained during the trial?"

Silence stretched across the courtroom. The stand-in prosecutor for Dale shook his head, seemingly unsure what to do when a win was about to be handed to him. Trask hesitated, glancing toward Billy, whose face remained impassive.

"That's what I thought," the judge said. He adjusted his glasses and looked at Billy. "Given your other recent actions, Mister McCray—actions that have demonstrated a distinct lack of restraint—you're fortunate to receive the sentence I'm about to impose."

The room held its breath as the judge lifted the paper before him.

"Forty-five days in the county jail and a fine of one hundred dollars. Sentence to begin immediately."

A ripple of shock swept through the crowd, while the toughs in the back snickered. Billy's expression hardened, but he said nothing. Trask blinked, momentarily speechless, before stepping forward again.

"Your Honor," Trask protested, his tone sharpened by disbelief, "forty-five days in jail for a fight and a drawn, but not used weapon? This is beyond excessive, especially considering the circumstances."

The judge's gaze didn't waver. "The circumstances, Mister Trask, were laid bare in the rustling trial. Mister McCray took it upon himself to act as judge, jury, and nearly executioner. I won't have this town descending back into frontier justice—not while I'm on the bench. If you have further complaints, I suggest you take them to the territorial court in Helena."

Elijah's fists tightened against the table as murmurs of protest rippled through the gallery. JT muttered under his breath, his face red with barely contained fury.

The judge rapped the gavel once. "This court is adjourned."

Elijah exchanged a glance with Moses, both men reading the same realization in each other's eyes. The fix had been in from the start. The trial, the testimony, even the judge's tone—it all pointed to one conclusion: someone had pulled the right strings to make sure Billy paid a price, no matter how unjust the means.

The room erupted in shouts, anger boiling over from the Barbers' supporters and frustrated townsfolk. Elijah rose, his presence commanding as he barked at his men. "Quiet. Keep your wits."

As deputies moved to escort Billy out, he glanced back at his supporters, his expression one of defiance. He then put on a determined face as he passed the Barbers and Summit Valley hands, then locked eyes with Elijah. "Reckon the law ain't always about the truth, is it, boss?"

Elijah met his gaze, his nod conveying a promise that this wasn't the end. "It ain't over, kid. Sit tight."

The courthouse emptied, the crowd spilling onto the steps and into the street. Voices rose again, angry words and accusations flying between the Barbers' supporters and Hill's shadowy enforcers. Sheriff Grant and Deputy Whitaker moved among the crowd, hands on their guns, trying to quiet the small mob to little avail.

Elijah and Moses stood their ground as Carson Hill's polished carriage rolled up, the man himself standing on the step with a practiced air of calm authority. His voice carried over the noise, calm and commanding. "Enough!" he called, his hands raised in a gesture of peace. "There's been too much violence already. Let the law handle what it must, and let's move forward."

"He runnin' for mayor now?" Moses grumbled. "Off to a good start with judges in his pocket and law too afraid to cross him."

The crowd hesitated, their anger checked by Hill's polished demeanor, giving Grant and Whitaker the opportunity to move the opposing sides apart.

As the townsfolk dispersed, Elijah stepped toward Hill, his voice low and dangerous. "I know what you've done, and who you're doing it with. I don't know how you got to that judge, but know this: Your days in this valley are numbered."

Hill's smile didn't falter, ensuring any onlooker was none the wiser, though his eyes glittered coldly. He leaned down and murmured just loud enough for Elijah to hear, "Ah, but ye know that isn't true. Wise of ye not to use Edward for your lawyer, and to ensure Dale recused himself on account of knowing ye. . . but I'm always a step ahead. With the jobs and new prosperity I've brought, and Jon Stratton wasting away on laudanum. . . Well, I'm the establishment of Bozeman, now. But your days, Mister Barber, will come to an end swiftly should you choose not to leave on your own."

"I ain't going anywhere," Elijah growled. "You'll find me at my ranch."

"*Your* ranch?" Hill raised an eyebrow. "Does Jonathan know that? Even his son sees that he became set in his ways, and is unwilling to change, even as he slowly dies." He smiled as someone passed them. "Nevertheless. If that's where you choose to die, I can arrange that."

The two men locked eyes.

"Go ahead and try," Elijah said.

"Very well," Hill hissed. He then stood up straight, addressing the remaining townsfolk with a measured smile. "Let's not let division tear us apart. Order through the law will protect the peace and prosperity we seek. Together, we can build a future for this town and the valley, side by side."

Elijah's gaze followed Hill as the carriage rolled away. Moses joined him, his voice grim. "Rotten."

Elijah nodded. "We need train tickets for first thing. We need to get back."

"Alright," Moses said. He turned and saw Maggie and Helen gathering the family, hands hovering around them as they moved down the street. He looked back at Elijah. "We gonna make a move?"

Elijah's eyes narrowed. "I'm tired of running and chasing, Mo." He gazed down the street at the disappearing carriage. "He can come to us."

Above them, snowflakes fell, dusting the courthouse steps with the quiet promise of winter—and the coming storm.

PART FOUR

— • —

WINTER

CHURCH MEETING

— · —

T he first real snow of the season fell softly on Summit Valley, blanketing the pastures in thin white as Elijah stood on the porch of the ranch house, staring toward the Absaroka Range. The mountains were already covered, and they'd pushed cattle to the protected winter pastures that would allow grazing for the longest. They'd soon start hauling hay when the snow completely covered the range, a heavy workload, but one that Elijah wished was his only concern.

The morning was clear and crisp, the winter air biting but invigorating as Elijah leaned against the post of the front porch, buttoning his sheepskin coat. His rocking chair creaked beside him, empty, but propelled by the wag of Scout's tail. He removed his pipe from his mouth and took a deep breath of the icy air, his mind heavy with worry. The past few weeks had been tense—Hill's encroachment into Summit Valley had grown more brazen, his men ever-present on Circle C's fringes. Edward Stratton's visits to the ranch had stopped—something they would have welcomed if not for the circumstances—and Jonathan's silence from Bozeman weighed on him like a stone.

A whine from Scout interrupted Elijah's thoughts, and then the sudden rumble of a distant explosion. The sound echoed across the valley, low and menacing, followed by a plume of smoke rising against the snow-covered backdrop. His heart sank as he realized the mining outfit Hill had established near Circle C was active again. That explosion wasn't just work—it was an ongoing messaging campaign.

Scout then bounded down the steps as riders approached from the north, drawing Elijah's gaze. It was Moses, and riding beside him was a weathered man Elijah recognized as the Circle C foreman.

The horses' hooves crunched on the frosted ground as they neared. The foreman dismounted first, his breath coming in quick, visible puffs as he turned up his coat collar. "Elijah," he began, his voice strained. "It's bad."

Elijah stepped into the yard, Moses holding back a moment to loosen his saddle girth. The foreman, a lanky man named Roy Harper, had the look of someone who had aged twice as fast as his years. His coat was patched, his gloves mismatched, and his face bore the lines of too many hard winters.

"What happened, Roy?" Elijah asked, his tone calm but firm.

Roy glanced at Moses before speaking. "Hill's men pushed a herd onto Circle C's northern range—our winter pasture—and they've started building a shack right on the border. Claimed the land is theirs—with cattle, a building, and mining claims on it. And that's not all—they've got more mining equipment moving in ahead of the weather. My hands saw them digging pits, and they've brought in armed guards." He glanced toward the recent explosion. "Reckon you've heard the rest."

Moses spat. "He's gonna have an entire operation running by the time anyone can contest it in any way. Knows we ain't gonna leave the ranch, not in this weather and not with everything goin' on." He rubbed his beard. "And the Strattons sure ain't gonna contest it."

"It's worse than that," Roy continued. "Missus Collins and Miss Emily feel unsafe with them so close. That Finn fella's got armed men ridin' back and forth, blocking our routes to water and any suitable winter range with their own cattle and operations. Our beeves are penned in like they're waitin' for the ax."

Elijah rubbed his beard, the news compounding the unease he'd already felt. It put a pit in his stomach after he promised James to watch over his family and ranch.

"Move your herd to the Slash V's winter ranges," he instructed. Talk to Travis about where but tell him it's my top priority. We'll supply you some punchers. Get any hay you've stored and bring it here. And tell the Collins family they're to pack what they need and come to Summit Valley. We've got beds, and I won't have them left defenseless."

Roy nodded, his gratitude evident. "Thank you, Elijah. I didn't know where else to turn."

Elijah nodded. "Of course." He pointed toward the bunkhouse. "Just saw Travis and Jax head in there to chat with the hands. You can likely catch them both and a few volunteers while you're at it."

Roy touched the brim of his hat, then departed to carry out Elijah's instructions. Moses crossed his arms. "That leaves the Circle C land empty. You think Hill's just gonna let it be?"

"I sure don't," Elijah replied. "But he moves in fully and that puts him right on our flank." He straightened, his jaw set with resolve as he realized his brother noticed his use of military speak. "I need your help getting a meeting together. Summit Valley needs to decide what we're going to do—as a community." Scout appeared at his side, and he scratched the dog behind the ears as he puffed on his pipe.

Moses nodded, already forming a list of names in his head. "I'll spread the word. Meeting at the church?"

Elijah nodded. "Tomorrow night."

THE SUMMIT VALLEY CHURCH stood as a sentinel against the encroaching night, its snow-covered steeple stark against the cold glow of the moonlight. Inside, a wood stove and the tightly packed crowd kept the sanctuary warm, but heavy with unease among the murmurs in the torchlight. The pews were packed with nervous Summit Valley hands and workers, farming neighbors, representatives from some of the smaller ranches, and displaced Circle C families.

Elijah stood at the front of the room, Moses at his side. Near the door, Reverend Harris held his Bible and greeted people with a brave face, as if it was any other church gathering. JT sat with Maggie, Helen, and the girls in the second pew, flanked by the Collins family. Emily Collins, her face pale and drawn, sat close to JT, her small hand occasionally brushing his as if seeking reassurance. JT's broad shoulders and calm presence seemed to provide the comfort she sought.

Roy Harper, the Circle C foreman, stood near the back with the reverend, his hat clutched in his hands. He nodded toward Elijah, a silent gesture of trust and respect.

Elijah cleared his throat, and the congregation quieted. He leaned on the lectern, his voice calm but resolute. "You all know why we're here. Hill's men are tightening the noose, and now they've taken Circle C's northern range. They've claimed it, thrown down mining stakes, and sent armed men to back it up. Those explosions we hear aren't just work—they're messages. Hill's showing us what he can do and daring us to stop him."

A ripple of murmurs passed through the pews. Emily's mother clutched her daughter's hand, her eyes brimming with fear.

Moses stepped forward, his deep voice cutting through the whispers. "We've got two choices, folks," he said plainly. "We either stand and fight, or we pack up and leave. Give Hill what he wants and walk away with our tails tucked—figure out a way to start elsewhere together."

The room erupted into heated debate. Voices overlapped, the congregation splintering into factions. A rancher near the front, his face reddened with frustration, stood abruptly. "This is all the Barbers' fault! You and that damn Billy Irons. If you hadn't pushed back against Hill so hard, he wouldn't be squeezing us like this!"

Another rancher, a wiry man from a modest spread, stood up, his voice calm but resolute. "I don't agree. The Barbers stood up when no one else would. If we don't fight now, what's stopping Hill from taking everything we've got left? Next year, it'll be my ranch, then yours." He looked around for support. "I'm too old to uproot my family, drive a herd to God knows where, and re-build."

"Easy for you to say," the first rancher shot back. "My family can't afford to fight. We've got no reserves, no help. What do you expect us to do?"

"What about the law?" someone shouted.

Elijah shook his head. "Not enough law in this county. A sheriff and a few deputies spread wide. And the unfortunate nature of things, is that—publicly at least—Hill is playing just on the right side of law and custom."

Reverend Harris raised a hand, his voice gentle but firm. "Brothers and sisters, this is no time for division. The Good Book tells us, 'Blessed are the peacemakers, for they shall be called the children of God.'" He paused, his kind eyes scanning the room. "But it also says, 'Resist the devil, and he will flee from you.' We must decide what peace means to us—and what resistance we're willing to give."

The room quieted, his words sinking in like a balm over an open wound. Maggie stood, her voice clear and cutting through the stillness. "And where will we go if we leave? What will we have left? Carson

Hill won't stop at Circle C or Summit Valley. He'll take what he wants, and he won't leave anything for any of us if nobody will resist him."

Roy Harper spoke up. "Missus Barber is right. And might I add, has already done more 'n near all of us to resist them." He nodded to her. "If we don't stand up to him now, we'll lose more than just land. We'll lose everything that makes this valley prosperous for all of us."

Before anyone else could respond, a voice shouted from outside, one of the hands in a series of those watching the ranch perimeter and grounds. "Riders comin' in boss."

There was silence in the church, and Elijah's heartbeat quickened. "How many, Gus?"

"Just two, boss." More silence, then, "It's Finn MacDonald... And he's got Edward Stratton with him."

A gasp went through the church, and Elijah and Moses exchanged a look. "Let 'em in, Gus."

The church door swung open with a loud creak, letting in a gust of icy wind and snowflakes. Heads turned as Finn strode in, his spurred boots striking the wooden floor like hammer blows. Behind him was Edward Stratton, his face sullen and drawn. The sight of Edward sent a ripple of confusion and anger through the room. Few had seen him in weeks, and his presence beside Finn spoke volumes.

Finn's grin was sharp as a blade as he surveyed the congregation. "Evenin', folks," he drawled, his brogue curling around the words. "Hope we're not interruptin' yer little meetin', but we heard ye were all in one place and wanted to chat."

Elijah stepped forward, his fists clenched at his sides. "What do you want, Finn?"

Finn removed his hat and shook off the snow, his pale eyes glittering with malice. "Just to pass a message from Mister Hill. He's a generous man, ye see. Wants to offer ye all a way out. Jobs in town, jobs in the mines, homes for your families, wages for hands ready to ride for the biggest ranch in the west. All ye have to do is stop the pushback and step out of his way. Recognize the situation for what it is. The Valley is Mister Hill's now. Includin' this ranch, soon."

A sharp intake of breath echoed through the room, followed by muttered curses. Finn showed his teeth. "Or," he continued, his tone darkening, "you can stay here, freeze through the winter, and see how long your herds last when there's no water or grass left for them." He looked around the room. "And those job offers will be gone if ye wait."

Edward stepped forward hesitantly, his voice low and unsteady. "I hate to admit it, but Summit Valley's been outmaneuvered. Mister Hill's offer might be the best option for some of you." He glanced around the room. "For all of us."

The room erupted into outrage. "Traitor!" someone shouted. "You're in Hill's pocket!"

Edward raised his hands defensively. "I'm being pragmatic! This isn't about loyalty—it's about survival." Elijah's eyes narrowed as he watched the man lie. "I simply want what's best for the longevity of this ranch, and those who helped my father grow it. But with his health fading, and Elijah Barber's questionable leadership. . ." There were groans and murmurs through the crowd as people looked at Elijah for a reaction. "Well, this is the situation we find ourselves in."

"That's enough out of you," Elijah said. The room fell silent as he turned his piercing gaze on Finn. "You tell your boss this land doesn't belong to him." He turned and stared at Edward. "And you. . . you tell your father I'm continuing to run this ranch until he tells me otherwise. Unless and until then, I ain't leavin'."

Finn pulled his hat back on and tapped the brim. "Suit yourself. But Mister Hill ain't the patient type. Ye've got three days to reconsider. You're a military man, Mister Barber. You know it's no good to move men and material in winter. We'd like to get this wrapped up before conditions deteriorate further. After that. . ." He let the threat hang in the air, then turned and strode out.

Edward remained, and eyes fell on him. "I really think that we—"

"You ain't part of any *we*, you sorry excuse for a man," Moses said.

Edward cocked his head. "Pardon?"

"You heard him," Elijah said. "Maybe we ought to tell everyone how deep in it you are with Hill? I bit my tongue long enough, not wanting to spur panic here while we deal with it, but you've forced our hand." Elijah turned to the group in the pews. "You all know what Carson Hill has done, and what we suspect he and Finn MacDonald were behind." Elijah composed himself. "But Edward here has been scheming with them to take the land right out from under his father's nose, getting rich while he's at it, without any regard for the land or its people. He was the one ordered the personal attacks here on the headquarters, my boy, and our wives and children. The one who ensured everything came out making Billy, Moses, and I look like the instigators."

The crowd gasped, with people whispering about having suspected it, or wondering if it was true.

Edward feigned disbelief at the accusation and opened his mouth to speak, but Elijah cut him off.

"You go on with your pal Finn. Ensure that bed you've made is comfortable and done up well. You're about to have to lie in it."

Edward bit his tongue, staring at Elijah and Moses for a moment, then straightened his coat collar and departed. The door slammed shut, and the church erupted once more. The arguments were fiercer now, the community splintering under the weight of fear and desperation. Some shouted that they should fight, while others, shaken by Finn's words, began voicing their doubts.

Maggie stood again, her voice rising above the din. "Friends! Please listen!" The room stilled as she fixed the congregation with a fiery gaze. "We've stood together through droughts, floods, and winters so cold they nearly broke us. Are we really going to let a man like Carson Hill tear us apart?"

Elijah stepped forward, his voice steady. "This is your decision. I won't force anyone into a fight they don't believe in. You're free to leave and make your own decision, and we'll wish you well and set you up as best we can. But if you stay, we will stand together. We fight for what's ours, and we fight to protect each other."

Travis, Jax, and all the Summit Valley Hands all stood, nodding to Elijah and Moses.

JT stood, his voice unwavering. "We're not running. Not now, not ever."

Emily glanced up at JT, her eyes wide with admiration and a glimmer of hope. She reached for his hand, and this time, he let her hold it.

The rancher who had rebuked Elijah shuffled out silently with his family, and two of the smaller spread ranchers and a farmer stood and moved to the door. One of them turned.

"I don't wish any of ya' bad and won't stand in your way. But I can't afford a fight." He lowered his head and departed.

"Alright." Elijah's gaze swept the room, meeting the eyes of all those remaining. "We'd better get ready."

MAKE READY

—·—

T he sun rose sluggishly over Summit Valley, casting a pale light
across the snow-blanketed landscape. Frost clung to every blade
of grass and fencepost, and the icy air sharpened the distant echoes
of ranch activity. Elijah stood on the porch of the main house, his
shoulders hunched against the cold, his sheepskin coat pulled tight.
His gaze drifted across the ranch, scanning for movement beyond the
bunkhouses and outbuildings, though his mind was elsewhere.

The past two days had been a blur of planning and tension. The
ranch hands worked tirelessly, but Elijah knew the odds were steep and
was deciding to send the women and children away with the bulk of
the hands to watch over them. No number of trenches or barricades
would match Hill's resources—or his ruthlessness.

Scout's tail thumped against the porch, the dog seated loyally beside Elijah's rocking chair. He puffed on his pipe, staring toward the
distant line of trees marking the ranch's northern border. Somewhere
beyond that horizon, Hill's forces were massing, preparing for whatever devilry they had planned. Elijah felt like a wartime general, wishing he knew what he was up against, so he might better prepare. He
thought of his old friend Matt Hobbs, who had provided just such
intelligence to a general during the war.

But even without that knowledge, Elijah could read the field. Summit Valley's buildings made use of the terrain, and nearby mountains and waterways, to leave only one likely route Hill's men could take. He didn't need to know the exact shape of the coming attack—he only needed to know how men like Hill fought. From the war and years spent matching wits with outlaws and raiders, Elijah had learned one truth: whatever was brought to bear first was never the whole of it. A good commander always held something back—a reserve force, a hidden weapon, or a trick just waiting to be played. Honest men did it, dishonest men did it. And he knew Hill, a man who trafficked in both power and deception, had more than one surprise waiting for them. But what Hill didn't know was that Elijah had learned from the best—and from the worst. And he had a few cards of his own.

The creak of the bunkhouse door drew Elijah's attention. JT, Travis, and Jax emerged, climbing onto their horses. All three men wore the solemn expressions of those shouldering burdens they'd never asked for. Elijah watched his son's movements closely, his chest tightening with a mix of pride and apprehension. The young man had more or less become number three after Travis and Jax, an unspoken acknowledgment that not a single hand seemed to oppose or hold ill will about.

Moses appeared next, rubbing his hands together as he approached the porch. "Looks like everyone's movin' already," he said, his breath misting in the frigid air. "Travis has the hands putting finishing touches on things before we have 'em slope out."

Elijah nodded. "Good. Keep them focused."

Moses kicked at the snowy ground. "You been out here long?"

"Long enough," Elijah replied, his gaze never leaving the horizon. "Was just thinking about Matt Hobbs, wishing we had him getting intelligence for us."

Moses chuckled. "Matt Hobbs," he said wistfully. He blew warm air into his hands. "There's a fella who would be helpful right now."

Elijah nodded. "Yes, he would, God rest his soul. What we could have, though, is a Billy McCray. Could sure use that, I reckon."

Moses leaned against the porch rail, glancing toward the outbuildings where women loaded wagons and children clung to their mother's skirts. He then looked up at the low gray snow clouds obscuring the mountains from view. "Storm's gonna come whether we're ready or not. Question is, how many'll make it through."

The words hung heavy in the air. Elijah finally turned to face his brother, his expression hard but not unkind. "Let it come. We'll make it through."

―――

THE RANCH YARD bustled with activity as women and children prepared to leave. Wagons groaned under the weight of supplies as their wheels crunched the frosty ground. Maggie and Helen directed the younger women, ensuring food, blankets, and provisions were accounted for. Despite their brisk movements and focused expressions, the weight of fear was palpable.

Maggie paused by one wagon, brushing a strand of hair from her face. She looked up as Elijah approached, her lips pressed into a thin line. "You sure about this?" she asked, her voice steady but strained.

Elijah placed a hand on her shoulder, his rough fingers brushing the fabric of her coat. "It's the only way. If Hill's comin', I can't risk you and the girls being here."

She searched his face, her eyes glistening. "You always think you can carry everything on your own, Elijah. But this. . . Folks are worried, wondering if you, Moses, and a couple hands can protect everyone's future."

He nodded, pulling her close. "I know they are. But this is the best way to keep you all safe. That's what matters."

The sound of approaching hooves drew their attention. Roy Harper rode into the yard, a farm wagon rumbling behind him, a canvas tarp covering its contents. Roy touched the brim of his hat and exchanged a knowing glance with Elijah as he dismounted.

Maggie nodded towards the wagon. "What's that Roy's brought? We have plenty of supplies for everyone leaving."

Elijah's eyes briefly met Roy's again before responding. "Just some things Hill's men left on Circle C land that we might make use of." He looked at the wagon once more, then turned to Maggie. "Everything will be fine," he said. He pulled her close. "You'll all be safe."

They stood like that for a moment, the chaos of the yard fading into the background. Finally, Maggie pulled away, composing herself. "You've always brought us through, Elijah. Just. . ." She paused, and a tear rolled down her face. "I fear you're willing to sacrifice yourself for all these people. I respect it, but I fear it."

He pulled her tight once more and kissed the top of her head. "I'll always come back to you," he said softly. Molly and Bridget appeared at their side, and Elijah kneeled and pulled them in as well. "I'll always come back to all of you." He stood and looked at Maggie. "We need you to get going now with plenty of daylight left." He stepped forward and kissed her, then stooped and kissed each girl.

Nearby, Moses crouched to hug his daughters, their small arms encircling his neck. Helen stood nearby, her expression stoic, though her eyes betrayed her worry. "You watch yourself, Moses Barber," she said firmly. "You be in one piece next time I see you, you hear me?"

Moses grinned, ruffling his youngest daughter's hair as he stood. "Wouldn't dream of doin' otherwise, darlin'."

At the wagons, JT helped Emily Collins climb into one, her hand lingering on his as she settled into her seat. The young woman's face was pale, her wide eyes scanning the yard. JT leaned, his voice low. "You'll be all right, Emily. You and your ma. I'll make sure of it."

She looked up at him, her expression softening. "You be careful, JT."

"I will," he said, straightening as the wagon shifted under the weight of another load. "I'll be riding just behind you all." He glanced toward his father, who was watching from a few yards away. Their eyes met, and JT gave a small nod before turning back to the wagon and helping Maggie, Helen, and the girls up.

As the wagons rolled out, the weight of the moment settled over the ranch like a shroud. Elijah stood beside Moses, his hands on his hips as he watched his family disappear into the distance. "That's hard," he muttered.

Moses nodded. Then, the gentle clatter of a horse-drawn buggy rolling across the snowy path caught their attention. Reverend Harris, guiding the reins with steady hands, arrived with his wife and daughter, covered by a blanket, sitting close. The Reverend's solemn yet hopeful gaze met Elijah's as he reined the buggy to a stop.

"Elijah, Moses, we're praying for swift justice and a speedy return," Reverend Harris said, his voice as calm and authoritative as a Sunday sermon. "My daughter is eager to get back to teaching the young minds of this community, and I yearn to preach in front of all of you."

"Thank you, Reverend. We're just hoping there's something to come back to," Elijah responded.

"Go with God," Reverend Harris intoned, lifting a hand in blessing. "He knows the righteousness of your cause."

Moses frowned. "Not sure how God feels about what might happen here."

"'Blessed are the peacemakers,'" Reverend Harris quoted softly, his eyes understanding the depths of their predicament, "'for they shall be called children of God.' Matthew 5:9. Remember, the Lord's paths are manifold, and He grants strength to the weary who fight in a noble cause for those they protect."

Moses nodded, the words giving him a moment's respite from his doubts, and Elijah felt a slight ease in his burden, comforted by the invocation of divine support.

They watched the reverend depart and saw him tip his hat to JT, approaching from the other direction. "Give us a moment, will ya, Mo?"

"Sure thing," Moses said, stepping away to confer with Travis and Jax.

JT approached, adjusting his gun belt as he led his mount. His movements were precise and calm, but Elijah could see the tension in his son's shoulders. As JT stopped a few feet away, Elijah gestured toward the hitching post.

"Leave him there for now," Elijah said. "We need to talk."

JT tied off his reins and stepped closer. Elijah clapped him on the shoulder, his grip firm but affectionate. "You've done good work these past few days," he said. "Folks are talking about you. Saying you've stepped up in ways they didn't expect. Beyond your years."

JT shifted, brushing snow off his coat. "Just doin' what needs doin'," he replied.

"Well, it's been a great help." Elijah scratched his beard. "Thank you."

JT bit his lip, as uncomfortable with receiving praise as his father was giving it. "You're welcome, pa."

Elijah nodded, his eyes scanning the horizon before settling back on his son. "And you know where you're headed?"

"Yessir," JT said. "I know the line shacks you're talkin' about. They'll be safe there. Cramped. But warm and safe."

Elijah studied him for a moment. "Good." He paused, rubbing the back of his neck as he searched for the right words. "Look, I hate to put all this on you, JT. You've had to grow up faster than most boys your age. Faster than I would've wanted for you."

JT shrugged, but his voice was quieter when he spoke. "Ain't much choice, is there? Not with everything that's happened."

"No," Elijah admitted. "Not with everything that's happened." But you've handled it. You're stronger for it. That doesn't mean I don't wish things had been different. . . That you hadn't needed to face these things like I did."

JT glanced away. "I'm fine, Pa. I've learned to handle it."

Elijah caught the flicker of emotion on his son's face, the brief crack in his brave front. He stepped closer, lowering his voice. "You don't have to pretend with me, son. I know it's been hard. I know what you've been through—what you've had to carry. It ain't fair." Elijah looked away, squinting. "I did a lot of 'did what I had to' self-talk during and after the war and. . . well, it's hard ain't it?"

JT hesitated, then met his father's gaze. "I just don't want to let anyone down. You, Uncle Mo, everyone counting on us."

Elijah placed a hand on his son's shoulder, squeezing gently. "You won't, JT. You've got your mother's heart and her way of bringing folks together, which counts for more than anything you've learned from me. You've got more to you than I ever did at your age. I know you'll do what needs to be done, and you'll do it right."

JT nodded, his expression firming, though the weight of Elijah's words lingered in his eyes. "And you?" he asked. "You'll hold things here?"

"We'll hold," Elijah said with certainty. He glanced toward the departing wagons, the tracks already filling with snow. "And you know what you're doin' once you get there?"

JT didn't hesitate. "I know."

Elijah studied him for a long moment, then nodded. "Good. I trust you, son. Now go. Get 'em there safe, and I'll see you again soon."

Before JT could move, a brindle and black shape trotted up from behind the barn, stopping at Elijah's side. Scout sniffed the air, then looked up at Elijah expectantly, his thick coat dusted with snow.

Elijah smirked. "And you," he said, scratching behind the dog's ears. "You go with him."

Scout's ears perked, and he turned his head toward JT, waiting for a command.

"C'mon, boy. You brought me back last time."

"And he'll do it again," Elijah answered.

JT stepped back and mounted his horse, settling into the saddle with practiced ease. He tipped his hat to Elijah, then rode off with a whistle to Scout, his silhouette blending into the procession of wagons. Elijah watched him go, the tension in his chest both lighter and heavier at the same time.

When JT was out of sight, Moses reappeared, his expression questioning. "He ready?"

Elijah nodded, his jaw set. "He's ready."

Moses glanced toward the horizon. "And you?"

Elijah's eyes narrowed as he turned back toward the ranch yard. "We'll find out soon enough."

THE HOUSE WAS QUIET, save for the occasional creak of the floorboards and the faint hum of wind against the shutters. Elijah and Moses sat in the front room, the fire crackling low in the hearth. The remnants of a simple but hearty meal lingered on the table—bread, beans, and dried beef. Travis and Jax had eaten with them earlier, the four men sharing a rare moment of camaraderie before retreating to their separate posts. Travis and Jax, now in the bunkhouse, insisted they would sleep lightly and be ready if needed.

Elijah and Moses had remained in the main house, partly to monitor the heart of the ranch and partly to allow for some solitude. Neither man had much appetite, but the quiet meal had steadied their nerves for what lay ahead. Still wearing their guns, the brothers sat across from each other, steaming cups of coffee in their hands and rifles propped within arm's reach of every door. Outside, carefully placed weapons dotted the yard—guns leaning against fence posts and trees, silent sentinels of the impending battle.

Elijah leaned back in his chair, puffing on his pipe. Smoke curled above his head, mixing with the firelight that danced on the log walls. His eyes were fixed on the flames, but his thoughts were far away. Moses sat forward, elbows on his knees, his own coffee untouched.

"You think Finn will come in with men, guns blazing or with a final threat?" Moses asked, breaking the silence. His voice was low, almost a whisper, as if speaking too loudly might bring the fight to their doorstep early.

Elijah exhaled a slow stream of smoke, his expression unreadable. "Reckon he'll put on a show for his folks but venture we're ready to chat after all his eyes saw folks riding away today. At least I hope so."

Moses nodded, his lips pressing into a thin line. "Reckon we've seen enough men like him to know how they operate."

Elijah shifted his gaze to his brother, his eyes softening. "Too many," he whispered. "Seems like we've spent more time fighting men like him than we have living."

Moses leaned back, his shoulders sagging. "Ain't that the truth. Thought maybe this would finally be different. That we could hang up the badges, put the guns away for good." He shook his head. "Guess it was for a while, but trouble follows men like us."

Elijah gave a small, bitter laugh. "I think about Talbot a lot in times like this."

Moses nodded. "Ain't that the truth."

Elijah continued. "I reckon he'd be as likely to say it's because we were too stubborn to stay away from it, as he would to say we're put in these positions to help folks and do some right."

A silence fell between them, heavy and contemplative. After a moment, Moses glanced toward the mantle, where a framed picture of the Barber family rested. His gaze lingered on JT, the young man's confident grin frozen in time. "We've been lucky men, brother. Two fine families. More comfort and security than we ever knew growing up, and families with secure futures." He took a drink of coffee, and a dark look came to his face. "Until lately, leastways."

Elijah looked at his brother, acknowledging him, but unsure of what to say.

Moses looked back at the photograph and pointed. "That boy of yours—he's the best of you and Maggie, and that's a helluva combination."

Elijah nodded. "He'll be a better man than me because of her, that's for sure. Too strong for his own good sometimes, but he's got that fire in him, like his ma. Wants to fix things, make 'em right. But this. . . this ain't the way I wanted him to grow up."

Moses sipped his coffee, his brow furrowing. "Ain't much choice, is there? World don't wait for boys to grow up when trouble comes knocking."

Elijah stared into the fire, his jaw tightening. "No, it doesn't. But I need you to promise me something, Mo."

Moses raised an eyebrow, setting his cup down. "What's that?"

Elijah turned to face him fully, his voice low and steady. "If something happens to me tomorrow—if I don't walk away from this—I need you to look after JT. And I don't just mean keep him alive. I mean keep him whole. JT'll want revenge. I need you to make sure he doesn't lose himself."

Moses's expression hardened. "You're talkin' like you've already made up your mind to die, Eli. I don't like it."

"It's not about what I want," Elijah said firmly. "It's about what needs doing. Hill and Edward need to pay for everything they've done. But if it comes down to it, I won't let this ranch or these people pay the price. You know that. But if Hill does win. . .I don't need my boy losing himself to boot."

Moses leaned forward, his voice sharp. "Damn it, Elijah, you're walkin' outta this just like the rest of us, just like we always have. You've gone and tried to get yourself killed for the greater good too many times, yet nary with a scratch. But you got a family now. So if you wanna be a hero, you go on and make sure you're a living one. Don't make me believe otherwise."

Elijah met his brother's gaze, his eyes unwavering.

Moses sighed heavily, rubbing a hand over his face. "Alright. But you damn well better not put me in a position to make good on it."

Elijah gave a faint smile, the tension in his face easing. "I'll do my best."

The brothers fell silent again, the crackling fire filling the space between them. After a long pause, Moses chuckled. "Speakin' of Talbot. You remember when we served paper in that boarding house on damn near our first day as deputy marshals? I bet you didn't think you were gonna get a face full of buckshot through a door."

Elijah smirked, shaking his head. "No, I sure didn't." He touched the scar on his face. "And I'd be dead sure enough had Talbot not realized we shouldn't be off gallivanting as lawmen without some proper guidance."

Moses laughed, the sound warm and familiar in the quiet room. "We always did have a knack for surviving when we shouldn't."

Elijah's smile faded, his gaze returning to the fire. "Let's hope that knack holds up one more time. It usually came with a Talbot, or a Matt Hobbs showing up to help save the day, though."

Moses reached for his coffee, his expression serious again. "It'll hold. And if it don't, we'll make sure Hill knows what it costs to take Summit Valley."

Elijah nodded. "For James. For Henry. For everyone who's sacrificed to make this place what it is. We owe them that much."

Moses raised his cup in a solemn toast. "And to make sure it's here for the ones who come after."

Elijah clinked his pipe against the tin mug, the sound small but resonant. "To that."

The two brothers sat together as the fire burned low, the weight of the night pressing down on them. Outside, the icy wind howled through the trees, a harbinger of the storm to come. But inside the house was resolve—and a promise that no matter what happened, the Barbers would stand.

TIME'S UP

— · —

E lijah woke with a start, his neck stiff from the chair he'd slumped in, the fire now a pile of dead embers. For a moment, he forgot where he was, the faint sound of wind against the shutters lulling him into a fleeting sense of calm. Then, reality settled in like the weight of an anvil on his chest. Today, the storm would come.

He rubbed his eyes and shuffled toward the kitchen, grabbing a log for the fire. The familiar rituals—stoking the flames, grinding coffee, heating the kettle—settled him, though the heavy silence of the house pressed in around him.

Moses emerged not long after, yawning and tugging on his boots. He grinned when he spotted Elijah at the stove. "Some things never change. You always wake early on days like this."

Elijah poured two cups of coffee, setting one on the table before grabbing a plate of leftover bacon from the counter. "Somebody's gotta make sure there's coffee ready."

Moses sat. "Well, if today's gonna end the way I fear it could, at least we'll go into it with warm bellies."

They ate in silence, each man lost in his own thoughts. Elijah's gaze drifted to the rifles leaning by the door and the shotgun resting against the far wall. The quiet was almost peaceful, but beneath it churned a tension that neither brother needed to name.

When the plates were empty and the coffee drained, Elijah stood. "Let's take some to Travis and Jax."

The snow crunched under their boots as they crossed the yard, their breath visible in the sharp morning air. Elijah followed the thin line of smoke coming from the bunkhouse up to see the first rays of sunlight creep over the Absaroka Range, painting the snow-covered valley in hues of gold and orange.

The bunkhouse door creaked open, and Jax emerged, rubbing his hands together against the cold. "Mornin'," he said, his voice low but steady.

"Got coffee and bacon," Elijah said, handing over the bundle. "Help you wake up."

Travis appeared next, his rifle slung over his shoulder. "Was hard to sleep much with the way things are."

Moses nodded, glancing toward the distant tree line. "No sign of movement yet."

"I'm sure he won't leave us to wait," Travis replied.

The four men stood together for a moment, sipping coffee in the crisp dawn air. Elijah glanced toward the horizon, his mind running over every scenario. The waiting was always the hardest part.

BY MID-MORNING, the men had settled on the porch of the main house. Elijah leaned against the rail, puffing his pipe while Moses sat nearby, sharpening his knife. Travis and Jax took positions on either side of the yard, their rifles close at hand.

The distant clomp and crunch of hooves on the snowy trail broke the quiet. Elijah straightened, his hands moving to his hips, where he cocked his revolvers. He could see them now—riders, perhaps half a dozen, moving with purpose.

"Here they come," Moses muttered, standing and stepping to Elijah's side.

"I count six," Travis called from his post.

"Doubt that's all," Moses muttered.

The riders came into view, they and their horses' breath visible in the cold air. At the front was Finn MacDonald, his wide-brimmed hat casting a shadow over his face. Edward Stratton rode beside him, pale and stiff in the saddle, flanked by armed men.

They stopped at the edge of the yard. Finn gave an exaggerated sigh, dusting snow from his coat. "Well, this is a sight," he said, his voice carrying easily in the stillness. "Just the four of ye."

Elijah stepped down from the porch, his expression hard.

Finn smiled, though it didn't reach his eyes. "I see ye sent yer women and children away. Smart move. Looks like ye sent most of yer hands, too. That leaves..." He glanced toward the porch, where Moses stood with his arms crossed. "Yer brother 'a course. And ye always need yer foreman and his number two at yer side. That's good sense, surrendering. Let's talk terms."

Elijah didn't respond, his gaze steady.

"Not a negotiator, eh Barber?" Finn chuckled. "I'll make it easy for ye. We need foremen—good ones. And you, Mister Carrington, well, you'd be perfect. Ye could keep these operations running smooth as silk, under Mister Hill's ownership that is. Better to work with us than starve out here tryin' to hold on to something ye can't."

Travis glared at the man as he pulled out the makings for a cigarette. "I wouldn't work for you or your boss if y'all were the last men hiring." He licked the paper and rolled it. "Or if you were paying all the money in the world."

Finn shook his head. "Enjoy that smoke. Might be your last."

Travis lit a match and puffed. "I intend to," Travis replied coldly.

Finn then looked to Jax. "How about you, negro? Smarter 'n him are ye?"

Jax stood straight, his head held high. "I ain't been nobody's negro in quite some time, 'n I fought to be free once, I'll do it again."

Hill's grin faded. "That's too bad."

"No offer for us?" Moses asked sardonically.

"Aye, no offer for the Barbers," Finn replied. "Other 'n lettin' you out of this country wi your hides, and those of your loved ones, intact if you don't force this to bloodshed." He studied Elijah for a moment, watching for a reaction, before looking back at Moses. "What say ye to that?"

Moses squinted into the sun, studying the riders, then shook his head. "Nothin' to say, just deciding which one of ya I'll shoot first if that's what you want."

I thought you might be stubborn, but I didn't expect foolish," Finn said, clearly agitated. He glanced at Edward, who looked visibly uncomfortable. "Ye know, I had to bring him with me. Couldn't have him slippin' away if things went bad. He's the one who made a mess of all this, after all, but I suppose it's come out to our favor."

Edward's face paled further. "I didn't—" he started, but Finn cut him off with a sharp look.

Elijah's gaze shifted to Edward. "This whole time, you've been hiding behind Hill. You didn't want to do the dirty work but wanted the results. No more hiding, Edward. You'll get what's coming to you."

Edward flinched, his shoulders hunching as if trying to disappear.

Finn sighed theatrically. "Aye, so you do still speak, eh Barber? Well, I thought we could keep this civil. But since you insist. . ." He nodded to one of his men, who turned and whistled sharply.

From behind a nearby hill, a rider emerged, leading another man whose hands were bound in front of him. Even at a distance, Elijah recognized Billy. His clothes were filthy and ill-suited to the weather, and his face bruised, but he was upright and walking.

Moses, Travis, and Jax all exchanged looks, but Elijah stared straight ahead at Finn, fighting not to react to the surprise and not knowing Finn's play.

Finn gestured toward Billy. "There he is. Can't say I never did anything for ye. I had to bust him out the county jail. Killed a couple deputies while we were at it. Left plenty 'a evidence pointing to yer boys having busted out one of your own. Sheriff'll be coming for you soon enough, so think twice about what you do next. Take yer man, go find yer families, and never return. Ye've no other way no, Barber."

Elijah's hands twitched at his sides, but he forced himself to stay still. His mind raced, searching for a way out of the noose tightening around them. He glanced at Moses, who gave the faintest shake of his head—a silent reminder to keep calm.

Finn smiled again. "So here's the deal. Ye surrender right here, and I let yer man live. No bloodshed." He turned to Billy. "What say ye to that, Billy Irons?"

Billy spat, glaring at his captor with disdain. "I say you're fixin' to bite off more than you can chew, and I can't wait to see it."

Finn laughed and turned to Elijah. "He's got a smart mouth to the end. Fight me on this, Barber, and. . ." He shrugged. "Well, I think you probably know I got more men waitin' beyond that rise, and you've just got the four of you." He shook his head. "Did I say it was smart to send all your hands away with the womenfolk?" He chuckled. "Smart for me, I guess. Nobody here to fight and will lend credit to my claim that they were off driving all the Slash V cattle we've recently found encroaching on our grazing land." He gave a sinister smile, happy he'd boxed the Barbers in on all sides.

The silence stretched, every second heavy. Elijah's fingers brushed his holster, his heartbeat thundering in his ears. "I reckon we're in a real bad way then," he said. He looked around the group, then locked eyes with Finn. "So, I'm surprised you'd ride right out front, ready to die before we do if you've got it all figured out."

Finn sneered, then his voice cut through the stillness. "You don't know when to quit, do you? Time's up."

He nodded to a rider who had moved behind Billy, and the man pulled a pistol, cocking it as he aimed, but Elijah was faster. His shot rang out, knocking the outlaw from his horse. The sudden crack of gunfire shattered the moment, and chaos erupted.

Billy seized the opportunity, yanking on the rope that bound him and pulling the man on the other end from the saddle. He twisted the rope around the man's neck, choking him as he reached for the revolver at the man's hip. The weapon came free, and Billy fired, hitting another of Finn's men in the chest.

Sporadic shooting broke out across the yard as Billy stumbled to his feet. Elijah, Moses, and Travis were returning fire as Billy ran toward Jax, who was already moving with a knife to cut him free.

Billy dove behind a barrel with Jax. "Happy to see me?"

Jax shook his head as he pulled Billy to cover. "Every time I hang out with you, there's shooting." He then handed Billy his second revolver. "Better in your hands than mine," Jax said.

A bullet smacked into the barrel and Billy flinched, then popped out and downed another man. "We got a plan? There was a whole mess of hired guns ridin' with them."

Before Jax could answer, Finn turned in his saddle, yelling something inaudible.

"Better cover your ears," Jax said to Billy.

Riders charged over the hill, twenty by Elijah's count.

Elijah returned fire as he sought cover, shouting over the pounding hooves. "Travis! Now!"

Taking a final drag from his cigarette, Travis flicked it toward a fuse connected to hidden charges—Carson Hill's repurposed mining supplies that Roy Harper and his hands had requisitioned. The cigarette end glowed as it contacted the fuse, igniting it with a sizzle.

Moments later, the ground beneath the charging riders erupted. A massive explosion threw men and horses into the air, their figures silhouetted against a flash of fire and smoke. The shockwave rolled through the yard, sending debris flying and knocking those closest to the blast off their feet.

As the dust settled and a brief, stunned silence fell over the yard, the sharp cracks of rifle fire resumed. Muzzle flashes lit up the nearby tree line, and Hill's men jerked in their saddles, some toppling like rag dolls before they could react. A racket of gunfire erupted as hidden men poured volleys into the ranks of reinforcements.

The outlaws wheeled in confusion, some pulling up their horses, others returning fire toward the hills. The advantage of surprise, and the elevated position of the hidden defenders, was immediately clear. Then, the collective battle cry of men, the likes Elijah hadn't heard from the war, sang out, and Slash V, Circle C, and a smattering of other riders came pouring into the yard.

Smoke hung heavy in the air, drifting among the debris and the newly formed crater that marred the landscape. Splintered wood and earth lay scattered in the snow. Moses gave a grunt of satisfaction as he fired from behind a stack of crates. "Bet they didn't expect to ride into that."

Elijah nodded, but kept his focus. "Ain't over yet."

The yard had transformed into a battlefield. Gunfire cracked in rapid succession, snow kicking up in white plumes as bullets struck the ground. Horses reared and screamed, some bolting into the chaos without riders.

Billy moved from cover to cover, his movements fluid and precise despite his recent ordeal. The rifle he'd grabbed from the porch barked as he picked off a rider trying to make a run for better cover. Another rider swung his mount toward Billy, revolver drawn, but Billy ducked low, rolling behind a trough and firing upward with his own pistol. The man fell, his body slumping in the saddle before tumbling to the ground.

Near the corral, Elijah, Moses, Travis, and Jax moved quickly, grabbing weapons from strategically placed caches, discarding their shot-out pistols in favor of fresh ones. Elijah swung into the saddle of a patiently waiting Duke, pulling his Winchester from the scabbard.

"Keep pressing!" Elijah shouted, spurring his horse toward a better vantage point. Moses followed close behind, his revolver raised as he fired at a group of men attempting to regroup near the barn. "Keep them away from the buildings."

The Barbers' hidden defenders continued to rain fire from the hills, their precise shots thinning the enemy ranks. But the reinforcements that hadn't succumbed to the blast weren't easily cowed. Several, who Elijah could see had soldier experience, dismounted and took up positions, returning fire with deadly accuracy.

Elijah rode hard, positioning himself behind an overturned wagon for cover. He leaned out, firing at a man who'd been targeting Jax. The man crumpled, and Elijah shouted, "Keep moving, Jax! Don't let them pin you down!"

For a moment, the tide seemed to turn in the Barbers' favor. Hill's men were scattered, many dead or wounded. The sound of gunfire ebbed, replaced by the panicked shouts of those still standing.

Elijah scanned the battlefield from his vantage point, his breath visible in the cold air. "We've got 'em," he muttered to himself. Then his stomach sank.

Another group of riders crested the hill. They moved with precision, their horses galloping in tight formation. It was clear they were no stragglers—these were Hill's second wave, sent to deliver the killing blow.

Carson Hill himself rode at the front of them, his expression one of irate determination, his coat smeared with grime and his hat askew. He looked like a man who had believed he held all the cards but had just been dealt an unexpected hand. "We'll finish this now!" Hill barked to his men as they aligned for another charge.

The remaining smoke from the explosion twisted around the men with Hill, and an uneasy weight settled in Elijah's gut. These weren't just cowhands turned fighters, or desperate men looking for a payday. These were the men who had sat in the back of the courthouse, intimidating anyone Hill asked them to—the hardened sort who had seen blood and sought it out again. Some wore the tattered remains of miner's garb, others had the look of men who had drifted from one boomtown to the next, leaving bodies in their wake. Their faces were rough, lined with cruelty, and their movements were sure—seasoned men who knew how to fight and kill without hesitation.

Elijah's breath slowed. Moses, crouching beside him, swore under his breath. "Hell. He ain't playin' around anymore."

Hill's eyes found Elijah across the battlefield. Even at this distance, Elijah could feel the weight of the man's stare, filled with deadly certainty. It wasn't the reckless ambition of Edward Stratton, or the cocksure bravado of Finn MacDonald. This was a man who had already decided the outcome in his mind, who believed the Barbers had made the wrong choice in resisting him, and now they would pay for it in blood.

For a long moment, neither man moved. The sounds of the fight faded to a dull roar in Elijah's ears as he locked eyes with Hill. The message was obvious: You should have taken the deal. Now I finish this.

Elijah cursed under his breath. He turned to Moses, who had taken cover beside him. "He had a plan for the unknown, I'll give Hill that."

Moses nodded grimly, reloading his revolver. "What's the play?"

Elijah didn't answer immediately, his eyes scanning the hills where their defenders had been positioned. He believed Hill had committed everything now—every fighter he had left was riding down on them. It was time to turn the table. Elijah knew from his own battle experience that when a fight reached its decisive point, it was often the leader in the field who could play the ultimate trump card that would win the day.

"Hold here," Elijah said as he gathered his reins.

"Huh?" Moses asked.

Elijah dug his heels into Duke's flanks, spurring forward hard and fast toward Hill.

Moses jerked in surprise. "Eli!" he bellowed, fear flickering across his face as he saw his brother charging forward alone.

Hill grinned, as if relishing that the overly-heroic Elijah Barber was going to make it easy for him. He leaned forward in the saddle, urging his horse forward, readying his rifle. The men surrounding him shouted and spurred their horses forward as well. Hill's advantage swelled as they rode toward their final kill, already emptying the saddles of ranch defenders.

Then a sound ripped through the air.

A cry.

Shrieking, war-painted figures surged from the ridge, their silhouettes stark against the sky. The ground trembled beneath a dozen pounding hooves as Crow warriors barreled down the slope, their shouts piercing and unrelenting. At the head of them was JT, his arm outstretched like a battle standard, pointing out the attackers, his own painted horse streaking down the hillside. Beside him, moving like a shadow in the snow, raced Scout, the brindled dog running low to the ground, his muscles rippling as he surged forward with them, his teeth bared at attacking strangers.

Hill's grin faltered. Then it disappeared entirely.

Some of his men slowed, trying to get their wits about them. A few, hardened killers that they were, raised their rifles to fire. But others stopped entirely, their horses rearing, some turning away, spurring into retreat before a shot was even fired. Panic rippled through the ranks like a wave, the advantage gone.

Carson Hill had already committed, however. He spurred his horse ahead, bearing down straight at Elijah.

Elijah clutched his reins in his teeth as both hands came up with Colts. The gunmetal gleamed in the snowy sunlight as he charged, reckless and unyielding. There was no turning away now.

Both men fired.

Hill's shot found its mark, a searing punch slamming into Elijah's arm, white-hot pain lancing through muscle and bone. But Elijah was already squeezing both triggers.

The first shot hit Hill squarely, jerking him sideways in the saddle. He grimaced but clung to the reins, snarling as he tried to keep himself upright. The second shot ripped through him, the force sending him backward, and this time, he couldn't hold on.

Hill tumbled from his mount, his rifle slipping from his fingers, his body crumpling into the snow.

Elijah didn't slow. He thundered past Hill's tumbling form, diving straight into the chaos as the Crow and Hill's men clashed. JT was already in the thick of it, his rifle cracking as he picked off a man trying to rally and Elijah dropped another who turned toward them. Scout was a streak of motion at JT's side, leaping at a man who had been fumbling to reload, knocking him backward into the mud with a guttural growl before darting back toward JT's horse.

"I was wondering what took you so damn long," Elijah called hoarsely as he pulled his horse up alongside JT. He touched the brim of his hat and gave his son a nod of approval, a simple gesture that he had shown to so many men he had commanded, conveying his respect for them in battle.

"I never seen him like that," JT said as he watched Scout.

"Me neither. . . he must get it from his father," Elijah said. He then saw JT staring at his arm, blood soaking through his coat. "I'll be fine. Stay with the Crow."

"Where you goin', Pa?" JT shouted.

Elijah jerked Duke's reins and spun him around. "To find Edward Stratton."

———

BILLY WAS MOVING FAST toward cover, reloading on the run, when he spotted a familiar figure stumbling through the wreckage of the battle. Finn MacDonald, his coat torn, his hat lost, was scrambling toward a riderless horse, slipping on the churned-up snow and mud. Billy slowed his pace, raising his revolver.

Finn turned, saw the gun leveled at him, and froze. His eyes darted, weighing his chances, but the set of Billy's jaw told him all he needed to know. Slowly, he moved his hands to his belt, unbuckled it, and held it at his side before offering a weary smirk despite the blood on his lip.

"Ah, Billy Irons," Finn drawled, his brogue thick with exhaustion. "Figured it might be ye who ended me. Always had a way of turnin' up at the worst possible time." He exhaled sharply. "Guess ye got the last laugh with me. Well, go on then. Get it over with."

Billy's thumb hovered over the hammer. "Might be the first honest thing I've ever heard you say."

Finn chuckled darkly. "I 'spose you ain't wrong. But listen, lad, Carson Hill's done for. You see it. The game's over." He licked his lips. "But his money ain't gone yet. I know where it is. You and me, we could go claim it. Walk away from this, rich men. Nae more takin' orders. Nae more ridin' for another man's cause."

Billy didn't lower the gun. "You think I want money so bad I'd partner up with a backstabber like you? The man who did Carson Hill's dirty work and set my course for landin' in jail?"

Finn's grin widened, but there was desperation in his eyes now. "Aye, well, that was business. You're a smart lad. But smarts only get you so far in this world, Billy. You got the guns, I got the know-how. I sprung ya from that jail, didn't I? Now ye could be a king out there, not some hired gun workin' for another man's dream."

Billy's hand was steady. "Elijah Barber's dream saved my life. I'll work for him as long as he'll have me. As for you and me? I'd rather finish what we started at the Big Montana. But you drop that gun belt, and I'll let you live long enough for 'em to string you up like I know you done to those Bar T hands to start this whole mess."

Finn sighed, shifting his weight ever so slightly. "Aye, then. I'll drop it."

Finn dropped the belt, his hand coming up with a pistol in it, but Billy was faster.

The shot cracked through the thinning smoke of the battlefield. Finn staggered, his mouth opening in surprise, as if he couldn't quite believe the bullet had found him. His knees buckled, and he hit the ground hard, a crimson stain blooming across his shirt.

Billy exhaled, stepping closer as Finn gasped for breath, his hand grasping at the wound in his chest. The smirk was gone now, replaced by something else—maybe regret, or the realization that his schemes had finally run out of trail.

"Fast," Finn managed, struggling to form even one word. His head lolled slightly, and then, with one last ragged breath, Finn MacDonald stilled.

Billy holstered his revolver, watching for a moment longer before turning toward the few remaining gunshots.

———※———

AS THE GUNFIRE all but dwindled, Elijah rode past the spot where he had dropped Carson Hill from his horse and his heart sank. Gone was the man's body, replaced by a smeared trail of blood in the snow.

Elijah dismounted and followed the blood trail with measured steps, his revolver drawn. His boots crunched in the snow, the sound muffled by the echoes of distant gunfire. His breath plumed in the frigid air as he scanned the tree line ahead, his pulse steady despite the situation.

Hill was wounded, and badly by the look of it. The crimson streak in the snow was erratic, dotted with footprints that suggested a limping man. Elijah crouched briefly to reload his revolver.

He was rising when the first shot cracked through the trees. Snow exploded in front of him, and he flinched, instinctively dropping low. Another shot rang out, this one grazing his thigh. Pain lanced through him, but he gritted his teeth and pressed forward, zigzagging between the trunks for cover.

"Coward!" Elijah bellowed, his voice echoing through the frosty stillness. "Come finish what you started!"

A faint rustling to his left drew his attention, and he fired blindly, the shots barking into the trees. The rustling stopped, replaced by a tense, suffocating silence. Blood seeped into Elijah's pants leg, the warmth a stark contrast to the bitter cold.

Elijah pressed on, his breaths labored. The trees thickened, their skeletal branches clawing at the pale sky. His eyes darted from shadow to shadow, every dark patch a potential threat. He thought of JT, of Moses, of Maggie and the girls—then he thought of the men and women who had bled to build Summit Valley. That thought steeled him.

Another shot cracked, this one splintering a branch near his head. Elijah dove into a patch of undergrowth, rolling to his feet with a grunt, his own blood now dotting the snow. He spotted movement ahead and fired, glimpsing Hill stumbling further into the trees, clutching his shoulder.

Elijah dug into his belt, removed six more rounds, and ejected the spent ones. Snapping the chamber shut again, Elijah pressed forward, grim determination etched into his face. He carefully emerged from behind a tree into a small clearing, freezing when he saw Hill was waiting, crouched low behind a fallen log. The man's face was pale, his lips trembling as he raised his revolver with a shaking hand.

"You should've taken the deal, Barber!" Hill spat.

Elijah didn't answer. He fired, the bullet grazing Hill's side. The man cried out, collapsing against the log before lurching upright again. Blood trickled from his mouth as he tried to steady his aim.

Hill fired, and the shot grazed Elijah's side, tearing through his coat. Elijah staggered but didn't falter. His next shot caught Hill in the leg, and the man screamed, dropping his gun as he clutched his thigh.

Elijah closed the distance, his own leg screaming in protest with every step. By the time he reached Hill, the man was slumped against the log, his face contorted in pain and fear. He reached for his gun, lifting it, and Elijah shot him again in the chest as Hill's pistol only clicked.

"They told me," Hill rasped, his voice weak but venomous, "They told me I shouldn't press you. But there lies the challenge for a man like me, aye?"

Elijah stood over him, panting, bleeding. "Guess they were right."

Hill's eyes darted to the side, searching for something—an escape, a weapon, anything. But there was nothing left. Elijah pulled back the hammer of his gun, his expression cold.

"Well played. . . usin' my own explosives against me." He chuckled. "I knew I'd blow a hole in this land." He spit, and the snow bloodied in front of him. "You'll never hold it, though," Hill said, his voice barely above a whisper. "The valley, the land—it'll be taken from you, one way or 'nother."

Elijah leaned closer, his voice low and firm. "Not while I'm breathing."

He pulled the trigger, and the forest fell silent.

Elijah stumbled back toward the yard, his body heavy with exhaustion and pain. The snow beneath his boots was streaked with red, and his breath came in shallow gasps. When he emerged from the trees, the scene before him was both a relief and a reminder of the cost.

Moses, Travis, Jax, Billy, and the rest of the remaining defenders were moving through the aftermath, searching for Elijah and checking the dead and wounded while tying up the few surviving prisoners. Scout barked and ran to Elijah, his tail wagging furiously. The others turned at the sound, their faces a mix of relief and alarm.

"Eli!" Moses called, hurrying over. He stopped short when he saw the blood staining his brother's clothes. "God almighty."

"I'm ok," Elijah said, though his voice was strained, and he struggled to stand. He leaned against a fence post for support, his eyes scanning the yard. "Where's Edward?"

Moses's expression darkened. "Lit out when the shooting started, I reckon. No sign of him."

Elijah nodded, his hand gripping the post. "Figures." He tried to walk, and his knees buckled. Moses caught him and held him up. "We'll find him."

"Brother, we gotta get you inside and get some help first. We'll have someone ride for Livingston to fetch the doc."

Elijah looked at him, a faint grin on his face. "First time you come outta one of these untouched."

"How 'bout that?" Moses managed.

"Is it over?" Elijah asked?

Moses lowered his head and nodded, then gestured toward the men checking the dead and wounded in the field. "Roy took every man still able to set out some pickets in case anyone else comes."

"Good, but I reckon that'll be it," Elijah managed.

JT appeared over a rise, his face pale but uninjured as the Crow rode alongside him. "Pa!" he called, spurring his mount toward Elijah. "Are you alright?"

"Let me see my boy before you haul me off like a casualty, will you, Mo?" Elijah forced a smile, stepping away from Moses, and staggering toward JT. "I'm good, son. It's okay now. You done real good, I'm proud of—"

The sharp report of a pistol shattered the moment.

NOT ABOUT THE LAW

— ◆ —

Elijah staggered forward, his body jerking as the bullet struck him in the back, falling to his knees.

"Pa!" JT cried, dismounting and pulling his weapon.

Moses turned toward the sound of the shot and, as he had done so many times before, brought his gun up and found the shooter. His mind tried to process what happened, but his body instinctively pulled the trigger. He watched the man drop his weapon, grab his side, and then fall—all seemingly before Elijah even hit the ground.

The shot echoed around the trees and outbuildings under the low, gray sky, and then a stillness fell over the yard. Moments ago, the ranch sounded like the battlefields of his younger days, and now, he felt, it had never been quieter.

He looked to the ground, and saw his brother laying face down, blood blossoming on the back of his heavy coat. Void of any emotion, he glanced toward Travis, Jax, and Billy, who he saw hobbling toward him, their wide eyes focused on Elijah. Then, the emotion rose to the surface, and he turned and saw JT across the yard, surrounded by the remaining Crow warriors. JT's eyes locked onto his father, and he took a few steps toward him before Moses stepped between him and Elijah.

"JT, wait just a second," Moses said. "Let me just see what—"

JT interrupted him, and his eyes flashed with anger as he turned toward the shooter, lying on his side, moaning near the tree line. "You back-shooting coward!"

JT marched across the yard, drawing his revolver as he approached. Moses hurried after him as he waved to Travis and Jax to attend to Elijah.

"JT, wait," Moses called after him. He could see the look in his nephew's eyes as he rushed to intercept him, a look he had seen on Elijah's face in such moments. His mind flooded with all the thoughts Elijah had shared over the years of not wanting to see his son become like him, and his promise of the night before to never let JT lose himself.

Now, reaching JT and standing over the wounded Edward Stratton, Moses could see that JT was ready to cross a line from which most men struggled to return.

Moses reached a tentative hand toward JT as he eyed Edward. "JT, gimmie that pistol."

JT jerked away, waving his revolver toward Edward as a tear ran down his face. "He did this." JT's voice cracked, but he cleared it and continued. "He caused all this, and then he shot him in the back like the coward he is. At least the rest of 'em fought honest. He's a murderer!"

Edward struggled to sit up against a tree, groaning. "Look around, boy," he spat as he cast a weak arm across the yard. "There are only murderers here."

Moses bit his lip and shook his head, then stared at Edward. "There's a difference between killin' and murdering you sonofabitch." He kneeled and retrieved Edward's revolver, opening the chamber. Moses laughed, a sound full of disdain. "You didn't fire but one shot in all that. . . a back-shooting, murdering coward shot."

"Murderer!" JT shouted again and pointed his revolver at Edward.

"He took what was mine from me!" Edward shouted. "Spare me your tears, boy. You're ready to do what you stand there and condemn."

"You never wanted it, and he put everything he had into it," JT retorted. "This place would be nothing without him."

Moses put his hand on JT's gun arm in a cautious movement. The young man's arm was steady, but Moses studied his face. There it was: The look of his father, a man of principle, a man who wanted to right a wrong. There was also, however, the look of someone who wanted a way out of this.

"He's wounded and un-armed, JT," Moses said. "You don't want to do this. Not after the way your ma and pa raised you." Moses turned and looked toward Travis, Jax, and Billy kneeling near Elijah, with Scout laying at his side whining.

"This ain't what your pa wants for you," Moses continued as he turned back to JT.

"Yeah boy," Edward sputtered. "You have to know the law like your uncle says."

Moses kicked Edward in his wounded side, eliciting a howl, then glared at the man. "This ain't about the law," he said, 'specially not around here, and 'specially not after all this."

JT scrunched his nose and wiped his eyes with the coat sleeve on his off-arm. He looked Moses in the eyes, and Moses nodded, conveying a look that the boy had done everything right, but there would be no more debate. Moses reached out his hand and jerked his head toward Elijah, and JT handed over the gun and started toward his father with a last glare at Edward.

Moses watched JT walk away, then looked toward Travis, who grimaced and shook his head, seeming to convey to Moses that the prognosis was grim at best. Moses could hear Edward mumbling behind him but tuned him out for a moment as he studied the gun he had taken from JT—a revolver he now realized was Elijah's from the war and their days as deputy U.S. Marshals.

Moses turned back to Edward. "What is it you're goin' on about then?"

Edward was mumbling, the pain of his wounding having drained him of his malice. "Thank you for sparing me," he sighed. "I—"

"Don't deserve it," Moses said as he snapped the revolver's chamber shut and held the weapon at his side. "You orchestrated all of this after years of only needing your father's name and money for your fancy East Coast life, never having a care in the world about what he'd built here or the life it provided people." Moses scoffed and shook his head. "You worshipped Eli as a boy, couldn't get enough of our stories and adventures. We made your father wealthy like few men are. This is how you repay us?"

Edward let his head fall back against a tree. "He aspired to be such an illustrious father when I was young, but then my mother died, and it was like he only did it for her. All I ever heard about was the example of the Barber brothers I should follow. Hard work, honesty, taking care of people."

Moses turned for a moment and saw JT laying next to Elijah, speaking to him. He looked back at Edward. "Guess you shoulda listened. Now there are fathers dead, lives ruined, the Stratton name tarnished, and you got none of what you wanted. You targeted our families in a range war. A pawn for a man who was always going to discard you afterward." He glanced around, then stared down at the man. "This ranch is ours now."

"What of my father?"

"I'll see to that," Moses said. "Real shame you brought him down into the mud with you."

Edward sighed. "Hill?" he asked.

"Dead," Moses answered. "MacDonald too. Billy enjoyed that, I reckon." He looked at the revolver, then pointed it at Edward. "Time to join 'em. I ain't real interested, but any last words for me or your maker?"

Edward struggled to hold a hand in front of his face, the little remaining color draining from it. "Please. . . you told the boy yourself. I'm wounded and unarmed. You don't want to cross that line."

"Well," Moses said as he thumbed the hammer back, "that was just for the boy's sake, and me keeping a promise to my brother. I already don't sleep much at night, and I'm pretty confident in what justice looks like on this one."

———

TRAVIS, JAX, JT, AND BILLY looked up when they heard the shot and relaxed when they saw Moses approaching. Reaching them, Moses returned the revolver to JT without a word or taking his eyes off Elijah. His brother was still lying on his stomach, his head turned to the side, and his eyes fluttered to stay open. The blood stain on his back had grown.

"Says he can't feel his legs," Travis said, shifting his weight gingerly. Moses saw their foreman had been shot in the leg.

Jax scratched his beard. "Blood ain't grown much in the last minute or two." Moses inspected Jax and saw a bullet hole in the lapel of his coat. Jax looked down and shook his head. "Musta been spent when it reached me," he said. "Coat and vest mostly ate it up."

Moses nodded, then looked at JT, and back at the other two men, his eyes showing he now wondered about the boy.

Travis limped closer to Moses and spoke in a low voice. "They been whisperin' to each other. Elijah ain't sayin much, and JT seems in shock." Travis turned and looked toward Edward Stratton's slumped body. "JT wanted to do it himself, didn't he?" Travis shook his head. "Eli woulda haunted you."

"Can't haunt me if he don't die." Moses eyed the men. "Can you three ride?"

"Painful, I reckon, but yes," Travis said.

Jax nodded.

"Just need a warm coat," Billy said.

Moses rubbed his beard and then saw the remaining Crow warriors approaching.

"We'll ride and get Maggie and the girls." He turned to the Crow and pointed to himself, Travis, Jax, and Billy, then the horses, before pointing in the distance. He opened his mouth to speak, then paused, searching his brain for the word. "*Baa-lay*?" He pointed to himself and the horses again, then to the distance.

"*Báale*," one of them said, as he nodded in understanding. "Family. Bring here."

Moses's eyes dropped. Even at this moment, he was embarrassed over the amount of English the Crow spoke as he struggled with a handful of words.

"We will protect," the Crow man said. He then pointed to Elijah, then the main house. "We will care for him. You go."

"*Aho*. Thank you," Moses said. He nodded to his men. "Grab our horses, or any four up to the task." The men departed, and JT stood as Moses looked at him. "You stay with him while I fetch your ma and sisters."

JT nodded, then looked back at his father. "He gonna make it, Uncle Mo?"

"Sure he is," Moses offered, unsure of himself. "If anyone can, he will." He looked at one of the Crow, who had retrieved a medicine bag from his horse, and others, who were fashioning a litter. "They're gonna help you for now, and I'll ride for the doc in Livingston when I get back."

JT looked past Moses toward Edward Stratton's body, then back at his uncle. "I couldn't do it."

"I know. . . and I'm glad. That'll be my burden."

JT nodded and moved to help the Crow men with their efforts. Moses bit his lip.

"JT?"

The young man turned.

"Say everything you ought to, though. Just in case."

JT looked at Moses momentarily, nodded slightly, and returned to his work. The three cowboys returned with four horses and as many rifles as they had found on the ground.

Moses swung aboard and looked down at his brother. "We're gonna get Maggie back here to you, Eli. You stay with us, you hear?" Moses bit his lip. "She might kill you when she learns about the stunt with JT and the Crow, but that bullet ain't."

Moses saw Elijah's eyes move toward him, and he blinked, then spoke in a barely audible voice. "It worked."

Moses took a deep breath. "Yeah brother, it sure did." He turned to Travis, Jax, and Billy. "We better be quick," he said, then spurred his horse to a gallop.

THE WIND KICKED UP SNOW across the yard, swirling through the battered remnants of the shootout as the Crow warriors crafted a stretcher from blankets and poles. The ranch, which had been a battleground just hours ago, now lay in eerie silence, punctuated only by the soft murmurs of the men working to bring Elijah inside.

They carried Elijah up the staircase of the main house, each footfall on the creaking boards rumbling like distant thunder. The Crow men worked in graceful unison, their hushed voices blending with Elijah's ragged breaths. JT rushed into the master bedroom, fumbling with tinder at the fireplace until a spark caught. Warm light flared, illuminating the strain on Elijah's face as the Crow men laid him on the bed.

A sheen of sweat glistened on Elijah's forehead despite the cold they'd just come inside from, and he winced with every jolt. Blood had soaked through his coat, darkening the worn fabric. Though his eyes were closed, they latched onto JT whenever they fluttered open. It was all the boy could do to keep the tremor from his hands as he stood back, letting the Crow men work.

The quiet was broken only by Elijah's labored breathing and the shuffling of the Crow men as they worked. One man kneeled by Elijah's side, pressing folded cloths to the wound with measured calm. Another gathered herbs from a worn leather pouch, crushing them and mixing them into a poultice. JT's eyes never left his father, watching every rise and fall of his chest. One man moved alongside Elijah and began a soft murmur, like a chant, and JT looked up, meeting the warrior's gaze.

"He ain't gonna die! There's no need for that!"

Elijah stirred, his eyes fluttering open for a moment, locking onto his son's. "JT. . ." he rasped, his voice barely audible, each word forced from his throat.

JT came, his voice a whisper. "Yeah, Pa. . . I'm here." His hand reached out, grasping his father's.

One of the Crow men looked at JT and gave a slight nod, as if to say they were doing all they could. Another pressed a bladder of water into JT's hand, encouraging him to let Elijah sip. JT carefully lifted his father's head, tipping a small amount of water into Elijah's mouth.

Elijah coughed weakly and blinked, focusing on his son. His voice rasped. "It's bad, ain't it?"

JT hesitated. He wasn't sure if he could bring himself to speak plainly. "They're doin' all they can, Pa. Uncle Mo rode for Ma and the girls, and then he'll fetch the doc from Livingston."

Elijah tried to shift, but the effort made him grimace in pain. Sensing his discomfort, the Crow man laid a steadying hand on his shoulder, murmuring a few words under his breath. Elijah nodded in gratitude, then gestured for the men to step away.

"*Aho,*" Elijah said. Then, shifting his gaze to JT, he added, "Give me a minute with my boy."

The Crow men dipped their heads in respect. One gestured for JT to kneel at his father's side while they moved to another corner of the room, sorting their medicine bag and bandages.

Elijah's eyes found JT's. His voice, barely audible. "You spared him. . . didn't cross that line." His words came slowly, every one an effort. "You could've ended him. . .but you didn't."

JT swallowed, his chest constricting at the memory of Edward Stratton in his sights. "I just—" His voice cracked, but he cleared his throat. "I couldn't do it." He lost his composure and wiped his eyes with his sleeve. "When they're attacking you, it's one thing. But when he was just laying there? Part of me wanted to, but. . . Uncle Mo did it."

"I'm proud of you," Elijah said. It was the first time JT had heard his father speak those words so plainly, even if barely audible. "Not because you're grown. . . or you fought for the ranch. . . but because you did right by yourself, your ma, and all of us."

JT blinked, a single tear escaping as he nodded. "I. . . I only did what you and Ma taught me."

A faint smile tugged at Elijah's lips. "Reckon that's the one lesson I always prayed you'd hold on to." Then, in a shaky gesture, Elijah pointed toward his gun belt laying on the floor—the old war-era rig he always wore no matter how many new pistols he owned.

Elijah coughed, then let out a ragged breath. "Take it," he whispered, nodding toward the worn Colt Peacemaker in the holster. The name was almost ironic, but there was a certain fitting grace to it. "That gun. . . well I hope you we've brought some peace that means you don't have to use it." He coughed again, winced, and laid his head back and wheezed for a moment. "That belt, though. . . I worn that like it was a piece of me ever since the war. You take care of it and it'll take care of you."

JT stared at the rig, stunned by the weight of what his father was giving him. "Pa, I don't know if— "

Elijah managed a faint squeeze of his son's arm. "Wear it. . . like you did today. With a clear heart. That's all I ask."

JT nodded, the tears flowing now. "Pa, I don't know if I like you givin' away things right now."

Elijah closed his eyes. "You won't like this either, then." The words were almost inaudible, and JT leaned in. "Take care of Duke for me."

"But Pa, tell me you ain't gonna—"

Elijah's head lolled back and forth. "Even if the Crow can keep me from bleeding anymore, and prevent all these holes in me from getting infected. . ." He trailed off, never able to speak more than a few words at a time. "I ain't gonna be getting on a horse again, I fear."

Before JT could muster any reply, there was a flurry of hoofbeats in the yard. Then a rush of footsteps sounded on the porch, followed by hurried voices, then boots up the stairs. Moments later, the door burst open, and Maggie swept in, teary-eyed Molly and Bridget clinging to her skirt. Her face was a palette of emotion: relief at finding Elijah alive, horror at his condition, and fury dancing behind her eyes. In the hallway, Travis, Jax, and Billy hovered, nursing their own injuries and exhausted from the brief, but hard, ride.

Elijah tried to speak, but the words caught in his throat. He lifted a trembling hand, wanting to reassure her, but the pain cut deeper than any answer. Finally, he managed a half-formed whisper, too low for them to catch. Maggie kneeled, fighting tears as she kissed Elijah's forehead, then gathered the girls to let him see them. Each child was crying, but there was a curious calm in their eyes as they looked upon their father, as though they sensed how much he needed that small comfort.

Elijah forced a faint smile, the effort evident in every crease of his face. "My girls," he rasped. The children bent closer, each touching his arm as if afraid even the gentlest contact might hurt him further.

Then Maggie's attention snapped to JT. Her eyes flickered to the guns on his hips, to the snowy grime and blood on his coat. She took in his hardened posture—how he stood like a young man who had seen more in a day than he ever should have. She let out a sharp breath. "I don't even want to know what role you had," she said in a trembling voice.

Before JT could respond, Elijah mustered a whisper, eyes still half-lidded from pain. "You surely don't."

JT allowed himself the smallest grin, a weary shake of the head in agreement.

"Now you find a sense of humor," Maggie said.

The Crow men stepped back in to check Elijah's wounds, murmuring to one another as they worked. Maggie rose, pressing the girls gently toward the doorway. "Go on, dears. Let our friends help your father," she said, her voice softening for them. When they had gone, her tone changed, turning firm as steel. She pointed a roving finger at JT, Billy, Jax, then Travis—who had hobbled into the room.

"This war is finished," she said, her voice carrying the authority of a woman who had played no small part in building this ranch at the frontier's edge. "No more bloodshed. No more retribution. Nobody rides off looking for any of Hill's remaining men. Nobody rides to Bozeman looking for Jon Stratton. We protected what's ours, but we've paid dearly. It ends here." She stared at each one of them individually, challenging them to question her.

For a breath, the only sound was the crackle of the fire and Elijah's unsteady breathing. Billy, Travis, and Jax exchanged glances, all trying to sneak a look toward Elijah, then answered in the same hushed chorus: "Yes, ma'am." JT, his hand on his father's shoulder, nodded in agreement.

Boots knocked in the hall, and Moses appeared in the doorway. He and Elijah exchanged a look that spanned a lifetime—pain, gratitude, and memories unspoken. It was the sort of look that said everything words could not.

Moses cleared his throat before speaking in a low voice that sought to hide emotion. "I gathered some things, and I'll be ridin' for Livingston," he said, looking at Maggie. "I'll swap horses with whoever is willing on the way there and ride straight through to fetch up the doctor."

"I'll go with," Billy said.

"Me too," JT added, moving away from his father.

Moses's eyes darted to Elijah, who closed his and shook his head.

"No, I reckon I'm on my own for this," Moses said, garnering a small nod from Elijah. "Fixin' to get awful frosty out there, and I want you all keepin' an eye on things here."

Maggie moved back to Elijah, her hand resting over her husband's. Everyone knew Moses would do everything he could to care for his brother. Her eyes flitted to Moses. "Thank you," she said simply. "Hurry back."

"I'll be sure he gets here quickly," Moses replied. He crossed the room and placed a firm hand on Elijah's shoulder. "I'll see you when I get back, you hear?" Elijah grimaced as he lifted his arm and placed his hand on his brother's.

They shared one more glance, the two seeming to communicate without words, then Moses turned to the men. "Three of ya outside always, watching the place. Be sure those fellas on picket duty got what they need to be comfortable tonight."

"You got it boss," Travis replied.

Moses dipped his head, paused for one more glance at Elijah, then he turned and slipped from the room, his boots echoing down the stairs. A moment later, the front door opened and shut. They all heard him tell Scout to stay, then moments later, hooves thundered off into the gathering dusk. Maggie exhaled a shaky breath, brushing Elijah's cheek. His eyes slid shut, his breath faltered, and a stubborn spark struggled to stay lit.

ABSOLUTION

— · —

B ozeman lay still in the early morning, the sky a deep indigo, on the cusp of dawn but still swallowed in the remnants of the night. A snow covered hush rested over the streets, the kind of quiet that only came when a town was in the deepest throes of sleep, unaware that the world had shifted while their eyes were closed.

Jonathan Stratton's unsteady steps echoed down the long, darkened hallway as he leaned on the banister, his breath shallow. The floorboards beneath his slippered feet groaned, the only other sound in the vast emptiness of the house. Somewhere outside, the wind howled against the windowpanes, rattling them in their frames. Snow had swept in overnight, leaving a cold so deep it had settled into the very bones of the house.

Stratton shivered as he reached the bottom of the stairs, pulling his robe tighter around him. His body felt weaker than usual this morning—his limbs heavier, his breath shorter. Each step sent a dull ache through his joints, a reminder of how much time had slipped from him. He had never been a man to fear aging. But now, in the dark hour before dawn, he feared everything.

He turned toward the parlor first, expecting to find a fire still smoldering in the hearth. But the room was dark. Cold. Lifeless.

That was strange. Harrison always saw that fires were burning early on days like this.

Stratton's frown deepened. "Harrison?" His voice came out hoarse, barely above a whisper. He cleared his throat and tried again. "Harrison?"

Nothing.

A flicker of unease twisted in his stomach.

Moving slower now, he turned toward his study, feeling along the shelves for the oil lamp. His fingers found it, and he fumbled with a match, striking it twice before the flame caught. A dim, flickering glow filled the room, casting long, shifting shadows along the walls.

His hands trembled as he reached for the decanter on his desk, sloshing whiskey into a glass before knocking it back. It did little to warm him. The cold had settled too deep.

His fingers drifted toward the drawer beneath the decanter, and he pried it open with great effort. Bottles rattled softly. His laudanum. He reached for it, but his hands fumbled, sending the bottle rolling.

He muttered a curse, rubbing his forehead. The cold. The quiet. The missing butler. Something was wrong.

He exhaled slowly, pushing himself upright and turning toward the fireplace. The logs inside sat untouched, the ashes from last night's fire nearly cold. He shook his head, scowling, muttering under his breath.

"Need a fire on a mornin' like this, Jon."

Stratton's breath caught. He stiffened, his heart slamming against his ribs as his gaze darted to the far corner of the study. A warm glow pulsed from the chair near the fireplace.

"Elijah?"

The figure leaned forward, the orange tip of a cigar burning bright in the dim room, and the face came into focus.

Stratton felt the blood drain from his face. His lips parted slightly, but no sound came.

Moses took another slow drag from the cigar, exhaling as he leaned back, utterly at ease, as if he had all the time in the world. "Couldn't be Elijah," he said evenly. "He's in bed dyin'. Shot in the back by your son." His eyes flickered with something dangerous. "I helped myself to a cigar. Hope you don't mind. Rode all night, barely ever warming myself while a fresh horse was saddled. Thought it might warm me up."

Stratton swallowed hard, his frail hands gripping the folds of his robe. "My God," he muttered, nearly stumbling as he moved toward his desk. "Elijah. . . is he. . .?"

Moses let the silence stretch, watching Stratton with a measured gaze. "If he ain't, he soon will be. Still breathin' when I left, though," he said finally, his voice devoid of comfort. "Barely."

Stratton collapsed into his chair, his hands shaking as he rubbed his forehead. "What happened?" His voice was a hoarse whisper.

Moses puffed on the cigar, then exhaled. "It's a real mess, Jon. A dozen or more dead. Double that wounded. Carson Hill's dead. Finn MacDonald, too." He paused. "Giant crater in the yard. I already told you about Elijah."

Stratton's fingers dug into the wood of his desk. He closed his eyes, wheezing, trying to brace himself against the reality of it all. "My son?" he rasped.

"Took care of him myself," Moses said quickly and without regret. "Had to save Eli's boy from doin' it. But can't say I'm gonna lose much sleep over it, Jon." He took a last draw from the cigar, then crushed out the remaining stub. "He turned rotten out east."

Stratton flinched as if the words themselves had struck him. His shoulders curled inward, his once-powerful frame folding under the weight of it all. A lion in his final winter.

Moses said nothing for a while, happy to let Stratton sit in it all. Then he saw Stratton look at his waist. "Don't worry, Jon," he said mockingly. "I dropped my guns off at the sheriff's door, just like your pal Carson wanted. I'd hate to be a rule breaker."

After a long silence, Stratton finally lifted his head. His eyes were bloodshot, hollow. "I should have stopped him," he murmured, more to himself than to Moses. "I should have. . . but what was I to do? He's my son." He stared at the ceiling.

Moses shot out of the chair and closed the distance between the corner and Stratton's desk. His expression darkened. "And Elijah's my brother," he said, a rising steel in his voice cutting through the room.

"I'll tell you what I told Edward before I put him down," Moses continued. "There's a difference between killing and murdering. You should've known better, Jon. You should've known that no matter what mess Edward got himself into, Elijah would've fixed it and kept everyone happy if you'd let him. . . If you'd asked him." Moses shook his head. "It mighta involved killing but it wouldn't have involved murdering, and it woulda saved an awful lot of mess and loss of life. You could have gone to the law, to the people of town, or shown up in court. But you chose self-preservation. Didn't risk your name or reputation." Moses shook his head. "A reputation I used to think stood for something."

Stratton closed his eyes, as if he couldn't even look at Moses.

"Like every damn battle he's ever faced, my brother didn't start this one," Moses said. "But he damn well finished it."

Stratton sucked in a breath, his lips quivering. His fingers clenched into fists on the desk.

Moses reached behind his back, pulling a revolver from his waistband in a swift motion. Stratton tensed, his breath freezing in his lungs.

"Like I said, I dropped mine off, but this one was your boy's," Moses said, spinning the weapon once before snapping open the cylinder. His eyes dropped to the loaded rounds. "Five left," he mused. "Only one fired." His gaze lifted, fixing Stratton with something ice-cold. "One bullet, Jon. We fought a skirmish bigger than some I saw in the war, and he fired one damn bullet. . . a back shot into my brother after it was all over."

Moses dumped all but one of the unfired bullets onto the desk with a sharp flick of his wrist. They rattled loudly in the suffocating quiet, rolling in uneven circles before stilling.

Stratton recoiled at the sound and ran a hand over his face.

Moses snapped the chamber shut, cocked the hammer, and pointed it at Stratton. "Now there's one left," he said, his voice quiet. "How's it feel, Jon? Maybe turn around and really get a sense of things. After all, that wasn't the only back shooting in this whole affair. Just the only one with a real bullet."

Stratton's breath shuddered. He stared at the gun, the single remaining bullet. His face twisted, his throat working around words that wouldn't come.

Moses dropped the hammer slowly, then set the gun on the desk. He leaned forward, his hands on the rich wood as he hovered over Stratton. His voice dropped lower, like a thunder before a storm. "I should end you myself," he said. "For stayin' quiet when you knew this was coming. For lettin' your son's greed and spite tear through my family and a whole bunch of good people." He shook his head. "But I can't do it."

Moses bit his lip, then continued. "I was good as dead when you found us all those years ago. If not for you, I'd have bled out in the dirt and Elijah would've been all alone. You gave us work. A future. A name. And now. . ." He straightened. "Well, Maggie says its over, and I'm inclined to believe my brother agrees. It don't absolve you of your sins. . . I just ain't gonna be the one to free you from them."

His eyes flickered to the gun once more, then back to Stratton. "You're sick, your name, and everything you worked for is tarnished, and your son is gone. I don't need to punish you any further. You can do that yourself, Jon."

Stratton looked down at the revolver. His whole body trembled. "I'm so sorry, Moses." He dropped his head, shuddering as tears came to his eyes. "To all of you. I'm so sorry."

"Me too." Moses turned from the desk. At the doorway, he paused, his back to Stratton. "Harrison and his family will be taken care of," he said, his voice final. "On the ranch. *Our* ranch." He eyed a safe in the corner. "Reckon we've got our work cut out for us, straightening everything out, but I'm hoping there's paper in there accounting for our original agreement. A letter from you might not hurt either."

Stratton nodded feebly, and Moses didn't wait for any further response.

Moses stepped out into the wintry morning air, the town of Bozeman still wrapped in sleep. The horizon was lightening, the faintest streaks of dawn creeping over the snow-covered mountains.

The streets were empty. Silent.

With a deep breath, he stepped off Stratton's porch and into the snow, walking slow and steady, like a man who had just put the past behind him.

The sun had not yet risen, but it would.

EPILOGUE

—·—

ONE YEAR LATER: CHRISTMAS EVE, 1885

J T Barber squatted down in front of the modest stone and brushed the thin layer of snow off the top, even though more was falling. He wiped his hands clean, blew into them, then stuffed them into his coat pocket as he sighed heavily.

"Well, we sure do miss you this time of year," he said. He looked at the grave, then chuckled. "More than usual, that is." He smiled. "Ma said she would come out tomorrow, but I remember how you always loved the whole family gathering on Christmas Eve, and I reckoned I better come say hello. That, and I was on my way in from hauling hay to the winter pasture."

He turned to face the church and scanned the trail leading through the yard toward the valley road. "Guess I don't know if we'll get a crowd tonight or not." He looked at the sky. "Hard to tell what this weather is going to do. Been a different winter so far, that's for sure."

The new archway at the entrance to the yard caught his eye, and he gazed up at the three large iron Bs. "Triple B, we're calling it now." JT smiled and turned back to the stone. "Guess I'm the third B. Folks say it's a good name. And you'll be glad to know the horse and livery business has kept pace, and the freighting has picked up as more folks come out this way. Grass grew greener than I ever seen this past summer, which is saying something these last few years. Lot of ranchers have brought herds this way after some wildfires north and east, but it don't seem like anything could ever ruin the cattle business here."

He stood, then realized there was, in fact, one thing that could bring the cattle boom to a halt. "They finally got that Cattle Growers' Association formed, and Uncle Mo has got a leadership role for the area. They gave him the badge of a special agent and said he was authorized to hire deputies and that he had jurisdiction over any legal matters related to livestock. He's gonna make sure nothing like all that happens again. How about that?"

A snowflake fell on his nose, and on cue, his body shivered in the cold. "Well, I best be getting back inside and on with the festivities now that chores are done." He stepped forward and put his hand on the stone before looking past the Absaroka peaks and to the sky. "Merry Christmas, Pop."

JT patted the stone, then turned his collar up and walked past the stones of the men who gave their lives for the ranch, wishing them a Merry Christmas as well, his footsteps the only disturbance on a fresh blanket of snow.

As he neared the churchyard gate, another figure stood waiting. Moses had his hands deep in the pockets of his coat, watching the falling snow settle on the archway above.

"There ya are," Moses said.

JT stopped at the gate and waited for his uncle. He noticed Moses was eyeing his nephew's trail. "Thought I'd stop and say Merry Christmas," JT said.

Moses nodded and smiled. "Yeah, he always did love everyone getting together Christmas Eve, didn't he?"

JT was silent for a moment as the heavy snowflakes gathered on their hat brims and shoulders. "Uncle Mo, I wanna thank you for everything you done for us the last year. It's been hard, but you've made it easier."

Moses twisted his face, as if to hide or prevent any sign of emotion. "Well, it ain't been easy for me either, and I reckon your pa would say it's the first time I've made something easier rather than harder, but. . ." Moses glanced around the ranch yard, his eyes settling on the Triple B above the iron gate. "It's what he woulda done, because it's what had to be done."

JT smiled, then laughed when Moses slapped him hard on the back, sending snow flying. "Alright, boy," Moses said, "ain't gettin' any warmer out here, and I smell a fire, and heard Harrison made some of his famous hot cider."

The pair stepped inside the boot room, closing the heavy wooden door behind them against the weather. As they shook out and hung their coats, a voice carried from further inside the house.

"If you want any of this cider, Moses Barber, you best not step inside here with anything wet still on," Helen called.

Moses smiled at JT as he sat and pulled his boots off. "Ought I head in there wearing just my birthday suit?"

JT laughed as he pulled off his boots. "Please don't."

"My boy with you?" came Maggie's voice.

"Yes, ma'am," Moses shouted back. He stood and checked himself over, ensuring he had shed all his wet clothes. "Find me when Travis, Jax, and Billy get here, and we'll add a bit of whiskey to that cider," he whispered to JT.

Inside the house, candles were lit everywhere, and a roaring fire in the great room threw light and, more importantly, heat throughout the first floor. Pine boughs with red ribbons adorned the walls and staircase banister, completing the festive decor of the season.

Moses stepped into the kitchen and slipped behind Helen, putting his hands on her cheeks.

Helen shrieked. "Your hands are freezing."

Maggie looked at JT with a raised eyebrow. "You stop and talk to your granddad?"

JT hesitated. "Yes, ma'am. Told him you'd be out tomorrow."

"You dress warm enough out there?"

"Yes, ma'am."

She handed him a cup of steaming hot cider, and JT saw Moses wink at him. "You can't help those cattle if you freeze to death, you know," Maggie said.

"No, ma'am," JT said before sipping the cider. "But we can't sell them if we don't get them some hay to survive the winter."

Maggie shook her head. "You sound just like your father."

Moses laughed as he nodded in agreement, then looked toward the fireplace. The girls were giggling and stringing up popcorn on a tall tree next to a form seated in front of the fire, watching them while attending to the fire. Curled up beside the chair, nearly blending into the dark rug, was Scout. His brindled coat rose and fell with slow, steady breaths, his head resting on his paws as he listened to the sounds of the house. He had stirred when JT entered, lifting his head in greeting before nuzzling against the leg of the form.

"There ain't any more fiddling to be done with that blaze," Moses called out. "I'm gonna need to start sheddin' clothes."

The figure in front of the fire leaned the poker against the stone and shifted in their chair. "Get hay to all three winter pastures?"

"Enough to outlast this weather," JT called out, moving toward the fireplace.

The chair turned on two wheels as its occupant maneuvered with two muscular arms. "Well done," Elijah said, speaking around his pipe and then smiling as he looked up at his son.

He then turned toward Moses and called out in an exasperated tone. "I fiddle with the fire because it's about as useful as I can be now." He glanced at JT and winked. "But I catch you putting any whiskey in this boy's cider, and I'll find a way to get out of this chair and come after you."

Moses smirked and watched Elijah take in the joy and warmth in the room. Then, they locked eyes, both of them knowing they had won—not just a fight, or some land, but something much greater.

Moses crossed the room, handed Elijah a mug, and leaned against the hearth. "Merry Christmas, Eli."

Elijah nodded. "Merry Christmas, Moses."

Outside, the snow kept falling, but inside, the fire burned strong.

THANK YOU FOR READING

— ⬩ —

Thank you for reading! Please consider leaving an honest review on Amazon and Goodreads. This is the most powerful way to support authors you love and help others discover them!

I hope, like me, you became close to the Barber Brothers and are sad to see their adventures end. But fear not! Keep your eyes peeled in the future for a Billy Irons story that is sure to have guest appearances from the Barbers. In the meantime, if you like short, classic Western gunslinger style stories, I have a series titled *The Vengeance of Reed Caine*. Books 1-3 are available now, and the fourth and final book will be released late spring 2025.

As always, I am thankful for my family, friends, and readers who support me. I'm eternally grateful to my wife. Her partnership in my life humbles me. Despite Western Adventures not being her preferred genre, she provides unwavering support for my writing. She's a fantastic friend, partner, and mother. No matter how many times I've wrote it, it's still true: I couldn't do this without her.

You can follow me on social media @Jason_Baker_Author, Book Bub, or JasonBakerAuthor.com, or sign up for my Substack newsletter to stay informed of future release dates.

ABOUT THE AUTHOR

— • —

J ason Baker is a career military officer and celebrated author deeply immersed in the Civil War era. His non-fiction book *Chicago To Appomattox* and his fiction series *The Barber Brothers' Adventures* and *The Vengeance of Reed Caine* are full of meticulous research and classic Western adventure, capturing the tumultuous period of American history.

An Illinois native, Jason resides in Northern Virginia with his wife and two young sons. He is a member of the Western Writers of America, Western Fictioneers, and a Color Bearer Donor to the American Battlefield Trust. Jason dedicates his work to preserving and exploring America's historical landscapes and battlefields. When he's not writing or hiking battlefields, he enjoys following Illinois and Chicago sports teams, waterfowl hunting, and traveling with his family.

Learn more at JasonBakerAuthor.com, or you can also sign up for Jason's Substack newsletter.